Sharon took a cautious step closer.

Another ripple, greater this time, the waves clearly shimmering across the surface of the lamppost. She reached out a cautious hand towards it, felt a cold too deep and sharp and localised to be real, drew in a slow, shaky breath, and brushed the metal with the tips of her fingers.

A hand shot out.

It came from the metal itself, and was of the metal, a hand wrapped in silver-steel skin, threaded with wires for veins, glass for nails; it came straight out of the spine of the post and locked itself round Sharon's wrist like a vice. She yelped and tried to pull away, but it clung on tight, visible to just past its own wrist. Thin yellow bursts of electric light rushed through it like pulses of blood. "Sammy!" wailed the shaman.

But the goblin just shrugged. "Think of it like...an intervention."

The wrist began to draw back into the lamppost, pulling Sharon's hand with it.

"Sammy, if I end up half lamppost, you'll never hear the end of it!"

"What's new?"

"Sammy!"

The hand gave a sudden tug, drawing right back into the lamppost, and, with a great heave of strength and a shuddering of liquid metal, it pulled Sharon through after it.

By Kate Griffin

Matthew Swift
A Madness of Angels
The Midnight Mayor
The Neon Court
The Minority Council

Magicals Anonymous
Stray Souls
The Glass God

KATE GRIFFIN

www.orbitbooks.net

Orbit
Hachette Book Group
237 Park Avenue, New York, NY 10017
HachetteBookGroup.com

First U.S. Edition: July 2013

First published in Great Britain in 2013 by Orbit, an imprint of Little, Brown
Book Group, 100 Victoria Embankment London EC4Y 0DY

Orbit is an imprint of Hachette Book Group, Inc. The Orbit name and logo are
trademarks of Little, Brown Book Group Limited.

The Hachette Speakers Bureau provides a wide range of authors for speaking
events. To find out more, go to www.hachettespeakersbureau.com or call (866)
376-6591.

The publisher is not responsible for websites (or their content) that are not
owned by the publisher.

Library of Congress Control Number: 2013932405
ISBN: 978-0-316-18727-5

10 9 8 7 6 5 4 3 2 1

RRD-C

Printed in the United States of America

"They be light, they be life, they be fire.
They be flame of blue, wrath of ice,
Dragon of stone, fury of blood.
They be life in flesh, death in sight.
They be the boss.
God help us all"

Anonymous graffiti, men's toilets,
twelfth floor, Harlun and Phelps

"While all and any are welcome to attend the regular meetings of Magicals Anonymous, or even pop by at our drop-in surgery, we do ask that if you are inclined to spontaneous combustion or actively leaking organic fluids from the unwinding hollows of your flesh, you use the overalls provided"

Notice pinned to the offices of Magicals Anonymous,
89C Little Lion Street, London WC1

Chapter 1

Listen to the Expert

He said, "No, wait, you don't want to . . ."

But, as was so often the case, no one listened.

Which was why the next thing they said was, "We told you so."

Things went downhill from there.

Chapter 2

Keep Your Feet on the Ground

He feels something press against his thigh, and half turns in indignation.

But the person who just brushed by is still walking calmly on, shoulders hunched, head down beneath a trilby hat, and Darren, as he brushes his leg, can't feel any blood, and is already half wondering if he imagined it. Perhaps he did. He's had a bit to drink and while he's okay – of course, he's fine! – it's easy to get jumpy on a lonely night.

He walks on, past the shuttered convenience store and the locked-up laundrette, beneath the painting on the wall of the grinning monkey, banana in hand, and through the accusing stare of the policeman drawn on the metal grille that guards the tattoo parlour, whose graffittoed face warns all passers-by that this shop is *his* shop. He turns the corner into the terraced road where he lives, six to the flat share, a house with a nice back garden where they sometimes try to have a barbecue in order to force the weather to turn to rain, walks three more paces, and pauses.

Stops.

Stares at nothing in particular, then down at the ground.

He seems . . . surprised.

It appears to Darren, and indeed to anyone who might be observing Darren at the time, that suddenly everything he's known up to this point has been meaningless. All that was has passed him by, and all that remains is everything which is, and yet to come. He is used to having such profound thoughts at two in the morning after a night in the pub, but it seems to him that this is, perhaps, revelatory. A feeling deeper, truer and more meaningful than anything he has ever experienced with or without the aid of illegal substances, ever before.

And so, for tomorrow can only come if we let go of today, he reaches down to his shoes, and carefully slips them off his feet. His socks are stripy, multicoloured, a reminder, he always felt, that underneath his veneer of clean white shirt and sensible trousers, he once fought for social freedoms and artistic expression. He flexes his toes on the ground, feeling the sudden damp chill of the paving stones rise up through the clean fabric, into the soles of his feet. He lifts up his shoes, carefully unpicking the knot in the laces, then, once they are free, ties the laces back together, one shoe to the other. He raises his head, looking for something suitable for his purposes, and sees a lamppost with a long neck sticking out over the street. He steps back a few paces, to get a better line of sight, then, whirling his shoes overhead, spins them like an Olympic champion and, with a great heave of his arm, lets the shoes fly. They tumble through the air, one over the other, and hook across the neck of the lamppost, tangling a few times round as they come to rest, to form a noose of shoelace across the metal top.

And, just like that, Darren is gone.

Chapter 3

Honour Your Ancestors

It wakes.

This is a long process, made longer by the great deal of time it has spent not waking. Its mouth is stuffed with soil, its bones pressed down by the crushing weight of earth above it. Not all the earth is pure dirt: it stirs, and something sharp and brown lodges against its back. It smells dust, skin-dust, that has seeped down through the grains of broken stone and rotting wool. The fibres of the clothing around it tangle and pull like the threads of a spider's web, and as it stirs into slow, irritated consciousness, one thought above all else intrudes into what, for want of an argument, shall be called its living mind.

How dare they?

How dare they?!

Chapter 4

Friendship Is Precious

It began as a Facebook group.

The name of the group was:

Weird Shit Keeps Happening To Me And I Don't Know Why But I Figure I Probably Need Help

As soon as he'd been granted admin privileges, Rhys had gone about changing that name, and the group had become known as: *Weird Shit Keeps Happening.* However, there were still too many people requesting permission to join who were simply troubled teenagers, or adults coming out of difficult relationships, or old folk who'd forgotten to take their medicine, and, of course, the ubiquitous spammers.

WEIRD SHIT HAPPENING TO YOU?? FOR ONLY $55 UNICURE WILL FIX IT!

Sharon had said, "Yeah, but isn't it kinda indiscreet to just put up a sign, on the internet, proclaiming 'magic is real and here we are'? Only I've seen movies, and usually what happens next is these government guys in black suits and glasses turn up and start asking you questions like 'Have you now or have you ever been an agent for the Soviet government?' and before you know it, there's medical experimentation going on, and I can't be having that."

Sharon Li, it turned out, couldn't be having a lot of things.

"Well, we can make it only open to friends of friends," suggested Rhys carefully. "And we could message any applicants first, just to make sure that they understand what they're getting into. And Facebook isn't the only way, of course; I mean, there are other tools on the internet for social networking, especially if the network contains two vampires, five witches, three necromancers and a troll, see?"

Sharon still didn't look happy. "But this is daft!" she exclaimed. "If every secret society the world over had an internet page, it'd be the death of conspiracy theories and late-night movies on Channel Five!"

"But ... we're not a secret society, are we? Aren't we open to everyone who has a problem with their mystic nature?"

Sharon considered. Rhys had always admired the way in which Sharon Li considered, her entire face drawn together and her body stiff as if to declare that, while the world might be passing her by, nothing was more important than getting this thing *right*. It was an attitude she had extended most of her life, from learning the skills of a shaman, seer of the truth, knower of the path, wanderer of the misty way and so on and so forth, through to getting her five fruit and veg a day and organising the once monthly pub quiz night for members of the society.

"Okay," she said at last. "Just call the damn thing Magicals Anonymous."

So he had.

Few people could have been more surprised than Rhys was himself when offered the job of IT manager for Magicals Anonymous. Then again, he'd quickly discovered that being an IT manager in an office of two – himself and Sharon – was in fact a polite way of expressing the notion of universal dogsbody, administrative minion, sometime sort-of-secretary and, above all else, regular purveyor of cups of tea to all who came through the door. Within days he'd raised this last skill to a high art form, and could now prepare the perfect cup of tea for goblins, sidhes, magus and tuatha de danaan, although his first attempt at providing tea for the danaan had nearly resulted in a diplomatic incident when he put in two lumps of sugar rather than one. The tuatha de danaan, it turned out, took these things seriously.

If Rhys minded that his job had, in fact, little to do with computers, he didn't show it. His last job had been heavily to do with computers, but had ended abruptly when it transpired that the computers in question were owned by a wendigo and his soul-enslaving committee of bankers: a termination process including no fewer than two trips to hospital and the destruction of a significant part of Tooting High Street. At heart, he concluded, he'd been a software man anyway, rather than a hardware kinda guy.

"But why hire me?" he'd asked Sharon, in a rare moment of boldness.

Sharon Li had looked up from her desk, with its magnificent collection of multicoloured highlighters, colour-coordinated folders and, stashed secretly in the lowest drawer, a book entitled *Management for Beginners*. "Well," she said, "I figure I was hired to do this gig, not because I've got office experience or know anything about local government, which is what, I guess, we are, in a kinda social services way, but because I can walk through walls, and the souls of the city whisper their secrets to me from beneath the stones of the streets. So, when I was asked to find someone to work with me, I guess I just figured I shouldn't get anyone who'd show me up too badly."

Two weeks later, Rhys still wasn't sure if this was a good thing or a bad.

The office of Magicals Anonymous was on the ground floor of a polite Georgian terrace, conveniently sited, Rhys couldn't help but feel, next to a walk-in medical, in one of the terraced streets that criss-crossed behind Coram's Fields. Little Lion Street was presumably named after an incident hundreds of years ago which concerned something little and almost certainly involved a street but, Rhys felt, had in no way included a lion. Not quite Islington but definitely not Holborn, it was in an area defined by the superb transport links making great efforts to avoid it. Since the former family homes lining these wide, tree-shadowed byways were too large, impressive and old to be affordable as somewhere to live, dozens of little offices and firms had sprung up within them. Magicals Anonymous sat on the ground floor across the hall from where five ladies of a certain age and one male youth of infinite despondency published little books on gardening, cooking and healthy living, RRP £1.99 from all good organic food shops. One floor up, and a solicitor who spoke in the brisk tones of the contracts she perused held meetings behind a closed black door; on the other side of the landing from her, three young men, with their sleeves rolled up to demonstrate masculinity where no other clues were available, struggled to develop the Perfect App for the modern age, and bickered about operating systems and mobile phones.

If anyone asked Rhys what Magicals Anonymous did, he told them it was a magicians' party service. Which, he realised, was unfortunate, as he had already received three letters asking if they did children's birthdays, and one enquiring about weddings.

"I'm not sure how the kids would react to seeing Gretel," Sharon had said. "Mind you ... seven-foot trolls probably *are* fascinating when you're five, and I'm sure she'd like making the cake."

Sharon Li.

Despite working in what she dubbed "local government", Sharon had made few concessions to the job in terms of personal appearance. For sure, on the first day she'd come into work in her mother's oversized and mismatched trouser suit. But next day she'd gone right back to what she usually wore: tatty blue jeans, purple ankleboots, bright orange tank top and, if she was feeling racy, a badge purloined from the vast collection pinned to the side of her battered green bag, proclaiming – Ask Me Anything, I'm A Shaman. With her straight black hair dyed bright blue at the front, and her almond skin polished to a well-fed glow, Sharon exuded the brightness of a firefly, the confidence of a double-decker bus, the optimism of a hedgehog and the tact of a small thermonuclear missile. However, aware perhaps that her CV mightn't be ideal for a guidance counsellor to the polymorphically unstable and mystically inclined, she had embraced a do-it-yourself approach to management that, for almost every five minutes of toil, generated nearly ten minutes of memos.

"It's important!" she'd exclaimed. "Apparently, when you're in management and have a position of care in the community, you have to have rigorous paperwork in order to reduce future liability. What would happen if some wannabe demigod comes walking in here complaining about feelings of inadequacy and, instead of saying, 'hey, you're a wannabe demigod, would you like a cuppa tea and a chat?' we give him a biscuit and tell him to get over it? The feelings of inadequacy will grow, with a sense of loneliness and confusion as he staggers through this uncaring mortal world, and, finally, explosions! Death! Fire! Destruction! Armageddon upon the earth! And when that comes, we, as responsible members of local government, have to make sure we documented our actions!"

"But . . . Ms Li . . . don't we answer to the office of the Midnight Mayor?"

"Absolutely!"

"And isn't the Midnight Mayor . . . I mean, doesn't he have this thing about how all paperwork is, pardon my language, Ms Li, pestilential putrefaction designed to confound the real work of society in a quagmire of bullshit?"

"What is a quagmire?"

"I'm not sure, Ms Li, that's just what I heard he said."

"Can a quagmire be made of bullshit?"

Rhys managed, just, to clamp down on his response. *Well, Ms Li, you are the shaman in this room, the one who is the knower of truth, and I'm just a humble web-designing druid; surely you should know?* Its utterance would have made no one happy.

Chapter 5

Through Education, Enlightenment

By day, community support officer for the magically inclined. It wasn't the job description Sharon had in mind when she left school. But then again, when she'd left school, hairdresser had seemed like a challenging prospect.

And by night . . . ?

"You gotta let 'em get used to you! You're being *thicko!*"

Sharon considered this proposition. At three foot nothing, the author of this idea had as many hairs on his head as inches to his stature, but made up for this loss with a truly astonishing growth of nasal and, she suspected, navel hair, in whose thick fibres viscous and largely unimaginable fluids clung with all too solid reality. Dressed in a faded green hoodie which proclaimed Skate Or Die, Sammy the Elbow – sage, seer, scholar, goblin and, as he frequently liked to point out, second greatest shaman the world had ever seen – had a remarkably black and white view of the world for one whose understanding of the multifaceted layers of reality went so deep. Things were either "okay all things considered" or they were, more often, "crap, innit?"

How she had wound up with a goblin as her teacher, she still wasn't sure. But he seemed the only thing going and, while Ofsted might not have approved of his methods, simply being there counted for something. Most of the time.

They stood, the goblin and his apprentice, in that grey world where reality falls away and all things that people choose not to perceive become visible at last. It was the invisible city, where the beggars dwelt, just out of sight, and where the shadows turned their heads to watch passers-by; a place where truths were written in the stones themselves, and the houses swayed with the weight of stories swimming against their darkened windows. Reality swept by, and occasionally through, the two shamans; great buses of lost faces, their wheels burning black rubber into the tarmac; taxis with only the yellow "for hire" sign blazing through the greyness like a dragon's eye; half-lost figures moving down the street, over ground sticky with embedded chewing gum and the rubbed-off soles of a thousand, thousand steps which had gone before, their pasts written in their footsteps, whispers of things which had gone before and which might, perhaps, be yet to come. It was easy to grow distracted in this place, to let the eye wander through glimpses of,

the door that slammed in the night as the woman stormed away, I hate you, I hate you, never coming back, to return tomorrow cold and damp
safety glass on the pavement as two kids, him thirteen, her twelve, smashed the window, first ever robbery, car radio far too well embedded for them to pull it out
police caught them two days later, a reprimand; don't ever do that again, smash again in the dark two days later, this time they stole a map, so they could say they'd stolen something
roar of the garbage truck which mistakenly crushed an old lady's cat
slipping of tiles down the roof in foul weather
shoe thrown over the telephone line, the man vanished beneath
soft earth breaking beneath the city streets
smell of . . .

"Oi! Focus, soggy-brains!"

A sharp rap on Sharon's shins snapped her back to attention. With his diminutive height, there were only so many parts of Sharon's body which lent themselves to easy abuse on the part of her goblin teacher; over the months in which she'd been studying, her shins had taken a lot of punishment.

She sighed, and examined the object of Sammy's interest. It was a lamppost, unremarkable in every way. It wasn't quaintly old-fashioned, or modern and sleek. It wasn't an old black Victorian job, where once a flame had burnt where now electricity shimmered; nor was there any aspect about it to denote a remarkable nature of any kind, not even a local planning permission sign cable-tied to its stalk.

"They're very shy animals," exclaimed Sammy. In this grey place his voice was so loud that Sharon half wondered if people passing by in the visible world just a breath away might hear it, and turn their heads, startled at the sound of a disembodied goblin giving a lecture. If they couldn't hear Sammy, they'd surely smell him. A shaman's invisibility didn't stem from any trick of the light, but from the simple attribute of being so at one with their surroundings that, like their surroundings, most people simply didn't bother to notice them. Which was a bit of a relief as, even on Streatham High Street, not the world's most conventional length of road, a three-foot goblin in a hoodie might have stood out.

"You gotta let 'em get a sense of you, like a cat," went on Sammy, his eyes glowing. "But, different from a cat, you don't get to throt-tle 'em and eat 'em raw after."

Sharon's gaze stayed fixed on the lamppost. "Sammy," she mur-mured, "I'm totally okay with you being a goblin and that – I mean, I've got used to it, because that's what you gotta do – but do *you* have to relish it so much? You know that tearing the flesh of some-one's cat with your bare teeth isn't going to make you popular, but you still talk about it like you really like doing it and then – and this is the bit which I've gotta take issue with – then you get all self-righteous about why no one likes you, and I'm just saying, there's a connection here."

"Don't try your self-help crap on me!" shrilled the goblin. "I'm the second greatest frickin' shaman to ever walk the earth!"

"Self-help would be you realising that you've got a problem with your social skills and trying to fix it," she sighed. "This is an intervention." In reply, Sammy kicked her shins again. "See," she went on wearily, barely noticing the pain. "That's just so hostile."

Sammy opened his mouth to say something, probably obscene, when a flicker of movement around the lamppost caught his eye. It caught Sharon's attention, too, for she suddenly became very still and stiff, eyes locked on the dull metal framed beneath its own yellow glow. There again – a tiny pulse of something that seemed to move through the frame itself, as if the post were a liquid rather than a solid, a ripple spreading out from an invisible join in the smooth, galvanised steel.

Sharon took a cautious step closer. Another ripple, greater this time, the waves clearly shimmering across the surface of the lamppost. She reached out a cautious hand towards it, felt a cold too deep and sharp and localised to be real, drew in a slow, shaky breath, and brushed the metal with the tips of her fingers.

A hand shot out.

It came from the metal itself, and was of the metal, a hand wrapped in silver-steel skin, threaded with wires for veins, glass for nails; it came straight out of the spine of the post and locked itself round Sharon's wrist like a vice. She yelped and tried to pull away, but it clung on tight, visible to just past its own wrist. Thin yellow bursts of electric light rushed through it like pulses of blood. "Sammy!" wailed the shaman.

But the goblin just shrugged. "Think of it like . . . an *intervention*."

The wrist began to draw back into the lamppost, pulling Sharon's hand with it.

"Sammy, if I end up half lamppost, you'll never hear the end of it!"

"What's new?"

"*Sammy!*"

The hand gave a sudden tug, drawing right back into the lamppost, and, with a great heave of strength and a shuddering of liquid metal, it pulled Sharon through after it.

There was a moment of uncertainty.

Sharon had an impression of the lamppost splitting open down the middle, a great black mouth full of humming and wires, the hand vanishing into its depths, her wrist trapped within it. It seemed that the darkness stretched and spread around her, curling out and then back in, smothering her, before, with a great, cold lurch, it swallowed her up.

Darkness.

Sharon opened her eyes.

Then closed them again.

She wasn't at all sure she was enjoying her own sense data, and wanted it to consider if this was really what they meant to tell her brain.

She risked opening her eyes again and, yes, there was no getting round it, she was inside a lamppost. And it was vast. Great cliffs of metal, huge humming cables, flashing bursts of brilliant streetlight; she was in a lamppost and it was a tower, a majestic tower heading to a point of yellow light overhead that shone through the metal interior like a private star. There was a continual buzz and hiss of electricity, and, as she turned to inspect her surroundings, beneath her feet the floor crackled and sparked.

There was no sign of an exit, but right now this was, she concluded a low priority. She turned back to face where she'd begun, and the dryad was there instantly, a city dryad: skin of steel, hair of flowing, billowing copper, body pulsing with yellow light, eyes curved with the Perspex shell that framed a streetlight bulb. At some point in their history, the old dryads of the forests had realised that trees weren't such reliable homes any more, and gone in search of a new forest to claim for their own; and what forests the cities had become, and how welcoming they had been. In a moment of panic, Sharon tried to remember what Sammy had told her about dryads, the ancient spirits linked to their lamppost homes; and came up a blank. Did they have any customs? Any dos and do nots for a first encounter? Almost certainly; but as it was, she was out of ideas. So, falling back on traditionalism, she thrust out her still-smarting hand and exclaimed, "Hi there! I'm Sharon! I love what you've done with the place."

The dryad stared down at the hand, its head twisting from side to side, like a slow-motion pigeon examining its target from every angle before making a decision. Sharon slowly withdrew her hand, flexing the fingers nervously as if that had been her plan all along. "My teacher didn't really tell me much about dryads, so sorry if I get anything wrong," she added hastily. "But it's really nice to meet you and, uh . . . your lamppost."

The dryad's head rose slowly from where Sharon's hand had retreated, to Sharon's eyes, as if trying now to fathom which part of its human guest served what function. Its eyes, she noticed, were the same streetlamp yellow that burnt in the real world, beyond the lamppost: unblinking, but flickering slightly with their own internal filament light. "If I'd known I was coming," she went on, "I'd have bought something to say hi. I don't know what kind of thing – I mean, usually it's tea, because I haven't met anyone who doesn't appreciate a cuppa tea – but you might not be so . . . into . . . that sorta . . . thing?" Her voice trailed away beneath the glow of the dryad's implacable stare.

"I'll uh . . . I'll be going now, shall I? I mean, this is great, but don't want to intrude and that . . ."

Sharon turned again, looking for an exit. She was perfectly comfortable with the notion of walking through walls; it was something she'd grown used to over the years, but the thought stayed with her – if she was inside a lamppost, and she tried to walk out through anything other than the front door, wasn't there a danger she'd re-emerge into the street two inches tall? It was something she wanted to ask her host about, but wasn't at all sure the communication barrier would sustain the exchange.

She took a slow, deep breath. "Okay," she sang out softly, to no one but herself. "No problem."

"He wakes."

The voice behind her was cracked, full of pops, as if being relayed through an ancient set of speakers. Sharon turned carefully to see the dryad, still staring at her as if she couldn't work out which part of Sharon was sentient. "He wakes," repeated the creature again, head bobbing slightly in an attempt to modulate the sound crackling up from her throat. "He wakes."

"Um . . . okay. Any 'he' in particular?"

"He wakes."

Sharon bit her lip. "Now, I don't want you to think that I'm not a positive kinda girl, because I am, always trying to think the best and that, but there's something about being sucked into a lamppost by a dryad to be told that 'he wakes' which just gives me this kinda queasy feeling – do you get that? Queasy feelings? I guess it's all psychological anyway, so maybe you're okay, but point is . . . this'd be way easier if you'd just send me an email. With, like, attachments and diagrams and that. I know I don't *look* stupid," she added, "but just this once, let's pretend that I am because, ironically, I figure that'd be the smart thing to do."

The dryad's head twitched again, processing Sharon's words. Then she stepped forward, so sharply that Sharon took an instinctive step back. The dryad hesitated, then unfolded one long finger and pointed it directly down at Sharon's feet. "He," she explained, emphasising first one purple boot, then the other. "Wakes."

Something clunked, deep in the lamppost, an electric fizz. The dryad's head whipped round, eyes flaring brightly yellow in the electric gloom. Then she reached up and grabbed Sharon by the shoulders, head turning slowly back like clockwork to look into the shaman's eyes. "Stop him," she hissed, and, with a shove, sent Sharon staggering backwards, into darkness.

Blackness.

Cold.

An unfolding.

A closing down.

Sharon stumbled bottom-first into the street, tripped on her own scrambling feet and fell over. She landed in a gangly heap on the paving stones, the world back in full city-night technicolour. In the shop windows lining the road, bright red hair extensions for the socialite lady jarred with ironing board covers and ripped-off hi-fi systems from truly impeccable sources, lined up for customer speculation and delight. The traffic was sparse, thinned out by the time of night, but what drivers there were had sensed a rhythm in the traffic lights and were hurling themselves uphill, determined to catch nothing but greens all the way to Morden. As a man on a bicycle pedalled by, his head swung round to glance at Sharon before he looked away, muttering under his breath. She swallowed and scrambled to her feet, walking a few quick steps to find that perfect place where what was gave way to the rather more shady question of what was perceived, to find Sammy standing in the greyness, waiting for her, arms folded and one foot tapping irritably on the paving stones.

"Took you long enough!" he fumed. "You never heard of getting on with things, pudding-brain?"

"I was talking," she retorted, "with a dryad. You may rush through these sorta social encounters like you're having a pee, but I wanted to appreciate the moment, so don't give me this crap."

To her surprise, Sammy's eyes widened. "The dryad *talked?*"

"Uh . . . yeah."

"What'd she say?"

"Why?" demanded Sharon, her face crinkling with suspicion.

Sammy's arms tightened in a knot across his small chest. "Dryads don't talk much, is all," he grumbled. "Sorta like . . . a privilege and that, if they say something to you. Which isn't to say you're any good at talking to dryads," he added. "Because falling on your arse on the way out is stupid for a shaman and you looked like a right lemon and, when you're being a professional on the job, that kinda thing can't be stood for. It's amateur, is what it is, and I'm not training up amateurs! But if the dryad spoke . . . that's summat."

Sharon was patting her knees and elbows down instinctively for any cuts or grazes from the fall, and murmured, only half aware of what she did, "'He wakes'."

"Who wakes?"

"Dunno. That's all she said."

"Is that it? You didn't *press* her?"

"Sammy, I was talking with a dryad, in a lamppost; it's not like I was gonna stick around for twenty questions!"

"But that could mean anything!" fumed the goblin. "Bloody hell, can't young people have a frickin' conversation these days?"

"I got the feeling it was bad news, if that's what you're asking."

To her surprise, the goblin flinched. "Lotsa prats walk around these days saying pretentious stupid things in stupid voices, cos there's plenty of cash in that line of work, but dryads only really talk when they got something important to say. You sure there was nothing else?"

"Uh . . . 'stop him'."

"Well that's useful, innit! Now we got twice the sense of death and half the information! What have I been telling you about *learning the truth* and *following the path* and all that? In one ear, out the other!"

"Hey!" Sharon gestured at the lamppost. "You want to go and have a chat with a dryad, be my guest!"

Sammy's nose crinkled with distaste. "Not good for one of us to spend too much time *in there*," he grumbled, gesturing with his chin at the lamppost. "People get . . . squishy."

"Lovely. Well, if you don't mind . . ." – Sharon straightened up, scanning the street with what she hoped was her best, decisive glare – " . . . I've got meetings at nine tomorrow morning. So, since 'he wakes' and 'stop him' is about as useful as roast beef at a vegan party, I'm gonna find a train." To her surprise, Sammy just nodded, distracted, eyes still fixed on the lamppost. "Hey . . . Sammy?"

"Eh?"

"There *isn't* anything we can do, is there?"

"What? No, 'course not, soggy-brains! It's friggin' cryptic, can't never do nothing with friggin' cryptic bollocks, that's why you should've done more of the truth stuff and less of the standing around like a lemon. Too late now," he added thoughtfully. "Not that it's probably none of our business anyway."

"Fine," she growled. "Maybe I'll put it in a memo."

Chapter 6

The Mind's a Prison

A phone rings.

After a while, the ringing stops.

A cheerful, recorded voice sings out in the dark, loud enough to stir the papers settled on the desk.

"Hi there! You've reached the office of Kelly Shiring. I'm afraid I'm not at my desk right now, please leave a message after the tone."

A tone.

Silence.

No – not quite silence.

Static.

A cacophony of hisses, cracks and pops. A chorus of electronic nothingness, an interpretation on a theme of void. Layers of busy, bustling emptiness, stretched out across each other like the skin on a drum, humming under tension. Press your ear to the speaker and you might think you can hear the sound of wind turning an antenna, or the pop of someone hanging up in Hong Kong, or perhaps, very, very faintly, somewhere beneath the sharp snaps of electrical interference, screaming out like a pinned butterfly, a voice that cries:

"Help me!"

Chapter 7

The Early Bird Catches the Worm

Sharon was not a morning person.

She sat behind her desk at 9 a.m., the second coffee of the day cooling beside her, and tried to look interested at a parade of:

"I've been on the night shift for thirty years now, and my boss says that I have to work days because of health and safety. Days! I've never worked days in all my life, and what's he going to do when my skin combusts spontaneously beneath the noonday sun?"

" . . . and I'm not saying we shouldn't let werewolves in, because some of my best friends are werewolves, it's just that . . . "

"And I said, 'You have got to be joking! I can't fight an ancient evil now, I've got three exams next week and a date!' and they weren't at all understanding."

"I'm really concerned about the blood banks. They say this year is going to be a crisis year, and unless I get my dose, I have to go and harvest my own and that causes all kinds of trouble . . . "

"I was, like, 'oh my God, what is he wearing?' and he was, like, 'babes, put the fangs away' and I was, like, 'Jesus, did he just say that' . . . "

"The use of minotaur horn is utterly outrageous in this modern age . . ."

" . . . Testing on imps . . . !"

"– my TV has started issuing prophecies . . ."

"They should have declared it was haunted *before* we exchanged contracts!"

"Just because she's dead doesn't mean she hasn't got feelings . . ."

Sharon's head hit her desk, and bounced lightly off the thick wad of notes and paperwork which had sprung up during the morning's meetings. She heard a polite cough by her elbow, and raised her head very, very slowly to see what new calamity awaited. Rhys was there, a fresh cup of tea in one hand and a small plastic bag in the other. "Um, Ms Li? What with the meetings running so long, you missed lunch, so I went out and got you a . . ." He fumbled in the bag. " . . . cheese and pickle sandwich, but then I thought you might not like pickle, because some people don't, see, so I also got cheese and ham, but some people are allergic to cheese, so I also got a BLT but then you might be vegetarian so there was egg and cress and I thought, who doesn't like egg and cress so I got one of those and also some crisps but I didn't really know what you liked so I got salt and vinegar, cheese and onion, smoky bacon and ready salted. And some orange juice. Oh – and some apple juice, too, because some-times you don't really want orange juice but you get this craving for apple and uh . . . well . . . see . . ." Rhys's words dissolved into silence in the face of Sharon's stare. Her hands felt their way across the desk to the plastic bag.

"Rhys," she said carefully, "I don't want you to get the wrong idea here, because I'm saying this in a strictly professional way, but I love you."

He flushed, an instant burst of redness from the roots of his hair to the ends of his fingertips.

"Thank you, M-M-M-Ms Li, that's v-v-v-very . . ." The end of his nose began to shake, the echoes rapidly spreading down through his whole body. Wordlessly, Sharon held out an industrial-strength tissue from the box by her desk. Working with Rhys, a stockpile of tissues had become something of an obligatory addition to the workplace, and now he grabbed it gratefully and held it to his nose as his body trembled, quivered, shook and finally jerked beneath the force of a great, lung-shattering sneeze.

Sharon waited for things to settle down again, then added, "What are you having?"

"I ate earlier, Ms Li," he explained, depositing the bag on her table like a box of crabs. "I hope there's something there you like!" The thin carpet almost smoked beneath his feet with the speed of Rhys's departure back to his own desk.

Sharon stared down at the great pile of food. There was enough to keep her going for a good four days, and yet somehow she knew it would all be gone within two. Even if she didn't eat all of it, Gretel the troll was always interested in trying new things, even if that new thing was Worcestershire Sauce drunk straight from the bottle; no one wanted to critique the culinary habits of a gourmet troll.

She reached out for the nearest sandwich, not caring which one it was, ran her finger down the join in the card, smelt the rich tang of yellow, plastic cheese, felt saliva spring unbidden in her mouth and heard . . .

"Oh my God, I just love the beanbags!"

The sandwich was already halfway to her lips. Sharon raised her eyes with the slow inevitability of the prisoner before the firing squad.

"And look at all the tea you have – where did you get this one? I've been trying to find this for months, but not even Waitrose has it any more!"

The woman speaking held up a packet of tea in a bright blue package. The packet was in fact the brightest thing about the picture, as the woman in question wore black. Black shoes, black trousers, black coat buttoned up with fat black buttons all the way to her neck, and even, tucked discreetly into the corner of her black bag, a black hat. Her pale skin and auburn hair should have mellowed the picture, but in fact the contrast only seemed to deepen the quality of black about her. However, if her wardrobe was worthy of a mortician, her smile was a burst of radiance to put any searchlight to shame. She used it now to sweep the room, taking in

Rhys at his desk, who tried to hide behind the nearest hard drive; and Sharon, her sandwich still hovering, ready to be consumed. Her gaze settled on Sharon and, if possible, the smile brightened to an almost dazzling luminescence.

"Ms Li!" exclaimed the woman, scampering forward to seize Sharon's fingers in a two-handed shake. "Such a pleasure to see you again – we met briefly before, I think – I'm Kelly Shiring, Mr Swift's PA? I bought you doughnuts ..."

A packet of doughnuts was deposited on Sharon's desk.

" ... and this umbrella ..."

An umbrella, long, blue, with a ripple effect carved into the handle either for greater grip or maybe artful whim, was propped up carefully.

" ... and congratulations!"

Sharon looked from the doughnuts, to the umbrella, to Kelly's brilliantly smiling face. In the doorway stood a man, also dressed head to toe in black, and holding back lest he disrupt the impeccable positivity of Kelly's presence. Kelly Shiring – magician, Alderman, personal assistant to the Midnight Mayor (defender of the city, guardian of the gate and so on and so forth) and truly fabulous cook, though she always denied the same, gazed down at Sharon Li and waited for the shaman to say something significant.

Carefully, aware that eating pickle might detract from the aura of sagely wisdom that a shaman was supposed to cultivate, Sharon laid her sandwich aside. "Uh ... thanks?" It was the best she could manage at short notice, and usually it did seem to do more good than trying to invent a profundity for every occasion.

"You're welcome!" sang out Kelly. "Now, if you need anything, you have my number, I think, and of course anything we can do to assist, you only have to ask."

"I do?"

"Of course! This project," Kelly gestured around the office, "is being financed almost entirely out of the Aldermen Development Fund, which, I must tell you, has taken a serious hit in recent months what with Burns and Stoke folding and the difficult financial times ... but look how well you've done with the resources available to you! I'm sure this little business will be absolutely fine, now that you're on it."

Sharon's stare deepened. "That's great," she ventured, still baking beneath the brilliance of Kelly's gaze. "And thanks for the doughnuts and everything but, uh . . . which little business?"

Something flickered across Kelly's face, a little harder and a little darker than the jubilation she usually projected, but it was gone so quickly Sharon wondered if she'd seen it at all. "Have a doughnut," the Alderman said.

"I was about to have a sandwich . . ."

"Oh, Miles!"

The man addressed as "Oh, Miles" detached himself from the doorframe and stepped inside, closing the door behind him lest rumours of his participation escape beyond the nearest four walls. He inclined his chin in the universal nod of manly-men-respecting-each-other's-masculinity to Rhys as he passed, inducing another quiver at the end of Rhys's already inflamed nose, and held out a polite hand for Sharon to shake. His grip was firm without being oppressive, loose without being limp, and as their fingers brushed she tasted

finest coffee beans ground beneath a brass handle in the morning
shoe polish, never too bright, never too polished
  laughter of children in the playground
stab of regret
    click of the gun in the night

before their hands parted. Pulling up a stool, the man called Miles settled by the corner of her desk. Kelly swung herself into the chair opposite Sharon, and began testing its manoeuvrability as if on the verge of shouting "whee!"

"I really feel you should have a doughnut," she declared, satisfied by the motion of the chair. "They're marvellous things. Did you know that the doughnut has a Jewish origin? During Hanukkah the Temple of Solomon was besieged, and they didn't have enough oil to keep the sacred flame alight but, would you believe it, the flame made it! And there was something to do with sacred oil as a result, and therefore doughnuts – I'm a little vague on the details but aren't doughnuts just the most marvellous thing to ever come out of organised religion?"

"Miss Shiring . . ."

"Kelly, please!"

"Kelly," corrected Sharon, "I'm really grateful for the doughnuts, and I'm sure Rhys is, like . . . giddy . . . about them, too, and I don't mean to seem rude or nothing, but why are you here?"

"I don't think you're rude, Ms Li – may I call you Sharon? – I don't think you're rude at all! Did you think she was rude, Miles?"

"Absolutely not," murmured the Alderman.

"Of course you'd want to know why we're here, why not? And of course the answer is, I'm here to give you the umbrella because Mr Swift specifically requested that you should have it, and to inform you that you've been deputised and the Midnight Mayor has vanished, and to bring you doughnuts because I believe in the project!"

Silence, punctuated by the sound of Rhys trying to blow his nose with all the discretion of a steam engine. Sharon gingerly pushed the doughnuts to one side, in case they were somehow contaminated by the news they'd arrived with. Kelly waited, her smile fixed in place. Her companion sat hunched forward, elbows on his knees, fingers twined together, watching Sharon, waiting for a reaction.

Sharon spoke slowly and carefully. It was, she'd found, the best way to create an illusion of shamanly wisdom, as people often mistook cautious speech for being thoughtful instead of panic-struck. "When you say . . . the Midnight Mayor has *vanished* . . . ?"

"Yes," sighed Kelly. "Embarrassing, really, as I'm supposed to be his PA."

"And 'vanished' . . . ?"

"Off the face of the earth. Well! Maybe not off the face of the earth, we have no evidence for that per se, and it seems a bit of a leap to assume that, because we can find no trace of him, he is in fact not here. But from what we can tell, he has disappeared completely, utterly and without a word. Which he has done before," she added. "But never like this, and never so . . . silently. Usually when he disappears it's to blow things up, or engage in nefarious acts with dark forces, but this time there's been none of that, and I'm a little concerned."

"You're concerned that things *aren't* blowing up?"

"You have met him," Kelly pointed out.

"Okay," Sharon admitted. "So maybe it is worrying. But I don't get why you've come to me!"

"Besides the doughnuts ..."

"Besides the doughnuts, yes. You're an Alderman, aren't you? You've got this whole ... scary people with guns thing – though I'm sure you're not scary," she added. "I'm sure you're very nice people and you use guns in a very safety conscious manner for the public good. But when I last checked, you were all about protecting the Midnight Mayor and the city and that, whereas we're more about ..." She glanced for support at Rhys, who ducked behind his computer, pretending he didn't exist.

" ... about social evenings and group therapy," she concluded with a sigh. "I don't get why you're here."

"Ms Li!" exclaimed Kelly, slapping the desk for emphasis, with depressing effect. "You're far too harsh on yourself! You are a shaman, a knower of the truth, and a figure of immense respect. Why, Miles here was only saying last week how much he was looking forward to meeting you, weren't you, Miles?"

"It's a pleasure, Ms Li," he confirmed, with a half-bow of his head.

"So really, you shouldn't do yourself down!"

Sharon glanced again towards Rhys, but a flurry of tissue was the only sign of life at his small, cluttered desk.

"Okay," she tried. "Not that I'm, like ... ungrateful for the ego boost and that, but still, I'm just saying, the Midnight Mayor deals with dudes with guns, and *you're* dudes with guns, and while I'm totally up for being mega-super-cool, which would be a nice change, Sammy hasn't yet taught me how to walk *through* bullets. So, uh, thanks for the doughnuts, and um ... good luck!"

Kelly looked at Miles. Across her face mild embarrassment blossomed like the evening primrose. "Well," she said. "There is of course the question of the umbrella."

Sharon's gaze roamed over to it. A long blue umbrella, not new, but hardly an antique; someone had knocked the point off, so that now it seemed stubbier than it had once been, and rested on the surface where the ribs came together. "Is it a mega-mystic umbrella?"

"I don't think so – do you think so, Miles?"

"Couldn't say, ma'am."

"Maybe it is, then!" exclaimed Kelly. "I'm really not sure! But Mr Swift did ask that I give it to you, should something bad happen to him. And of course he requested that you be informed that you have now been made Deputy Mayor and that you were to, as he so charmingly put it, shift your bottom into gear."

Sharon's eyes flashed up from the umbrella to Kelly. "I'm *what*?"

"Deputy Mayor."

"Since when?"

"About forty-eight hours ago. I'm sure Mr Swift sent you an email ..."

"He bloody did not!"

" ... and if he didn't, I'm sure he *meant* to."

"I can't be Deputy Mayor!" wailed Sharon. "I've got paperwork to do! I've got a social evening to arrange, health and safety assessments to fill out, bookings for singles dating night for all those unable to flirt during full moon, bingo for retired witches! I can't go around being Deputy Mayor! I refuse!" She thumped the desk, then flinched as the noise sunk away into the walls. The Aldermen were silent.

Kelly gazed at Sharon. Across her brow there flickered a mixture of sympathy and, much worse, mild disappointment. "I understand," she said, "that this must be difficult ..."

"Difficult! Do you know how many Post-it notes this office gets through?"

" ... and it's a pleasure to see you taking such interest in your work, really it is! They say that the private sector motivates people more than the public one, but I've always felt that the public sector is where people with a genuine passion go to find their path, and you clearly have that passion and I think we should respect that, shouldn't we?"

"Absolutely," chorused Miles.

"And if you're too busy to help us find out what fate has befallen the defender of the city, guardian of the night, watchman of the slumbering dark, then of course it's your decision and I fully understand how, in this difficult day and age, you'd want to abide by that. Obviously a shaman's unique skills could be of great service in this hour of need, but I'm sure, despite the circumstance, we'll find our way and, hopefully, we can do so without any unnecessary loss of life, don't you agree, Miles?"

"We can but try our best."

"So, Ms Li." Kelly stood up briskly, the chair coasting out on its wheels behind her. "I hope you have a marvellous day and, please, do keep the doughnuts, and the umbrella, and we'll . . ."

"Wait," groaned Sharon. Kelly waited, eyebrows raised. Sharon looked from Alderman to Alderman, then gave another, louder groan and let her head bang once more against the top of her desk. Soon there would be a groove in the paperwork where her forehead had carved out a path. "Fine," she grumbled, looking back up, chin first. "And don't think I'm doing this just because of your manipulation, because I'm not and because I don't believe in falling for cheap tricks. I'm just . . . taking an interest because of my civic spirit, and . . ." She snatched up the doughnuts. "I'm keeping these. Rhys!"

Rhys stuck his head out from behind the computer with the innocence of a man who has absolutely not been eavesdropping. "Yes, Ms Li?"

"Get your coat!"

The day outside was cold and bright, dazzling through the falling leaves, with the Aldermen incongruously dark beneath a baby-blue sky. Sharon juggled the blue umbrella and the bag containing sandwiches and doughnuts, and Kelly, indicating the noise of traffic from Theobalds Road, said, "I hope no one minds if we get a bus?"

"A bus?" echoed Sharon, scampering after the two Aldermen. They were heading south, past tall terraced houses of coal-grey brick with bone-white window frames. "What happened to swanning around in chauffeur-driven cars?"

"Financial consequences," sighed Kelly. "When Mr Swift and

yourself did that marvellous job removing the wendigo from Burns and Stoke, and freeing the imprisoned spirits of the city from their lair, of course it was fabulous for the welfare of London as a whole. It was, however, a teensy bit detrimental to the fiscal stability of the brokerages market, and Harlun and Phelps suffered some not inconsiderable financial losses as a result. Alas, as Harlun and Phelps is the prime employer and supplier for the Aldermen, this means we've had to make a few cutbacks in one or two administrative areas. Do you have your own travel cards?"

Sharon looked at Rhys. "I cycle to work," he offered.

"That's excellent, absolutely what people should do! Well, if you have to take public transport in the course of this investigation, please do keep the receipt."

"Is this an investigation?" queried the druid. "Only I've got the boiler man coming round tomorrow at eight, see, and it's been very hard to arrange . . ." Sharon glared at Rhys, who dissolved into " . . . but I suppose that's not very important in the scheme of things, is it?"

They walked on past expensive cars parked outside expensive houses. Commemorative plaques occurred in this part of town with mocking regularity, assuring passers-by that, while their own lives up to this point may have been futile, great works had nevertheless distinguished these streets, even in an age when most people were lucky to have butter with their bread. Sharon was uncharacteristically silent, and, Rhys thought, slightly thin around the edges, her brisk walk taking her close to where shamans began to disappear from sight: that precise speed where the brain seemed to say, 'oh look, a native' before disregarding anything further including, for example, whether that native was solid all the way through.

They turned onto Theobalds Road, a busy place of sandwich bars, expensive hairdressers and lawyers. The bus, to Rhys's surprise, came quickly. If asked to define who or what he was, he would usually explain that he was the man who had to wait fourteen minutes for every train which ran on a fifteen-minute interval, and so could only attribute the miraculous appearance of transport to the luck of the company he now kept. People stared at the Aldermen, but not at him. Even with a shock of straight ginger hair, and dressed in a thick tartan-pattern shirt and slightly too short jeans, Rhys had never been an object of interest even to those who specialised in spotting style calamities. In a way, that gave him comfort. If he didn't look like much, at least small children didn't cry at the sight of him.

They sat at the very back of the top deck, in the seats Rhys had marked out in his imagination as the naughty seats for naughty schoolchildren. Sharon at once had her boots up on the plastic back of the seats in front, and was reaching for her cheese and pickle sandwich.

"Okay," she said. "Tell me about the 'vanished' thing."

Kelly looked round the bus with what was either the shrewd look of a woman careful about eavesdroppers, or the brilliant face of all urban tourists enjoying an unfamiliar experience, or possibly both. She leant back in her seat and said, "It's been two days. Or has it, hard to say . . . I suppose it depends when he vanished, as compared to when I saw him last . . . but I saw him last two days ago, so that's probably the best we've got to go on."

Sharon shifted uncomfortably, pushing the blue umbrella into a corner and spraying her lap with crumbs. If she cared, she didn't show it.

"He came into my office, gave me the umbrella, said, 'Kelly, if anything happens to me, get this to Sharon' and walked out. Then he walked back in again and said, 'buy her doughnuts' and then walked out again; he does that a lot, you see, always thinks of the important things when he's halfway to the lift. I've tried to convince him to buy a smartphone but he refuses, which I think is ironic considering . . ."

"That was the last time you saw him?" demanded Sharon.

"Yes."

"And why do you think he's vanished, instead of just done a bunk?"

"Well," murmured Kelly, fixing her eyes on some point at the opposite end of the bus as it rattled its way down Clerkenwell Road. "I do occasionally keep tabs on Mr Swift, just for his own sake, of course, and when he didn't answer his phone yesterday we did a little bit of a scry, and got nothing. Nothing at all. And of course – of course! – a good sorcerer can shield himself from these things, but then he really isn't answering his phone and there are so many things about Mr Swift that we can scry for. There's the blue electric angels, of course, embedded in his soul, or the power of the Midnight Mayor, branded into his hand – frankly he usually stands out like a kangaroo in a coal mine – so the fact that we've got nothing is a little concerning. Then of course there's that," Kelly inclined her head towards the umbrella. "It may be nothing at all, of course, but Mr Swift isn't widely regarded for his consideration of the weather, or indeed of others who may experience it, so quite why he'd be so specific that you receive both the umbrella and the doughnuts, I cannot say."

Sharon's hand, which had been groping for a doughnut, drew back sharply. "Jesus! You don't think the doughnuts could be mystic, do you?"

Kelly looked thoughtful. "No," she concluded. "At least, I find it very unlikely, as I bought them from Londis half an hour ago."

"Okay," Sharon muttered, settling for another cheese and pickle sandwich. "Well, I guess that's something."

"Also, I hate to say it, but there have been other signs that Mr Swift may have thought he was heading for trouble."

"What . . . signs?"

"Well . . . " Kelly's face was a picture of organisational distress. " . . . He sent his apprentice to New York."

"Wait there a moment! Swift's got an apprentice?"

"Oh, yes. Ms Ngwenya. Charming woman – we go to a book group together on the first Friday of the month. This month we're reading *Little Dorrit* and I must admit I am struggling, but then . . . I can see you're not interested in this."

Sharon tried to fix her expression in the polite, open look she used for obsessive vampires and outraged necromancers, and hoped it would do for Kelly Shiring, too. "And this apprentice . . . she gets to go to New York? As part of her teaching?" She just about managed to keep the acid from her voice.

"Absolutely!" exclaimed Kelly, oblivious to most things which might dampen the day. "Mr Swift says it's very important that sorcerers experience all sorts of urban magic, not just the peculiarities of London; however, he also says that when the shit hits the fan the last thing he wants is his apprentice in town, as he can neither guarantee that she won't get hurt nor that she won't hurt others recklessly, and so you see . . ."

"You think he sent her away to keep her safe?"

Kelly flinched. "The possibility must be considered, distressing though it is."

Sharon drummed her fingers on the window of the bus. Outside, the terraced houses of Clerkenwell were giving way to the glass offices and imperial facades of the City, the Golden Mile. Without looking at Kelly she murmured, "So, I don't wanna ask this, but I guess I gotta, seeing as how I'm now involved and that . . . how'd you know he isn't just dead?"

Rhys swallowed, and wrestled his expression into one of concerned astonishment. Kelly twiddled her thumbs nervously. "I don't think so," she said. "Not to dismiss the notion, of course, but he *is* the Midnight Mayor. And while Mr Swift might die – which would be terrible! – the power of the Midnight Mayor, the essence of what *it* is, well, that's as old as the city, and will last as long as its stones themselves. So if he were dead, I do feel that the power would have been transferred to a successor. Someone like you, perhaps!"

Sharon choked on her sandwich, sending a spray of crumbs and cheese across the seat in front of her. Kelly waited for the shaman to stop suffocating before she added, "You haven't developed any unusual scars lately, have you? Or found yourself communing with dragons, for example?"

"I bloody well have not! Why would any arsehole make *me* Midnight Mayor?"

"Ms Li," chided Kelly, "did we not already establish what a truly marvellous person you are? Miles, back me up here!"

Sharon swung round to glower at the man called Miles. The tube-like shape of his Alderman's black coat only seemed to increase his impressive height; his carefully trimmed blond hair completed the appearance of royalty in mourning. Unwavering grey eyes, flecked with blue, met Sharon's glare full-on. "I must admit, Ms Li," he murmured, "based only on having read your file, of course, I think you would be an excellent choice of Midnight Mayor. You have admirable civic spirit, and I feel that your management style could infuse a great deal of thought innovation into our working environment."

Sharon's mouth dropped open.

So, for that matter, did Rhys's.

"Of course, if you *were* Midnight Mayor, it would suggest that Mr Swift is, in fact, deceased, and I'm sure no one here wants that."

"Well, quite!" exclaimed Kelly, rising to her feet with the purposefulness of a woman who saw a bus stop coming up. "And I'm sure the sooner we find him, the easier it will be to prevent that from happening!"

She trotted down the stairs and Sharon followed, still trying to recompose her expression into something suitably shamanesque, as the four of them stepped out onto Cheapside.

Once a place of dubious repute, the Cheapside of recent times had undergone a series of face-lifts, whereby the frontage of Victorian offices, and former guilds still bearing Latin mottoes of yore as a reminder of the time when you did not mess with the candle-makers of London, had been replaced with glass facades. Nowadays passers-by had access to window displays of mobile phones and greetings cards for every occasion, and banks accessible to the public from five minutes after the start of normal office hours to five minutes before their end, please don't try and visit during lunch breaks. The assumption on Cheapside was that nobody much would pay for anything with cash.

Kelly strode north, down a road barely wide enough for the sandwich delivery man to pedal his bicycle and trolley between its black bollards embossed with the crimson cross of the City of London. She led the way past the fire exits of great financial firms, where smokers huddled on their breaks to pass on the gossip of the day; past the wine and sushi bar where each night men in suits greeted old friends to compete over various triumphs; and around the square tower of a church whose nave was long gone, but which nonetheless remained, defiant and alone.

Harlun and Phelps was situated on Aldermansbury Square, a crooked open space framed by modern sheet glass and the white stone walls of the ancient Guildhall, which squatted like an angry badger at a pedigree dog show. Inside the foyer, the theme of the month appeared to be great stalks of bamboo, seemingly taller than the block of flats where Sharon lived.

"Enjoy this place while you can!" exclaimed Kelly as the lift pinged in greeting. "With things as they are, we won't be able to afford the rent for much longer."

Harlun and Phelps itself was, to Sharon's surprise, a fully functional office. Desks were divided from each other by low partitions, behind which men and women in suits sat hunched over computers with the look of people determined not to be caught playing solitaire. Coffee machines hummed in closets off the open floors, and harsh fluorescent light flooded the place, even in the middle of the day. Sharon looked for some sign of mystic inclinings, and, seeing none, looked again, as only a shaman can. The office was . . .

. . . ordinary. There in the shadows, the ghost of a manager who'd stood on a table and screamed at his workers, three days before he lost his job; there, hovering just behind the back of a man scrabbling away at a keyboard, head bowed and shoulders hunched, a woman with a mouth opened so her chin nearly bumped her collar, whispering *harder, harder, harder, don't you realise there's a family to feed?* From behind the closed door of the cleaning cupboard, the sound of whispered promises broken, *anything you want babes, anything you want, just a kiss, that's all, just a kiss . . .*

Sharon looked away, before the walls in that particular corner could tell much more of their tale.

"I'm not getting much magic," she murmured, as Kelly swept through the office with the imperious stride of one who belonged and, to a degree, ruled.

"Of course not, Ms Li! The majority of Harlun and Phelps is a strictly for-profit corporation. Bonds, futures, all that stuff – really, it goes far over my head," confessed the PA. "While the Aldermen are often employed in the company, and while we do prefer to hire members of the magical community, if only to keep them out of trouble, one must concede that not every macroeconomics graduate of the London School of Economics is going to know how to banish a ghoul. It was our more . . . mundane . . . which is to say the more financially profitable . . . departments which were so heavily invested in Burns and Stoke, and we all saw how poorly that worked out. Here we are!"

She stopped before a door, like any other. Taped across it was a name neatly written in black felt-tip pen – M. Swift. Sharon looked from this to where a name plate sat, bare and empty.

"He said that having a name plate was like putting your signature in the devil's logbook. Well," added Kelly, unlocking the door, "he may have included a few expletives. But I'm sure you appreciate the sentiment."

She pushed the door open. Beyond it Sharon saw . . .

. . . a disaster.

Piles of paper hid every part of the floor, save for five neat, foot-sized trenches which had been left at just the right distance to make stepping from one to the next, strenuously uncomfortable. The twisted mind that contrived this round-your-footsteps school of filing, hadn't spared the walls or windows either: every available inch was covered with maps, memos, notes, diagrams and, in one or two cases, what looked to Sharon like mystic wards, inscribed in marker pen onto the wall itself. One map dominated all the others. Wider than Sharon's outstretched arms, longer than the bed she slept in, it showed all of London from the M25 in, and was pinned to the wall over a slew of other documents which stuck out around it like nested fledglings peeping from under their mother. Red dots were stuck across its surface, forming a thick mess across large parts of north London, and a slightly thinner mess south of the river. Each dot had a date – a day and a month – scratched next to it in tiny writing, but there was no other indication of its purpose.

In the middle of the room, encased by all this junk and sagging under the weight of many unwashed coffee mugs, was a desk; a computer sat huddled on one corner, as if embarrassed to be so digital in this analogue room. The only chair had also fallen victim to the mess of paperwork and was burdened by seven copies of the Yellow Pages, the earliest dating back to 1992. Sharon thought about moving them, then couldn't work out where they'd go; so, stepping carefully towards the desk, across the paper-infested floor, she balanced precariously on top of them, like a toddler on a bar stool. The others lurked in the doorway, waiting to see what fell first.

"This," said Sharon, "is not good office practice."

There was a small sigh of relief. It came from Kelly, who appeared to know exactly what good office practice was and to hope someone else might too. "Ms Li," she exclaimed, "I'm so glad you're here, you have such a can-do attitude! Obviously, call me if you need anything, I'm just next door, and good luck with your investigation!"

She turned to go, and was somehow out of sight before Sharon had a chance to say, "Oi, don't you bloody go, you can't just leave me with ..."

The door to the neighbouring office slammed, with, Sharon felt, perhaps more emphasis than necessary. She looked down at the desk, and the pile of Yellow Pages shifted beneath her. Things were growing at the bottom of one of the abandoned coffee mugs. Since the things weren't about to utter prophetic truths, she averted her gaze.

"Um ... Ms Li?" Rhys stood in the doorway. So, to Sharon's surprise, did Miles. "Can we, uh ... do anything?" hazarded the druid.

Sharon looked at him, then stared around the room, searching for inspiration. "Dunno," she said. "Ever gone looking for the missing guardian of the city before?"

"Um ... no. Sorry."

"I haven't either," offered Miles, "but I do have Google maps on my phone, should we require them."

Sharon's eyes narrowed. "That's great," she muttered, in the tone of one who still didn't trust technology to know the difference between a canal path and a motorway. "But, and I don't mean this in a negative way, what exactly *is* your job in this?"

"Oh, I'm here to assist!" Miles exclaimed. "I am, in fact, your minion. I believe that's not the politically correct term, but I don't mind it. Anything you need, anything you desire, be it menial, demanding or dangerous, and I will be only too happy to assist."

Rhys sensed an itching at the back of this throat. He felt that if anyone was going to do menial, demanding or dangerous jobs, it should be him. He eyed Miles up and down, noticed the healthy glow to his skin, the well-muscled neck leading into what he deeply suspected were toned and rippling chest and shoulder muscles; the fine posture, the excellent speech, the educated tones ringing through, and felt a surge of itching all the way to his eyes and nose.

"A minion, huh?" murmured Sharon, trying out the sound. "Cool. So, uh . . . you're an Alderman, right?"

"That's correct."

"And I'm guessing you have mega-useful skills, in case guns and death start happening?"

"I wouldn't say *mega*-skills," offered Miles. "I can score five perfect hits with a handgun at thirty paces, have a Brown Belt in taekwondo and a Purple in judo, practise fencing every Sunday and have been rated 'superior' on my evocation and abjuration exams by leading members of the Westminster Coven of Wizards; whether any of that will be appropriate, who can say?"

Sharon's eyes met Rhys's, unable to hide a flicker of alarm. "Cool," she mumbled. "So, uh . . . do you know where to get a cuppa coffee round here?"

Chapter 8

Nothing Is Impossible

Two hours and several doughnuts later, Sharon sat with her head in her hands and tried not to whimper. In her time spent in Swift's office, the only definitive conclusion she'd reached was that this was a man for whom the notion of multicoloured highlighter pens and neatly labelled ring binders was anathema.

At her feet, Rhys squatted in one of the few clear patches of floor, evidently fascinated by the contents of a folder.

"Did you know," he said, "that wyverns have a kerosene problem?"

Sharon looked up from the depths of her despair. "Do they." The ice in her voice could have liquefied nitrogen, but Rhys was too enthused to notice.

"Apparently their second stomach is the perfect environment for cracking hydrocarbons – wyverns could be very useful in the petrochemical industry, couldn't they?"

"Anything about one of them eating sorcerers?"

"No. It's mostly long-chain alkenes. Sorry."

Sharon glared about her in frustration. Miles had somehow found a stool and, impressively, somewhere to plant it. He was likewise engrossed, in a report on the sanitary conditions of the kelkie nests at Twickenham. His feet were balanced on a pile of books, the top one of which was entitled *Black Grimoires – The Cautious Approach*. Sharon's gaze swept back to Swift's desk. Through a great deal of cursing, and some subtler encouragement from Rhys, they'd coaxed Swift's computer into turning on, only for the entire system to spend fifteen minutes auto-updating with no regard for Sharon's blood pressure. Now it was whirring like an asthmatic motorbike, with a screen laid out for her confusion that was almost as messy as the floor itself. She flicked through spreadsheets detailing annual expenditure on wands, wards, exorcists and transport; scrolled aimlessly through a guide to the latest techniques in three-circle summoning spells; then stared with furrowed brow at a news report from the *Archway Chronicle* detailing the disappearance of yet another one of its trusted readers, sometime around three in the morning on Tuesday last.

She hesitated, then clicked through to the full article.

Darren Clarke, digital rights executive, left the King's Head, Islington, at one a.m. on Tuesday morning, heading for his home in Highgate. Friends reported that he was sober and appeared to be in good spirits. When he didn't show up for work the next morning, colleagues attempted to contact him and, receiving no reply, went round to visit his abode. There was no sign that Darren had made it home. Police report the investigation as ongoing, but as this was the fourth resident to vanish from within the north London area in the last two weeks, speculation is mounting that there may be a criminal organisation at work. No bodies have been found, and police say that it is too early to speculate as to the fate of Darren, and others like him.

Sharon looked up from the computer. "Anyone got anything generally on people disappearing?"

Miles shook his head, and tossed the file on kelkie nests back into the mess of paper on the floor. He fumbled at random for another document.

"Um . . . newspaper clippings?" suggested Rhys, holding up a file. Sharon snatched it from his hand. A note on the front declared in Swift's scrawled handwriting, Bad Stuff. She scowled. If ever a man had needed to buy himself a copy of *Management for Beginners* it was the Midnight Mayor. If he was lucky, she'd even lend him hers, once she was through the chapter on successful negotiation strategies for the executive team.

She flicked through the clippings. They were sparse, but well fingered. The oldest dated from three weeks before, and reported that Kathleen Briars, a twenty-one-year-old mathematics student living in Roehampton, hadn't returned to her home, and parents and police were worried. The most recent reported that Yusef Kanun, sixty-seven-year-old former car dealer, had also vanished. Said the police spokesperson:

"We have received no evidence of foul play. It is sad but true that people often leave their homes for reasons which are not, of themselves, criminal, nor constitute a criminal act."

In one photo a much younger Yusef Kanun was beaming at the camera, his hand resting on the bonnet of a convertible car. Another showed a pair of shoes, their laces tied together, thrown over a leafless tree branch. The caption read: "Mr Kanun's shoes were spotted by his nephew a few hours after he was reported missing. There were no reported signs of violence in the area."

Sharon closed the file of clippings and slipped it into her shoulder bag. Looking up at the map on the wall, she wondered how many little red dots there were on it, and guessed at least thirty. Indicating the map, she murmured, "Anyone know what this is?"

After a pause, Miles said, "The Midnight Mayor was a rather private person. As far as I'm aware, the map was entirely his own work."

Sharon sighed. "Bloody typical. Hasn't this guy heard of ccing his emails?"

A thought snapped into her mind. She turned back to the computer, and went to Swift's email. A box appeared requesting the password. She glanced up at the Alderman. "Hey – you know how to get into this guy's email?"

"I believe that the Midnight Mayor's system is designed to be secure against both technological and magical attack," replied Miles. "He *is* the defender of the city, after all."

Rhys, however, was on his feet. "Email?" he asked, eyes glowing. "I'm good with email."

Sharon clambered off her perch, and balanced with one foot in a patch of empty floor and the other on a pile of reports, so that Rhys could position himself atop the volumes piled on Swift's chair. He leant over the keyboard, frowning with concentration. "Passwords," he murmured. "Passwords . . ."

He tried a couple out.

"Well, at least the password isn't 'password'," he mused. "Embarrassing how often you see that."

"I'm kinda hoping you've got more tricks up your sleeve than just typing 'password'?"

"I am an IT manager!" he replied with a little huff.

Sharon shrugged, and made her way carefully across the floor towards the map. On the other side of the room, Miles called out, "More tea, anyone?"

"God, yes."

"Yes, please!"

He bounded up and headed for the door. It closed behind him, and Sharon caught sight of Rhys's expression as he looked up from the keyboard. "Hey," she said, "he did offer to make the tea. It's not like I actually told him to be a minion."

Sharon scanned the map once more. Little red dots on a big piece of paper. She pulled out the file of newspaper clippings, checked a couple of dates, then looked up and ran her fingers over the map. A dot for the day of Darren's disappearance was marked, and labelled, Archway. There was also a dot for the day that Yusef had vanished, carefully annotated. Dozens of other dots had no corresponding mention in the newspaper cuttings; but then, she suspected, they didn't need one.

At the desk, Rhys muttered something, and hit Delete with unusual agitation. Keys clattered like falling rain beneath his fingers. Sharon watched, and Rhys, aware of her, began to turn red. The end of his nose twitched. His eyes were locked on the computer screen, but the swelling around his nostrils and eyelids grew manifest. Sharon fumbled automatically in her bag for a pack of tissues, having taken in recent weeks to having a reserve. He grabbed it from her even as one hand continued to type, and as the sneeze welled up to unstoppable proportions he exclaimed, "Aaaa . . . aaatchooo!" and slammed down on the Enter key.

The screen changed.

Sharon peered over Rhys's shoulder. He'd been working in the command prompt, and, as she looked, a series of commands self-perpetuated down the screen. She caught a glimpse of . . .

"Incantation equals one?"

"Um, yes," said Rhys, dabbing at his nose. "You could have said it equals true. But I always use this script because it's easier when you need to . . ."

"It was the 'incantation' part I'm querying, actually."

"Oh! Sorry! . . . Well, the druids always said that words had power, see? And in the old days sometimes you'd write the words with special inks or on human skin or things like that, and then they really had power . . ."

"Is 'ew' something shamans say?"

"Um, I don't know. I don't think druids say it, but then we have to become comfortable with organic fluids very early in the training process."

Sharon's face was a battlefield of warring curiosities. "Let's talk about computers," she said at length.

"Oh, yes! So, well, if words and books were sacred in the old days, then obviously now, what with magic evolving to suit the urban environment, binary data and server racks are becoming hubs of the new power. The trick," Rhys sat up straighter, warming to his subject, "is to find a proxy rack with a suitable energy tag, obviously not situated too close to a fibre ley line because – well – we all know what would happen then" – Sharon tried a bit of sage nodding. It seemed her safest bet – "and then you route it back here and use it as a focus for the invocation which you implant at the base level to allow it to percolate and multiply, until finally . . ."

The screen changed again. A little message box appeared. It read:

'Did You Know You Can Use Flags To Organise Your Inbox? Just One Of The Great New Features Of Mail 8.1!'

"... you can access some bugger's email?" suggested Sharon.

"Um ... yes."

Sharon contemplated this, while the screen filled up with Swift's email. Then, "Rhys ..."

"Yes, Ms Li?"

"I just gotta ask this, in my capacity as a knower of the truth and all that, but ..."

"Yes, Ms Li?"

"It seems like a lot of hard work, doesn't it?"

Rhys hesitated, then shrugged. "At least it's open source," he said. Sharon leant past him, examining the screen. Matthew Swift's approach to his email was not unlike his attitude to paper filing. Most of the items on the screen were unread, even those labelled URGENT or marked out with a big red flag. She did her best not to tut. *Management for Beginners* would have had critical things to say about all this. Only one or two had been read, standing out among the detritus.

[P. Ngwenya] Re: New York Expenses.

[K. Shiring] URGENT – Imp infestation in N. London.

[D. Sinclair] Invitation to dinner.

[P. Ngwenya] Re: re: New York Expenses – PAID.

[M. Seah] Re: your undead problem.

... and so on. As Rhys scrolled down, more emails appeared, and shuffled in through the server as if embarrassed at contributing to the volume of unread strangers already on Swift's hard drive.

She said, "Anything recent? Like in the last forty-eight hours?"

Rhys scrolled back to the top. A note from P. Ngwenya turned out to be a picture of a woman – presumably the P. Ngwenya in question – making a giant thumbs-up sign from on top of the Statue of Liberty. A caption underneath read:

WISHED YOU WERE HERE, BUT THE LOCALS SAID THEY LIKED THE QUIET LIFE

A quick note from one A. Huntley wished Mr Swift well in his enquiries, and invited him to drop by the Fields any time he needed further advice. An even shorter note from C. Wijesuriya informed the Midnight Mayor that the matter was being looked into, but, personally, she didn't think it likely.

A few emails down from the still-populating top of the screen was one headed:

[A. Hacq] Re: umbrella

"That one!" Sharon exclaimed. "Umbrellas! That one there!"

Rhys clicked it. It seemed to take a very long time to open. As it did, Miles came through the door, holding, with some dexterity, three steaming mugs of tea. "You got into the emails?" he asked, laying the mugs down wherever he could find.

"Rhys did."

"Ah – of course. I suppose you used the base incantation, routed through a proxy rack, yes?"

"Um . . . yes," said Rhys.

"Good trick that – lovely to see it still works."

Rhys bit his lip, and didn't answer. On the screen, the email from A. Hacq unfolded with the softness of a stick insect. Sharon peered at it. It was one line long.

Found the needle. Tonight, 11 p.m., Longshore Quay, Deptford. Bring money. A.A.

That was all.

Sharon looked at Rhys, and Rhys shrugged. She turned to Miles. "Know anything about a needle?"

"I'm afraid not. Should I?"

"Dunno – guess it depends whether you're a minion or a swot."

Miles beamed, which Rhys couldn't help but feel was the wrong reaction.

"Anything else from this guy?" she asked.

Rhys peered through the inbox. "One today." It, too, was headed as re: umbrella. Rhys went to click on it, then froze. "Uh . . ." he began.

The screen shimmered. It seemed, to Sharon's eye, that half the screen decided to go one way, while the other half went the other.

It happened in the blink of an eye, and then settled back to normal service, but there was no denying the moment had happened. Rhys's finger was frozen over the mouse button, ready to strike. But strike it did not.

"It's got an attachment," he murmured.

"Is that good?"

"It's a hex file."

"And ..."

"*Uh* ..." This time, Rhys's "uh" was the protracted, painful "uh" of someone seeking to give very bad news. The screen flickered again, and this time Sharon saw something move within it. It was a shadow, there only when the picture distorted, but, for a second, just a second, something was staring out at her from inside the screen.

The something was grey, pixellated, twisted, and had eyes.

Rhys lunged forward and turned the screen off with a sudden, decisive movement. "It's a hex!" he called, pushing Sharon away from the computer hard enough that she stumbled over a pile of paper and fell sprawling into a great mass of files. "I need magnets!" he cried, diving under the desk and pulling the power cable out of the back of the computer. Miles was already making for the door with the not-quite-run of a man who wishes to be seen as making merely a strategic withdrawal, not a full-blown retreat. Rhys continued clawing cables out of the machine, but it still went on giving a rising, determined whine. Sharon looked up at the screen, and, though it was black, the glass was warping; something was trying to push its way out like the screen itself was liquid, trapped within a barrier no thicker than a sheet of cling film. Something long and thin; something which, as it pushed, developed shape, grew protrusions, grew, unmistakably, claws.

"Rhys!"

Sharon scrambled to her feet. Rhys stuck his head up from under the desk, saw the claw and exclaimed, "I really need m-m-m-magne ... atchoo!"

"Rhys, this would be a great time to take your antihistamines!"

The claw was now all the way out of the screen, a thing of three talons that rounded to a sharpened point. It wasn't solid, in the sense of skin and bone, but, rather, seemed composed of static greys and flashing whites, of dull sparks and flashing blacknesses, as if its essence were pulled from the base stuff of the computer.

Rhys was fumbling desperately for his antihistamines, and now the arm had grown a shoulder.

Sharon looked around for a weapon. Finding nothing, she grabbed her shoulder bag and slammed it like a slingshot into the emerging arm. She felt resistance, an undeniable something in the air, but the arm just splattered into two where her bag struck and immediately reformed, the parts fusing back together with an electric fizz, like follicles of hair dragged towards a static balloon. Almost immediately a shoulder had moved all the way out of the screen, and the beginning of a head emerged: a sharp chin of static, a jaw that sparked and crackled as it opened wide, eyes of spinning data and rolling numbers, hair of bursting code that spat and scarred the screen as it wriggled its way out. Still looking for his antihistamines, Rhys sent wads of used tissues and old receipts tumbling out onto the floor, while water filled his eyes, but as the creature coming into view now turned its head and seemed to see Sharon, he gave a cry of, "I think I left them at the office!"

Sharon yelped with exasperation. "Tell me how to stop it!"

"I need magnets!" he wailed again, wiping the back of his nose with his sleeve.

Sharon swung her bag again, slamming through the head of the creature as it began to pull its torso out of the now-smoking screen. The head dissolved, and reformed, all in a smooth, hissing crackle of static. She hit it again, and as the creature flopped out across the desk, only its legs yet to come, she reached out for Rhys and prepared to run. The world was already shimmering grey around her, the cold drizzle of invisibility ready to drop over them both.

Then someone was at the door. She glimpsed blond hair and a flowing black coat, and with a cry of "Don't mind me, now!" Miles the Alderman burst into the room, leapt dexterously between the drifts of paperwork heaped on the floor, slid easily beneath the desk and with a great metallic thump, slammed a pair of magnets the size of frying pans against either side of Swift's machine.

The creature, nearly all out of the screen by now, screamed.

It was an electronic scream, the high beep of an error sound, prolonged into a great whine of distress. The thing's body rippled with static, great pulses of whiteness surging out of the screen and down to its fingertips, and with each pulse it writhed and twisted, the fingers dissolving to dull grey sparks that fizzed as they dissolved on the air, then hands, arms, shoulders, head, back and bony hips, as with a final burst of whiteness the creature pressed against the screen and vanished.

Silence settled over the office.

Rhys gave a huge sneeze.

Miles stood back, laying down the two magnets on the desk. Something caught his eye, and a smile burst across his features. "Tea!" he exclaimed, seeing the three mugs gently steaming. "That was what we were doing, wasn't it?"

Chapter 9

If at First You Don't Succeed...

Sharon, Miles and Rhys sat on a sofa in the lofty glass-walled reception area of Harlun and Phelps and drank tea in thoughtful silence.

At length Rhys said, "I . . . I think I found my antihistamines, Ms Li."

Sharon looked up from her mug of tea. A foil packet containing one white pill was gripped in the druid's hand. Fluff clung to it, from the ultimate depths of his pocket.

"Oh, good," she murmured. "That's great."

Miles's voice, when he spoke, seemed suddenly far too loud. "You know, it takes a lot to get a hex file through the firewalls in this place. Which I think is something positive we can take from the experience." At the stare that Sharon and Rhys each gave him, lesser men would have squirmed. Miles was not a lesser man. "If someone is attempting to cover up their activities by attacking us with a binary hex," he said, "then it does rather imply that we are in danger of stumbling on their activities, doesn't it? Which is a marvellous indicator of positive progress!"

Sharon hesitated. To her irritation, the Alderman had a point.

She rolled the handle of the umbrella between her palms, then turned it over to examine the end. There was a small hollow where the point of the umbrella had been removed. The inside of the hollow was rusted; clearly this operation had happened some time ago. She ran her finger carefully along the curve and for a moment there was,

Snap snap snap umbrella snap along street surface
        pouring rain drum
water running off the edges
    pain in sharp and hot and
forgotten
        taste of dirt
in the mouth
    in the throat
        suffocating
            choking
                hot!
                can't
                    breathe!
                Can't breathe!
                CAN'T BREATHE!
                CAN'T BREATHE HOW DARE THEY

She choked and dropped the umbrella, clawing at her throat and gasping for air. The world was spinning, her eyes watering; and as she choked she simultaneously tried to cough, to spit, to splutter, to get air in and dust out, her chest contracting and bursting all at once within her.

"Ms Li!" Rhys was by her side, pushing Miles out of the way, grabbing her by the shoulders as she leant forward. She hauled down air and almost at once gasped it out, as if her need for oxygen was too great for one petty lungful of air to satisfy it. The umbrella had fallen between her feet; instinctively she kicked it away as she shuddered and pulled down more air.

Slowly, the rushing of her heart retreated from her ears and throat. She looked up, and managed to wheeze, "Mega-fucking-mystic-fucking-umbrella!"

Gingerly, Miles picked it up, examining every inch. "Interesting," he mused. "I really can't detect anything mystic about it."

"It's bloody magical!" she retorted. "Who the hell has a magical umbrella?"

"Mary Poppins?" suggested Rhys. She trod on his foot. "Sorry," he said.

"I'm sure you're correct, Ms Li," said the Alderman, "but we did have a good look at it and I'm sorry to say that no one detected a glimmer of any spell. Which isn't to say that it hasn't been used for mystic purposes in the past; merely that, at the moment, the umbrella's purpose seems entirely related to the weather."

Sharon's scowl deepened. Briefly and, she felt, perhaps naïvely, she wondered if the time hadn't come to consult her spirit guide. All shamans, so she'd been told, had one – a psychological manifestation of their deepest thoughts, feelings and strengths made visible to them alone – but it was a continual irritation to her that her own spirit guide, far from the majestic being of light she'd hoped for, was a cheap talk-show host by the name of Dez. Particularly irksome was the feeling that Dez's manifestation, from the inner recesses of her consciousness, could be no one's fault but hers. She looked up and saw Rhys's face set in an expression of expectant optimism. He was, she reminded herself, a believer. It was just bizarre that the thing he believed in was her.

"Right," she said, and felt surprised to hear herself. Then, firmer, to make sure it wasn't a mistake, "Right!" She got to her feet. "Well, there's no point arsing about here, hoping it'll get better by itself. Time to ... fulfil our management obligations, yes?"

"Absolutely, Ms Li!" enthused Miles. "How do you propose following this excellent plan?"

She thought; but the answer, it seemed, was obvious. "What's the best way to Deptford?"

Chapter 10

... Try, Try Again

They took the Overground.

This surprised Sharon. It wasn't just that the line through Whitechapel and across the river was new; it was that it was new, sleek, punctual and all things for which the words 'National Rail' seemed destined to reject. It wound through that transitional part of town where the City met the East End, humming above the streets whose occupants looked up from bus stops and cracked old benches as if they couldn't quite believe what they were seeing. Posters at the stations warned passengers heading towards Camden Road and Willesden that, during this season, leaves might fall on the line and this could be a problem. But such reassurance that the Overground was, in fact, a part of London's transport network and fulfilled the requisite clichés of the same, was countered by the promise, then arrival, of trains to within a few seconds of when they were due.

But if Shoreditch was shocked at finding itself accessible by public transport, Deptford was having no such crisis. Set between the royal palaces of Greenwich and the solid, unpretentious housing of Bermondsey, Deptford was an industrial embarrassment. Into its tangle of one-way streets and drive-through burger bars, great splats of aluminium-walled warehouses and grubby-faced offices had been thrown like dirty droppings from the urban paint brush. Century Industrial Complex ("A Legacy Of Success") hid a cardboard-box company, a sandwich maker and a printer of quirky T-shirts; Cannon Wharf Business Centre ("For All Your Commercial Needs") contained the offices of a company which supplied ushers for large public events, a coffee importer and three men who hired lights for far too little to people who couldn't afford to pay a penny more. A potted plant in its reception area assured visitors that no matter how bleak, functional and cold this place might seem, they were, in fact, welcome guests in a dynamic environment.

The white warehouses of Longshore Quay ("Bringing Innovation To Your Working Environment") were lined up like warriors squaring off for battle in long ranks that ran from the gateway down to the river, in units each consisting of a small metal door for humans, and a far larger metal shutter for lorries to back through when making deliveries and connections. Stepping past a barrier by the abandoned entrance, Sharon could smell diesel and hear the distant long-ago cries of foremen and porters as they juggled their loads in and out in a perpetual flow of cut flowers, fresh eggs, pasteurised milk, clean paper, soft toilet roll and all the unseen essentials of city commerce – now faded to nothing more nor less than echoes that whispered in the shaman's mind. She looked down and now saw cracked grey tarmac through which grass and sharp-leaved weeds were pushing their way up. The signs that had stood above the lorry bays were gone, leaving no more than outlines on the wall, or odd letters dangling by a single nail from scarred concrete and crumbling brick. Even the nearby waters of the Thames, in an ancient timber-lined inlet where wooden vessels had once offloaded their cargos from the Empire, seemed sullen and dull as they slapped against the quay.

"Why would the Midnight Mayor come here?" Miles spoke in the breathy tone of one who'd hoped his companions would have put the question first, and spared him from betraying his own bewilderment.

Sharon didn't answer. She walked on, between the shuttered bays and faded signs, and listened. For all that commerce had long since abandoned Longshore Quay, life, with pesky unstoppability, had pushed its way in through the rusting chain fence, and as she walked she heard

Soft step of the fox padding through the night
Scuttle of the rat hiding from the hunter
    clatter of a saucepan – a family of travellers, thirty to the clan, who rested here for three nights on their way to somewhere better, hate the cops, fuck the state, this is the way to live, this is freedom!
    giggle of the children from the estate
        who came here to try some things that were legal, and several which were not and loved it
    until the bad trip
        when they got scared
and never came back

She half closed her eyes, trying to hear something more specific. Every part of the city, every corner, was, she knew, infused with a kind of life. Not necessarily sentient, not always something that would come out of the walls and secret places and tell her its secrets face to face, although that, too, could happen, when the situation was right – but a life which left its scars on the very stones and which, if you knew how to use it, could be a kind of magic.

And as Sharon moved, listening, she began, very gently, to turn invisible. It wasn't a fading. It wasn't a greying-at-the-edges. It was simply an ever-increasing difficulty in noticing that Sharon was there at all, as by degrees she became so much a part of her environment that there was, to the watching eye, nothing to distinguish her from the background until . . .

"I say, does Ms Li vanish into thin air on a regular basis?" asked Miles.

"Oh, yes," Rhys exclaimed. "It's part of being a shaman, see?"

"Well, yes, I did know that; I just wasn't aware that shamans disappeared habitually, rather than on, say, special occasions."

"Isn't this a special occasion? I mean . . . investigating?"

"Good God, I suppose it must seem that way to you, yes!" exclaimed the Alderman. "How thoughtless of me!"

In the grey place where shamans walked, and where the truth of what really was slipped out of hiding and did battle with the truth of what was simply perceived, Sharon walked, and looked, and listened. The ghosts of lorries past moved around her; the shadows of faceless men were burnt into the ground in the moment when their colleague was hit by a truck, his blood bright in this shimmering place, leg twisted to one side and he would live, but it would be all that management needed to shut this place down, no longer effective, no longer efficient, goodbye the Longshore Quay. She scratched irritably at the palm of her hand and looked for the Midnight Mayor, for some sign of him, unable to comprehend how someone as inclined for calamity as Matthew Swift could have moved through this place and not left his mark.

And there he was, a brief flicker. He stood directly in front of her, right hand raised, a hand wearing fingerless black gloves which hid the scars of his office; he was staring her in the eye and his face was set in an expression which was almost inhuman in its emptiness, its cold impassivity. He was gone as quickly as he was there, a shadow swept up in the rest of the spinning mass that swirled around this place; but it was good enough. Sharon stepped forward, the movement snapping her back into visibility and the world into colour, and she heard the slight grunt of recognition – for he was not one to be outright surprised – from Miles as she reappeared.

"He was here," she declared. "Swift came here, just like the email told him to."

"Um . . . the email from the man who sent a binary hex into the computer system?" queried Rhys. "Which isn't to say I'm not excited by the detective work, Ms Li, I am, but it's just that binary hexes take a lot of effort, see, and I'm not very good at . . . "

"I'll handle any unpleasantries," interrupted Miles. "You can just hang back, and leave that sort of thing to me."

He was already marching after Sharon as she moved on between the abandoned lorry bays, which was why he didn't see the glare the druid shot at his back.

They made their way down one row of parking bays, then back past another. The shutters were nearly all down and locked in place by rusting padlocks, the keys long since lost, but one or two had been broken open in recent years, and gaps left for the wind to explore. Now and then Sharon paused to peer into one of the darkened bays, looking for, at best, a sign declaring "Swift was 'ere" and, at the very least, a drop of blood, an abandoned gun or perhaps a smoking umbrella. Rhys carried the big blue umbrella under one arm. The shaman herself hadn't wanted to go near it, but he was already wondering whether having an umbrella didn't give him a distinguished look which his tendency towards oversized shirts and saggy jeans had never quite achieved.

At the end of the quay, the river was hidden beneath the sharp drop of a concrete embankment. Its waters slapped muddily at low tide. Ships drifted by as though floating on air: the little police boat bouncing on its way to another call; a sleek catamaran powering round the Isle of Dogs in a roar of speed; a tug dragging three floating pallets of metal boxes and rubber pipes. The world slid by, busy and uninterested.

Then Sharon stopped, and stared.

A unit like any other, the metal shutter pulled down and locked tight. There were no graffiti, no blood pooled on the ground, not even a helpful note pinned up and explaining everything, though Sharon had lived in hope. What there was, however, was a very shiny, very new, padlock holding the shutter down.

"So," she said, "call me, like, Sherlock friggin' Holmes, but how many new padlocks have you guys seen in this place?"

Miles seized the padlock, testing it. "Ah," he declared. "Now, I have just the spell for this sort of occasion . . . "

But Sharon had already walked straight through the nearest wall.

Darkness, reduced a little by two high, narrow windows so dirty it was a miracle any daylight made it through the grime. There was a strong smell of bleach. The walls were white-painted breeze blocks; and a notice by the door warned employees not to smoke.

Sharon peered at the cement floor. Great pale streaks had been washed across its settled dirt, and recently, too: cloud-like patterns of grubby and clean had been made by the rubbing of a cloth, the swirling of a mop, the scrubbing of a brush.

A moment later, light flooded in as Miles unlocked the shutter and rolled it up, letting in daytime and the smell of the river. As Rhys stepped inside, his nose crinkled in distaste at the raw smell of chemical detergents.

"Cleaned recently?" mused Miles.

"Recently scrubbed bare," corrected Sharon. "Which sucks for the investigation thing, but is kinda cool in the at-least-there's-a-cover-up sorta sense."

Rhys raised a hand in enquiry. "Are we pleased there's a cover-up?" he asked.

"Well, it's better than there being *nothing*. Positive thinking!" Sharon beamed to hear herself speak such reassuring words. "Positive thinking is the way to . . . to do stuff. Positively."

Rhys's smile was strained. "What we need," she persisted, "are *clues*. Maybe a mystic anorak, that'd be kinda in the zone, or a letter beginning 'dear reader' and ending with 'so I confess to everything' – I mean, we'd get fewer brownie points for investigative coolness, but it'd save a lot of time."

"How about a burnt telephone line?"

Miles was squatting to look at something by the back wall. There were two electrical sockets, and a single, scorched-looking telephone line, with no wires attached but a great scar of soot still curling from its interior. The Alderman sniffed, and beamed. "I love the smell of fried circuitry in the morning."

The others hurried over to look. Sharon brushed her fingers against the edge of the outlet, and there was

WE TOLD YOU SO!

a shout, gone as quickly as it had come, in a voice that was strange, unnatural, furious. "So," she murmured, straightening up and looking round the bare unit. "Matthew Swift . . . he's not *just* human, is he? I mean, there's the blue electric angels, too, and they're big on phones, yeah?"

"They are, in fact, a composite life form created from the magic of the telephones." Miles spoke in the prim voice of a man who's read a textbook and hopes everyone else will appreciate the same. "If we take the old adage that life is magic, then wherever life goes, so magic will spring, and of course the telephones are just screaming with life . . ."

"And boom, blue electric angels?"

"Exactly so – boom. I hadn't thought of saying 'boom' before, but yes, that's highly apt, where these creatures are concerned."

"And they're part of Swift?"

"Or he's part of them. No one is really sure of the distinction, any more. What are you thinking, Ms Li?"

Sharon shrugged. "Stinky commercial unit in Deptford, mystic umbrella, missing sorcerer, crispy telephone line . . . dunno. Am I supposed to know already? I mean, I get that it's a big responsibility, investigating a missing Midnight Mayor and that, but I kinda assumed that there was a difference between brilliant, incisive leaps and rushing into things like a pillock." She looked to Rhys for assurance, but he merely widened his helpless smile.

Sharon looked around once more, then bent down until her nose almost brushed the floor, examining the swirls left in the dirt by a wet cloth. She stood up, walked towards a wall and pressed her shoulder blades against it, then got back down on her hands and knees and turned her head this way and that, scrutinising the floor.

"It's okay," said Rhys, seeing Miles's frown of speculation. "I'm sure this is a shaman thing."

"You seeing this?" asked Sharon, still on all fours.

"Um . . . seeing what, Ms Li?"

"Someone's cleaned this place up, right? I mean, really scrubbed it."

"Yes . . ."

"But they didn't bother with cleaning everything, only the stuff they'd made dirty."

"Um . . ."

Sharon sprang back up and grabbed Rhys by the elbow, pulling him back until he could see nearly all the floor. "They cleaned up their mess," she exclaimed, "so now the things what were dirty are much cleaner than everything else! Look at where the floor is clean, and what do you see?"

Rhys looked. He saw great sweeps of floor made pale by scrubbing, splashes where water had sloshed from a bucket, a mess of tide marks in one corner where someone had scrubbed so hard they'd almost peeled the sand out of the concrete itself. And, if he looked in just the right way, then perhaps, in all the ebbs and flows of dirt, he saw . . .

"A circle."

Rhys bit his lip as Miles spoke, then managed a manly nod of assent.

The Alderman walked along the edge of a stretch of cleaned floor, marking out with his black polished toe the course of a cleaner stretch of clean that did indeed make, quite distinctly, a circle.

"Too small to be a summoning circle," he mused. "You need more room, just to ensure enough oxygen content in the atmosphere. Maybe an enchanting or binding circle? Hard to tell now they've washed it away. Not meant to be used again, otherwise they'd have used paint to draw it. Chalk, maybe? Bit old-fashioned, but all right as a temporary solution."

Sharon opened her mouth, then closed it. Then, very slowly, she said, "So, will it undermine my super-cool investigative vibe if I admit that we haven't done magic circles in class yet?"

"Oh no, Ms Li!" blurted Rhys.

"Do shamans use magic circles?" asked Miles.

"Dunno. Maybe we don't. Maybe that's why we haven't covered them in class. You know what it's like being taught by a goblin – he's great on things to do with carved wyvern bone, but not so hot when it comes to syllabus breakdowns. Then again," Sharon brightened, "you gotta know your limitations and trust your friends, so that's why you guys are here, and pride *is* the failing of great men."

"Is it?" asked Rhys.

"I dunno. Isn't it?" Turning to Miles to avoid Rhys's stare, she asked, "Is it safe?"

"Safe? Oh yes, once the circle itself is washed away there's really no residual energy left. Detergent, in fact, almost guarantees that the original purpose of the circle is neutralised. That's why, I suspect, this place has such a pungent aroma."

"Oh. Good." Cautiously, she stepped into the circle, looking for a shadow of its purpose.

As her foot brushed the centre, her fingers spasmed into fists. Her head twisted up and back, mouth opening in pain, and for a moment she stood there, her heel not yet on the floor, a silent cry of pain at the back of her throat as her body rocked and twisted. Then her own momentum pushed her onward and she staggered out of the circle again. Her hands were shaking, and her eyes rippled with water. "Bloody hell," she wheezed, leaning against the nearest wall for support. "I thought you said it was safe!"

Miles was by her side in an instant. "I'm so sorry, Ms Li! What happened?"

"What happened? That thing," she stabbed a quavering finger across the floor, "is hotter than a chippy's frying pan! So much for the fricking training!"

Miles edged towards the centre of the circle. He knelt down just off-centre, and brushed his fingers over the floor. "Perhaps . . . something," he mused at last. "A residual glow, maybe, but . . . it's very unlikely. For there to be any lingering magical activity after this time, and after the clean that this place was given, would imply a spell of incredible power – dangerous power – being performed here."

"Great," Sharon grumbled. "Because all I wanted to make my day complete were the words 'dangerous power'. Rhys, do you have . . . ?"

But Rhys wasn't looking at Sharon. His attention had been drawn to the base of the wall. There was something dark on one of the breeze blocks, a speck of brown against the white paint. He bent down until his eyes were almost level with it. "Um . . . I think it's blood."

Sharon hurried to look. The mark on the wall was tiny, barely noticeable, a fleck of drying, rust-brown particles. "Dunno," she said. "It's either blood or a really unlucky fly."

"I can call a forensic team . . . " offered Miles.

"How long'll that take?"

"Well, what with our recent budgetary ... upheavals ... We've had to sub-contract some of this work, and it'll take a while to process the lab results, but the work they do is highly professional and I really feel ..."

"Only I'm thinking," she cut in, "if we're dealing with blood, then I know this real expert we could call."

"Do you?"

"Totally," she said, straightening up and reaching for her mobile phone. "Only thing is, he's not much good in daylight."

Chapter 11

Some Skills Come Naturally

The sun was down over London, slipping beneath a cold, grey sky.

The onset of darkness – if not yet night – brought a shift in the speed and volume of the city's traffic. Commuters huddled in tighter under the bus shelters, pressing shoulder to shoulder against the wind; hot air flowed out of the doors of packed, sweating bars where men rolled up their sleeves and women let down their hair for a night of warm wine to drive away the darkness. The smell of garlic and saffron tumbled out of the curry houses, stronger now that the light was gone and the mind grew more reliant on other senses. On the steamed-up windows of the buses, schoolchildren wrote messages in the condensation, which faded to grease smears on the glass. Streetlamps snapped on with a washed-out light which swelled to pink, orange or yellow intensity as the last rays of daylight retreated, and children were called in for dinner, muddy trousered as they kicked their shoes off inside the door.

Darkness fell, and, as it did, two rather special things happened.

In a tiny square of land, hemmed in by offices and roads, where plane trees towered over lichen-crusted stone, the warden drew a padlock across an iron gate, snapped it shut for the night and headed for his bike, propped against the sign warning travellers not to rest their cycles here. He reached for the first of the two chains that bound it, and thought he heard, at his back, the gentle tumbling of damp earth. From habit he looked around, ready to curse the local kids, or the squirrels or the foxes that played havoc with his neatly kept graveyard, but none were to be seen. He stepped close to the iron railings around this little patch of greenery in the heart of the city, and listened again, but the slow sound he had heard had now faded. He shrugged, a little self-consciously, embarrassed to have felt the need even to pause and look, and turned, and unchained his bicycle, and pedalled away, dinging his bell at those who didn't get in his way, and muttering obscenities at any who might.

Behind him, in the darkness beneath the gravestones, something stirred. Limbs of bone and black rotten leather pressed upwards and felt the earth, very softly, give. It was slow going, hard going, but they were getting closer.

That was the first thing that happened as darkness fell.

The second thing was this:

A curtain is opened.

A shutter pulled back from a window.

Then a second shutter, solid metal, slid away.

A pair of watery eyes flick back from the final lingering glow of sunset.

A phone is turned on, the white glow from its screen only highlighting the extreme pallor of the skin which touches it. A text has been received. The eyes scan it, the eyebrows waggle at it, and a voice declares,

"Oh God, that is so totally *gross*."

It was forty minutes later, but the quality of moan had a depth and persistency that could not be measured in mere time.

"Babes, while I'm, like, totally flattered that you think I'm some sort of expert in blood, I gotta tell you I can't be working in unsterilised environments. There might be pathogens!"

His name is Kevin and he is, to everyone's surprise, a vampire. It's surprising – not because he doesn't try – pale skin, pale hair, clingy jeans are all, potentially very much In Season for that most fashion-conscious species (or perhaps ethnic grouping, Sharon's not sure) of the ebon night – but because somehow, with his bag of sterile wipes, latex gloves and dental floss, he just doesn't give off the traditional vibe.

"So, like, what happened here?"

Rhys looked at Sharon. Sharon looked at Miles. Miles looked at Kevin, smile locked in place ready for battle, and tried to work him out. While vampires were, technically, very dangerous, the Aldermen's attitude towards them was generally one of, you don't mind us, we won't mind you – just remember to register with your local NHS blood bank and no midnight snacks. No one said it was a happy arrangement, but at least it was an understanding. One which he couldn't fully extend in his mind to cover Kevin.

Seeing that no one else was about to volunteer, Sharon cleared her throat, and said, "Uh . . . so, we think that the Midnight Mayor was lured here with something to do with an umbrella – maybe this mega-mystic umbrella . . . " – she waved it in the air – " . . . where he probably met some kind of dire magic end which I don't know much about but which I'm feeling was pretty catastrophic owing to, you know, the cover-up and smell of bleach and that, and Rhys found blood. And Miles here . . . " a helpful wave towards Miles, "thought maybe a forensic team but then I thought," a note of urgency seeped into Sharon's tone, "why wait three days for lab results when we could get an expert, a *real*, qualified, totally on it expert, to come down and do the blood thing right now?"

Kevin considered. "Well, babes, it's, like, really sweet that you thought of me, and I'm touched, yeah, but thing is . . . this blood you've found . . . it might have been anywhere. I mean, do you know how long tetanus can live outside the body? Fucking ages, that's how long."

"I don't think anyone here died of tetanus," offered Sharon, shrinking before Kevin's hygienic disapproval. "Although maybe they did, we don't know, but it would be seriously unlucky for this whole vanishing-blood-umbrella-mystery thing to coincide with someone going into the dying throes of a rare disease. Unless actually tetanus is involved somehow, in which case I guess that's something we oughtta know. Either way, I'm sure you can see why we need you?"

The vampire sniffed, inducing an involuntary mirror-sniff in Rhys. "You mentioned bleach?"

Sharon's face lit up. "Yeah! Bleach everywhere! I mean, it's so sterile in there, you could perform brain surgery or that! Just a tiny bit of blood, and we've been very clean, haven't we?" – she shot a warning glare at Rhys and Miles – " . . . so I'm thinking that even if there is tetanus involved, the odds of uncontrolled infection and death are really, really low."

Kevin swayed almost imperceptibly, considering his options. Seeing him waver, Sharon added, "Also, did I mention . . . fate of the city and that? I feel kinda guilty bringing it up, because I know it's manipulative to bring in the whole 'oh God we might die' quality here when we don't know anything, and it might actually not be the case, but I just want you to know that this is how strongly I feel about it."

The vampire sighed, revealing a hint of sharpened teeth. "Fine," he grumbled. "But if I get something *disgusting* from this, I think you should know that I'm totally going private, not NHS."

Sharon beamed. "Knew we could count on you."

"Yeah yeah yeah . . . "

Kevin ducked beneath the metal shutter, into the white-walled unit; the others followed. Rhys, Miles and Sharon stood uneasily as he prowled, examining the floor and walls with distaste expressed in face, shoulders, arms and back, his whole body unified in apathy. Finally, "Okay, so yeah, I'm getting some blood. Fresh-ish, I think, although bacteria can divide in less than twenty minutes and that's, like, long enough for some serious contamination." Kevin looked at the others for reassurance, but was met with blankness. He sighed at his unhygienic companions. "Most of the blood's human; kinda hard to tell anything about it, though, what with the clean-up. Some of it is . . . " He sniffed again, then wrinkled his nose and reached for his shoulder bag. "Oh God, that's just, so disgusting!" he whimpered, pulling out a white face mask in a sterile wrap and, to Sharon's surprise, a small plastic nasal spray. Inserting the spray first in one nostril, then the other, he gave two great puffs of vapour and slipped the mask over his nose and mouth with a rubber band, before turning to the others and offering them the same.

"Um ... thanks, but no thanks?" said Sharon. "What's so disgusting – specifically, I mean?"

"Babes, some of this blood is, like, totally not human," Kevin confided. "I mean, it *might* be a bit human, there's kinda some haemoglobin and plasma and stuff, but if you could smell it, you'd be, like, that's gross, I mean, *uch*. Like, I wouldn't drink it even if you put it through a dialysis machine and three months of antibiotics." Seeing that Miles's mouth was hanging open, Kevin shifted uneasily and added, "Uh, have I, like, got something on my face?"

Miles switched to default battle-smile. In a voice of drifting serenity, he breathed, "Do you do much blood work?"

"My God," groaned the vampire. "Getting a decent pint of O Negative is, like, such fucking hard work these days. You've gotta get a whole medical history before you know the stuff is any good, and, you know, one in ten people under twenty-five has a sexually transmitted disease, and probably doesn't even know it?"

"Kevin has Seah's Syndrome," explained Sharon. "He can only drink a certain blood type."

"A certain fucking rare blood type, usually given to wankers in the same section of DNA that codes for living an unsanitary life."

Miles's head nodded almost by itself. "I see," he murmured. "I can understand how that would be problematic."

"But if we can briefly turn our attention back to the fate of the city ...?" ventured the shaman.

"Uh, babes, dunno what else I can tell you. Loads of human blood, I mean, like, way too much to be healthy, and some of this weird-crap not-quite-human blood, all over the place. Chemicals," he added sourly, "are usually only good for spreading the stuff around."

"Does any of the blood go outside?"

"Uh, a bit. I mean, I think someone tried to do a bit of a tidy-up in here, cos they get the human outside and it's still dribbling but, like, way less, so I'm guessing that the human bleeder did most of its shit indoors. The non-human stuff smells pretty much the same outside, too, but we're talking, way lighter, I mean, like a surface wound or something like that – ew but not icky."

"I hadn't thought of it like that," Sharon murmured. "Can you follow it?"

Kevin's eyes narrowed in suspicion. "So long as there's no danger or anything like that," he said. "I mean, I totally get the fate of the city thing, but, like, do you know how long it takes for nails to grow after you're dead?"

They followed him out into the night.

"How did you meet Kevin?" asked Miles, falling into step beside Sharon and Rhys.

"He attends Magicals Anonymous meetings," she explained. "Also, he's trying to sue his dentist for ethnic discrimination."

"Uh, guys?" called out Kevin, half turning towards them. "I can, like, totally hear everything you're saying, what with these amazing hunter-predator instincts I've got going."

"Stop me if I say anything wrong," Sharon called back.

"I was just going to congratulate you on your civic spirit and modern attitude," added Miles. "So refreshing to meet a vampire who isn't stuck in the 1890s."

They reached the river. Kevin stopped at the edge of the quay, turning this way and that to sample the air. The tide was out, revealing glistening black mud beneath the embankment walls, and a flight of four rotted wooden steps, the remnants of what had been a proud stairway. "So," he said, "I'm thinking the human bleeder got thrown into the water. There's, like, a definite stop in the scent, and a bit of mould, which is, like, uch, because there'll be spores. But, yeah."

"What about the not-quite-human bleeder?" asked Sharon. "What happens to him?"

"Trail's a bit faint," admitted Kevin. "But he's still dribbling, and whoever did the bleach job back in the unit hasn't bothered to do anything out here, so . . ." He prowled along the waterfront for several yards, head bent towards the ground, before giving a cry of triumph.

"Bodily fluids right ahead!"

In the faded light, the smear was almost invisible, and under other circumstances Sharon might have dismissed it as another streak of dirt or an erratic spill of shadow on the cracked tarmac. But as Kevin took another precautionary dose of nasal spray, and Rhys fumbled for his tissues, she looked again at the thin, diamond-shaped splash. "Looks human," said Miles. "Directional droplets, indicating the victim is moving."

"Babes, it may *look* human, but I'm telling you, that red stuff is, like, such a big no-no."

Miles gave the vampire a look. It occurred to Sharon that this might be the first time anyone had called the Alderman "babes". Kevin, meanwhile, stepped round the blood and nodded towards a small prefabricated building by the water's edge. "Trail goes that way, if you're, like, determined to follow it."

No one seemed determined. Sharon sighed, and with a rallying cry of, "Come on, minions," marched onward.

The building had been an office. Like elsewhere in that place it seemed to have been abandoned overnight. Desks still stood against the walls; venetian blinds were crookedly locked across the cracked windows. A series of pictures up on the wall showed men in yellow jackets and hard hats beaming at the camera. The oldest photos were yellowing, with grey mould beneath the glass, and painted a picture of the times. In a group from 1982 a hundred men were lined up; seventy smiled out from 1989. In 1993 the first and only woman stood with her fifty comrades for the shot, her white hard hat at a jaunty angle, her hi-vis jacket defiantly bright among the stained garments of the men; by 1997 she was gone, as were another twenty employees. By 2003, in the last photo, twenty-six grim-faced men, all young save three veterans, with knee-high orange boots and chipped hard hats, stared out at the photographer as if trying to warn through silence all who came after to beware the things they themselves had seen. A bronze plaque above an abandoned coffee table read:

Industry Safety Standards Award 2002–2003. Making Britain Better.

Across this, and a large section of the wall, someone had written in giant orange paint:

GOODBYE

That was all.

Sharon thought about looking at the shadow of the thing, peering into the ghostly depths of the building's past; then thought again. It was too easily evident right here on the surface of things: a truth that could not but be perceived, and needed no shaman's vision to penetrate. The line of not-quite-human blood had run in a thin trail of droplets from the water's edge up to the door of the building. A couple of fingerprints, stained red, showed where the door had been pushed open. The source of the blood trail had then wandered into a corner of the room and, judging by a streak of discolouration down the wall, sunk into a corner to bleed a while longer. There it had gone on bleeding, long enough to leave a still-sticky pool on the floor. "Uch uch uch!" wailed Kevin, flapping like a man troubled by a swarm of invisible flies. "So gross!"

Sharon leant down to examine the small puddle of blood with what she hoped was a suitably professional expression. There was a small indent along one edge, filled with viscous, solidifying blood. It was the tiny corner of a shoeprint, the toe turned towards the wall. Another door stood open; this one led to a smaller yard behind the cabin where thick white pipes still protruded from the earth, a promise of plumbing left unrepaired. Thin drops of blood moved from the cabin to a metal cover set in the ground. From beneath it came the sound of rushing water. Sharon prodded the cover with her toe, and it shifted. "Sewers?" she asked.

"Oh *God* . . . " whimpered Kevin.

Miles knelt down beside the manhole, tracing with his finger round a drop of blood on its rim. "We must be near an outlet," he mused. "Whoever's bleeding went down there."

"Babes, I *am* on board with the fate of the city stuff," said Kevin, "but I am *not* going into a sewer."

Rhys said, "I-I-I can't say I'd enjoy it, Ms Li, but if someone bleeding did go down there this is very important so if you think someone ought to go into the sewer then, of course, I'll do what needs to be done . . . "

Sharon raised a hand to silence the rest of this unhappy thought. "Whoa there. Let's not get ahead of ourselves, yeah? Because, while I think Kevin has got some issues with hygiene – which we all respect that you're working through – I've only got one good pair of boots and even I think it might be time to go health and safety on this one. Let's just . . . lever this thing up," she kicked the manhole cover, "and if there's not a body obviously in sight, then maybe we should call the professionals. Which isn't to say that we *aren't* professional," she added. "Just that sometimes it's *professional* to call the professionals."

Miles already had a blade in his hand. It was kitchen-knife long, and white, like it was made of pottery. He slipped it under the edge of the manhole cover, teeth clenching as he twisted the knife to give more leverage. Sharon, then Rhys, seized the raised edge of the metal, while Kevin lurked behind them with a cry of, "So I'll just, like, keep watch?"

The heavy cover slid to one side, cold and damp from condensation. There was darkness below, flecked with the glow of rushing if-only-it-were-water. The cool night air suppressed the worst of the smell, but it was still there, a throat-twisting assault that made every pore clench up. Miles reached out a hand over the gap; his lips moved in an incantation as he opened up his palm to create a small bauble of light, white and fluorescent, which drifted away and down into the shaft. It revealed no bodies, but a certain brownness to the waters rushing below that Sharon could have done without seeing illuminated. Thick grey-green growths clung to the walls of the shaft, and an unignorable warmth drifted up. Then:

"Stop!" In the dull glow of Miles's light, Rhys had seen something on the walls. "There!"

Miles pulled the light back up to where Rhys was pointing. Sharon edged round the manhole to see better. Scratched in black, burnt onto the wall as if with a smouldering charcoal stick, was a set of stick figures. One, wearing a baseball cap, hurled a bunch of flowers at a woman in a triangular skirt, who in reply held a bazooka aloft. Between them a child stood, a balloon shaped like a bleeding heart attached limply to her wrist by a string. They were crude and small, but it was clear enough what they were meant to show.

Sharon said, "Okay. We definitely didn't cover this in shaman club."

Miles lay belly-down next to her and peered at the figures, the light flickering erratically as his concentration wavered between the spell and the drawings. "Damn," he breathed. "Tags."

"Tags? As in 'yo dis is my hood' tags?" suggested Sharon. "Who tags a sewer?"

The light went out as Miles stood up, brushing dust and slime off, or perhaps further over, his neatly buttoned black jacket. He turned to survey the area before murmuring, "Kevin, if you wouldn't mind ... With your vampire senses, can you tell at the moment if we are being observed?"

From behind the white shield of a face mask, Kevin said, "Darling, my vampire senses are getting nothing but sewage and I seriously think this is getting unhealthy."

Sharon got back up, and Rhys wrested the manhole cover back over the shaft. "Miles?" she asked. "You're doing this concerned-but-okay thing, which, being as I am, a knower of the truth, I kinda feel is about nine parts concerned to only one part groovy. What the hell is up with the scratchy street art in the sewer?"

Miles sighed, turning at last back to Sharon and looking her in the eye. "It's a tag," he repeated, voice flecked with sorrow. "It's the mark of the Tribe."

There was an intake of breath from Rhys, and a sharp, "Goddamn" from Kevin. "Okay," the vampire added, "well, this has been, like, totally great and I'm feeling, like, so positive about all this, but, actually, I think I'm gonna go now so ... "

Sharon's eyes didn't leave Miles. "Kevin!" she barked. "Stay!"

He froze, as if embarrassed even to have been caught considering departure. "The Tribe," Sharon repeated. "Now, I'm gonna make a great investigative leap here, which might be brilliant or could be wank, but which I'm thinking based on the aura of 'oh crap' currently going on here in so many ways ... when you say 'the Tribe' like that, I'm guessing we're not talking an association of tea-loving teddy-bear fanciers?"

"No, Ms Li," confessed Miles. "Not so much."

"And," Sharon went on, "I'm imagining that when one of your hobbies is drawing stuff on the inside of sewer walls beneath abandoned industrial estates in Deptford where only a few hours ago lotsa blood, some human, some not, got cleared away, I'm imagining that the word you're gonna use to describe 'the Tribe' is not going to be ... " – she held back the sound for a moment, considering how best to form it – " ... *fluffy*."

Chapter 12

The Tribe

fck u fck u fck u wrld!!!
fck u fck u fck u 4 finkin u woz betr dan us 4 finkin u woz gr8, u woz
ligt u woz beutiful
we is da tribe we is da 1s u cal stupid ugly wrng
u is many
we is few
but jus cos u is many n we is few
dont mean we aint rigt
so fck u 4 finkin u kno us
fck u 4 finkin u culd jus let us die

Chapter 13

Adversity Is Sent to Test Us

Miles said, " ... self-mutilation is not strictly ... "

Kevin said, "They cut themselves with knives! With *unsterilised* knives!"

Rhys said, "They certainly have uno-o-o-orthodox approaches to their physical wellbeing, but maybe they just don't want to be judged by s-s-societal norms?"

Sharon sat with her arms folded behind a high plastic orange table in an all-night café on Jamaica Road whose services included, if you believed the sign, free wi fi, smoothies, shakes, sandwiches, burgers, salads, hot drinks, cold drinks, fresh coffee, herbal tea, ice cream, sorbet, Turkish Delight and international money transfers. The owner, a man missing two front teeth and wearing a poorly glued toupee above his freckled head, beamed disconcertingly at his only four customers as they sat pressed up against the window, bickering.

Miles sat with a small untouched cup of very strong almost-espresso before him. With each point he made, he pressed his index finger against the orange table top for emphasis. "The Tribe believe that the key to power – to self-empowerment – is to rid yourself of concern for physical flesh."

"Sounds kinda okay . . ." Sharon's voice was the drone of one who can't shake the feeling that, somehow, it won't be.

"To this end," went on Miles, the firm teacher with a difficult class, "they do indeed cut their own skin, and often take pride in achieving what society would define as . . . ugliness."

"Disgusting!" wailed Kevin, shrill enough to make Rhys flinch in the seat closest to the paper napkins.

"They say," Miles concluded, "that mankind is trapped by illusions of what it is to be man. They say that by cutting into themselves they become truly human, whatever that means."

Sharon drummed her fingers. Feeling the need for comfort, she'd ordered a Danish pastry and had been surprised to discover a solid pillow of icing and fat deposited in front of her, its radius nearly greater than the circle of her skull.

"Okay," she said. "So I can see how these guys might have issues. But hell! We're Magicals Anonymous! We're issues-central! And, sure, knives – especially unsterilised knives – are a big no-no at MA meetings, and I can see how the Tribe might have a more relaxed attitude towards that. But you can't force people to conform to your social expectations, can you?"

"No, Ms Li," ventured Rhys. He wasn't sure he believed his own words, even as he uttered them. But Sharon seemed certain enough, and who could trust a knower of the truth and seer of the hidden path?

"Right! So why don't we just pop along to talk to these Tribe people, and ask them . . ."

"Like hell no!" wailed Kevin.

"I'm not sure that would be . . ." put in Rhys.

"There are complexities . . ." added Miles.

Sharon groaned. "All right, what's the problem here?"

Three grown men cowered beneath the force of Sharon's practicality. "Well," offered Miles, "the relationship between the Aldermen and the Tribe has always been . . . strained. In recent years, we've had an alliance with the Neon Court, who have traditionally been rivals of the Tribe, and this has rather . . . coloured arrangements."

"'In recent years'?"

"Subsequent events have perhaps altered the situation," he conceded. "And, diplomatically speaking, we are now in a better position, perhaps, to negotiate with the Tribe. However, the fact remains that the last shaman of the Tribe was murdered while fighting a pitched battle with Lady Neon in Covent Garden during an endless night, and the political consequences of this action do remain . . . somewhat clouded."

Sharon leant forward to rest her chin on the bridge of her hands, and narrowed her eyes. "Now," she said, "I've been reading up on management speak, and I'm guessing that where you say, 'somewhat clouded', what you really mean is 'totally down the pan and in the shit'?"

"Well . . ."

"Which isn't to say I don't respect you trying to be diplomatic," she added. "Because it's bad to colour people's perceptions before they have a chance to make up their own mind. But, then, Kevin here has been talking about unsterilised knives, and Rhys does look like he's having an asthma attack. So I'm guessing that, just this once, I should maybe pull in my positive attitude?"

"That does sound . . . sensible, Ms Li. Also, we have to consider . . . if a blood trail led us to a sewer tagged by the Tribe, then does this not imply that the Tribe are involved in these events? And, if so, should this not further dent your otherwise admirably positive attitude?"

Sharon considered this. "A Positive Attitude," she intoned, "Is Healthier Than Negativity."

"Even with knives involved?" queried Kevin.

"*Especially*," she declared, "with knives involved. So, Alderman . . . in your capacity as my minion, which I'm still totally groovy about, by the way, I need you to do a coupla things for me."

"How may I assist, Ms Li?"

"I need you to do that Alderman thing you do, and find out if any bodies have been discovered in the river in, say, the last forty-eight hours."

"Of course."

" . . . and I need you to get me a meeting with the Tribe."

Miles hesitated. "While I'd love to oblige, Ms Li . . ."

"Is that a 'shan't' or a 'won't'?"

A vein throbbed in the Alderman's neck, where it pressed against his high collar. "Not at all, Ms Li," he said. "Merely that the Aldermen and the Tribe . . . our relationship is poor, and any overtrees from our office are likely to be met with . . . difficulty. Perhaps if you had contacts with someone else, who might make an overture? Do you know any imps, for example?"

Sharon's eyes narrowed. "Goblins?" she asked.

"I believe some goblin clans have made tentative diplomatic approaches to the Tribe in the past . . ."

"I know just the one. You won't believe how diplomatic he can be. What about the body in the river?"

"I can absolutely conduct a search via the relevant authorities; that's no problem."

Sharon sat back slowly. "Okay," she said. "Then I guess we're getting somewhere." She thought, then added, eyes fixed on some distant place, "Yay team."

Chapter 14

Find a Peaceful Space

It was one in the morning when Sharon walked through the locked door of her flat. It wasn't that she didn't have keys – although recently she'd got out of the habit of carrying them – but that the door itself was heavy, and would have thudded in the dark, and it seemed more civilised just to walk straight through it without disturbing her housemates.

She felt warm, tingle-skinned, exhausted, and depressingly, insufferably, awake. She crept upstairs to her room, one of three in what the estate agent had termed a "fashionable maisonette" and which her mother called "that grubby little flat". In the sense that it had stairs, the estate agent was probably right. In the sense that you could stand in the middle of Sharon's room, extend your arms out to either side and touch a wall, her mother was clearly onto something. She sat down on the edge of the bed, displacing a small alp of unsorted clothes whose fate would have to wait, as it had for nearly four days already.

The blue umbrella, with its missing point, balanced between her knees. She hadn't wanted to leave it with Miles. Swift had very specifically left her the umbrella; also, she had detected an aura of mystic calamity about it that no one else seemed to have picked up on, and that, too, made it her problem. She tucked it in a drawer under her bed, burying it beneath a mess of unpaired socks and scrunched pyjamas. Then she sat and stared at nothing and wondered what it would take to go to sleep.

Finding a body in the river would take Miles some time.

Getting in touch with the Tribe would also take time.

Somewhere she'd heard a policeman say that if a case wasn't solved in the first seventy-two hours it was unlikely to be solved at all. How long since Swift had disappeared? She wasn't even sure she knew. She turned on her small bedside lamp and lay on her belly, pulling out her notebook and a collection of multicoloured biros from her bag. Flicking through the pages – notes on curse victims, agoraphobic djinn and claustrophobic gnomes, on gargoyles with pigeon problems and how many sugars you should and should not offer to the tuatha de danaan – she found a clear page and wrote, very carefully, in bright red ink:

MISSING MIDNIGHT MAYOR

She felt the note sufficient to merit capital letters and red ink, which she underlined twice in black, just to make it clear how important this was. Underneath this she also wrote:

Umbrella. Why? Mega-mystic.

Email. About umbrella. Requesting meeting in Deptford. Why? Cover-up. Email ate the computer.

Deptford. Cover-up. Blood. Two bleeding. Human and 'nearly' human (Swift?). Body in the river? Bleeder into the sewer?

Magic circle. Burnt telephone wire. Doing a spell? What spell? The Tribe.

She paused at this last one, then carefully, this time in neat blue ink, added at the bottom of the page:

??!?!?!?!???!

Feeling a little more weary and far more satisfied, she stared at the words, then closed the book and stuffed it back in her satchel, returned the pens to their small internal pouch, rolled over and turned off the light.

*

Sharon Li slept.

Or, perhaps more importantly, she dreamed.

And as she dreamed, she walked.

She walked out of her body and out of her room.

Out of her flat and out of the small brick estate in Hoxton that housed it.

She walked out of the dreams of a child, surprised to find a blue-haired woman suddenly staring at him from across his nightmare of an assembly hall, and into the dreams of an old man recalling a day when recollection was easier. She walked through the dreams of a postman, whose cart rattled in his sleeping ear and whose fingers were turned black with ink. She walked between two tower blocks whose windows flashed and shimmered with the projected thoughts of the sleepers lying within; nightmares and wonders, fantasies and the dark churnings of a mind which would rather choose to forget. She walked the slow, changing paths of the dream walk, and, as she walked, a figure fell into step beside her, brilliant and bright in this flickering world of unravelled thoughts. She barely glanced at him, and said, though no sound could exist in this slumbering world,

"Evening, Dez."

Dez Cliff Jnr, white suit surgically plastered to his orange-adjusted skin, beamed at her from the nether reaches of Sharon's subconscious mind. She knew, in some objective part of her soul, that she had only herself to blame for her spirit guide being, essentially, a cheap talk show host instead of, say, a glowing unicorn or radiant spirit of light. However, knowing a thing and coming to accept it were two different, and still-ongoing, processes.

"And this evening in Sharon's dream walk," sang out Dez, "we ask ourselves . . . what the hell is going on?"

Sharon sighed, as the great-bellied snake of a train driver's nightmare hissed and spat at her from where it had coiled itself around the small yellow-brick house within which the dreamer slumbered. "It's okay," she said, voice flattened by the swirling shadows of the dream walk. "I think I've got this one."

"Sharon," – a microphone appeared spontaneously in Dez's hand and was waved towards her face – "you have no experience of criminal investigation, or magical investigation, or investigation of any kind – tell me, how does that make you feel?"

"It's gonna be fine," she repeated. "Totally on it."

"Sharon," insisted Dez as they stepped over the rising black waters of a teenager's thoughts recalling humiliation in the school showers and the laughter of his peers, "are you not concerned that you're gonna screw this one up entirely?"

Sharon stopped so abruptly that Dez walked right through her, emerging flustered and smoothing down his white suit, the microphone gone.

"Positive bloody attitude!" she exclaimed. "Jesus, what's the point of having a positive bloody attitude if the deepest manifestation of my unconscious mind has to turn up every night and go negativity on everything?"

Dez hesitated, tugging the ends of his shirtsleeves a little stiffer over his unnaturally tanned, orange wrists. "But," he protested, "surely if you strive so hard to have a positive mental attitude towards everything, it's only because unconsciously you believe yourself to be deeply, truly, stuffed?"

Sharon threw her hands up in speechless rage and marched on, leaving Dez to dissolve into the shadows whence he had come.

She walked over the chittering insects of a student's nightmares, and around the floating umbrellas of a midwife's dream as they soared into a starry sky. She walked across the waters of the Regents Canal, past the beggar man who dreamt, fitfully, of falling ice and caverns, before she drifted up towards King's Cross, where cranes and bulldozers lined up before the old brick warehouses like a welcoming committee to an architectural funeral, and the water of the canal shimmered with spilt oil. Here she drifted through the walls of the abandoned workshops and up, until she came to what some might have called a den, others a nest, made of cardboard and pilfered blankets, rusty boxes and bent pieces of pipe. Here a small figure lay curled beneath a stolen waxy coat, and his dreams were of . . .

"Oi oi!"

. . . Sharon had never actually known what Sammy dreamt of,

mostly because he was far too attuned to the presence of another dream walker ever to let them detect the content of his slumbers. He stood now, a figure above his own sleeping form, and Sharon couldn't help but notice that the dream-walking Sammy was a little taller, a little prouder, and in possession of far less nasal hair than the real Sammy. A faint odour of toothpaste trailed after him as Sammy slipped through the walls and away from his own slumbering body, Sharon following in his dusty wake. "Ain't seen you practising your dream walking much," he grumbled. "Not that you're any good at it anyways."

"I need your help," she said, as the two of them descended back into the street, where the still-churning dreams of the city slipped across the paving stones, and twisted their black-smoke shapes beneath cones of streetlight.

"Everyone does, but they're usually too thick to notice till it's too late."

"It's about the Tribe. I need to get a meeting."

"Which tribe?"

"The Tribe. With a 'the' and unsterilised knives."

Sammy rolled his eyes, always an impressive sight, considering how disproportionate they were to the rest of his head. "Self-mutilating tossers!" he exclaimed. "Bunch of incompetents!"

"Nevertheless," she persisted, "there's this whole fate of the city thing, a missing-Midnight-Mayor thing, and apparently I've been made Swift's deputy, which I think means I'm supposed to clean it all up, which is really kinda crap actually, but okay, so if you'd do that expert goblin thing you do so well, that'd be really great."

Sammy fumed. In the real world, this might have consisted of little more than a certain firmness of step. In the dream walk, steam rose off him in thin blue-grey clouds which fizzled and dissolved around his walking spectral form. "Thing is," he grumbled, "the Tribe ain't never really forgiven me for that time with the garbage truck and the naiad's foot . . ."

"Sammy. Fate of the city and that."

Sammy the Elbow gave a profound, lingering sigh. "Fine fine fine!" he declared, flapping his stubby-fingered hands in indignation.

"I'll go out and just fix everyone's problems, shall I, because that's what I do, don't you worry about me. Sammy do this, Sammy do that – just don't expect 'em to be pleased to see you, is all, cos damned if I'm gonna do your dirty work all the time."

"Thanks, Sammy."

"'Fate of the city'," muttered the goblin, even as he began to fade back into the swirling ether. "'Deputy Midnight Mayor' what a load of swollen bollocks . . ."

He shimmered into nothing. Sharon stood a moment longer, listening to the sound of a song half remembered in the wandering mind of a shop assistant who can't get this tune out of her head, before sighing, closing her eyes, and drifting finally, and at last, off to sleep.

Chapter 15

Please Leave a Message

Sharon turned her mobile phone off at night.

Later, when she stopped to think things through, she decided this was probably a mistake as, being responsible for the fate of the city, you couldn't expect to be working to sensible hours. However, in the age of instant messaging, smartphones and text messages sent drunkenly at two o'clock in the morning, the fact was that Sharon Li, in an act of technological defiance, *had* turned her mobile off and this was why, when he rang, all he got was a message which went:

"Hi, you've reached the phone of Sharon Li. Sorry I can't pick up at the moment, but I'm probably in a meeting or walking the misty path right now, so please leave your message, after the beep. Thank you!"

Beeeep!

A static whine which hisses like a snake, the open sound of transmission with no breath. It whispered:

Hhhhsssssssssssss . . .

Listen.

Beneath.

hhhhssssssssssssssssshhhhhhhhaarrooon!!
sssssssssssssshhhhhhaaarrrrroonnnnn!
SSSSSSSSHARON!!!!
There may have, perhaps, been more.
But the caller seemed to run out of credit.

Chapter 16

Seek New Horizons

Rhys was halfway to the office when the text message came. He was going to the office because, frankly, that was all he knew what to do on a weekday at 8.45 a.m., and, even though he couldn't shake the feeling that today would not be an ordinary working day, the day had to start somewhere and not turning up at the office could well be deemed worthy cause for disciplinary action. As it was, the text message forced him to hop off the bus, cross over the street and return from whence he'd come.

He arrived, twenty-five minutes later, breathless and red-faced, halfway up Hampstead Hill. Sharon was already there, leaning against the burgundy tiles of the Underground station, a cup of coffee in one hand, a sign at her back declaring that the recent hike in fares was entirely in the public interest. She was hunched into a black padded jacket against the cold. As Rhys sidled beside her she glanced up and exclaimed, "Do you know how much a cuppa coffee is in Hampstead?"

"Um . . . two pound thirty?" Hearing him get it right, her mouth dropped open.

"I go to a book group on the first Friday of every month round the corner," he explained. "Last month we read *Wild Swans* which I didn't really like but everyone else said was amazing, and this month we're reading *Do Androids Dream of Electric Sheep?* and everyone has said that it's going to be crap but I'm really enjoying it so far, so . . . uh . . . "

"You go . . . to a book group?"

"Um. Y-yes?"

"For druids?"

"Oh, no! For feminists, mostly."

Sharon's voice was the slow see-saw of one trying to solve a difficult problem. "But . . . you're a druid. And . . . also a feminist?"

"I don't think you have to be either, or not be either, or be neither one nor the other, or not either or, in fact, to join."

Sharon stared, a woman attempting to adjust her long-held views on another soul; then gave up and blurted, "So I figured we'd do more incisive-detective stuff, if you're okay with that?"

"Of course, Ms Li. I packed a thermos, just in case."

"Good!" She opened up her bag, fumbling among its mess of biros, notebooks and half-eaten sandwiches.

"Is . . . Miles joining us today?" asked Rhys, and felt a momentary flush of pride at how level his voice was.

"What?" Sharon mumbled, focused on her task. " . . . No. He's doing the whole Alderman thing, trying to see if anyone got thrown into the river last night. And Kevin's tucked up for the day, so it's just you and me. That's . . . okay, isn't it?"

"Oh yes, Ms Li! I mean, of course it is, I wouldn't want you to think that it's not, which isn't to say it would ever not be, not that I don't like Miles because of course I do . . . " And here it came, the beginning of the sneeze. Rhys swallowed it back down so hard his ears popped.

With a great upsurge of paper and sandwich, Sharon pulled the object of her desire from the depths of her bag. "Ta-da!" she exclaimed, flourishing it aloft.

The document, folded down a dozen times, revealed itself when unfolded to be a map. Fully opened up, it proved too big for Sharon to hold without it sagging around the edge, even in her outstretched arms. Rhys helped her struggle with it as they tried to fold the thing into a manageable form.

This done, Rhys actually paused to look at the map. He saw a surface punctuated with coloured dots, and said, "Swift's map?"

"Yup! Pinched it off his wall," Sharon explained. "Which I know some people might call theft, but others would say is initiative. That's the trouble with management. It's all about some other bastard's point of view."

Rhys looked uneasy. Stealing was stealing, especially when the theft involved a semi-possessed, mythically empowered, almost undead sorcerer.

"So I was having a gander at it," she went on. "And I figured that all the coloured dots probably meant something, and that maybe it would be dynamic and proactive," – relishing the words – "to go and have a look at some of the places they marked. Also, I thought sitting around on our arses in the office, while technically what we're paid to do, would be really uncool considering the whole missing Midnight Mayor/blood thing, and it's good to get out and about sometimes, isn't it? It's like a staff away-day, only with death on the line!"

Rhys sagged. "Yes, Ms Li."

"Don't be like that – it'll be fun!"

Hampstead. If you believed the signs in the window of the local deli, Hampstead wasn't just a nice corner of a pleasant borough, it was a *Village*. A small oasis in the chaos of the city, a peaceful place where you need not visit the supermarket for your meat, nor wait at the chemist for your medicines, but where the happy butcher in his bright red apron would greet you by name as he carved up fillet steak for your consumption, and the pharmacist at the back of the apothecary beneath the masseuse's lavender-scented rooms would offer discreet and well-informed conversation as she filled in your prescription. In Hampstead Village, mothers could sit outside the coffee houses while their babies slumbered in buggies designed like a space mission; freshly baked bread would be lined up on the rustic wooden shelves of the patisserie, the aroma of yeast wafting out on a warm breeze through the inviting open door. In Hampstead Village, crime was unseen, littering not tolerated and public transport a traffic annoyance that passed through, on its way to somewhere else. It was beautiful, clean, welcoming, friendly, quaint, historical, modern and, Rhys couldn't help but feel, judging him.

"You can't be judged by a borough," said Sharon, as they wandered downhill past white mansions with iron arches above their gates where flaming torches had once burnt through the night.

"B-b-but boroughs do have a distinct personality." Rhys dabbed at his nose, as the city spread wide beneath them. "Not just ethnically, I mean, though there are trends, but also financially, and based on employment and literacy and that. Which isn't to say that a borough where more people can read will be *nicer*, just that if all these things happen together at once – ethnicity and money and everything – then maybe you do get a collective personality, see?"

"But why would a borough judge *you?*" demanded Sharon. "You attend a non-druidic feminist book group!"

She did have a point.

They took a turning towards the edge of the Heath. The houses became wider, grander, lower, and marked by the individual character of their original makers. A white-timbered mansion in a colonial style; a grand, orange-bricked building with a white portico and two cars parked out on a lovingly raked gravel crescent outside; a cluster of buildings painted the colour of ice-cream flavours in a posh Italian shop, 100 per cent organic and adorned by the front door with little signs declaring "Heath Lodge" or "Wildflower Cottage" as if, for this small set-back piece of street alone, the double-decker bus had never happened.

They stopped before one of these cottages of three bedrooms, two living rooms and a Mercedes, and Sharon examined her purloined map. "Okay," she said. "We're at a spot." She looked up at Rhys, only to find that her expectation, which wasn't great to begin with, nonetheless trumped the look on Rhys's face. "Um ... do druids do much communing with the secrets of the universe?" she ventured. "I only ask, because that might be, like, seriously useful in this sorta situation."

"Not really," admitted Rhys. "I mean, I'm sure at higher levels maybe some of the really good druids can. But usually we just make potions and commune with the natural environment, see? Which isn't to say natural, not in the strict sense any more, but is more to say . . . the fixed environment, you know?"

Sharon's face didn't know, but Sharon's voice proclaimed, "Ah. Okay. That's . . . So I'm guessing you're not having any great insight into why Swift put a red dot on this street on the map?"

Rhys looked around helplessly. "Maybe he was house hunting?"

A scowl flickered on Sharon's mouth as she turned to examine the street. Bins for families of four or more; cars with an annual insurance value that probably exceeded her yearly rent; clean windows and professionally tended gardens; hedges neatly trimmed into either very solid, or occasionally mildly artful shapes, depending on how radical the trimmer was feeling that month. Trees, taller than the houses themselves, and more varied than the plane trees in the city landscape below. On one of them, some wit had slung a pair of shoes, while below, carved into the bark itself, J had declared undying love for P. A small, single-decker bus built for little old ladies and women with prams, hummed by on an electric engine, heading downhill towards the railway line, while overhead little white clouds puffed through a great expanse of pale blue sky above the Heath itself.

Sharon turned and took in all of this, then turned again and, growing faint around the edges as she did so, looked with a shaman's eye. Flashes of things which had been, and things which might yet come, melted together and danced before her. Kites soared above the Heath, while clouds rumbled and rolled, promising rain at the picnic; cars blurred into a streak that stopped and started like a swollen snake as vehicles turned off in search of a place to park for the family's day on the hill. A woman screamed at her husband, caught in an act of betrayal; an engine backfired in a burst of yellow-sooty flame. Music shimmered from an open window, swirled in clouds of steam from a radio standing near a boiling saucepan, and the smell of fresh rain bloomed on the hillside. Bracken swayed and flourished, shrank and withered with the seasons; trees put forth new leaves, then shed them in a firestorm of orange and red; and still the shoes hung upon the branch.

Sharon saw all of this, but as she looked and looked again she could see nothing that seemed unnatural. Her eyes passed over Rhys and even he, in allergic distress, had a glow, a luminescence more than just the natural warmth of blood, that hinted at his magical inclinations. She wondered how she would look if she could see herself in this shadow-place. Would there be anything even to see?

"I'm getting nothing," she admitted, stepping back into the bright, hard reality of the street. "This would all be way easier if Swift had just left a note."

"Apparently the Midnight Mayor doesn't like memos."

Sharon scowled. "Memos," she asserted, "are a vital part of good office practice and management procedure. Keeping a record of events is essential in this age of litigation and complicated, multi-faceted organisational operations!"

Rhys smiled wanly at this, and waited for Sharon to deflate. "At any rate," she persisted, "that's what I've heard . . . Right! Let's go and look at another of Swift's red dot things and maybe we'll find a pattern . . . what are you doing?"

Rhys had his mobile phone out and was taking pictures, "Um . . . scene of the crime photos?"

"That's . . . actually kinda a good idea."

"Th-thank you, Ms Li, I thought it might help, see, as we're doing this professional investigation, so we want to learn from professionals. I mean, I think it makes sense."

Sharon patted him on the shoulder. "I think that all sounds very sensible." Then, aware that she was still, technically, the boss, "Carry on!"

Chapter 17

Persistence Is Not Stubbornness

They visited six other dots on Swift's map, scattered across Hampstead, Highgate and Haringey, and ended up in a small café in Wood Green. With a name like Wood Green, the place should have been a pleasant retreat of ivy-clad trees, maybe threaded with streams. What it in fact was, was a shopping mall. There was perhaps some small redemption in that the mall itself seemed confused about its social intentions and economic purpose. While it held the usual chain stores, advertising goods from expensive moisturiser to cheap DVDs, in its lower halls a sort of bazaar had sprung up, where ramshackle stores and trestle tables competed with each other to sell vivid fabrics off the roll, dubious electrical goods and brightly coloured spices shovelled out of great sacks. In the small local library, inserted by a ground-floor entrance, where a vending machine dispensed gobstoppers at 20p a shot, the shelves offered books in Punjabi, Bengali, Russian, Hindi and Hebrew for the literary local community.

Yet however varied the visitors to this part of the mall, the coffee served here was that brand of thin liquid known universally as bad. Sharon and Rhys sat in silence as the world tumbled by, and sought a way to consume their drinks without tasting them.

The day had been, as Sharon was forced to admit, disappointing.

It wasn't that she didn't feel proactive – they'd done a great deal of walking and ridden a lot of buses – it was simply that, in the 150 or more photos Rhys had taken that day, not one had included anything you could call nefarious. The dots on Swift's map had corresponded to scenes of ordinariness: neat terraced roads, quiet backstreets, and residential cul-de-sacs off well-ordered estates. They'd all been within easy reach of a bus, occasionally a little isolated, never overlooked by CCTV, and, from what Sharon could tell, about as remarkable as slate on an entire roof.

"Well," said Rhys. "Actually . . ." he began again, then added, "I thought it went well, don't you?"

Sharon looked at him in disbelief, and waited. Seeing her expression, at length he mumbled, "Maybe I can print up my photos, and we can see if there's any pattern?"

Sharon nodded mutely. Pressing her hands around her mug of coffee, feeding on its warmth, for a moment she listened to the world passing by, to the voices of . . .

Come on for God's sake we'll be late!

and then yeah then I was like mate, you cannot fucking say that and he was like uh whatever?

three for a pound three for a pound you madam you you know you want three for a pound . . .

Are you sure you want that one?

Well, it's your money.

Her eyes began to drift shut as she let the sounds wash over her, the high-speed babble of the schoolgirls playing truant from chemistry; the loud cry of the salesman making a hard sale to the wrong crowd, the snapping of the tired mother at her wailing child, the burble of the toddler who's just discovered the wonders of the Postman Pat machine by the library door and wants another go, and the grumble of the old woman paying for her meal in nothing but two- and five-pence coins, laying them one at a time before the despairing gaze of the pie seller in her little steaming stall.

The sounds comforted her, warmed her. Sharon's eyes drifted open again, and she managed a smile. "Righto, Rhys," she said. "Let's go bloody home."

Chapter 18

What We Do Defines Us

"Home", it turned out, meant the office.

There was paperwork to do.

Tea to make.

It was, Rhys recalled, Meeting Day.

He sat at his computer, hearing the printer creak and chug its way through printing out the photos from his mobile phone. Sharon fussed around, plumping up beanbags and putting out collapsible chairs. The two of them had recently got better at organising Meeting Days, falling into something of a system, down to working out exactly how many biscuits they needed for an average room of wizards, witches, magi and banshees. But Sharon's request for a larger kettle still hadn't been processed by head office, and much of Rhys's function during each meeting was to stand over their small plastic job, topping it up and reboiling it for the supply of tea, coffee and herbal concoctions that were the members' mainstay.

They began to arrive at 8.40 p.m., knocking on the already open door of Magicals Anonymous. Rhys had finished printing the photos of the day, and was pinning them up on the board when the first member arrived, a small woman with mousy hair who went by the name of Jess, and who had a problem with morphic stability, pigeons and domestic cats. A rap on a window looking into an over-shadowed grey space laughingly called the back garden, announced the arrival of Sally, descending from the sky with a snap of leathery wing. It had taken Sally some time to stop coming to the weekly meetings of Magicals Anonymous under the protection of her chameleon spell, and the day she'd finally arrived without it, her banshee features clear for all the world to see, everyone had stood up and applauded her great courage and community spirit. Beneath the guise of perception-alerting magics, Sally had turned out to have a small, neat face, with tiny pinched-in nose and pasty, cream-tinted skin, entirely hairless but not, to Rhys's surprise, repulsive. She never spoke, out of consideration for the eardrums her voice would shatter and the blood her scream could boil. But on those few occasions when she could be tempted to sample a biscuit, holding it gingerly between razor-black talons at the end of her great grey wings, the lipless flesh across her mouth would curl back to reveal huge spines of tooth, assuring anyone who looked upon them that the banshee was indeed a piranha of the sky. All of which, Rhys concluded, must contribute to Sally's reluctance to attend the exhi-bitions of Impressionist art that were her chief interest and hobby, during daylight hours.

Hello Rhys, she wrote in her immaculate, old-fashioned hand once she'd come through the window. It had taken Sally a long time to master the art of holding a pen in her talons without spraying ink everywhere, and Rhys wondered if the skill of writing had not, with its slow, careful strokes and elegant, practised slopes, coloured the language of the banshee herself. *May I say how marvellously your shirt complements your complexion today?*

By 9 p.m. the room was almost full; beanbags and chairs were overloaded with legs, bums and claws. There was Gretel, seven foot nothing, troll by birth, gourmet chef by inclination; across from her, Mr Roding with his perpetually peeling skin and nails, who couldn't understand why necromancers had such a bad press. Chris was there, who believed that exorcism was a conversation, not an imposition; Amy, who possibly kept a kingdom in her black sequined bag, but hoped no one would tell; and, of course, Kevin the vampire, who couldn't believe just how disgusting human eating habits had become in recent years.

At five past nine, Sharon pushed back her chair, swallowed a last mouthful of tea, laid her mug to one side and straightened up.

"Hello everybody," she began.

"Hello Sharon!" chorused the room.

"For new members – and I think I see a few new faces tonight – let me quickly introduce myself and what we do. My name's Sharon, and a few years ago I became one with the city . . ."

Chapter 19

Panic Is Your Own Worst Enemy

Same time, different place, and she says,

"I'm tired."

He says, "I know. You're doing very well."

"I'm so tired, Daddy, I'm so . . ."

"I'm very proud of you."

"But Brid . . ."

"Brid understood."

"I don't know if I can do this much longer."

"You can. You're strong. You're so strong."

She smiles, but there is no light left in it. He holds her by the arm, pulls her close. "Just a few more," he breathes. "A few more nights, just a few, and that's it, that's all we'll need. Then you can stop."

"They'll all be so disappointed . . ."

"They won't matter. It'll all be how it was, how it should be. You understand that, don't you?"

"Yes, Daddy."

"You want to make things better?"

"Yes, Daddy."

"You want for us to be happy again?"

"Yes, Daddy."

"Then just a little bit more. A little longer, and you can put the glass one back to sleep."

"I know."

"You're my girl. And I'm proud of you."

"Yes, Daddy."

He gives her another squeeze of the arm, then lets her go. "It's all right," he murmurs. "Soon we won't need any gods at all."

Chapter 20

Put Other People First

"The price of good summoning supplies these days . . . !"

" . . . and I said to him, it's not like I don't want to, it's just that full moon is a really bad time for me . . ."

"What kind of curse is unto the hundredth generation? That's, like, two thousand years of warts!"

" . . . and I said, it's not 'frigid' this isn't me being 'frigid' this is me thinking about you, thinking about the surface wounds, because they can go really nasty if not disinfected . . ."

" . . . cheap knock-off dragon claw, made in China, naturally, and when I put it into the pan the entire potion went . . ."

"So hard to dry clean sacred robes . . ."

"Is a wand an offensive weapon? Only, the police have been really cracking down in Peckham lately and if I get stopped, I don't really know what to say . . ."

" . . . and my flat stank for months and the neighbours complained so the council sent a man round and when he saw the pentagram he was incredibly judgemental and told me that unless I found a way to store the dry products in an air-tight container, he'd have to contact the local health authority . . ."

"'Undead' is such a pejorative term . . ."

"The pigeon-only diet is just so . . ."

"O- blood, like, eight per cent of the population have it and what do they do? They eat at McDonald's, fuckers!"

" . . . so . . ."

"All I want is a man who understands the lunar cycle . . ."

" . . . so chewy, and I was thinking, some garlic and a bit of rosemary . . ."

"And that's the problem."

" . . . would make all the difference."

"It's just so nice to talk to someone about it."

"But things can only get better, can't they?"

Sharon sat and nodded and smiled as the words washed over her. No one was obliged to speak at Magicals Anonymous meetings, and indeed most new members took several hours even to give a name or hint at their various mystical problems. However, once people had become comfortable among their undeniably eclectic fellow members, it would all come out at once. Great sighs of:

" . . . just because I do it as a hobby doesn't mean I don't seal my wards properly . . ."

"Getting the ectoplasm off the walls has been incredibly hard . . ."

"He keeps buying it for me, and it's incredibly generous, but how do I explain why I can't wear silver?"

" . . . relationships when you have armour-plated scales . . ."

" . . . finding trousers where you can fit a tail . . ."

" . . . she just doesn't understand . . ."

" . . . sometimes I feel so . . ."

" . . . confused . . ."

" . . . lonely . . ."

" . . . lost . . ."

It had occurred to Sharon early on that Magicals Anonymous was potentially disastrous for its members. What if someone came to the meetings who *didn't* understand the difference between abjuration and ensorcelment? What if a journalist caught on to their activities, or a social worker with an inflexible approach to community support? Or what if she herself did damage? She had no experience of community counselling; yet, through the dubious fact of being a knower of the truth, here she was in this frightening position of responsibility, looked to by seers and sages, necromancers and pyromancers for wisdom, guidance and insight. It was bad enough giving the wrong directions to a stranger in the street – how much worse could it be when that stranger exhaled ethane gas and had incisors of flint in their mouths for striking a spark to the same?

Then again, as conversation grew louder and more personal, and sorrows more true, it had become evident that there was a need for Magicals Anonymous, a lack in the life of the city's magic practitioners that had to be fulfilled. A life of secrecy, of working spells beneath the streets, produced in many a need for company and self-expression that could not be found in your average pub or meeting place. Sharon had read a lot of books on the subject of human society and psychology, and after a great deal about social identity and pack spirit, had taken away this simple conclusion:

It is far better to talk bollocks at great length and feel okay about it, than to talk about nothing at all and end up killing people. With an axe. Or a fireball, or talons, or razor-glass teeth, whichever came most naturally. The point was – death = bad. And if talking = decrease in psychological stress = decrease in violent outbursts of a magical nature = less death, then who was she to get worked up about the finer implications? The point was – the point *was* that . . . look, just because she was in her early twenties with two dubious A-levels and seven even more questionable GCSEs, plus six weeks' experience as a barista, five weeks as a call-centre assistant and twelve months in a posh soap shop . . . well, that didn't mean she wasn't *right*. About whatever it was people expected her to be right about, dammit.

Then there was Rhys. The ginger druid toiled silently in the background of all things, never complaining; and, as if that wasn't bad enough, he had *faith*. In her. She'd say something that, to her ears, was ridiculous, and Rhys, rather than leap upon it with a snarl and a rousing cry of "what total bollocks is this, get back to serving coffee!" would nod, and smile, and ask quietly if there was anything he could do to help. And this, more than anything else, terrified her.

The meeting wound on.

At the end, there were comments and suggestions.

"How about a singles' night?"

"Craft workshops – how to enchant jewellery for beginners."

"Health and safety tutorials for exothermic invocation."

A late-night trip to the Royal Academy, no questions asked?

"Pub quiz? Maybe with a theme of gnomes, goblins and grimoires?"

When it was done, Sharon shook the various appendages of attending guests, and as her skin brushed theirs, so her thoughts filled up with fragments of their lives, slipping off them like dust from an overcoat, telling stories of the places they had been, the people they had seen, and the dreams they wanted to make come true. Gretel the troll was one of the last to leave, the blur of her chameleon spell shimmering across her skin. The spell didn't exactly alter her appearance, but merely made it hard to look too closely, before the mind decided that what it saw it could not possibly be bothered to comprehend. It was a kind of invisibility, a comfort in a busy city street, and a vital protection for a seven-foot-tall troll.

"I was thinking," she murmured, her voice the roar of an engine, her murmur the blast of a backfire in a silent night, "that next time I might bring canapés?"

If there had been consternation in the society as to the hygiene of eating food prepared by a troll whose present domestic address was 1, The Tunnels, Under Tower Bridge, London E1W 3RP, this had been quickly dispelled by Gretel's first attempts at gourmet cooking. Once you saw past the slime-encrusted Tupperware boxes, and adjusted your point of view to consider fairly the fist-sized nibbles tucked up inside, an awareness dawned that here, in food form, was a genius which could not be denied. Even Kevin tried some, grumbling all the way, and, having grumbled, he stole some more and hoped no one would notice.

"That sounds great," said Sharon, craning up to peer into the troll's hard-to-focus-on face. A bit of a smile burst beneath the spell, a flash of small eye in round, brick-built features. Then, as Gretel turned towards the door, she hesitated and said, "What are the pictures for?"

Sharon glanced at the wall behind her desk, where Rhys had painstakingly pinned up photos from their day of wandering. "Oh," she said with a shrug. "We're saving the city again."

Gretel considered this, nodding slowly. Every gesture she made took a while, partially because she didn't want to hurt anyone or damage anything by rapid movement, but mostly, Sharon suspected, because the laws of inertia just weren't on the troll's side. At last, and having considered all the implications, Gretel said, "If you need any help with that, I'll bring sandwiches."

And the troll departed.

Sharon sighed and turned. A flapping of leathery wing briefly obscured her view as, with a hop and a spin, Sally detached herself from where she'd been hanging off a ceiling light, and flopped down onto the floor in front of the pictures. The banshee had struggled with modern fashion, trying to find clothes that provided discretion, protection and decency, while allowing her wings to spread in flight, and even letting a little of her personality shine through. A great robe of black was her usual garb, with strategic holes permitting her limbs to protrude. Fabric which might sag was pinned in place to minimise a disruption to the flow of air, while on her legs, which bent backwards sharply at both knee and ankle, Sally wore black and white striped leggings, which clung with elastic determination to the skeletal structure of her limbs. It was, Sharon felt, an interesting means of self-expression, but one she could find surprisingly easy to respect.

Now Sally stared up at Rhys's pictures on the wall and, as she looked, the banshee reached unconsciously for the whiteboard and pen she wore on a string around her neck, and wrote:

Interesting composition. Nice use of light. Not sure about the exposure. Symbolic, or simply a natural representation of urban life? Interesting shoes motif. Rather samey angle.

Sharon peered down at the proffered text, then back up at the pictures. "Shoes?" she murmured, as much for herself as for the banshee.

Sally was already rubbing out the message to replace it with another.

Could it be argued that they present a form of social chiaroscuro to the overall work?

Sharon stared from the message, to the banshee, to the pictures, and back. Then, "You know, for years, I thought chiaroscuro was something that people did to their feet, but I'm guessing, based on context and that, that I got it wrong."

The banshee shrugged, great shoulders of bone sending ripples down to the tips of her wings.

Chiaroscuro is the interplay between the conflicting forces of light and dark across an artistic motif. That, at least, is how I have always thought of it, though I might have misunderstood. Thank you for another pleasant evening, Ms Li. It's always so nice to drop by.

"Any time."

So saying, Sally waved with a talon, hopped up onto the ledge of the open window and, with a great beat of wing, was gone.

Sharon watched her vanish into the sky, then turned back to stare at the pictures on the wall. Behind her, Rhys was clearing biscuits away. "I think it went well tonight, don't you, Ms Li?"

She didn't answer. Her eyes wandered up and down, over and across Rhys's photos, moving from shrub to car, road to house, window to door, a picture of a journey from Hampstead to Haringey, marked out by little red dots on a missing man's map . . .

Her jaw dropped.

"Bloody hell."

"Ms Li?"

"Bloody hell!" she repeated, louder.

"Is everything all right?"

She grabbed a picture off the wall, then another, and another. "Shoes!" she exclaimed. "Bloody shoes!" Rhys drifted over with the sidling half-step of a man who wants to know, but doesn't want to put himself in danger. "Shoes!" she repeated, slamming the photos into the desk. "Bloody shoes!"

He looked from one photo to the next, and, as he did, the light of revelation began to shine. There, hanging off the branches of a tree on the edge of Hampstead Heath, the pair of brown leather shoes tied together by their laces that he'd noticed on their very first stop. Here, slung over a telephone line between an office block and an off-licence, a pair of white trainers, laces threaded in a neat bow. A streetlight in Highgate was draped with a couple of black loafers; in Alexandra Palace, against a background of broadcasting masts above the rows of neat, red-brick houses, a pair of trendy blue sneakers dangled off the arm supporting a giant satellite dish, while from a municipal hanging basket whose flowers had long since withered among the commercial walkways of Wood Green, two smart, black, polished ankle boots, with deadly heels, swung above a sign warning dog owners to clean up after their pets. Sharon stabbed her finger at the pile of photos, and barked, "It's frickin' bloody stupid bloody shoes!"

Rhys looked again, his eye drifting from one photo to the next. It wasn't that he couldn't see the pattern, it was simply . . .

"Why shoes?" he asked.

"How the hell should I know?"

"But . . . it must mean something . . ."

"Of course it means something! Midnight Mayor vanishes, Midnight Mayor has map, map has dots, dots indicate a place where some tosser has thrown shoes over something – it's so connected it's like mafia fashion week!" She paused to draw in air, before concluding, "But – and I say this strictly in a humble-but-hopeful way – bugger me if I know *why*."

"That," said a voice behind them, "is cos you two are thick as two short planks – which makes you actually thick as one short plank each – and you don't know shit about crap."

Rhys felt an itch start at the back of his throat and, yes, if he inhaled – very slowly – through his nose, there it was, the unmistakable, unforgettable smell that could only be that of one unwashed goblin shaman, shimmering into existence out of the empty air. He turned, and Sammy the Elbow was right there, grinning up into the druid's face with all three of his great yellow teeth.

"Oi oi," said the goblin. "Someone said summat about wantin' to talk to the Tribe?"

Chapter 21

In My Reflection, I Find Myself

Midnight in the City.

It was called "the City" to distinguish it from merely The Rest of London. In "the City" men who worked in that impenetrable industry known only as "Finance" discussed matters of great merit in a language composed almost entirely of acronyms and capital letters, with surprisingly few verbs or adjectives. By day, the streets were a sluggish river of stop-start traffic and broken traffic lights, their congestion worsened by the local council's perpetual-seeming quest to discover oil beneath its streets; by night, they were empty, silent, apart from the occasional delivery van offloading its daily quota of silk suits and stuffed olives. The night buses, what few there were, took every stretch of open road as a challenge to the laws of inertia. The Underground was closed, its shutters pulled across the entrances down to the intestinal maze of Bank station. Streetlight fell, pink-orange, on the statues of proud colonial generals riding proud English steeds, swords raised aloft as if to declare that what we have won can never be lost; CCTV cameras nestled beneath the great stone walls of the Bank of England.

A street cleaner trudged down King William Street, two buckets rattling on his cart, a plastic claw in one hand ready to grasp at floating litter. Framed in a square of glowing glass, a security guard slumbered, cap pulled low, while on Gracechurch Street three voices could be heard, rising through the night . . .

"Are you sure . . . ?"

"Yes."

"But do you really . . . ?"

"Yes!"

"I don't want to be difficult, but are they . . . ?"

"*Yes!*"

Look closely, and two figures could be seen, or perhaps . . . two figures, and the shadow of a third, much smaller, but carrying about it a smell which cut through all senses like capuchin chilli.

One said, "Ms Li, the Tribe are really rather antisocial, and I understand how we might want to . . . but is it such a good idea to . . . ?"

One said, and it seemed that this voice came almost entirely from the empty air, "Shut it, runny-nose!"

One, the girl dressed in orange, with blue in her hair, said, "Rhys, I understand that the Tribe are perhaps not the most friendly of dudes. But I really think if we're polite and sympathetic, then they'll see where we're coming from and maybe we can get something positive from this experience."

Rhys managed to suppress a groan.

They walked on through the night.

Sammy said, "Finding the Tribe ain't just about knowin' where to look. They do a lot of hiding, some of it in plain sight, some of it deeper. Gettin' to 'em ain't just about geography. Some say you can ask Fat Rat, what lives down in the sewers, and if you give 'im an offering, he'll give you a ride. But I've had this thing with Fat Rat ever since the business with the chimera infestation and the toast rack. So I figured you'd be wanting to try something smarter."

"You're not coming with us?" asked Sharon.

Sammy shifted uneasily. "It's like I said," he muttered. "I've got . . .

history . . . with the Tribe. I can show you the way, but you're gonna have to do the talkin' by yourselves."

"Okay," Sharon groaned. "Let's wander that misty path, shall we?"

They walked on, beneath the wrought-iron roof and low-hanging lights of Spitalfields market, towards the great, dark-glass base of the Gherkin, whose true name had been lost even before it was built. Lights still burnt high up, and bright fluorescence shone in the reception areas, behind the white columns that curved down like twists of DNA. With the streetlight at their backs, Sharon and Rhys could see their own reflections in the building's glass walls: pasty, faded figures against the shining interior, while Sammy flickered in and out of vision as he drifted from the shaman's unseen walk into reality and back again.

"So what do we do once we're inside?" asked Sharon, as they circled the base of the Gherkin.

"Follow the path, like the sages say, duh!" Whatever Sammy's strengths as a teacher, people skills were not one of them. Rhys's eyes flickered towards Sharon; a scowl twisted in the corner of her mouth. "And remember," Sammy went on cheerfully, voice fading as he did, "just cos they've got principles, don't mean they've got brains!"

And the goblin was gone.

Sharon's scowl deepened. "Sammy," she grumbled, "has gotta work harder at his attitude."

Rhys said nothing. He found it hard to meet the gaze of his own reflection in the window, and every time he did, he flinched away, not sure if he could take the guilt implicit in his own stare. Sharon, on the other hand, was stopping at almost every other pane of glass, leaning in and out to consider her warping double, before declaring, "No! No good!" They kept on marching round, Sharon grabbing Rhys by the sleeve whenever he slowed down, with a cry of, "Come on! Work work work!"

And "No good, no good!" she sighed, readying for another circuit round the Gherkin's base. As they strode past reception, Rhys saw a security guard by the door, examining them from inside his pool of light, radio in hand, face wrinkled with confusion. He tried a wan smile at the guard, and hoped his middle-class demeanour and possibly his ginger hair would convince the powers that be to disregard him as a criminal threat.

When Sharon stopped, it was so suddenly that Rhys almost walked into her. She swayed this way and that, examining her own reflection in the glass, before exclaiming, "Ah ha! This'd be it!"

Rhys followed her gaze, and saw ...

... not himself. Certainly it was him, in that the colour of his skin, hair and clothes suggested the same; but somehow, on that curved surface, every aspect of his appearance had been warped. His hair was a swaying burst of colour, his head was three times too big and grotesquely deformed, while his body was withered down to almost nothing: a stick, from which obscene, twisted limbs dangled like tentacles off a dead octopus. Next to him, Sharon was an elongated stretch of colour: a great orange belly swollen above two purple boots which seemed to have been elasticated round the edge of the glass. Her head was a sheet of black falling hair around a tiny slit of a face, as if she'd grown ashamed of her features and tried to hide them from sight. As she leant into the glass, her face swelled up to fill it almost to bursting, two huge, popping white eyes, two black nostrils and a tiny pinpoint mouth which huffed cold breath onto the glass. The condensation from her lips settled in a thin, grey cloud, lingered for a second, then dissolved, sinking, it seemed to Rhys's eye, *into* the glass itself, like moisture into a sponge.

Sharon stood back in triumph. Before he could protest or waver, she grabbed him by the hand, exclaimed, "Positive attitude, Rhys!" and marched him, face-first, into the wall of the Gherkin.

A moment of uncertainty.

It was not, he realised, the cold, grey twist he sometimes felt when Sharon pulled him after her into the spirit walk, but a damper, harder pressure against the skin, like walking face-first through thick wet laundry left out in the rain. His eyes closed instinctively, there was a sound in his ear, like the faintest tinkling of water on glass, and then he stepped forward and found that there was nothing to step onto. Terror gripped him, and as he overbalanced and began to topple, his eyes snapped open and he looked down, and down, and down a little bit further, into a black pit with a tiny silver bottom, before a hand closed around his collar and yanked him back against a cold, black wall. Gasping down lungfuls of freezing air, he turned to see Sharon, her hand still locked on the back of his shirt, peering at the drop into which he'd nearly plummeted. As he looked around he saw, by the thin light crawling in through cracks above, that they were on a great circular staircase, which led to the unknown glow far beneath. The steps were concrete, damp, slippy and steep; the walls were black glass, with the same helix curves as the Gherkin exterior. Moisture clung to the glass; and if he strained, he could hear, very faintly, the sound of running water far below.

"Hey," said Sharon, forcing a cheerful lilt into her voice, "Sammy did say follow the path, to get to the Tribe."

Rhys looked back and was bleakly unimpressed to see that there was no doorway, no crack, no great gap in the wall through which they'd stepped, but just more black glass, solid and impenetrable, giving no clue as to the world from which they'd come. He nodded, unfolding a tissue from a fresh pack, ready to deploy. "Yes, Ms Li," he intoned, managing to keep the despair from his voice. "I suppose he did."

Her smile was a little too bright, too white and too cheerful in the gloom, but Rhys managed to swallow his sneeze as they began to descend.

Chapter 22

Be Careful Where You Walk

Her name is . . .

Her name *is* . . .

. . . it's not important right now, what matters is . . .

. . . what matters . . .

. . . the shoes.

She examines them.

They are in her hands.

Not on her feet.

In her hands.

They are yellow, tough, hard leather, lightly embossed with a pinpoint pattern that runs round the edges of every join.

There is something she has to do to them.

Something important.

Something essential.

Remember . . .

. . . it is . . .

Oh yes.

Here we go.

She ties the laces together.

Looks up for a sign, an object, a dangling pipe.

There – a cable stretches across the street, which sometimes carries power for Christmas lights or festival banners. She takes one shoe in her hand, the other hanging down by the laces, and swings it round and round, building up momentum with each turn of her arm until finally – lift!

The shoes fly through the air.

The laces catch around the waiting wire.

The shoes tumble, one over the other, tightening the knot.

They come, at last, to rest, hanging down evenly, side by side, overhead.

And she, whoever she was, not that it really mattered, is gone.

Only this time, for the first time since it all began, he watches.

And it feels fantastic.

And he wants more.

Chapter 23

The Getting There Matters

The staircase went down until Sharon's breath steamed in icy puffs.

Then it went further.

An Underground train whooshed through the night, and its whoosh was overhead, sending vibrations through the glass. Goosebumps stood out on Rhys's arms and back; his teeth knocked audibly in the gloom. The source of light was thin, far off, but still somehow illuminated a place where the staircase ran out, above a rusty iron ladder that descended the last few feet down into a tunnel of fast-flowing, shallow water. Sharon sniffed the air, then said, "Well, it doesn't *smell* like a sewer."

She slipped onto the edge of the stair, then gingerly levered herself onto the ladder. The metal sang beneath her at a high-pitched note, a thrum passing upwards that echoed off the glass walls, and seemed to send shivers all the way up the stair to the unseen entrance through which they'd come, far away. With each step she took down the ladder, a new note sounded, the echoes melding back to create a harmonic dirge of sound, which sang on even after she'd jumped into the cold running waters below. Rhys peered down as Sharon turned this way and that, assessing the chilly tunnel

where she stood, the water running round her ankles. At length she
looked up at Rhys. "You didn't bring any dry socks, did you?"

"No, Ms Li . . . Sorry."

A profound sigh from below. "Magic *sucks*."

With a great sneeze, which resounded up through the dark to
join the other echoes, Rhys crawled out over the ladder and down,
splashing into the water below with a cry of, "Ow! Cold!"

"Aren't druids supposed to be at one with nature?"

"Um . . . yes?"

"I only query that, because 'ow, cold' doesn't seem a very druidic
utterance. Although—," a thought struck Sharon, "I've been reading
lotsa books about management and that, and nowhere did anyone
say anything about carrying spare socks." Her gaze drifted forlornly
down to her submerged boots beneath the running water. "I guess
we're a bit beyond traditional social roles."

This sounded like an escape from blame, so Rhys nodded fer-
vently.

The light was running out rapidly now they were in the tunnel.
"Do druids do illumination?" asked Sharon.

Rhys fumbled in his jacket pockets. "Um . . . I think I may have
a potion for that . . ." Little plastic pots bumped against each other,
their labels Sellotaped with neurotic precision. He pulled each out
in turn, squinting in the dark to read his own words, until finally he
gave a cry of triumph. "Try this, Ms Li!"

Sharon took the bottle, and peered at its label. "Baby Shampoo –
Travel Size?"

"Oh, no, that's just what the bottle used to hold," he exclaimed.
"I keep all the bottles, though, because they're useful now you can't
take liquids through customs at the airport, and because it's difficult
finding good containers for your potions and powders and
Tupperware is expensive so . . ." He became aware that Sharon was
staring at him, and his babble dissolved into the tumble of the water.
"I'm s-sure this one is safe," he said. "I even preheated my ingredients."

Carefully, Sharon twisted the lid off, and sniffed the clear contents. "Smells . . . soapy."

"That's probably just a little leftover shampoo ..."

"You sure this stuff ain't gonna blow up in my face? Because I'm already dealing with a wet-sock disaster, and getting bad hair now would just piss me off."

"N-no explosions, Ms Li. I never really got into exploding things," he added. "At least, never on purpose."

Sharon held out the bottle as far away from her as she could. With her face scrunched up in a preemptive grimace of pain, she emptied it into the water. The potion was swallowed up at once, rushing away into the surging mass.

A moment, a silence.

Sharon said, "Uh ..."

... and the water burst into light. It was a golden-yellow, flecked with foam, a great rush of sunset warmth in the tunnel, itself lined with glass, amid which little bubbles of shampoo rose and popped like mud above a volcano. It rushed away, following the flow of the stream, eddying out into stray currents, and there was a smell, an overwhelming, irrefutable smell of ...

"Fresh towels and babies?" suggested Sharon.

"Eucalyptus and fabric softener?" offered Rhys.

"What the hell do you put into this stuff?"

Rhys shrugged. "Um ... a bit of this, a bit of that. I'm glad it works, see, because last time I tried I just burnt the saucepan." In the warm light now filling the tunnel, Sharon's expression was either one of absolute admiration or limitless horror. Rhys shifted in the cold flowing water, and added, "Do you think the T-Tribe have warm socks?"

The shaman turned away, her eye following the direction of the water. "Dunno." She sloshed through the tunnel, golden light breaking and parting around her ankles. "So far they haven't given off that kinda vibe."

Chapter 24

Welcome the Uninvited Guest

The tunnel, as they walked, grew colder, narrower, darker and, undeniably, smelly. The smooth glass walls grew patched with worn, slime-covered brick. At first these reminders of the old Victorian watercourses were merely intrusions into the otherwise perfect curve of the passage, but after a few minutes the tunnel became entirely brick-lined.

The potion that lit their path began to fade, not so much from a lack of ingredients as an addition of others. The clear water grew muddy, fed from the ceiling by pipes that spat orange goo into the dimness, so that the golden foaming light became brownish, and the initial brightness was broken into sallow patches of illumination which floated on the surface like oil. Walking ahead of Rhys, Sharon briefly vanished and, for a moment, terror gripped the druid's stomach, before the shaman reappeared with a cry of "Well, it's not pretty, but at least it doesn't stink so much in the spirit walk!"

So saying, and before he could protest, she grabbed him by the arm and pulled him after her, into the silver-grey walk of the shamans.

Still the same tunnel, still the same place. The spirit walk of the shamans was, Rhys knew, not so much about a change in geography as an altered perception. He looked, sharing Sharon's perceptions. The tunnel now had its own light, great splotches of illumination from ancient fungus fed on unnameable sources, and tendrils of slime that writhed like the tentacles of living creatures. He looked down and saw that the water which ran around his ankles was full of faces, sinking and bobbing up from the depths, a thousand thousand faces with empty black eyes, bubbles bursting from their mouths as they opened their lips to scream, before they drowned. The shadows of rats ran in his wake, great fat bodies and dark red eyes, one or two more enterprising creatures passing straight through him before they, too, dissolved into the shadow of what had been, or might be, or might yet come to be. He looked up at Sharon, and even here, even in the spirit walk, it seemed that she wasn't there, a bare outline in the dark, a tiny scratched shadow moving through the gloom, and it occurred to him that if she let go of his wrist he might not believe she was there at all.

As they moved further, scratches on the wall, almost invisible to the normal seeing eye, burst into light around them. Here, the image of a child holding a gun; there, a policeman scratched crudely into stone, a bag of swag over his shoulder. There, a beautiful lady cleaning her nails with the razored end of a stiletto heel; there, an eye embedded in a CCTV camera, which wept silvery tears down the brick walls as they passed. The tags of the Tribe, their symbols, brilliant to the shaman's eye, glimmered as they passed them, until, with a great squelch of ooze beneath their feet, they ducked out beneath a metal rim and emerged onto a plain of mud.

Sharon slowed, the world reasserting itself around them as she paused, and Rhys looked down to discover thick, green-grey mud had embraced his feet halfway up the length of his shins. Looking up, he saw a flat stretch of reeds and long grass, heading to a sudden stop that might have been a riverbank. The yellow lights of the Isle of Dogs glowed in the distance, and the white summits of the Thames Barrier, like clothes irons sticking up from the river's surface. A thin green laser, its beam caught in low cloud, stabbed upwards from the black mound of Greenwich Hill, marking the meridian. On the waters of the Thames itself, a tug grumbled by, hauling yellow containers freighted with landfill.

Rhys looked back and saw a narrow brick portal gushing grey slime into the muddy mess where he stood, the last glow of his potion now the merest shimmer in the blacker-than-black tunnel from which they'd come. Sharon was looking down at her feet with disgust. "Magic," she repeated, "totally and utterly *sucks*."

She tried lifting a foot, and the mud slurped and clung to it. She sighed and, bending down, scraped off enough mud to reveal the laces of her boots, then untied them and took off her sodden, grimy socks. Pulling her boots out of the mud, she knotted their laces together, then hesitated.

"Jesus," she said. "Do you think there's something mystical about tying your shoes together? Am I about to be smitten by the wrath of God or something?"

Rhys's instinctive shuffle back from this proposed calamity was only prevented by the sticking of his own shoes in the mud. They both waited. A smiting from the Almighty did not occur. Sharon relaxed and, holding her boots by their laces, looked about her, across the muddy plain. "Maybe it's okay," she muttered. "Mustn't let the death and danger stuff get to you. Or compromise your personal values and that."

By that count, Rhys couldn't help but wonder what you *could* let get to you. "Um . . . do you think the Tribe are . . . here?" he asked.

Sharon looked again. A small brick stump, little more than an architectural accident in the mess of mud, stood some few hundred yards away, its back turned to the light of the city. Around it were clustered poles and wireless pylons, their cables long since stripped away, metal corpses in a dead forest. "Well," she muttered, "let's go find out."

There were the remnants of a chain fence around the brick hut.

The fence had been torn up in so many places that it hardly counted any more.

A sign on what was left of the rusted links proclaimed:

WA NING – NO U AUTHO ISE ACCE S

The sign swung freely from its one remaining bond, as the wind brushed it by.

The brick hut was silent, dark, locked.

A single metal door was the only way in. One tiny window was covered over with chipboard on the inside. The paint on the door had popped and burst in little rusted flakes. There was no one in sight, no sign of life. Sharon went up to the door and knocked.

The long shoreline grass rippled in the breeze.

Sharon knocked again.

It occurred to Rhys that he had no idea how they were going to get back, assuming there was anything left of them afterwards to go back. He could see no obvious roads, or nearby means of transport, and tried in vain to imagine that a kindly bargee would give them a lift on his tug to the nearest bridge or quay.

Sharon knocked one more time, then called out, "Look, it's not like we're from the Inland Revenue or nothing!"

No response.

"It's cold," she went on, face turned to the closed door. "It's late, or maybe it's early. I'm muddy and my socks are soggy and there's nothing worse than wet feet, they get all wrinkled and blue, and then they stink for days and it's just disgusting, so, look, could you just let us in? We'd seriously appreciate it, wouldn't we, Rhys?"

He nodded, pretending fervour.

Still silence.

"Okay," she sighed. "We're gonna come through the door, but, and I feel you oughtta know this, it's in a strictly need-to-get-on way."

Once again, she grabbed Rhys by the hand, and, before he could explain that, actually, he wasn't really a fan of walking through the translucent boundaries between reality, the world went silver-grey, and she dragged him wrist-first through the locked metal door.

A moment as the world closed and parted around him, and they were on the other side of the still-shut door. He had a second to appreciate a sense of tight brick walls, low ceiling, and silent metal banks of equipment, before someone came up behind him and hit him very hard on the head.

Chapter 25

Hospitality Is a Social Gift

Someone said, " . . . Really quite unnecessary!"

Rhys opened his eyes.

Pain shot through from his retina to the back of his skull, but that wasn't his main source of anxiety. A face – or what had once been a face – filled his vision. Certainly, the usual features – eyes, nose, ears, lips – were still there in principle, but this seemed to be despite their owner's intentions, rather than owing to any great care of them. Scars, great ridges of purple and red, ran criss-cross across the shabby remnants of the man's cheeks. The flesh had been methodically pulled back from the ends of his nose, so now two great slits opened up directly into black hollows of cartilage and calcified tissue. The tops and bottoms of his lips were shot through with needle points where once thread had bound the whole together, and the lobes of either ear had been hacked off, the edge cut round and spikes of silver and aluminium thrust through what little remained of the protruding spirals of skin. As the head moved, tendons rippled beneath the flayed skin of his neck, standing out and sinking in, white bands no longer hidden by the missing skin, and, though there was a pattern to the cutting, an order to the disfigurement, what Rhys beheld was, nevertheless, the face of a monster.

Instinctively he tried to get away, felt a chair at his back, clawed at it for support, and saw the throat of the man ripple and flex with the faintest of laughs.

"u is weak lil fin, is u," murmured the man.

Rhys bit his bottom lip hard enough to draw blood, but it was too late. The pressure welled up at the back of his throat, clawed its way across the ridged pallet above his mouth and with a great burst of sound and dampness, exploded into the room. "Aaaatchoo!"

The face recoiled, and in the momentary widening of his vision which this offered Rhys saw more faces, more people, slunk round the brick walls of this windowless cell, men and women, some with still-bleeding wounds glowing red across their skins, some with fingers missing, or bolts of steel pushed through the tenderest pieces of their flesh, to make the skin sag and hang low with the weight of metal. He recoiled, felt another sneeze rise up inside him and, as he turned to look, he heard a voice say,

"I don't suppose you guys have antihistamines?"

The voice was calm, clear, polite and blessedly familiar.

" . . . atchoo!"

Through the haze of moisture rimming up in the bottom of his eyes, Rhys saw Sharon, sitting on a metal chair next to him, hands folded politely in her lap, knees crossed. She was staring at the man with the savaged face, with that very special look that Rhys had seen deployed on vampires and wendigos with an attitude problem.

"Failing that," she went on, "tissues? I did have some in my bag, but I see you've taken my bag away, which was unhelpful. Also, I heard rumours of unsterilised knives, and I do hope that someone is going to offer appropriate medical attention to my druid here, seeing as how you took it upon yourselves to attack him without provocation."

The man with the ruined face slunk across the floor towards Sharon. He moved with an animal-lowness, his weight dropped towards his knees, his back bent forward, his fingers splayed, a hunter waiting to strike. He slunk over to Sharon and the room of disfigured men and woman watched him, lips parted, tongues wet, eager to see a fight. The scarred man leant down until his face was almost close enough for the tatty remnants of skin to brush Sharon's own, and breathed, "u wnt 2 play, lil girl?"

Sharon's dark brown eyes locked into the red-rimmed blueness of the man's. A muscle tightened around Sharon's jaw. Her fingers clenched into fists. Then she said, "You know, personal issues are no excuse for bad manners." The scarred face drew back, a ridge where eyebrows might once have been, tightening in confusion at her words.

"Now, I can see that you, Mr ... well, I can see that you have clearly got a few issues, a few personal issues, which now may not be the right time to discuss, not least because we barely know each other. But while no self-respecting member of society is entitled to disregard the concerns of another, I do feel that taking your angst out on well-meaning strangers is uncalled for, and, frankly, gives off a bad impression. So if you don't mind, I'd like my bag back, please, because Rhys has got this thing with nerves and allergies, and if he doesn't look after himself he'll get a very raw nose and no one here wants that, and if you've got a kettle I'd love a cuppa tea for myself."

In the silence that followed, the open mouths of the assembled people were, Rhys noticed, now dangling a bit wider. The scarred man stared, trying to work out what he was supposed to do next. Requests for tea were clearly not in his usual understanding of things.

Aware that this mightn't be getting her anywhere, Sharon cleared her throat and added, "If, on the other hand, you're enjoying the notion of unsterilised knives in all the wrong ways, I do feel that some might interpret that as indicative of deeper psychological issues. I'm not saying that society has all the answers, but there has to be a less radical means of self-expression than blindly attacking anyone who walks through your front door."

At length, as if the question had come out despite the speaker's best intentions, the scarred man said, "Who r u?!"

Sharon beamed and held out her hand. The man stared at it,

horrified, confused, backing away half a pace as if expecting a blade to appear from somewhere within the depths of Sharon's orange top.

"I'm Sharon," she explained. "This is Rhys . . ."

"Hello," mumbled Rhys, feeling round the back of his head, where a lump was swelling up from the disordered surface of his scalp.

" . . . we're from Magicals Anonymous, the community support group!"

They looked at her without moving.

"Okay, I'm guessing you guys haven't heard of us, but, seriously, it's great and you'd be welcome at the meetings. I mean, it's not just meetings, is it, Rhys . . . ?"

"No, Ms Li."

" . . . we also give advice on local council issues, the latest legislations and what to do if you get an imp infestation."

"And health and safety," added Rhys. "I th-th-think someone wanted classes in that . . ."

" . . . which sounds like an excellent idea!" concluded Sharon. "I mean, these things are important, aren't they? And also it's, like, you get these magicians, right, and they're into all their blood and darkness and stuff, and I honestly think that if more of these guys just got out a bit and had a nice time with colleagues who understood, then there'd be fewer roaming nightmares haunting the city streets, don't you?"

The scarred man looked from Sharon, to Rhys, and back again, and didn't understand. And because he didn't understand, and his social responses were limited, and because his friends were watching and they, too, didn't have enough knowledge of what to do in these circumstances, he drew his hand back and swung his fist as hard as he could towards Sharon's face.

She saw it a moment before it struck, and vanished.

His fist sailed through empty air, and there was an audible gasp. A moment later, the chair toppled back. The scarred man turned in horror and surprise to Rhys, who shrugged. Then a voice, drifting out of nowhere, proclaimed,

"Wow, you have so many issues, it's actually quite sad?"

The man lunged at the voice, swinging his fists at random, and struck nothing. Round the room, men and women were tensing up, murmurs rippling in consternation.

"And when I say sad," went on the voice, "I don't mean it in the 'uncool' way. I mean properly sad, as in, like, upsetting. You know, there's a bit of me that really goes out to you, now I can see just how much shit you've been going through and just what that's done for your self-esteem."

The scarred man swung again at nothing, overbalanced and went tumbling into the arms of several others. They just laughed, pushing him back into the centre of the floor.

"Though the part of me that *does* feel sorry," Sharon went on, "is being seriously undermined by this whole beating-people-up thing, which I totally think is overcompensating."

"Wer r u?!"

She made no answer.

"Wer r u?!" he screamed.

Something moved behind him, where, in fact, it had always been. It was a pair of once-purple boots, now coated with mud which flew off them in great splats. It went sailing out of nowhere on a pair of laces and sliced squarely across the back of the scarred man's skull. He staggered, falling onto his hands and knees; and there Sharon was, where she'd always been, in her soggy socks. She stood over the fallen man, boots raised high for another strike and yelled, "And this is what happens when you let your problems get out of control!"

The man rolled onto his back, staring up into the shaman's face and raising his hands protectively. She drew back a touch, and slowly he relaxed. His mouth twisted into tight shapes, before finally, incredulously, opening up into what might have been the beginnings of a smile.

"U . . . r shaman," he breathed.

"Uh . . . yeah?" Realising this might not have much force to it, Sharon raised her muddy boots again. "And I can't be having gratuitous violence and that!"

Rhys sneezed. It wasn't easy for an auto-immune response to be pointed, but he managed.

"Violence in the cause of self-defence," Sharon went on, "is a sad but occasionally necessary evil, but it's still evil and only necessary because society hasn't sussed a smarter way of handling shit, so, and if I can just make this clear, I am, overall, very disappointed."

The face of the man on the floor was still struggling with its own purpose. "U r shaman!" he repeated.

"Yeah, I did mention that, you know?"

He scrambled away from her, wriggling backwards, then flopped forwards again on his hands and knees before her. "U r shaman!" he cried out, and there was no denying it now, the joy in his voice. "U r shaman!" Around the room, others picked up the murmur, swelling it to a cacophony of strange voices.

"Right ..." murmured Sharon. "So this isn't quite how ..."

"@ lst!" cried the man. "A shaman @ lst!"

It was a few minutes later.

Rhys sat on a metal junction box which had been torn off the walls, while a woman with a great purple scar sliced across her face from crown to chin, examined the back of his skull for blood or signs of permanent damage. A cardboard mug of what might have been tea with no milk had been pushed into his hands, but when he'd given it a cautious stir, something which might once have been living had floated to the surface, and now he was trying to find a tactful way to get rid of it. Not, he concluded, that the Tribe were necessarily big on tact.

Huddled in the near-dark of tyre-fuelled firelight, the Tribe, old and young, men and women, the dispossessed, shunned and forgotten, huddled safe from the night. The newer the member, the less scarred their features seemed to be, but the oldest among them had fingers of metal, skins of cling film, and only the occasional white of an eye suggested that anything about their faces had ever once been human. Rhys looked away, whenever those bright eyeballs in ruined features had rolled onto him, clutching his not-really-tea, and wondering how long was left until the dawn.

A few paces away, Sharon stood by a burning oil drum with a huddle of Tribesmen, warming her damp socks over the flame. The bare concrete beneath her feet was cold, but dry. Bare pipes and split cable housing in the ceiling and around the walls whispered of an electricity which had once been, and was now no more, in this dead place.

Dressed in a lacerated leather coat and torn trousers made of old hemp sack, the man who had recently been in contact with Sharon's boots across the back of his head said, "i m 8ft."

"Sharon," she replied, as her socks steamed gently above the fire. "Sharon Li. Hi there."

8ft, along with the rest of the Tribe, stared at her in wonder, and some in fear, like cats eyeing an angry bulldog. They talked, not so much with an accent, Sharon concluded, but with a dialect of their own, an assault on English bred from the era of the mobile phone, where vowels were decadent and punctuation a waste of space.

"w dnt no u wer shaman," breathed 8ft reverently. "som com ere sayin dat dey r shaman, dat dey r leder, but no 1 is. u is. u r shaman."

"Um . . . I am, but I don't get why everyone's so worked up about it."

"u r shaman!" he repeated urgently. "we is tribe! we had shaman, but neon cort bitches kil im n now we av nofin. we is tribe wif no leader we is ppl wif no hed. mst rspct shaman," he added, inducing sagely nods of agreement from his colleagues. "no law no lies no skin but da shaman . . . da shaman is da truf n u mst rspct truf."

"And that's great," said Sharon brightly, turning the socks over for another round. "I'm loving the attitude there, and I hope you guys are completely cool if I just lay down, right here for the record, that while I'm open to discussion with you guys about, you know, the truth and stuff, I've already got this full-time job thing, so if you're thinking that I should get with the . . . you know . . . " – a flapping of sock, which might have been indicative of cutting knives and skin – " . . . then I gotta tell you I'll need to seriously think about that one before doing anything reckless."

8ft just stared at her. So did the others, their gazes locked and curious, expression still seeping through the ruined faces. Sharon swallowed and looked back at 8ft, his features no less disfigured but acquiring a certain familiarity which she chose to take for comfort.

"Don't take this the wrong way," she said, turning her sodden socks over to steam on the other side above the flames, "but usually when I tell people I'm a shaman, they look kinda . . . confused. Which isn't to say I'm not, because I totally am," she added quickly. "But everyone seems to want their shamans to be all . . . you know . . . feathery and profound and maybe have their own bongo drums, so the fact that you guys are all so . . . accepting . . . is a bit odd, especially what with the stuff that everyone says."

8ft scowled, lines of skin opening and closing across his face. "Ppl lie," he explained. "ppl mk truf wat dey wnt truf 2 b. ppl wnt us 2 b othr, aprt, bcos den dey dnt hv 2 fink bout us, dnt hv 2 lstn 2 us, n can prtend dat der lives got meanin, got truf, got wat dey wnt 2 fink dey got, evn tho its al lie. All lies n dey jst dont wana c. Bt u!" His eyes were bright in the glow of firelight. "U r shaman! U c truf, even dat wat is hid benef!"

"Um . . . I guess that is fair. And I don't want to push my luck here, but uh . . . you haven't seen the Midnight Mayor, have you?" Something flickered over 8ft's face, a contraction, a curling in. "Average kinda guy, dark hair, blue eyes," she went on hopefully. "Almost human? Only something almost human went down into the sewers near Deptford a few nights ago, and it was bleeding, and the sewers were tagged, and I kinda figured . . . " She drew in a long, slow breath, "In my capacity as someone who knows the truth, I mean, I kinda figured you guys might know something. Although, " she beamed, "if it turns out that you're actually bad guys in all this, and you're doing a kidnapping, murdering thing, then I gotta tell you that's really anti-social and I can see why you guys get such a bad rap after all, not that I'm judging because that's just not what we do, is it, Rhys?"

"No, Ms Li."

Sharon speared 8ft with her best smile and added, so sweet her teeth ached, "Hope that's all okay?"

8ft glanced round the brick hall, and this time, even the glare-fixed Tribe members turned away. "Y u wnt da mdnght mayr?" he muttered, voice dropping low.

"Apparently he's the protector of the city," said Sharon. "Which I think is such a stupid job title I just don't know where to begin. I mean, no wonder the guy's got problems with his management style, right?" These words were clearly not something even 8ft, liberal-minded as he could be, expected from a shaman. "Thing is," she went on, "seems like there's stuff that the city needs protecting *from* and that's why it's got a protector; otherwise it'd be a redundant role and not a very efficient use of resources. So when the Midnight Mayor goes missing, someone's gotta get him back. Is that okay?" she added, sudden worry flickering over her face. "He didn't say something stupid, did he? He's like that, but then he's got tact problems like you would not believe."

8ft's knuckles were raw red and bloodless white. "Da mdnght mayr woz nvr our frnd," he muttered. "Nvr. 4 yrs we wer atacked, we 4ght, we bled n we died n da mdnght mayr stnd der n say 'u r ugly n u cnt b gud' b cos dat woz wat ppl wntd 2 belive n he woz no difrnt. but dis 1 . . . dis mdnght mayr . . . he isnt lik dat."

"Well . . . good?"

8ft shook his head sharply, a quick one-two. "No! he says he difrnt, says he want 2 b frnd, but der is somthin beneath, somethin in da blod . . . he not human. he not human. dis mdnght mayr, he b devil. he b angel. he b god."

Sharon's eyes went to Rhys, who gave a feeble shrug. "Um . . .when you say 'god'," she ventured, "I mean, it may just be a communication thing, but there's something about that which suggests . . . something happened. Something has happened. Something . . . theological?" she suggested. "Maybe not theological, maybe more . . ."

"Spiritual?" offered Rhys.

"Spiritual, yes, that's exactly it. Something a bit beyond the comfort zone, if you get what I'm saying?"

8ft shifted uneasily, but didn't need to give more than a brief nod.

"Fantastic," sighed Sharon. "Okay, just a few more questions, you

know, the important ones, because I'm already paying Rhys overtime here and apparently you're supposed to have a break every
other hour or so in order to increase efficiency, so, here's the big-
gies . . . this god-devil-angel thing which may or may not be going
down right now, does it involve any of the following: blood, death,
horror, magic, gore, screaming, betrayal, misery and ritual dancing?"

8ft thought about it. "yeh," he grunted.

"Yeah? Which bits?"

He thought again. "al of it. cept da dancin."

Sharon's smile was a lighthouse on a foggy night. "Fantastic," she
breathed. "Well, there's some small comfort, isn't there? Final question . . . do you have the Midnight Mayor?"

8ft shifted uneasily. "sorta," he grumbled.

"Sorta? Oh God, there's not, like, body parts are there, because
I'm seriously not up for that."

"I'm not either," said Rhys, grateful that someone shared his
response.

"u shuld com c 4 urslf."

Chapter 26

Never Forget Your Roots

It's coming.

It's coming.

It's coming.

Someone stop it.

Someone stop it.

Someone stop it!!

Stop it! Stop it before the soil cracks, before the stone splits, before the bones reach up! Stop it before the light goes out, before the iron rusts, before the pipes burst, before the walls crumble to dust! Stop it! STOP HIM!

Too late.

Too late.

Too late.

It's here.

Chapter 27

Misery Loves Company

Sharon felt a shudder run up the length of her spine, and didn't know why. She looked back at the receding firelight, and knew that whatever it was that had clattered her teeth, it wasn't a fear of the dark.

"Rhys?" she muttered. "You hear anything?"

"Um . . . no, Ms Li? Do you?"

She didn't answer, but turned to follow 8ft as he led them deeper into the tunnels beneath the mud. The light here was little more than a shadow thrown by the fading fires, or came from the occasional dying bulb dangling from the slimy brick wall. The mess of copper cables and pipes was thicker here, heading down with the slope of the ground towards a heavy, shut metal door; and if Sharon looked, and if she listened, there were still the echoes of things that had passed through the wires, still a memory embedded in the metal, a whisper of . . .

hello, putting you through now caller . . .

. . . yes, I'm trying to find . . .

. . . 745 Aldwych . . .

please hold while I connect you to

BEEP!
   an operator
   will be with you to
beeeeeeeeeepp . . .
transferring!
   hello?
   hello?!
     HELLO?
beeeeeeeeee freeeeeeeeeeee

"Ms Li," hissed Rhys. "You're going invisible again!"

At the sound of his voice, and with a shake like a shaggy dog throwing off water, she shimmered back into full solidity. 8ft stared at her, a hard, fascinated stare, which she met and held until he looked away.

At the bottom of the passage, by the door itself, two figures sat guard beneath the glow of a single bulb: a boy and a girl, barely more than fifteen years old. Their faces were only lightly scarred, with bands of metal through their ears, lips, noses. The girl carried a fresh red pair of scars lightly incised above each eyebrow, a sign, Rhys realised, of seniority. They rose from where they'd been crouched, dog-like in the gloom, as 8ft approached, and glared at Sharon and Rhys with defiance and doubt.

"dis is Gold Mnkey n Hobo Grlz," explained 8ft. "dey fnd im."

"Found . . . the Midnight Mayor?" asked Sharon, eyeing up the locked metal door. There was a taint on the air, a sharp iron smell, and when Gold Mnkey and Hobo Grlz glanced towards the door, fear stirred across their features.

"yeh." 8ft glowered at the two teenagers, and barked, "dis is a fckin shaman n 1 who nos da truf so u fckin bow u heds!"

To Rhys's surprise and Sharon's astonishment, the two teenagers bobbed their heads respectfully at her, shuffling a little further back from the door. A sudden crackling, as of metal tearing in two, muffled behind the thick walls at their back, made both Tribesmen jump. 8ft lashed out at Hobo Grlz, catching her hard across the skull, sending the girl staggering, catching her balance badly against the wall. "no fear!" he barked. "lok @ me!" She did, flushed face locking with fury onto 8ft's own. "u is a Tribesman now," he hissed. "fear is lies, jus lik beauty."

The girl nodded, once, chin tilting up high. Another sound came from behind the door, a high-pitched, slow shriek of tortured metal. The door creaked, and brilliant blue light flashed with ultra-violet intensity around its edges; and with it came another sound cutting through the twisting of metal. A human sound, but only in that there was breath and air somewhere in its composition; a voice, shrieking in key with the tortured room.

"Okay," murmured Sharon, eyeing up the door. "So I'm guessing Swift's in there?"

"no," muttered 8ft, "dats da prblm."

Chapter 28

Don't Let It Get You Down

They didn't open the door.

Though no one would say it, they didn't dare.

Sharon took Rhys by the arm and said, "You – with me."

"Oh, but, Ms Li, do you think . . . ?"

She didn't give him time to finish, but walked straight through the door.

A room on the other side.

Banks of machinery, old, cracked, dusty, lined every wall. Once, nimble-fingered operators had sat in this place, and moved jacks between sockets, transferring calls from one place to another, and sparks had flown and numbers had tripped through the system with the sound of knitting-needle clatter. Now it was dark, silent, the door sealed tight, the chairs gone, the wires gnawed, the numbers long since faded into obscurity. The machines had been left behind, simply because no one could think of anything better to do with them, and the lights had long since burnt out.

Yet as Sharon and Rhys shimmered back into the real world, there was illumination. A clear blue glow spilt out from the centre of the room and up the walls, spreading and fading with the regularity of a beating heart. Its source was hidden from view, tucked away behind a bank of shattered terminal boxes. But as Sharon shifted her weight, broken copper fragments crackled beneath her feet; and with that tiny sound, the room seemed to shudder and stretch, the light flaring up and a voice calling out wordlessly in unison with the noises of the metal, as if tongue and cable had fused into one.

Rhys pinched the bridge of his nose, and declared, "Aaaaa ... Aaaaattttcc ... aaattcchhh ... "

"One moment," requested Sharon, and before he could complete his sneeze she once again vanished from view.

A moment later she reappeared, hauling the startled 8ft by the arm through the thick door. He staggered back into visible perception with a gasp, clutching at the walls, and stammered, "i-i-i-i saw da da da ... "

"The truth of things, yup; happens like that," exclaimed Sharon. "You see things in the spirit talk that you don't usually see elsewhere, and frankly that's probably for the best because you know what, reality is tricky and perception kinda helps make things easier, but maybe that's a conversation for another time when there's not scary pulsing blue light and the sound of someone screaming."

8ft stared at her. His mouth hung open to reveal gummy ridges where there hung a few metal-clad teeth. "how do u bare it?" he breathed. "seein wat u see?"

"Evening classes," she replied. "And lotsa positive thinking. That said ... " Another burst of brightness, and with it there was a perceptible flash of heat, a hair-curling, skin-cracking warmth that passed almost as quickly as it had appeared. " ... the sounds of mystic pain are really putting me off."

Somewhere in the blue-lit gloom, a gasp dissolved into a groan, which spread out in both sound and illumination. Sharon hopped back with a yelp as blue sparks flashed across the wrecked cables over the floor, and burst into splotches of light where they hit the wall, or wriggled in puddles of electric flame as they dug their way down into the earth. "Right!" she squeaked. "No point delaying!"

Rhys could think of lots of good reasons for delaying, but one look at Sharon's face suggested that now might not be the time to air them. With a determined stride, the shaman marched towards the brightest part of the pulsing blue light. 8ft glanced at Rhys, and Rhys smiled helplessly, hoping that 8ft would take the initiative in terms of manly pursuit. The Tribesman shuffled forward reluctantly.

Sharon climbed over a fallen mess of cable tray, stepped past a burst pile of rusted metal trunking, and looked up to see . . .

She supposed that "man" just about covered it. But even in the most liberal of biological senses, the individual pinned by a mess of copper to the tallest telephone exchange was having an evolutionarily tricky day. Certainly, he still possessed two arms, two legs and all the bits above and in between; but as his fingers opened and closed, great bursts of ragged blue flame spread outwards and back across his flesh, rippling over the blood-soaked rags of his clothes, and his hair stood on end, bursting with static. His bright blue eyes opened and closed erratically, and his lips worked at words that would not form; and as he writhed, great copper cables, lashed across his legs, wrists, shoulders, chest and neck, spat white electric chaos onto the floor.

He was – or at least, had been – a man Sharon knew. Sorcerer, protector of the city, not-quite-human with the consciousness of an angel or, more to the point, of the blue electric angels, spawn of the telephone wires and about as holy as cauliflower: Matthew Swift, the Midnight Mayor, and, as if all that weren't bad enough, the man who she was supposed to think of as the boss. Tacked to the shattered remnants of a telephone exchange by a cage of copper, he now twisted and screamed; and when his eyes opened, there was no white in them, but only burning, mad electric blue.

His eyes opened now, and locked onto Sharon. His body arched, spilling more sparks across the floor, as if muscle could no longer contain the energy bursting from the inside out. For a moment it seemed that there was recognition in his face.

Then the man who should have been Matthew Swift raised his head, and screamed.

"dwn!" roared 8ft, knocking Sharon to the floor as he dived for shelter. From his place on the wall, Swift's whole body arched with the force of air passing from his lungs, and kept on arching, until the skin seemed to stretch thin across his bones, unable to contain them. Cracks broke out on his forehead, his neck, his hands, his arms, through his clothes, great ragged fault lines bursting out from inside him. But where there should have been blood, there was only fire, brilliant burning blue; and, as he screamed, the fire flared up, burst into roaring light and sound, and rippled outwards in a sheet of flame that sheared through the dead machines, lit up the torn copper cables, snapped pipes from across the ceiling and sent arcs of electricity dancing from every metal surface and every nail.

Sharon looked up from the floor, socks steaming on her feet; beside her 8ft lay awkwardly sprawled.

Swift's head hung motionless on his chest. The cracks in his skin, which should have been enough to reveal bone beneath, were closing up as quickly as they had formed, and from them red blood now ran, only wriggling and shimmering blue a little as they ceased dripping from his flesh. His chest rose and fell slowly, and with each breath the blue light still playing around him pulsed in and out with the slower beating of his heart.

"it'l b stil a whil now," murmured 8ft, easing himself up. "den it'l wak, n screm agin."

Sharon saw Rhys a few feet away, patting at the smoking ends of his hair. She staggered to her feet, brushing the worst of the soot and seared dust off her clothes, and stared into the now-empty face of the Midnight Mayor.

"Is he ... a prisoner?" she asked, as the cables around him stretched and contracted with each breath.

8ft shook his head. "we culdnt hld it if we wnted 2. it com 2 us, mak dis cag 4 itself. i fink it wer tryin 2 prtect us, n itself, frm wat it wer bcom."

Sharon nodded, eyes still fixed on Swift's slowly breathing form. She took a step closer, and at once 8ft reached after her, then froze, afraid to touch. "it is dangrous," he breathed. "it is a tru dangr. it is angel. it is devil. it is god."

"No," murmured Sharon, moving another step away from 8ft, and closer to the dangling man. "It's none of that." She reached up gingerly towards the still-glowing flesh; the blue light shimmered over her skin like silk. "It's the blue electric angels."

Her fingers brushed the man's skin. For a second her face twisted in pain as it came, all of it, the truth all at once, a deafening, roaring cry of:

weee beeeee!!

  weeeee beeeeee!!

  WEEE BEE LIGHT WE BEEEEEE

LIFE!!

  WE BE FIRE!!

She snatched her hand away, and a little of the blue glow travelled with it, spilling over her skin, then tumbling away. "Jesus," she breathed. "He's not there any more."

Weeee beeeeee . . .

A sound that began with the dialling tone in the telephone wire, a voice that came out of the nothing. And there it was, waiting to be heard; she didn't even need to touch him, it was so strong: a cry, a shriek, a scream tumbling silently off Swift's flesh, and it said,

Weeee be light, we be life, we be fire!

We sing electric flame, we dance underground wind, we touch heaven!

Come beeee we and beeee free!

Weeeee beeee . . .

"Blue electric angels," she whispered. "Swift's gone. There's nothing there."

Swift – or rather, not-Swift, the body that should-have-been-Swift, gave a sudden shudder, as of a restless sleeper, and the flames flickered with renewed heat across his skin.

"we shuld go b4 he waks again," hissed 8ft. "we shuld go now!"

Sharon nodded, then hesitated, and reached forward again for Swift. "shaman!" he hissed, desperation edging into his voice.

She ignored him, easing the scorched, smoking remnant of Swift's shirt up from his middle. Blood had soaked through the cloth in a thin line, and though the cracks on Swift's skin had healed as quickly as they had come, there was still a shallow wound across his side, just above his lowest rib, where the blood was clotting black. She let the tatty shirt fall, and turning, scrambled away from the sorcerer.

"Ms Li?" asked Rhys, as they scuttled for the door. "Is he going to be all right?"

"You know what," she murmured. "I'm kinda starting to doubt it."

Chapter 29

Persevere and You Shall Succeed

Rhys and Sharon were not the only people pulling overtime that night.

In the offices of Harlun and Phelps, financiers to the very obscure and legally dubious, a light burnt above a lone desk. The desk itself was immaculate. The in-tray was empty, the out-tray was neatly stacked, labelled and colour-coded for dispatch in the morning, when the rest of the world would arrive to receive its gifts. Where most people liked to have one, or, at most, two screens on which to work, the owner of this computer had felt the urge to have three, and rather than, as was traditionally the case, keep his third monitor clear for playing cards and updating Twitter with such witty remarks as:

#workinglatetonight

or:

#feelinghungry

. . . or other such matters of great import and moment, the owner of this machine had split the screen down even further to provide rolling data on stock markets across the globe, local and international news, a live CCTV feed from the security cameras around the building, and an internet forum for Scryers Incorporated – 24/7 updates on mystic activity near YOU!

As if this wasn't enough, the man sat in immaculate, stiff black behind the desk, and was drinking coffee from a mug labelled – **KEEP CALM AND DON'T PANIC**, quite possibly without irony.

Miles lays his cup of coffee down to one side, and for a moment is the living embodiment of exactly these words. He stares at the second of his three available screens, considers the information on it, then smiles and reaches for his mobile phone.

Well, he muses, *fancy that.*

Chapter 30

We Are Different for Everyone We Meet

She said, "He's gone. Swift's gone."

They stood round the black-smoke-belching fire in its scarred metal can, Gold Mnkey and Hobo Grlz hovering uncertainly behind them, and Sharon said, "Matthew Swift's brain is no longer in Matthew Swift's body."

There was silence. Then Rhys asked, "Really?"

Sharon scowled at him. "I mean, it's still there," she pointed out. "It's not like there's this big empty space full of foam where there should be grey squelchy stuff!"

"Oh. Sorry, Ms Li . . . "

"But," she asserted, "his *consciousness* has fucked right off. Which would be fine, were it not for what got left behind."

"blu electric angels," murmured 8ft, eyes fixed on the firelight. "dey r stil in da body."

"Right. And, I'm no expert in the thought processes of mystic entities, but I'm guessing, based on the screaming and the burning and that, they're really not coping well."

"Um . . . excuse me?" Rhys had a hand raised in polite enquiry. "I know this is probably a very foolish question, but I think it might be important, see . . . *why* isn't Swift's brain in his body any more? I mean, doesn't that seem a little . . . excessive?"

"Excessive?"

"I just mean, considering the times and the economy and the problems of people management and the current political and social climate . . . "

"Rhys!" barked Sharon, impatiently.

" . . . wouldn't it be easier just to kill him?" he persisted. "I mean, not us, of course not us, we wouldn't, but if you wanted to hurt him, why not just kill Swift? Why . . . do this?" he gestured back down the darkened hall.

8ft didn't appear to have an answer. Sharon turned and met the nervous stares of Gold Mnkey and Hobo Grlz. "Hi, there," she said with a forced smile. "You two found him, right?"

Brief half-nods.

"Before or after he went blue and shouty?"

Eyes flickered from one to the other, and at their hesitation, 8ft lurched a step towards them, fist raised in warning. "she is da 1 wat knos da truf!" he barked. "u tel her everthin els she tak it from u!"

They cowered before 8ft. Sharon laid a placating hand on his arm. "And while all that is kinda true, did I mention my thing about gratuitous violence? If we had a kettle, I'd suggest we have a cuppa tea and a sit-down, but I'm guessing that's not the vibe here, and while I don't want to question your social choices, I think that's a bit of a shame. But!" She clapped her hands together, sending an echo down the darkened halls. "Now probably isn't the time to have a cultural revolution, so let's just talk about the Midnight Mayor. Where did you find him?"

Hobo Grlz spoke first, her left foot twisting in and out beneath her, shoulders down, chin up, a contorted picture of a body infuriated by its own skeleton. "@ da hospitl."

"Swift was at the hospital?"

She shook her head. "B-Man woz @ da hospitl. we went der 2 c B-Man, but B-Man wer alredy ded."

Sharon looked at 8ft, whose face was hard and set, and who said nothing. "Okay," she sighed. "Who's B-Man?"

"he wer of da Tribe," replied Hobo Grlz, voice rising, daring the world to disapprove. "he wer . . . doin fins 2 get by. dat wat u do. u get by. al els is jus feelin, n feelin is lies." Here she glanced at 8ft for approval of her philosophy, and received a single, brisk nod for her pains. "he wnt 2 do dis thin, but wen he didnt com bak, we wnt 2 find im. he wer in da hospitl, he wer sick, he wer dyin. den he wer ded."

"Um . . . what 'thing'?" asked Rhys. Already he wore a grimace, in expectation of not liking the answer.

Hobo Grlz shrugged. "dunno. he wer fast. he wer smrt. he did fins 2 get by."

"he tok fins," explained 8ft briskly. "ownin fins is a lie 2."

Sharon looked from 8ft to Hobo Grlz then back again. "Okay," she said. "There's a whole ethical can of worms there which I'm not gonna go into right now, but one day, when there's not a screaming Midnight Mayor doing the blue-fire thing in the room behind us, I really think we should sit down and have a proper chat about society and shit."

No one responded to this. Rhys shifted his weight from foot to foot, and avoided Sharon's eye. "Look," she insisted. "No one ever said that being able to see the truth of things extended to academic or philosophical ideas, okay? Otherwise I wouldn't be here, I'd be a frickin' captain of industry or whatever, so can we move on? B-Man was in hospital and he was dying . . . "

"he ded," corrected Gold Mnkey sharply. "he ded."

"Sorry. How'd he . . . ?"

"dey say it woz blck deth."

A moment. Rhys managed not to step involuntarily back; Sharon stood still, head on one side, and tried to work out if she felt the itching of fleas, or just general grime on her skin. "Black Death, huh?" she said, soft and low. "That's kinda . . . unusual." Gold Mnkey shrugged. "'Unusual" clearly didn't mean much to the Tribe.

"And the Midnight Mayor . . . "

"he woz der."

"At the hospital?"

"yeh."

"Which one?"

"U – C – H." She pronounced the letters slowly, with difficulty, as if the clarity of the sounds had somehow been lost from her over the years.

"Did Swift ... hurt B-Man?" suggested Sharon, trying not to wince. She wasn't sure if giving someone bubonic plague was within the Midnight Mayor's remit; but, then, she *could* imagine Swift doing it, if he was really, really angry and, frankly, when wasn't he?

Hobo Grlz shook her head. "dunno. dont fink so. he wer tryin to tlk 2 im, tryin 2 spek 2 B-Man, but den B-Man ded and mdnight mayr he real angry, he shout n curs n bang his fist inna wall. den he get phoncal n he go n we folow cos we dont kno wat hapned 2 B-Man n we wnt 2 find out. n he go inna city, n we hid n we watch, n he go to offic, n stay der a whil, den he com out n tak da tran n we folow n now its dark n he stil lok angry n wen we get to dept-ford he c us n say 'u! wat do u kno bout B-Man?' n we run awy."

"In Deptford? When was this?"

"nght b4 lst."

"Why did you run away?"

Hobo Grlz's body curled in a little tighter on itself, her arms pinning each other across her chest. "he da mdnght mayr. mdnght mayr sometim enemy. n he ... blu electric angel. angel. devil. god. wat u say 2 dem?"

"But he was still Swift, right? I mean, he wasn't yet doing the blue fire, screaming stuff?"

"no. dat woz later."

"So what happened?"

Hobo Grlz glanced at Gold Mnkey for support, but the boy stubbornly refused to meet her glare. "we run ... den we c ligt ovr da estat, big, brigt ligt, n we hear shoutin n voics n den dis truck com out of da estat n der r faces in it, ppl, den silenc. somthin hapned, n we go bck, cos," her voice lifted in defiance, "cos fear is somfin mad up, cos der aint nofin 2 fear, cos we woz taugt 2 fear is 2 kep us in our place n cos we ... we dont fear n we r free."

This little pep talk earned another grudging nod of approval from 8ft.

"we go bak," she repeated. "n der is blod on da wals of dis place, n a woman is lyin der, ded, she is ded n he – da blu electric angels – r jus standin der, lokin @ her, standin der in dis mesed up place, n der skin is cracked n blu, n der hair is on fire, n der hands burn n dey r red wif blood but der blood is burnin blu n dey lok @ us n ... n u dont fear death neithr, cos death is jus a plac wer all thins stop, so we wernt afrad, but he loked @ us n it wer not a 'im' no more, it wer an 'it' an its fac wer death. it wer death. n it say ... "

"help us." Gold Mnkey spoke soft, the words a distant whisper, a memory of a thing still burning strong. "it say 'help us'."

For several moments no one spoke.

"wat shuld we do?" breathed Hobo Grlz. "wat do u do 4 a god?"

Sharon stared into the girl's ravaged young face. "Dunno," she confessed. "I guess you do as it asks."

"we tok it ere," concluded Hobo Grlz with a sad little nod. "it said no mor, jus walkd inna dis rom, tok off its coat n mad itself a cage. it stod der n da wires tied demselves round it, n it stood der lik it wantd 2 b trapd. its skin wer crackin, its fac burnin, but in der ... somtimes da screamin stops."

As the girl finished speaking, Sharon was nodding with fatigue in the firelight. The warmth was making her sleepy, driving the last of the damp from her bones. She wondered how long it was until sunrise, how many hours they'd spent down in these blackened brick tunnels, and how they were going to get home. "Okay," she said. "All right." A moment or two passed, while she thought it through. "Well, I guess things could be worse."

"Um ... could they, Ms Li?" asked Rhys.

She shot him a glare. "He could be dead," she pointed out. "That's kinda worse."

A thought crawled through the muddied mess of her thoughts, made a request for attention and wriggled through the barbed wire of her fatigue to hoist its flag somewhere on the edge of her tongue. Her head turned slowly, puppet-like, and she fixed Hobo Grlz with a steady gaze. "Hold on a second ... " she said. "He gave you his coat?"

*

The coat of the Midnight Mayor should, Rhys felt, have been long, black, thick and possibly inscribed with mystic sigils. The fact that it was beige, splotched, smelly and hemmed with grease around the cuffs did not enhance the gravity of the office.

Sharon patted it down, and with each touch of her fingertips she exclaimed, "Uch old curry uch old coffee uch bad night sleeping uch uch uch uch . . ."

"I could look, if it helps?" suggested Rhys. "I mean, if you don't want to see *all* the truth all the time, that is?"

"It's fine," she grumbled. "Always figured Swift for a slob, and now I know it's true."

She rifled through the pockets, producing old paper napkins, stubs of chewed pencil, grubby receipts and, in one pocket, a single, grey sock which she threw on the ground with a cry of, "Oh, for God's sake."

"Do you . . . see anything?" hazarded Rhys.

"Bad food, sleepless nights and long walks," she retorted, pulling yet another receipt from the pocket and holding it up to the faint glow of firelight. "Hey – you ever seen Swift smoke?"

"Um . . ."

She stuck her nose into the coat, sniffing deeply. This turned out to be a mistake, as a moment later she was reeling back, trying to cough through her nostrils. "Oh, God, there's way too much sewer-to-starch happening there."

"Cigarette smoke, too?" asked Rhys.

"No. Everything else, but no cigarettes. Here." She handed Rhys the receipt. He peered at it, a scrunched-up, grubby piece of paper which proclaimed at the top:

Archway News & Films

Beneath this was an address, a date and an itemised list of purchases. "He renewed his travel card and bought . . . pouch tobacco?" murmured Rhys. "Day before he disappeared."

"Uh-huh," replied Sharon, brushing her hands off on her trousers, in the hope that a very dirty object could cleanse the effects of an obscenely dirty one. "Also, Archway? Lotsa little red dots on his map in that area."

"Do you think it could be significant?" Rhys liked saying "significant"; he felt it carried a sense of importance.

"Buggered if I know. But I think we'd feel right pillocks if we ignored it and then it turned out it was."

Sharon turned back to where 8ft was waiting uneasily, his fists clenched at his side. "I know I'm gonna regret asking this," she said, "but if the Aldermen wanted to pop down here and take a gander at . . ." 8ft's face had collapsed into a snarl of contempt. "Yes, well, I'm guessing you guys aren't that pally with the Aldermen."

"dey r da bigst liars of al."

"Are they?"

"yeh. dey fink dat der is order 2 da world."

"Yes," she admitted. "I guess they do at that. Thing is, I feel kinda bad leaving you down here with this screaming, glowing, burning blue dude . . ."

"he com 2 us. we protect."

" . . . which is really sweet of you, I mean, I'm so impressed, aren't you impressed, Rhys?"

"Yes, Ms Li."

" . . . but I'm sure there's health and safety implications here, questions of moral and maybe legal responsibility and that. I mean, the guy is my boss, and I gotta think about what I'll do if he, like, spontaneously combusts on my watch. You see what I'm saying?"

8ft's pained expression said more than words could.

Sharon tried one last time. "Let me put it like this . . . I get where you guys are coming from with your whole truth and lies thing, I really do. And, in a way, I respect that, because it takes a lot of personal courage and perception to turn round and say that everything you've ever been taught is a lie, including some of the basic human instincts, like fear and that – in fact, I think it's really cool the way you've done that, isn't it, Rhys?"

"Oh yes, Ms Li!" chorused the druid.

"But you guys do believe in the truth, I mean, the *real* truth, the truth that's underneath once you've got through the lies about work and the lies about beauty and the lies about who we are and the lies about who we want to be, yeah? I mean, that's what it's all about, isn't it?"

A hesitation; then 8ft nodded, his eyes fixed on her, the veins thick and dark on his neck.

"Well then," she sighed. "Here's a truth for you, one of the ones that's underneath, and the truth is this . . . the psycho-screaming guy in there," she jerked a thumb back towards the metal door at the end of the dark passage, "could kill you all by accident. And you wouldn't be afraid, and once it'd happened, you wouldn't be sad, because you'd be dead and that, and I'm not gonna wax theological about the afterlife because, frankly, I ain't got the training, but whatever it is, whatever you may think about it, it would be a bloody stupid fucking waste. So," her smile stretched a little thinner, a little wider, "how about letting me help?"

8ft hesitated. There was a long, slow silence as his eyes roamed around, examining unseen thoughts from the hidden reaches of his mind. Then his head bowed, and his pupils drifted up, and locked onto Sharon's. "u r shaman," he breathed. "so u must kno dis truf too."

"Which one?"

"dat carin is a lie. dat ppl only care 4 wat it is dat mak em feel betr, or mak em fel mor gr8, or giv em somthin els, in a tim not yet com. u kno dis. u r shaman. u must kno."

"Possibly," she said. "Maybe that's all it is, just . . . another selfish act. Maybe you're right. But I figure, in the grand scheme of things, even if that is so, even if the world is as messed up as you say it is . . . caring is still caring, right, so who gives a damn?" A brilliant grin suddenly spread across her face. "Jesus," she exclaimed. "I should totally write this down and print it on a T-shirt. Rhys!"

"Yes, Ms Li?"

"Remind me, when all this is done – caring and giving a damn and all that – on a T-shirt!"

"Um . . . yes, Ms Li."

8ft cowered beneath the full force of Sharon's optimism, and stared in horror at her hand as she thrust it out for him to shake. "You clasp it in a symbol of friendship," she explained. "Leaving aside that friendship is probably just another social construct invented to make life easier and that. But . . . " – she held out her hand closer to him – " . . . stop thinking so hard for just five minutes, and trust me?"

8ft looked from Sharon's hand, to her eyes, and back again. Slowly, he closed his own fingers, torn up and metal-plated, over hers, and shook. Sharon's grin, bordering on inane, relaxed. "There," she breathed. "Could've gone worse, couldn't it?"

Chapter 31

Out with the Old

It stands in the mud and watches.

The river washes up to it, breaks around its knees, its ankles, and, as it does, foam rises, great, grey bubbles bursting from the surface of the water, catching luminescent bubbles, like oil on a pond, before slipping away, still frothing, back to the river's depths. The reeds sway in the breeze around it, and as the air carries the smell of it across the grasses, so they begin to turn brown, to shrink into themselves, dry, crack, wither, decay, wherever it is that the wind has blown.

And still it watches.

And it is angry.

Chapter 32

A Transport of Delight

There was a sign for the bus in the middle of an empty concrete road framed by empty grass banks. The wind blew and the grass stirred, and orange lights burnt in the streetlamps, and nothing moved. Sharon stood in the middle of the road itself, looked left, looked right, looked back again, and saw only more road, framed by mud. Rhys sat at the base of the bus sign – shelter implied a roof – and tried not to yawn.

Sharon prodded him with her foot. He jerked, eyes flying open wide. "Is it here yet?"

Sharon's frown deepened. She stared down the empty road and said, "You know, when 'Greater London' started including parts of Essex, I really think the urban planners cocked up."

Grasses swayed in the breeze, and the road was silent.

Getting to the Tribe, Rhys was beginning to think, wasn't nearly as hard as getting back. At least with magical portals and mystic byways, you had a reasonably good chance that economics and time constraints confined the journey to just a few minutes of scrambling around through geographically unsound temporal mists. In the small hours of the morning, the air cold and damp, and the sun not yet even a glow on the eastern horizon, it was more of a challenge to get back using nothing more than the urban travel infrastructure.

"What the hell kind of a bus comes *here* anyway?" demanded Sharon. "What a stupid bloody place for a bus stop!"

What a stupid bloody place for a secret Tribe, thought Rhys. His eyelids were drifting shut and his mind was slipping into that surreal, disordered place where madness made sense and sleep was the only solution . . .

Seeing this, Sharon delivered a kick to his shin. "You're still on the clock, you know! If I have to be awake at stupid a.m., then so do you!"

Rhys managed to swallow any response behind a great yawn.

"I hate transport zone six!" wailed Sharon, throwing her arms up in despair.

The reeds whistled in the flat fields of mud at her back, and for a moment Rhys, struggling to maintain some semblance of coherent thought, imagined he could smell . . .

He gagged, but no sooner had his body reacted than his mind dismissed the notion as absurd. Sharon glanced down at him as he tried to suck away the taste of the sudden stench that the breeze had wafted towards him. "You all right?" she asked. Then Sharon's nose crinkled. "You smell that? Something . . ."

She turned slowly. A figure stood, some hundred yards off, a low squat shape in the thick windswept blackness. She paused, and as she looked at it, her nose crinkled again and her face distorted at the smell of . . .

rotting flesh?

Rhys pulled himself onto his feet, and followed Sharon's gaze.

The figure, shrouded in the night, stood between two pools of orange streetlight. A huddled creature in black, it stood in the middle of the road, staring, assuming it did have eyes to see, straight at them.

"From the Tribe?" asked Rhys, knowing it wasn't so.

Sharon didn't answer. She stepped out into the cracked, pot-holed centre of the street, looking fixedly at the figure. "Hi there!" she called out. "I'm Sharon – this is Rhys. Are you waiting for the bus?"

The figure didn't move.

"I don't think it is," hissed Rhys.

"Well, you bloody say something then," she retorted.

Rhys swallowed, and shuffled out into the middle of the road. "Um . . . hello. I'm a druid, see?"

He sensed the force of Sharon's glare. "'I'm a druid, see'? That's rubbish!" she declared.

"At least it's honest."

"I didn't lie! I just asked if he was interested in the bus!"

"Um . . . but it's a lone figure in the middle of an empty road on a dark night during uncertain times," he persisted. "And I think we should maybe try getting to the heart of the matter, see?"

For a second Sharon just seethed. "Fine!" she said, and stepped in front of Rhys, putting herself between him and the huddled figure. "Yo there!" she sang out. "Rhys here isn't just a druid, he's, like, almost the chosen one of his circle and you – you would not like to see him on antihistamines, so you just stop standing there freaking the crap out of us and get on with it, because it's really late and there's a busy day tomorrow and I can't be having any of this spooky crap without my morning coffee!" So saying, she turned back to Rhys. "There? Heart of the matter enough for you?"

Wordlessly, Rhys pointed.

The man was gone.

Sharon said, "um . . . "

The smell hit them again, with almost physical strength. Rhys made a choking sound, pulling his sleeve over his mouth, even as Sharon turned first white, then grey. It rose up from the mud around them, spun with the breeze over the reeds; and as the smell grew, so something else drifted up from the ground beneath their feet. It happened fast, in barely a few heartbeats: the mist swelled, a sludgy greyness that surged up around them, amplifying, liquefying the smell into puffy little breaths, crawling up the lampposts and smothering the bus shelter in its embrace. And there it was, the smell, undeniable, irrefutable – rotting flesh.

"Sharon?"

Rhys was already half lost from view, a colourless shape in the gloom. Holding her hand across her nose and mouth, Sharon reached out for him, felt nothing, saw him drift further into the dark. "Rhys? Rhys, keep talking!"

"Sharon?"

Something moved behind her; she turned, calling out again, and reached out a hand to feel . . .

Soft.

Warm.

Sticky.

Her fingers came away and thick red goo clung to them, dried, coagulated blood, flecked with ancient black clots. "Rhys!" She turned to run, but a hand came out of nowhere and caught her by the back of the neck, pulling her back. The hand was hot and damp; but thin, barely any flesh on it. An unnatural heat came off its fingers of loose skin and jagged bone; the smell was overwhelming. She glimpsed dangling grey skin hanging off in flags.

Then a burst of red-yellow light to one side was accompanied by a voice, shouting;

"Don't you touch her!"

Rhys staggered out of the mist, with streaming reddened eyes, and a potion burning in one hand. His skin crackled with erratic energy, tarmac popped and gravel split beneath his feet, and the ground shimmered and shuddered with the force of his stride. He plummeted into the side of whatever held Sharon by the neck, hard enough to send both of them flying onto the grass verge. Sharon rolled to one side, crawled up groggily, and saw Rhys fall on top of the thing in the dark, his potion still blazing. Coils of wire were rising up and splitting the ground beneath him, and wrapping, ivy-like, around his and the fallen figure's feet.

"Don't . . . you . . . touch her!" he screamed, and slammed his fist into the unseen face of the black-clad figure.

A hand rose up from the creature on the ground, all yellow bone and discoloured, fleshless skin. It pushed, very gently, against Rhys's chest. The druid flew backwards, wires snapping beneath him, potion tumbling from his hand, like he'd been struck by a lorry, and landed with a bone-sharp crack on the road, arms flopping, eyes going wide. He fell, and he lay, and he did not move.

The figure picked itself back up. And now Sharon could see its face. Ears, lips and nose had withered away to cavities in its sagging skin. His eyes were hollows of burst inky-red, the whites long since lost to blood, jaundice and time; and his great, oversized back was bent almost double over the curve of a rag-clad body, so he seemed small and short, though he might have been a giant, for all she could tell. He wore a coat of lacerated brown leather, rotted away to hanging strips that dangled off stick-arms and a spine-stretched back. His nails were great bark-like curves, forming thick loops of bone; his feet were bare, each metatarsal clearly visible as they moved beneath his almost translucent skin. His face turned slowly, barely lit by the flickering remains of Rhys's potion, and as his gaze settled on Sharon there was

taste of mud

weight

heat

worms in skin

and she gasped for sudden breath, choking on ash and dust, scrambling back up the grassy bank as the creature took one step, then another, feet barely lifting off the ground, towards her.

"Whatever you want," she stammered, "this is a seriously bad way of getting it."

Another step, then another. The smell of rot tumbling off his body was almost overwhelming, but to puke was to divert attention from the thing as he staggered towards her, it was to look away from those curling nails and blood-filled eyes, and neither of these were things she could do. Rhys stirred on the road behind, tried to lift his head, and flopped back down.

"Now look," she babbled, as the creature came another step nearer, then another; so close now, she could touch the hem of its tatty leather robe. "I'm guessing, based on circumstances only, that you've got some issues you need to work through, and I'm just telling you, that this is not the most productive way of doing it . . . "

A hand reached down towards her and instinctively Sharon moved. She moved without moving, a slipping down, rather than a rolling out, a drop into the greyness of the spirit walk, into the place where all things were true and nothing was real; and for a second, as she looked up into the face of the monstrous man, she saw ...

A mask. A leather mask, with a great pointed beak at one end, and two round hollows for eyes.

Then the hand came down towards her and, here, the flesh wasn't hanging off, wasn't dangling limp – here, the flesh was a living, writhing thing, coated over with a living, heaving mass of maggots and Sharon drew in a breath and, not quite knowing what she was doing, and having nowhere else to go, she pushed herself up and ran straight *through* the hand.

A moment.

A second, and it lasted a hundred years.

For a moment, maggots coated her skin.

For a century, she breathed dirt.

For an instant, rats chewed at the end of her toes.

For a millennium, fleas sucked on her hot blood.

Bare feet curled in dirt.

Toes pressed down deep and beneath them, dead flesh moved.

Just for a second.

Only forever.

Then she stumbled *through* the man in his rag coat, his body jerking hard as she passed out the other side, his fingers opening and snapping back. She stumbled onto the ground behind him, wiping not-there maggots off her skin, spitting not-there ash from out her mouth and, with the violence of her own revulsion, she stumbled back into the visible world, back into the mist and the smell of flesh. Realising this, she turned again and looked behind her; and there he still stood, turning in the faint glow-light to stare at her. It was perhaps too much to attribute any expression to his face, if it could be called a face at all; but if it wore any look, any glimmer of feeling, then that look was ...

surprise.

For a moment, the two stayed there, frozen in place, while Rhys rolled over on the ground and tried to work out which way was up and which was down.

Then the rotting man in the rotten coat reached out, slowly, one curled bone-hand, and there was no threat in it, and perhaps an invitation.

Sharon stood up, a limb at a time, her body shaking with effort, revulsion, fear.

The hand gestured, once, calling closer.

Sharon shook her head. "Sorry," she mumbled. "Not a bloody chance." The figure hesitated. Then pointed at the ground, at his bare feet, then at Sharon's own. "Um . . . this is gonna be a tricky kinda conversation, isn't it?" she said.

The creature gestured in exasperation, and pointed again at her shoes.

"You got vocal chords left?" she asked. "Or how about charades?"

His head tilted to one side, hesitant, struggling to understand. Then it moved forward and back, chicken-like, a gesture which began with the chin and thrust outwards, almost clucking, and with it came a sound, a little puff on the air.

"Uh – uh – uh – uh . . . "

Rhys was on his hands and knees, groggy and bewildered. Sharon glanced at him, saw no blood, stared back at the gasping creature. "What do you want?" she breathed, quiet in the dark.

"Uh – uh – uh – I – I – I – . . . " The words came slow, little half-wheezes.

"Yes?"

"I – I – I – . . . ?" The creature's fingers twisted at its side, and with a sudden heave it threw up its arms, releasing a great stench and sending the mist swirling around it. "I – I – I – " The reeds at its back began to wither and crack, turning brown, then black, curling down to burnt ashes in an expanding circle around him. The tarmac beneath his feet split, jagged fault lines rushing outwards, dust billowing up from the surface of the road. Mud bubbled and foamed, great bursts of gas popping from the still earth, and Sharon could feel it now, a dryness on her skin, a sucking out and a pulling in, a suffocation on the air, and she tried not to breathe, tried not to run as the creature raised its hands to the sky and shrieked,

"I – I – I – want – want – want what I – I – am owed!"

The sound was a wheeze, a bare gasp, but it tore the mist around it and rolled down the empty street.

Faded slowly away.

The creature raised its right hand, palm-out, towards her. The lines in its flesh were drooping sags of skin, holes peeking through to suggest darkness and rotten muscle below. "You – you – you – you – give – it – it back."

"Give what back?" breathed Sharon. "What was taken?"

The creature's face twisted as it tried to find the sound, then, with a great hiss of frustration, it pointed again towards Sharon's feet. "Give – it – back!"

She stared down at her feet, then up again at the not-man, who again raised the palm of his hand. Sharon looked at her own hand, saw nothing amiss except perhaps a bit too much dirt and . . .

No.

Looked again.

A little bit closer.

Looked with the eyes of a shaman, and there it was, a distortion to the mist, like a knife cutting through silk, a tiny after-image which clung to the surface of her skin and moved, a little out of time, with her hand, when it moved. An indelible, impossible, invisible set of crosses, one smaller than the other, set in its neighbour's top left corner: the mark of the Midnight Mayor.

"Oh, shite," she whispered. Her eyes flashed up again to the creature. "Look," she babbled, "I think I gotta warn you, I'm only a shaman. I mean, Swift made me deputy Midnight Mayor and that, but it's not like I've got any power, it's not like I'm up for the whole . . . you know, bang, boom, blast kinda stuff. I just run a support group! Counselling within the community. I can't be dealing with missing things and owed things and all that crap. You want the . . . the . . . " Her voice trailed off. "Okay," she said. "So you probably *do* want the real Midnight Mayor, but he's kinda . . . so I can see why you might . . . but, really, I don't think you're reasoning this one through properly! It'll all go crappy with me in charge! I mean, nine times out of ten I've no idea what I'm saying and I'm only ever nice to people because I don't have the charisma or the knowledge or any of that to get away with witty put-downs, so really, honestly, this seems like a terrible mistake!"

The creature pointed again at her feet, then back at her hand. "Give me – me – me – what I – I – I am owed."

"Okay, okay . . ." Sharon tried a deep breath, then regretted it, coughing on the foul air. "Any clues as to what that might be?"

"Give me!" he hissed, and before Sharon could start forward, or scamper back, he turned in a sweep of ragged robe and flapping skin, and marched away, back down the bare and empty road.

"Hey, wait, that's so unhelpful it's like, I mean, I don't even know what it's like, it's like so . . . " The mist spun around him, eating the figure up. "Hey! You can't get all doomy on me and then not contribute to the overall affair!" she called out, as the darkness swallowed the creature up. "That's just bad working practice!"

Silence from the fog.

Sharon stood there, staring up the road after him.

There was a flash of light at her back, white and sharp. She turned and saw a pair of bright white spots moving through the gloom. She looked back; there was no sign of the creature. The mist was already rising, drifting up into the air as if it had decided it was interested in being a cloud after all. Rhys was staggering to his feet, running his hands over his head, his neck, his chest, feeling for disaster.

A crunch of gears changing in the dark, the rattle of an under-maintained diesel engine trying to shake itself loose.

"Ms Li?" called the druid, leaning against the bus post for support. "Did he . . . ?"

Sharon stood in the middle of the road, hands clutching her elbows, like one trying to fight off a deep, damp coldness. "Damn," she muttered. "We are in so much shite."

A parp of horn, a glow of fluorescent light.

She turned, and the bus, a lonely single-decker, slid to a halt by the bus post, its doors slamming open with the thump of rubber on Perspex. At his wide black wheel the driver motioned, urging them on board.

"Come on Rhys," said Sharon. "Let's go home."

Chapter 33

Blue Electric Angels

We beeee
   we beeeee!
      weeee BEEEEE
immortal eternal brilliant bright beautiful fire light magic dancing
death burning sky falling burning falling voice screaming scream
dance sing sing sing songs of
trapped
weeeee beeeeee ...
   flesh
      flesh wither
         flesh die
help us
   we beeeeeeeeeeeee
free?

Chapter 34

Clean in Word and Deed

Trish said, "Oh, my God, Sharon? What the fuck is that smell?"

Sharon looked down at herself, at her mud-stained, sewer-splattered trousers and boots, at her scorched top and trousers, black-lined fingernails and dirt-encrusted hair. Then she looked up at Trish. At eight in the morning, most of Sharon's trip back from the shores of the Thames Estuary had consisted of waiting for the trains to start, and, by the time she'd crossed London Bridge, the morning sun had risen. From a fleck of gold in the east, it had become a burning white brightness that filled the dawn sky with so much light, it became impossible to see where sun ended and light began. She'd walked through the front door of her flat, bleary, forgetting to open it as she did so, just in time for Trish – the loud one – to come downstairs in search of breakfast. And now she stood in the hall, muddy, grubby, tired and greasy, staring into the perfectly polished face of her flatmate, and found that she had nothing whatsoever to say.

"There was a thing," she confessed. Then, thinking this might not be enough, she added, "I'm not sure if I'm ready to talk about it yet."

This last sentence, was, objectively speaking, an absolute lie, as she was more than ready to find a nice, sympathetic ear, not necessarily human, and preferably a pair of lungs geared up for traditional feedback sounds such as "um" and "ah" and maybe even an "oh really", at which she could scream the horrors of her day. However, Trish was clearly not about to provide either source of comfort, and so there she was, falling back on the default position of, "I'm not ready". It wasn't a rejection, a denial or a rebuff, but, rather, in those few magic words, Sharon informed her flatmate, woman to woman, that behind such a simple sentiment lay a world of emotional pain, best not explored.

Trish hovered, torn between the desire for breakfast and her duty as a flatmate to explore the unexplorable. Breakfast won out. "Okay, babes," she said, "but you seriously gotta have a bath and those clothes – *write off.*"

Sharon smiled wanly. "Thanks, Trish." She started upstairs.

"And, hey – no offence, yeah, but will you clean the bath after?"

Sharon had a bath.

Amid the smells of lavender and lemon, she nearly fell asleep.

Her chin sunk beneath the steaming water and foam went up her nose. This was enough to wake her with a start. She sluiced herself off with cold water and, wrapped in towels and with the heater on full blast, she cleaned out the bath. She didn't feel like the bath *needed* the cleaning, but then she'd become used to the smell of soot and sewage, so who was she to judge?

Afterwards, with a feeling of odd sadness and strange inadequacy, she binned her slime-stained clothes, then took the rubbish to the communal skip outside.

At 9.15, as the door slammed behind the departing Trish, Sharon Li curled up in her bed. Her eyes drifted shut, her mind passing straight through restless fatigue and half dreaming, plummeting for the deepest, darkest depths of sleep, and . . .

Her phone rang.

Groaning, she fumbled out of bed towards her mobile and, with her eyes still not open, she flipped it on. "Yeah?" she rasped, testing the sound to make sure it was still English.

"Hello? Hello, Ms Li? Ms Li?"

Sharon rolled over onto her back. Her limbs flopped heavily around her. "Hi, Miles," she groaned. "What time is it?"

"About a quarter past nine, Ms Li. I'm terribly sorry – you aren't busy, are you?"

"Aren't I? I guess I'm not."

"I'm so sorry it's taken me this long to get back to you . . ."

"Take your time," she sighed, pressing her free hand in a fist against her forehead. "Totally okay."

"But I think I may have some information on the body dumped in the river . . ." Sharon opened her eyes. In the few minutes since they'd drifted inexorably shut, the world seemed to have become unbearably bright.

"The river police picked up a body last night, and took it to the morgue. It was rather badly damaged, but they think . . ."

"Don't tell me," sighed Sharon. "It's a woman."

"Ms Li!" exclaimed Miles, not missing a beat. "I can see that you're already on top of this!"

"Not really. Just a hunch. You seen . . . you know . . . the body?"

"I was going to head over there now, and wondered if you would like to . . . ?"

Miles let the words fade tactfully away. "Gimme the address," she muttered, rolling out of bed and landing bum-first on the floor. "This is me, getting totally on it."

Her mud-splattered shoes were too sodden to be worn in polite society, let alone dead polite society. She crawled under her bed and fumbled around between cardboard boxes and unmentionable pieces of mail strategically ignored, until she found her emergency backup shoes. They, like all the best things in life, were also pale purple, but adorned with white swirls and faint traces of blue flowers along the canvas, which laced up around her ankles to leave just enough lace dangling down at the end of the bow to present a subtle but potent trip hazard. As she pulled the left shoe out from under her bed, her hand brushed something metal and rusted and there it was the *can't breathe can't breathe can't breathe can't*

how dare they how dare how dare
      GIVE ME WHAT I'M

She snatched her hand away from the end of the umbrella, where she'd stowed it, what felt like a week ago, before the images could overwhelm her. Then, very gingerly, she reached back under, gripping it by the wooden handle instead, and pulled it out. Blue, oversized, missing its end, the mega-mystic umbrella was still as infuriatingly mundane-looking as ever. She turned it over a few times in her hands, but each time the rusted end was visible, where a spike should have been, she somehow couldn't bring herself to look too closely, let alone touch it. The idea of carrying it around all day was faintly appalling, but then . . .

How much worse could things get?

Her green canvas bag still whiffed of sewer. She sprayed it with lemon-scented air freshener before putting it on her back; and, this time, she remembered to take the chain off the door on her way out of the house.

Chapter 35

The Dead Have No Fear

They met at St Thomas's Hospital.

As medical institutions went, St Thomas's – Tommy's to its staff – was more of a city state than a place for sickness and disease. With its view across the river to the Houses of Parliament, it towered over the waterside like a great beached whale, occasionally hanging banners out from its topmost windows to offer advice and protest to the MPs dining opposite. Inland – and by the time you'd got there it felt distinctly inland – ambulances swept to and from the swishing glass portals of A & E, while deeper in the hospital itself could be found not merely wards and laboratories, but kitchens, shops, hairdressers, shoe-shiners and various chapels and prayer rooms for different faiths seeking a moment of solace.

It also had a morgue.

Finding the morgue was hard work, as it was one of the few parts of the hospital that didn't particularly advertise. Sharon stopped to ask one blue-shirted orderly, who gave her such rich and detailed instructions that she'd followed only half of them before having to ask the way again. Being the knower of truth, it turned out, didn't necessarily equate to geographical savvy.

The morgue itself was down in the bottom of the hospital, washed with the sounds of grumbling boilers and huge chugging thermostats, each striving to keep the building hot, and cold, and all comfortable things in between. Stepping through the swinging heavy fire doors to the morgue itself was like crossing over a weather front, and Sharon half expected a tiny chemical cloudburst to open above her head as the sudden cold air of the morgue hit, along with a stench of disinfectant. The colour of all things to do with death, she realised, wasn't black, or even white, but pink – a garish, alcohol-laced pink with which every other surface had been scrubbed, every tile mopped and every hand scrubbed that had buzzed on the buzzer at reception. A bored man, with grey hair combed over a freckled scalp, drifted to the reception counter, heard her name and let her in without a word.

A long corridor, the floor rubber-scarred from a thousand passing gurneys. A notice board offered leaflets on what to do when a loved one passed away, your legal responsibilities and the support you might want to get. Walking past it, Sharon couldn't look. Even without shifting into the spirit walk, she could hear the echoes of people who had passed this way before, feel their clenching grief in the pit of her stomach. It was hard, sometimes, keeping such things out.

Miles was waiting for her, sitting with his legs crossed on one of a row of plastic chairs. He sprang to his feet, taking in her emergency wardrobe: tatty jeans, random T-shirt and reserve pair of canvas lace-ups.

"Good morning, Ms Li, I hope you're well today?" She scowled. Miles, though his eyes were shadowed and heavy, still hadn't so much as a crease on his long black coat and tight-buttoned shirt. "No Rhys?" he asked.

"Druid's sleeping," she grumbled. "Or if he isn't, then he oughtta be."

"Long night?"

"Kinda. Had a meeting, met the Tribe, found Swift – well, no, didn't find Swift, it's complicated – and got shouted at by this mega-sticky guy with serious issues while waiting for a bus. You?"

Miles's face was all pained concern. "Well, I was feeling rather pleased with myself at having spent all night phoning every mortuary in the city and calling every favour I could with our police contacts. But now I hear about your evening, I must admit, my self-satisfaction diminishes. So, when you say you found Swift . . ."

"Yeah, about that . . ."

"I take it our situation has not improved?"

Sharon's face scrunched up tight. The cold air was helping to keep her awake, but Miles's look of concern seemed to produce in her a spontaneous ageing effect. "Kinda no, really. I mean, he's not dead, technically, which I think is a win. But he's . . . not all there. Which would be fine, except . . . someone else is there."

Miles kept his face from falling, but only just. "The . . . electric angels?" His voice was the sigh of a man hoping he's wrong.

"Yeah."

"They . . . control his body?"

"I dunno if we should say 'control'. I mean, 'control' implies possession, unless that's just a social stereotype. It also suggests they don't shoot blue fire whenever they feel stressed, and their skin isn't cracking open, and they aren't screaming all the time. I think maybe the word we're looking at here is . . . inhabit?"

"And you learnt this from the Tribe?"

"Yup."

"May I ask . . . how?"

She stared at him. "I asked them." Sensing that his surprise threatened to burst out into astonishment, she added, "I asked them nicely."

There was a body to examine.

Sharon realised she'd never examined a body before. She'd seen death, up far too close, but that had been in the heat of the moment, a thing which was, and then was not.

This, however, was formalised death.

A body had been laid out on a slab, a pathologist covering it with a sheet. "It" was definitely an "it", even if it had once been a "she". "It" was only organs and skin, whereas "she" might once have had a name. It had been found, according to Miles, by the river police, when it washed up with the tide near London Bridge. It had been wrapped up tight in bin bags and masking tape, but a human body was naturally buoyant. Besides, there were gases. Sharon hadn't asked about the gases and, seeing her face, Miles hadn't offered to tell.

The bags had protected the body from the worst that the river could do. As the pathologist, a Dr Nikookam, five foot two with stubby, trimmed nails that looked like they'd given up on growing, talked in a professional, nasal voice through the discovery of the body and the process of decay, Sharon stared at the white sheet still covering the corpse. She wondered how long until the pathologist performed his magic trick, whisked away the sheet and revealed nothing underneath but bunny rabbits.

When Dr Nikookam did pull the sheet back, to point out a particularly interesting laceration to the flesh, Sharon was shocked at how unshocked she was. The body was just a thing, which had been a woman, aged somewhere between twenty-five and thirty, with dyed black hair and dead blue lips: a picture of a body, not a real person. Her neck had been incised in several places by something jagged and sharp; but the morgue had washed away the blood, and all that remained were red marks in grey flesh, forming a blast pattern across one side of her body, perhaps from broken glass exploding close at hand, or maybe from a furnace exploding, though no trace of glass or metal had been found in the wounds. The electrical burns running across her body in the same motion, from left to right, had barely formed before the body itself had died, preventing the swellings and expulsions which Sharon had dreaded as an accompaniment to death. The woman's broken right arm had been carefully laid back in place for the funeral, as soon as anyone came to claim the corpse. This injury was, so Dr Nikookam concluded, the result of the body itself being hurled with considerable force against some sort of solid object – maybe a concrete wall?

In conclusion, he could find many causes of death – trauma, laceration, electrocution – but as all of them appeared to have happened at the same time, and as the body itself had then been removed from the scene of the crime, he could give no hypothesis as to the circumstances surrounding the event. At least, no hypothesis which he, as a professional, would be willing to write down.

"Obviously," he explained, "her death was the result of serious impact from a high-level expulsion of electro-magical forces."

Sharon's eyes flashed up to the doctor's face, and there was Dr Nikookam quietly rolling the sheet back up over the woman's naked form.

"I'd say that she was no more than two metres from the centre of the blast. The burn patterns suggest an exothermic spell, probably an uncontrolled expulsion of pent-up energies. The lacerations to the skin, naturally indicative of a defensive ward being broken from the inside out. Or, to put it crudely," he added, seeing the look on Sharon's face, "something which she wanted kept inside a ward, got out. Stomach contents – she drank far too much Coca-cola and her last meal was a sandwich. Body moved post-mortem, presumably to be disposed of in the river, and analysis of her bone density indicates that she's been a frequent user of wand-fuelled incantations, cast primarily through the right hand. The wand method, you see ..." – a tiny smile from an expert doing a thorough job and hoping to impress – "... can often affect the calcium levels on the limbs used in greatest proximity to the casting node."

Sharon realised her mouth was hanging open.

"Thank you." Miles filled the gap. "This is all very helpful."

A polite nod from Dr Nikookam, who began peeling off his white latex gloves.

Sharon stared at the corpse, and wondered what she'd see if she touched it.

Perhaps nothing.

Life was magic, Sammy said. And death was only death. You didn't get much truer than that.

"Anything on the body itself?" asked Miles, one dispassionate professional to another. "Personal items?"

"Clothes, no wallet, but a phone."

A clear plastic bag was handed to Miles. And here it was; this was where the blood had gone, a great brown stain which had soaked through every fibre of clothing on the body, diluted and spread by the river water seeping into the bin bags that had held her corpse.

"I suspect" – Dr Nikookam disliked suspecting anything without proof, but for Miles he'd make an exception – "that the perpetrators removed anything which could identify the woman, but failed to notice her mobile phone. It was kept in her bra, you see. No pockets in her skirt. We can't turn it on – the river – but maybe you'll have more luck."

Miles smiled wanly, and wrapped his fingers tighter round the plastic bag. "Your report . . . ?"

"I'll send it to the relevant authorities," said Dr Nikookam. "I know how this works . . . And if you find the individual responsible for this young woman's death," warned the pathologist, as they turned to go, "do be careful. The injuries are indicative of . . . shall we say, an unstable character."

The Alderman nodded in thanks, and hurried Sharon out of the door.

The blood-soaked clothes were of no interest to Miles.

"We'll give them to the scryers, see if they get anything," he said, hiding them deep in a blue shopping bag to avoid unwelcome questions. "But after two days in the river . . . ?"

Sharon kept her eyes forward and her feet moving, down the cold, grey corridor, and tried not to inhale through her nose. "What about the mobile phone?" she asked. "Any use?"

Miles pulled it from its plastic bag and tried to turn it on. Nothing. It was a smartphone – smart enough, Sharon felt, that its owner probably didn't need her own brains for much of the time – and, beneath its clear surface and delicate touch-screen, a whole life could be contained in tiny electronic bits. "We could give it to the techie boys," he conceded. "Let them work their magic."

"I don't suppose they've got a spell entitled 'fix everything and make it better'? Or even just a spell for drying out mobile phones?"

"Sorry," he grinned. "Although I don't see why the latter should be hard to create." He thought, then added, "Ms Li . . . about the Midnight Mayor . . . "

"What? Oh, yes. What about him?"

"We really do have to talk about what we're going to do if he's . . . incapacitated."

"Not dead."

"What?"

"Not dead – if he's incapacitated, not dead. It's something Rhys pointed out," she murmured, as they wound their way upstairs towards the exit, through corridors of samey wheelchairs stacked like shopping trolleys, doctors with busy walks and important clipboards, and porters with the shamble of the not-at-all-bothered. "Why wouldn't you just kill him? I mean, in a nice way, but he's a bit of a tit, isn't he? So why not just kill Matthew Swift?"

"I think your error, if I may be so bold," replied Miles, dodging an oncoming gurney, "is in thinking that this is about Matthew Swift. He's just a person, if you'll pardon me saying so, and can be killed. But the Midnight Mayor . . . that's a power. That's a force, a thing that is a part of the city. If you kill the current Midnight Mayor, a new one will arise, and as a new one has not arisen . . . how's your hand?"

Sharon stopped so suddenly he nearly walked into her.

"My what?"

"Your hand. If you were to become Midnight Mayor, your hand would . . ."

"Me?!"

Miles's smile scintillated with infinite patience. "You *are* Swift's deputy," he pointed out. "And while the job comes with no appreciable power of its own, it is if nothing else a useful indication of where he thinks the succession should lie, were the worst to happen. And I for one can understand his reasoning."

Sharon stared down at her hand, remembering the ghostly set of crosses that had floated above her skin the night before.

Nothing. By the cold light of a hospital corridor, there was nothing on her palm except the lingering scent of bubble bath. She breathed out slowly, then in, counting silently to ten, and waited for her heart rate to drift back down into double figures.

"Okay," she replied. "Let's say Swift isn't dead, and, even if he was, there's no reason to think he'd be so bloody stupid as to make *me* his successor."

"Why would it be stupid? It's clear that you're highly qualified."

Sharon threw up her hands in despair. "I'm a barista!" she shrieked. Heads turned in the bustling halls. She swallowed hard, her knuckles white where they gripped the umbrella. "I'm a community support worker," she corrected angrily. "I tell people that it's okay for them to be weird, so long as they don't hurt anyone; *that's* my job. I can't be doing this ... Midnight Mayor, fate of the city crap, I just can't! I've got meetings to chair, I've got minutes to take, biscuits to buy and a bingo night to arrange! That's what I do, that's my job, and this ..." – she gestured feebly round the hall – "... this is just someone else's idea of a bad day at the office!"

Miles waited for the worst of her fury to drain away.

"But, Ms Li ... you *are* here, aren't you? You *are* part of this, and that, more than anything else, counts."

Sharon drooped, leaning on the umbrella. "They killed the woman. The blue electric angels did it."

Miles drew back. "Are you ...?"

"Yes. I'm pretty sure it was self-defence, or they were scared, or she was trying to hurt them somehow, but I still think they did it. And now Swift's gone, but he's not dead, or at least, I don't think he was dead – but that's the point, isn't it? If you can't kill a power, if you can't kill the Midnight Mayor, then what's the next best thing? You remove it, get rid of it somehow, but you don't kill. Swift's gone, but he's not dead, and last night this dude with the worst breath you've ever smelt came out of the mist and said 'give me what I'm owed' and it was really disgusting and I thought, me and Rhys, I thought ... this isn't what I signed up for, you know?"

Miles hesitated, then laid a hand on her shoulder. When she didn't pull away, he said, "And in light of all that, Ms Li, may I say how well you seem to be doing?"

Sharon gave a tired, hollow smile. "Cheers, Miles. You know, for a guy who wears nothing but black, you're okay."

"Thank you, Ms Li."

"I mean, I personally think it gives out all the wrong vibes." She straightened, warming to her theme. "It's all very well having this 'fuck with me and you're dead' vibe. But if you think about it, I bet at least half the people you meet are just ordinary guys having a difficult day, and maybe even less than fifty per cent are actually blood-sucking monsters, and if they are, do you think that black, as a style choice, is going to put them off? Pastel colours," she concluded. "You can't go wrong with a judicious mix of pastels."

"I'll take your word for it, Ms Li."

Sharon's smile widened. "Right then!" she exclaimed. "Let's go sort this crap out – hey . . ." A thought struck, and she spun, levelling the tip of the umbrella at Miles. "What do you know about the Black Death?"

Chapter 36

In My Friends I Find Myself

Rhys woke at 1 p.m. to the sound of his phone.

As he scrambled towards it, it stopped, just as his finger hit receive.

He checked the number.

Sharon Li x3

He rolled out of bed, and stepped onto yesterday's clothes. He groaned as smell and memory hit, just as his knee bumped against the portable can of gas that fuelled his tiny stove.

Rhys lived in a studio apartment.

It was an apartment, because it was on the fourth floor of a building that was full of apartments.

It was a studio because there was only four foot between the bed, the desk and the stove. Light found its way in through a skylight above the bed. Downstairs, his neighbour was practising for *The X Factor* – or so Rhys assumed, because he only sang one song, on a theme of acoustic pop, rendered loudly, flat, and with added choruses of "aaaaahhhi!".

Rhys's phone beeped: a text message.

Goin 2 Archway. U awake yet? Bring thermos flask and tea.

Sharon xx

It had disconcerted him the first few times Sharon had signed her text messages with a pair of kisses; he'd had nightmares on the theme, nearly all of which had ended with a three-foot dash to the kitchen cupboard and a squirt of nasal spray. However, as acquaintance between them had bloomed to association, he'd come to realise that 'xx' at the end of a text message meant absolutely nothing. Memos on the topic of office utilities had been signed "lots of love", while the worst he'd seen was an email to a minotaur who'd demanded a throne of gold to sit on, should he deign to attend the meetings, but who had received for his pains a note from Sharon informing him that his needs would be considered, but unless he could provide a medical or chemical reason why his chair had to be specifically gold, budget restraints would limit the office's willingness to comply. That email had been signed "yours sincerely"; and the sight of those two words had made Rhys shudder. The minotaur had not contested the point.

Rhys wasn't a morning – or even much of an afternoon – person but, seeing Sharon's email, he still made it from unconscious to out of the door in seven and a half minutes.

Archway was not an inspiring place to meet: a great roundabout where glum Upper Holloway met the steep ascent towards elegant Highgate, it was cursed with thunderous roads, dubiously phased traffic lights, a maze of obscurely labelled bus stops and architecture described at best as accidental. No one, surely, had *intended* for Archway to be so ugly?

"Morning – or maybe afternoon."

Sharon Li didn't so much appear in the air beside Rhys as manifest the obvious fact that she'd been present all along. She held a cup of hot coffee in one hand, and a Cornish pasty in the other; and the realisation struck Rhys that his life was not complete without coffee, scalding hot and rich in caffeine, never mind concerns of flavour and price. "Or," she said, seeing him enraptured with this notion, "maybe it's still last night?"

She fixed him with the frowning stare he associated with her perceiving the mystic void, or the hidden truth, or whatever it was shamans were seeing whenever they looked like that; then held out the coffee cup.

"Miles is running round lotsa hospitals trying to see if anyone died of Black Death recently," she said. "Last night he sat up trying to find if anyone had been drowned in the river during the last few days, and today it's plague all the way. You and me, though, we're just going to pop down to a newsagent and see if anyone saw Swift before he went all explosive and that. But if you want," her eyes gleamed maliciously, "you and Miles could totally swap?"

His fingers closed round the hot cardboard cup. "Thank you, Ms Li," he said, inhaling the smell of coffee before savouring the big event. "I'm not sure I'm very good with Black Death."

"This is why Miles is doing it," she replied. "You know, while this whole deputy Midnight Mayor thing sucks, I kinda like having a minion?"

Rhys nearly choked out hot coffee across the pavement, but Sharon had already turned away. Trying not to blow caffeine out of his nostrils, he scurried after her as, jauntily swinging the umbrella, she began to march uphill, away from the Underground station.

"Get home safe last night?" she asked.

"Yes, Ms Li, although the bus driver was very rude about how I smelt."

"No mystic encounters? No gibbering monsters come crawling out of the night at you?"

"No." He tried not to sound relieved about this. As an afterthought: "There weren't any after you, were there? Only I do think that would be unfair, not that the rest of us want to have monsters come after us. I'm just saying . . ."

"I got home fine. Had a bath, went to bed, got woken up immediately, but I figure . . ." She grabbed the coffee cup out of his hand before he could squeak in protest and took a slurp. "I'm sure union regulations have something to say about working conditions and that."

"Are you a member of a union?"

"No . . ."

"Are there any unions for mages, magicians and associated professions?" mused Rhys.

Even before he realised he'd spoken out loud, he noticed Sharon growing intense.

"You mean . . . magicians could be being *exploited?* Casting spells for less than the minimum wage, working in unacceptable conditions, no health and safety, no national insurance . . . oh, my God." She stopped and turned so suddenly that Rhys nearly bumped into her. "What about gender equality? What if you have to be male to be a warlock?"

"But . . . you're not a warlock, Ms Li . . ."

"Not the point!"

"No, no," he conceded. "I see that, but I think what I mean is, uh, that legislating for something which isn't there, as it were, I mean that when you are part of a secret, hidden society . . ."

"Just because it's secret doesn't mean it mustn't respect modern social realities!" declared Sharon. "I mean, magic moved from the countryside to the cities, yeah, because that's where the life went. Life makes magic and life went urban and so magic went urban but life – life . . ." She waggled the umbrella for emphasis. "Life has got to wear appropriate protective footwear!" Seeing Rhys's look of bafflement, Sharon awkwardly concluded, "Anyway, that's what I think." She started walking again, faster. "Look," she blurted, "I don't want you to think I'm a scary feminist or that, because I know that's the fear some people have when they see a woman get worked up about gender equality and that; I'm not scary, it's just that I think there's this problem of people going 'she's a girl and she's trying to do that' like somehow it's surprising or a bit radical when really . . . I guess what I'm saying is . . . I'm not a scary feminist person, I'm just a scary people person. What do you think?"

Posterity was not to know Rhys's response, as Sharon stopped again, at that moment, looked up, and exclaimed, "This must be it!"

Rhys followed her gaze. In white letters on a blue background, a lit-up sign above a doorway proclaimed:

ARCHWAY NEWS AND FILMS

A bright blue-painted door jangled as Sharon pushed it open, pausing to let three schoolgirls in brown uniforms make their way out past a notice board offering singing lessons to locals and French translation on a freelance basis, and warning that only two school-children and one dog would be permitted inside the shop at any time. The "films" section of the store was, in fact, a small stand offer-ing a mixture of kung fu action movies, and last year's straight-to-DVD thrillers starring actors who you'd almost heard of but who'd never quite made it off daytime TV. The news section was wider – great shelves of it, from concerned headlines about the breakdown of climate change talks, through to trumpeted tales of **Jilted Ex's Anger At Celebrity Scandal!** A cheerful collection of cheap stationery ranged from biros of the kind that got chewed, to Christmas wrapping paper depicting reindeers in silly hats. Two glowing fridge compartments offered chilled drinks, and a tiny freezer held lollipops and ice creams, positioned just too high for thieving children to reach.

At the back was a counter, guarded by two men with identical haircuts, coffee-brown skin, almond eyes and a pet dog. The dog, fat, black, with a great wet nose in a squashed little face, lay with its head on its paws, and looked about as vicious as a gerbil. The two men were clearly brothers. The elder sat behind the counter read-ing a magazine; the younger was sticking yellow price tags on huge suspicious jars of chilli pickle. Sharon looked at the brothers, then at the chilli, then at the shop itself; and for a moment she observed as only a shaman can, and saw . . .

children thieving children nabbing the chocolate bars
dog grows teeth when the robber comes, gentle in rest, furious when roused
ghost of our father standing behind the counter, his face sad, his back
bent, he leans in over the till, barely human, as the infant brothers look on
pages turn and fly in the news racks
boxes line the walls
count every penny
count every copper
Good morning sir!
Good morning ma'am
father sinking into the counter, eaten alive by it, swallowed whole . . .

She looked away.

Rhys had found a small box of children's modelling clay, for sale above the glitter pens and fairy dust, and was twisting a sample piece between his fingers uncertainly, trying to work out what he'd use it for. Sharon walked up to the counter, laid her umbrella on the top and said, "Hello, I'm looking for . . ."

"You found it!" exclaimed the younger brother, looking up from his jar of chillis.

"I . . . did?"

"Where was it?"

Sharon followed his exultant gaze down to the blue umbrella, lying on the counter. "Um . . . I'm not sure I'm gonna be able to answer that one. Is it yours?"

The elder brother's gaze flickered from the magazine to Sharon, then back again. Clearly, customer service was left to the junior of the two.

"Oh no, no – Mr Crompton's, he lost it last week, very distressing." The younger brother spoke with a faint Indian accent, but years of north London living had eroded it away to the odd lilt at the beginning and end of sentences. "He left a sign up – in the window."

In the window at the front of the store, amid the notices from women who sought men who sought women, there was a small, neatly inscribed piece of card. It read:

LOST
BLUE UMBRELLA, GOLF-STYLE, WOODEN HANDLE,
RUSTED POINT.
NO MATERIAL VALUE, OF GREAT SENTIMENTAL VALUE
TO OWNER.
REWARD FOR RETURN: £250

Beneath, the same immaculate hand had written out a contact number and address, then signed itself,

T.J. CROMPTON

Rhys detached the notice from the wall and took it over to

Sharon, who scanned it quickly, then turned it over in her hand to check the back, just in case someone had written something mystic, or possibly enlightening, on the reverse. No such luck.

"Who's Crompton?" she asked.

"Mr Crompton? Nice man, very nice man, always says hello."

"And this is his umbrella?"

"Yes – definitely. He never went anywhere without it, though ..." the younger brother's face fell a little, "it seems to be missing its point."

Sharon swallowed, and kept her fingers as far as she could from the rusted hollow where the point should have been. "Has ... someone else come in here recently, asking about the umbrella?" she asked, trying to radiate innocence. When the brothers didn't answer, she added, "A man, for example? Dark hair, blue eyes, maybe bought some tobacco, renewed a travel card ..."

"We get a lot of customers ..."

"Yes." The elder brother cut in before the younger could finish. "There was a man like that. He came in here a few days ago. Bought tobacco but was surprised at how much it cost – I remember that. Also blue eyes. Very blue. Noticed that too."

Sharon smiled at him, but he'd already gone back to his magazine. Flustered to find her charms so ineffectual, she turned to the younger brother, who returned her smile with a dazzling one of his own, causing Rhys to snuffle even more snottily than usual. "My brother has a better memory for faces," he explained. "Is this man a friend? Boyfriend?"

This time, Rhys sneezed profoundly.

"Nah," said Sharon. "Mind if we take this ...?" she asked, waggling the card.

"Of course! Mr Crompton will be pleased."

"I'm sure he will."

Chapter 37

Don't Judge People Until You Know Them

Mr T. J. Crompton lived up the nearby hill, in one of the side streets between Archway and Highgate, ordinary in themselves but which, here and there, enjoyed a far from ordinary view across the city. Victorian red brick featured throughout, with most terraces never more than two floors high, plus a hint of back garden and a polite little patch at the front where the inhabitants grew defensive hedges and passing teenagers threw their litter. The further up the hill, the more expensive the parked cars became in their designated bays; but a few of the larger buildings still had a dozen buzzers on the front door, and a tangle of bicycles inside the hall.

There were two buzzers on Crompton's house; and above the small letterbox, a sign proclaiming NO JUNK MAIL. Wedged casually in the letterbox was the menu for a local pizza house. Sharon buzzed on the intercom and waited.

Then she buzzed again.

"Maybe he's not home?" suggested Rhys, and immediately regretted his words, as Sharon reached out, grabbed him by the sleeve and, before he could offer even a sniffle of protest, dragged him bodily through the front door.

A cool hall, painted baby-blue, thinning grey carpet on the floor. The house had been divided into one flat below, one above. The stairs were narrow and a little too steep, high enough to trick home-owners into thinking they could fit a sofa up them, but tight enough to guarantee entrapment on the bends.

The door to flat A was white, old, locked. This time Rhys managed a cry of, "Oh, but, should ..." before Sharon dragged him through that, too.

The smell of tobacco struck even before the colours of reality had reasserted themselves on the druid's senses. Thick, chest-tightening tobacco. It had embedded itself in the walls, spread over the floor, formed black tar drops along the ceiling, stained the windows grey. Some effort had been made to disguise the full effect of this, by painting the walls themselves a smudgy brown and the ceiling a thick, eggshell orange, and by laying beige lino on the floor. Even so, the effect was overwhelming. Small watercolour paintings lined the wall, nearly all of men in cricket whites, and executed in a photographic style. The narrow hall received little natural light, except indirectly, from a single bedroom, a mouldering bathroom where the damp was almost as thick as the smell of smoke, a larger living room lined with more cricketing prints, and a kitchen, where the owner had decided that the theme of brown was getting a little tedious, and opted instead for thick, dark puke-yellow on the walls, ceiling and floor.

A sudden noise from outside made Rhys jump – a klaxon, followed by a deep, automated voice warning all passers-by to stand clear, as a vehicle was reversing. Somewhere in the flat, a boiler grumbled to itself; and he could make out the course of each pipe in the walls and floor as straight lines where spotty, dark mould had congregated, drawn by the heat.

Once you saw through the discoloration and damp, the flat itself was neatly kept. One plate, one knife and one fork had all been carefully cleaned and propped up in the drying rack by the kitchen sink. One small shelf contained four plastic tubs of different teas, each tub carefully labelled by a neat hand as lapsang, mint, camomile and chai, the original packets long since recycled in the small green bag kept pinned to one wall for the purpose.

Rhys drifted from room to room, his guilt at being an intruder in a stranger's house briefly undermined by his fascination with all things to be seen therein. He found Sharon in the living room, staring up at a wall of bookshelves that sagged under the weight of reference guides and much-fingered travel journals.

"Maybe he's on holiday?"

Sharon scowled and didn't answer. With the trepidation of someone half expecting a bomb, she prised open a couple of tiny drawers in a wide chest tucked away beneath the lowest shelf.

Maps, odd assorted batteries, carefully labelled ancient cassette tapes, manuals on How to Use Your New Iron, guides on how to clean a carpet. Boxes of matches, bundles of paper, carefully folded bills and statements from the pension authority, solidifying pots of sample wall paint. She dug deeper and further, as Rhys hopped from foot to foot and sensed allergic disaster building at the back of his nose. Another drawer, more bits of junk accumulated over the years with the righteous thought of 'maybe one day . . . ?' and left to rot; another drawer, and this one . . .

Sharon froze. Very carefully she moved to pick up the single, small object lying amid a jumble of loose change, from the bottom of its wooden coffin. It was a badge, shaped like a shield. White, metal, it rested in the palm of her hand and her skin was perceptibly colder for its touch. A pair of red crosses marked the symbol; a large one across the middle, and a far smaller one, resting in the top left-hand corner of the shield, which might not have been a cross at all, but a tiny crimson sword.

Sharon looked at Rhys, Rhys dabbed at his nose.

"An A-Alderman?"

Her fingers tightened over the badge; and there it was, obvious, irrefutable, a power in the sign, a freezing of her skin, solidifying, grounding, a kind of . . .

"Ms Li!"

The panic in Rhys's voice focused her attention. Looking down at the hand in which she held the badge, she saw that her fist had begun, without any pain, to turn to iron. She dropped the badge, which landed silently on the floor; and at once the metal retreated, rolling back into her own skin as if it had never been there, like sunlight caught behind a passing raincloud. "Bloody hell," she muttered.

A rattle of the door.

A key in the lock.

Rhys gestured impotently. Sharon swung the umbrella up in front of her like a weapon, then hesitated, dropped the umbrella, picked up the badge, bounced it from hand to hand indecisively, put it back down, and picked up the umbrella.

The door opened, a swush of draught excluder on a lino floor. A footstep in the corridor, then another. They stopped. Another step, and another stop. A voice said, "I have a gun."

It was old, male, matter-of-fact. Rhys turned grey. Sharon grabbed him by the sleeve, pulling him towards her, and still holding the umbrella aloft called back, "Yeah? Well, I've got a druid!"

Rhys bit his hand, leaving a great purple curve along the palm.

Silence from the corridor. Then, "I'm calling the police."

Another footstep, a shuffle towards the bedroom.

"And your umbrella!" she called out.

The footsteps stopped. Then, "Show me."

"Hey – you just said you've got a gun!"

"I lied."

"Well, that's bloody great," she called back. "But, seriously, that's a really freaky conversational opener you've got going there so you'll forgive me if I don't go running straight in for the hug."

"For the . . . who are you?"

"Now he asks," exclaimed Sharon. "Why couldn't people ever just be pleased to see us?"

"You broke into my flat!"

"No, no, because that implies *broke*, and we didn't break anything, did we, Rhys?"

"Um . . . no?"

"See?"

Silence from the corridor. Then loud, outraged, incredulous, "Who the hell *are* you people?!"

"Well, my druid here is Rhys . . . "

"Hello," essayed Rhys.

"And I'm Sharon Li, community support officer and senior manager at Magicals Anonymous, a confidential, informal, personal service for the mystically inclined. And I'm deputy Midnight Mayor, I guess I'm that, too, but you know, that job's kinda a bit . . . whatever."

"You're . . . the deputy Midnight Mayor?"

"Yeah – I said it like that, too, when I heard."

A sudden thunder of footsteps and before Sharon could shift into invisibility the man was there, filling the door. He stared from Sharon to Rhys and back again, before exclaiming, "But who the hell *are* you?"

The kettle was boiling.

There was something, Rhys concluded, in the sound of rising steam that lent itself to calm. Essentially, water was being excited to dangerous temperatures; so this calm had to be a cultural thing, born out of four hundred years of the British drinking tea. But it was hard to imagine that anyone could get really fraught when there was a cup of tea in the offing.

They stood in the kitchen, the three of them, doing their best not to glare too suspiciously.

The man called Crompton was old. Not the magically fuelled old of Mr Roding the necromancer, or the bent-double old of a pensioner who'd borne too much and lived too little, but a weathered, wind-swept old, of stiff straight joints, proper bearing, canyoned skin and salt and pepper hair cut to stiff military length. He wore a sleeveless woollen jumper over a thick yellow shirt, and had tufts of half-hearted moustache clinging to his top lip. He had snatched the blue umbrella from Sharon's hand when offered, and his eyes went straight to the tip – or to where the tip should have been. Now he leant against the kitchen counter and seethed in tune with the boiling kettle.

Sharon malingered. It was the only word she could think of to describe her presence in Crompton's flat; she was not an invited guest, and it was evident he didn't want her there. And yet, until she had an answer, preferably all the answers, she felt she had no option but to linger. Up to and including maliciously.

"How'd you end up deputy Midnight Mayor?" he asked at last, the words tumbling out past all self-restraint.

Sharon shrugged. "Dunno," she said. "I think it's a stupid idea, too."

By the look on Crompton's face, he agreed.

"But seriously," she said. "Midnight Mayor job: there's fire, there's lightning, there's all sorts of heavy artillery stuff – and me? I'm only good for the truth and the walking through stuff, stuff."

"Which is rude," added Crompton.

"Which is rude," Sharon agreed. "But, I figured, fate of the city and that. Besides, you . . . You said you wanted your umbrella back, and I brought you your umbrella back, and I *know* that, the day he went missing, Swift came to see you, and . . . "

"Swift is missing?"

Sharon paused, irritated at having her flow interrupted. "Yeah. Well – no. Well – sorta. Look, I'd give you the full story, but I kinda feel like I'm here doing the deductive bit and you're supposed to be doing the helpful bit so can we just focus on that?"

"I don't see why I should say anything to people who break into my flat . . . "

"And return your umbrella!" added Rhys.

"And who are the deputy Midnight fucking Mayor!" exclaimed Sharon. "I mean, I'm sorry, I know it's kinda having your cake and eating it to be all 'I don't want the job' and then pull rank, but these are difficult circumstances and interesting times and so can everyone just shut up and do what I say?"

To her surprise, everyone did shut up. She waited to see if the moment would last. It did. "Okay," she said, shifting uneasily before the two men's gaze. "Sorry about that. But . . . long day. Uh . . . so I'm right, yeah, about Swift coming to visit you?"

"What? Yes," grumbled Crompton. "Or, rather, I went to visit him; then he came to visit me. Actually, I sent him several emails, but I don't think he read them. So I went to visit him and explain the situation, and he agreed to help because, really, it's his bloody job and the man was being difficult about a very important issue. Then he came to visit."

"And bought you some tobacco, right?"

Crompton's eyes narrowed. "Yes," he murmured. "And you know this . . . ?"

Sharon waved the receipt, purloined from Swift's coat. "He renewed a travel card and bought you some tobacco a few days ago. I'm guessing the tobacco was to say sorry for being a tit with the important issue stuff?"

"More or less," murmured the old man. "He began, I believe, to appreciate both the importance of my office and the danger we are all in, and, lacking the emotional intelligence to simply apologise, he attempted to make up for it in other ways. Difficult man, this Midnight Mayor. Maybe it does make sense, having you as his deputy."

Sharon wasn't sure if that was a compliment or not.

"Now," she persisted, "when you say 'important issue' . . . ?" She let the words hang. Crompton glanced at Rhys, who was occupying himself with an almost spiritual dedication to the pouring out of tea. "Rhys is my IT manager," explained Sharon, seeing the look. "You can trust him with anything."

"Your . . . you are investigating this with an IT manager?"

"Yes." Sharon's smile didn't shed a tooth. "And I used to be a barista, until I became at one with the city and the city became at one with me, at which point I began to blend into the background of all things and become a part of all things around me, which are in fact in me, and I saw the truth that is hidden beneath the reality we make for ourselves, the world of perception, you see, and the walls of things were as shadow before me, and I had panic attacks sometimes because in my sleep I walked through the dreams of men. Then a goblin called Sammy turned up at work and ordered a really large cuppa tea, and I guess you could say I've become more grounded since then. So I guess the point *is* . . . " – she drew in a

long, shuddering breath – "... you just shouldn't go around judging people until you know them." She treated Crompton to another,
dazzling smile. "Whatcha say?"

Crompton almost writhed beneath the force of her optimism. He
said, "What do you know about Old Man Bone?"

"Old Man Bone ..." Sharon tried the words out, to see if they felt
better than they sounded. They did not. "... nothing. What's he?"

So Crompton explained.

Chapter 38

Crompton

I've got a job to do. Not pretty, not nice, but gotta be done. Started hundreds of years ago, even before the first plague came. We're always told that life is magic, and death is the end, but people never think it through, because even dead things, when they decay and change, have a power. Always been a problem in a big city, what to do with the dead.

They say that Old Man Bone started out as the gravedigger who dug the holes in unsanctified ground. Suicides, witches, beggars with no names, bastard babies what died before they could breathe – that lot, he was the one who took them, dragged their rotting corpses out of the city streets and gave 'em rest underground, out of sight and out of mind. The city's got more bones beneath it than most people think, the living moving in so quick they didn't have time or space to move the dead. Victorians had a real problem with it; nowhere to put the corpses, you see, so they built this railway that carried the bodies out in the dead of night, whole carriages of them laid out on wooden bunks, like the sleeper train to Scotland, only these sleepers were never going to wake up. Some folks said they saw him there too, Old Man Bone, driving the necropolis engine, scarf blowing in the wind, like a rider of the apocalypse, they said, but, then, they were Victorians, bit hysterical, bit fanciful about stuff like that, and, personally, I don't believe it.

What I do believe is the bit about the plague pits. When the Black Death first came to this country in the fleas on the backs of the rats, it killed whole villages and towns, and no one knew why. Every family lost someone – some families lost everyone. You could walk into places where the houses stood empty, and those people that were left did not have the strength to bury the dead. The crops rotted; children ran wild, living on dead human flesh. That, the stories said, was when he truly became Old Man Bone, the raggedy man. He walked among the corpses and buried the dead, never asking reward, never stopping for the moon or sun. He cleared the dead things from the streets and houses, and when it was done, and the survivors came out from the shadows to scrub the filth from their homes and reseed the fields, Old Man Bone went back into the earth, to sleep with the dead.

They say he walked again in 1665, when the plague returned to London, only this time he wore a doctor's mask over his face, and great black gloves, and he could carry a corpse over either arm, and pulled his cart of the dead over the muddy cobbles without ever a word or a sign. His feet were bare, and you could hear him work by the slopping of soil over the plague pits, long into the night. When, next year, the fires which burnt down the city, also burnt out the plague, he was gone, blown away like ash. He was not seen nor heard of again until the Blitz, when they say a man with no shoes on his feet and lime in his hair, helped bury those bodies what were too damaged to be recognised, in the great tombs they dug on the edge of the city. He is a part of the city, is Old Man Bone, just like the Bag Lady and the Midnight Mayor. He caters for the dead, and when others cater for the dead, he sleeps at the bottom of the old plague pits with the bones of those he has buried, and all he ever asks is . . .

What he is owed.

This is my part. I am the undertaker. The city has a debt to Old Man Bone, there is a price which must be paid, and I . . . am asked to pay it. To make others pay it for me, perhaps I should say. Pay it for us. There must be . . . recompense.

I was asked to take these duties by the Midnight Mayor. Not Swift – this was a long time before Swift, before most of the Aldermen, in fact. I was one of them, an Alderman, but I had a daughter, and she . . . I felt unable to continue my duties to the city, shall we say, and resigned to care for her. When she passed away, I was lost. This . . . job . . . was a way out. A responsibility which I could bear, which someone had to bear, and, in my way, I have always tried to fulfil it with mercy.

There must be a sacrifice, you see. An offering made to Old Man Bone. It comes rarely, a dozen years or so, but he sleeps so long, and so deep beneath the earth, and even sleep is a form of life. Old Man Bone deals in death, but he needs life to sustain him, and so I . . . give it to him.

Before you judge me too hard, before you condemn my actions, let me say this: that he, like the power of the Midnight Mayor, cannot be killed. He cannot be contained, cannot be reasoned with, for he is a part of the city, and to try and control him would be like saying you shall command that every house in London no longer be made from bricks. What we are left with, therefore, is not control, but . . . containment.

There's a dagger. It was used thousands of years ago in the temple of Mithras to sacrifice to the gods and, when it was not being used for sanctified purposes, it was used by more malign forces within the cult itself, to sacrifice people. How Old Man Bone found it, and why he kept it, I have never asked, but over the years it became imbued with his nature. It is rusted, ancient, scarred beyond recognition, and has been worked and worked and worked again so that now barely the point remains, hardly a needle of the original embedded in many more layers of iron. Touch any person with that blade, and they are marked by Old Man Bone, as sacrifices to his cause. He isn't greedy. He has never asked for more than a few, and I have tried so hard with my selection. That is my responsibility, my duty. I chose those who must be given to the sleeping rag man. I hope I have chosen kindly.

When the time comes, I go out into the street with my rusted blade, and mark one, maybe two, for sacrifice. They feel no pain. It is ... simply a not-being. One moment they are, the next they are not. And there are never any corpses left behind. Only ...

"Shoes."

Sharon spoke so softly she hardly realised the words had passed her lips. As the others looked at her, she nodded down at nothing in particular and murmured again, "Only their shoes are left behind."

Chapter 39

Sacrifice unto Others

Rhys blurted, "But you *kill* . . . "

"If Old Man Bone was not appeased," snapped Crompton, "far worse would befall the city, I assure you."

The druid turned to Sharon, gesturing with indignation. "But . . . "

"Why the umbrella?" Her voice was hard and sharp. "What's so special about it?" Crompton opened his mouth to answer, but before he could, Sharon interrupted. "No, wait, got it. Way ahead here. You can't exactly walk around with an ancient Roman dagger, stabbing people, yeah? So you had the blade embedded in the point of your umbrella, am I right?"

Before he could agree or disagree, she snapped her fingers and added, "And the shoes that have been thrown over things, the points on Swift's map? That's what gets left behind when you make an offering to Old Man Bone, because those are what are stolen from the dead, and left for the living. But – wait a second . . . if your umbrella got stolen with the dagger in it, then you couldn't go around making sacrifices. But Swift's been monitoring shoes for weeks now, which means that someone pinched your umbrella, took

the point out of it, and is going around doing your job for you, am
I right?"

Again Crompton moved to speak, and again Sharon cut him off.
"Except! We met Old Man Bone – I mean, either him, or his freaky
twin brother – last night, and he was all pissed off and 'give me what
I'm owed'. And I guess he came to talk to me, because the real
Midnight Mayor is currently off in swanny angel land; but, point is,
Old Man Bone was kinda pissed and a bit cranky – would you say
he was cranky, Rhys?"

"Not my first choice of word, Ms Li," he said. "But I suppose it is
one of several which we could try?"

"Okay, maybe even a bit more than cranky, maybe he had *concerns*," Sharon went on. "But, point being, didn't sound much to me
like he was getting these sacrifices you've been talking about. And
you said one or two, but Swift had tracked, like, dozens of these
shoes hanging over things, and, hell, I'm not saying that every pair
of shoes you see hanging off something in the street means an
ancient gravedigger has come back for payment. I'm just saying
that's a lot of sacrifices going down if they have which means . . . "

She paused to collect air and thoughts, "Which so bloody means
that someone else has pinched your rusty blade, done something
nasty with it, made lotsa sacrifices, but clearly not to Old Man Bone,
got rid of the Midnight Mayor without actually killing him – luring
him, in fact, to a sticky end with this very same umbrella, minus seriously mystic magic object, in Deptford, where that all went horribly
wrong, and guess who has to clean it up? Middle management, that's
who. All of which brings us to the following situation." She paused,
while the two men stared at her, chins against their chests, waiting
for her conclusion. When it didn't come, Rhys raised one cautious
hand.

"Um . . . which following situation, Ms Li?"

"Oh, yeah, sorry, I was just going over all that in my head to see
if I got it right so far. Hey – this investigation thing isn't so tough,
is it?"

"I think you're marvellous," he replied. "I mean, the investigation,
that it is in fact, proceeding, all things considered . . . "

"What do you do again?" demanded Crompton, turning on Rhys. "No – I remember now. *IT manager.*"

"Hey – Rhys is my bloody druid and I won't have a word against him," snapped Sharon. Rhys blushed almost the same colour as his hair. "You be respectful! Our situation is that we are facing . . . several challenging issues and potentially some tricky opportunities and we will need a unified strategy in order to develop as a team and surmount the present climate of . . . of it's all gone to buggery."

A moment while the two men translated these words. "Do you mean . . . we're in trouble?" asked Rhys.

"Did I say that, did you hear me say that?"

"Yes," grunted Crompton.

"Positive attitude!" she snapped. "Just because it looks like we're seriously stuffed, doesn't mean we have to undermine the process of getting unstuffed by having a stuffed approach! Look at the three hundred Greeks what defended that mountain pass against a million bloody Persians or however many it was. They didn't have an 'oh shit it's a bit dodgy out here let's go home' approach, did they?"

"But . . . they died!" Rhys managed to keep his voice a bat's shrill below a shriek.

"Not the point!"

"I'm sorry, are you *sure* you're the deputy Midnight Mayor?" demanded Crompton.

Sharon turned her indignation on him like a blowtorch. "Hey – did I get anything wrong in any of that deductive crap? Was it not, in fact, a really mature bit of incisive insight? I'm not fishing for compliments here, I'm just looking for that bit of respect I feel is lacking from you, the guy who goes around finding human bloody sacrifices!"

She hadn't noticed that she was shouting, until the volume was well advanced.

"Sorry," she blurted. Then, "That was unprofessional." Then, "Sorry."

Rhys cleared his throat. "But . . . you *are* right, Ms Li, aren't you?" Sharon glanced at Crompton, whose face, while hardly picturesque, wasn't bothering to deny it. "And . . . Mr Crompton here *has* made a career out of picking people to be sacrificed to a mystic sleeping entity, yes? Which I think limits his entitlement to complain, see?"

Crompton gave a grunt. "I did what had to be done."

"He did what had to be done," grumbled Sharon. "That's gotta be on so many gravestones. You!" Her glare fixed its unstoppable power on Crompton. "If you're this Old Man Bone's undertaker guy, then you oughtta have an idea how to fix it, right?" He opened his mouth to answer, but Sharon's face had already scrunched up in distaste as an idea struck. "Except you bloody don't, do you? Because if you could just fix it, you wouldn't have asked Swift for help, and if you hadn't asked Swift for help, he wouldn't be missing right now. So I'm guessing you're as stuffe— as *challenged* by this situation as we are. What did you ask Swift to do for you, anyway?"

"I asked him to find my umbrella."

"Your mega-mystic umbrella."

"If we must be so crude."

"And did he?"

"Clearly. But the vital component, as I'm sure you've noticed, was missing."

"And there are shoes on the line," she murmured, not really to anyone else in the room.

"And there are, indeed, shoes on the line."

"This . . . Old Man Bone . . . what will he do if he *doesn't* get these offerings of yours?"

"I imagine he'll withdraw his services from the city."

"Is that a bad thing? Considering the lack of Black Death around these days?"

Crompton barely twitched an eyebrow. "The gravestones will crack, the ground will open, the plague pits will boil their bones to the surface, the streets will fill with the stench of the dead, the taste of rotting flesh will float upon the air, and plague will spread like fog under the cracks of every door. At least, that's how it was explained to me."

Rhys smiled wanly and said, "Maybe it's just a myth?"

"If you've met Old Man Bone, as you say you have," the older man pointed out, "I find it hard to believe you would consider it so."

Sharon said, "I know I'm not going to like the answer, but I'd feel a tit if I didn't ask – is there any way at all we can convince this Old Man Bone dude to sit tight and *not* unleash, say, the stinking smell of death across the city?"

"Other than sacrifice . . ."

"Yeah, other than that."

"None that I am aware of, or would consider trying. If, however, you wanted a more expert view on the subject, you could ask Arthur."

"Arthur . . . ?"

"He is a warden in Bunhill Fields, where they say Old Man Bone was last buried. He is also something of an expert, and may have more . . . radical ideas on the subject, than I do. As far as I'm concerned, the only way to appease the Old Man is to give him what he asks for, and the only way to give him what he asks for is to recover the rusted blade which should rest at the end of my umbrella."

Sharon sighed. Her tea remained untouched on the counter beside her, rapidly cooling. "How'd Swift find your umbrella, do you know?"

"I do not. I left the matter entirely in his hands."

"Of course you did," she groaned. "Because nothing ever goes wrong when people do that."

"Um . . . Ms Li? The T-t-tribe said one of their own had died of Black Death, recently? B-Man?"

"You talked to the Tribe?" Crompton asked Rhys. It was hard to tell if his voice held respect or incredulity.

"Black Death," went on Rhys, "isn't a very common disease these days, and is actually quite treatable with antibiotics."

"And Swift went looking for B-Man," murmured Sharon thoughtfully. "A kid who pinched things for his tribe. You know, I think I'm getting used to this whole mystic business. I'm thinking that if you went around stealing the mega-mystic umbrella of Old Man Bone, there's bound to be a few snags. I'm thinking there might be questions asked, curses cast, nasty, depths-of-all-evil kinda curses, curses like . . ."

"Bubonic plague?" concluded Rhys.

"Right." She looked at Crompton, dislike flashing in her eyes. "Sound smart?"

"As no one has ever attempted to steal Old Man Bone's blade, I can't say for certain. But I imagine ... there would be repercussions, yes."

"Rhys," Sharon's eyes stayed fixed on Crompton, "remind me, when this is all over, and I've sorted out bingo, speed dating and council tax for Magicals Anonymous, to have a serious talk to someone about this vigilante, above-and-beneath-the-law thing that urban magic, as an institution, seems to have going for it. Don't get me wrong," she added, as Crompton's face twitched. "I see how having the plague pits burst and the stench of death drifting through the streets could be a serious issue. But I just want to make sure we get magical retaliation on some sort of equal footing. Steal a mystic umbrella – get Black Death. Borrow a sacred pencil, maybe that's only acne. You see where I'm going with this?"

"No," barked the old man.

"Yes," corrected Rhys. "I think it sounds very reasonable, see?"

"But B-Man must have given the umbrella away first. Otherwise Swift would have found it when he went to the hospital," mused Sharon, her eyes focused on a place only she could see. "Which means the only guy who'd know where the blade is now, is ... " She gestured, not sure how best to avoid the words "dead of the plague".

"Well, I can see the welfare of the city is in good hands," grunted Crompton.

"You ... " Sharon squared up to him, shoulders back and chin out. "You sit alone in here day after day, year after year, smoking those cigarettes and watching *Countdown*, and when the sun goes down and the instinct calls, you pick up a sacrificial blade and walk through the streets searching for a stranger who looks alone, and cold, and unloved, and you walk by them as casual as anything and prick them as you pass and then they die. I mean, it may not be death, it may not be blood and rot and flesh left after, but they cease to be. And *you* do that, so I'm really not sure you get to judge, no matter what you say about death and plague and that, because actually . . . " – she swayed with the effort of not shouting – " . . . it may be what has to be done but it's still fucking murder!"

"I save you." Crompton spoke so low he was barely audible. "I save you. I do what you won't. I *save* you. And you know it."

For a second, they glared at each other, Alderman and shaman. Then, her eyes not moving from Crompton's face, she said, "Rhys. We're going."

"Yes, Ms Li."

"Keep the umbrella," she snapped, as she and Rhys made their way towards the door. "Looks like it'll rain later."

Chapter 40

A Pleasant Walk Clears the Mind

His name is Paul, hers is Ele, and they are in love.

They've been in love for seven years, but they still hold hands – that's how in love they are.

They walk through the graveyard, not because they're interested in graves, but because it's an interesting, historical shortcut between *here* and *there* and, moreover, it's always a pleasure for them to discover these little patches of greenery, places where the streets still stand tall, in the very heart of the city.

Then she stops, abruptly, mouth opening in horror and disgust and says, "What is that smell?"

He tries to smile, to laugh it off, but there is no laughing away this stench; it hits like a battering ram against plywood walls.

"Maybe . . . they're doing building works?" he suggests.

She is the indignant one; he quietly takes it. "In a graveyard?!"

"Maybe they broke something?"

Her face contorts in disgust; she begins to turn a little green. With one sleeve over her mouth, and needing no more words, she pushes him towards the nearest bus and they do not hold hands again for the rest of the day.

Chapter 41

Healthy Body, Healthy Mind

Miles said, "Let's do lunch."

It was something management types did, Sharon had concluded. Ordinary people, living ordinary lives, simply ate lunch. Busy office workers grabbed a bite to eat – grabbing because they were in a hurry, desperate to get back to their desks – and a bite because they were, presumably, on high intensity diets in accordance with their high intensity lifestyles. But management – management *did* lunch, with all the dedication and panache of a kung fu master doing his exercises.

Lunch, in this case, turned out to be a sushi bar on the busy junction where Clerkenwell met Farringdon; trains ran beneath, buses swept along one side, and bicycle lanes danced through it all, a haphazard afterthought of painted lines and warning signs.

Sharon, Rhys and Miles sat at a conveyor belt of tiny, overpriced dishes of rice and some fish, each waiting for The Perfect One to sweep by, before getting bored of waiting and taking what happened to be within their line of sight.

"I would treat us to somewhere a little less . . . commercial," the word slipped from Miles's tongue like discarded snakeskin, "but, times being what they are, the wining and dining budget can only go so far."

So saying, he grabbed a dish of wasabi beans, popping the little green bobbles from their shell with the casual expertise of a man who had long since forgone sensory pleasure in aid of sleek, well-nourished physique. Rhys eyed the beans sideways, not at all convinced he could trust in such a creature. Sharon toyed with a couple of dumplings, eyes wandering over the collection of sauces and condiments before her with the expertise of a bomb maker, wondering which would be a sauce too far.

"How did you do with the dead woman's phone?" she asked, making a plunge for a suspicious tub of green goo.

"The tech boys are having a look at it," said Miles. "Trying to coax it back to life. They say it's fifty-fifty, which isn't bad for them, as usually they just laugh if you ask them to do anything technical at all. I see you no longer have the umbrella, though. Is this a positive development?"

Sharon tried a lick of the suspicious green goo off her finger, and blanched. She reached across Rhys, and swallowed the remaining water from his glass in a great gulp. Miles waited politely, sliding a fingernail into another wasabi shell.

"Uh, the umbrella,' Sharon wheezed as she recovered from her attack. "Well, I think it was positive, if you ignore the sorta death-plague-doomy overtones."

"Potential plague-doomy," added Rhys. "I mean, the plague-doomy overtones are things yet to come, aren't they? The death isn't, though; the death is definitely happening. And has happened. And will probably happen again. But I think we're on top of the plague-doomy, see?"

"You ever heard of Old Man Bone?"

Miles rolled a bean between his fingers, then popped it into his mouth like a pill. Rhys watched, hypnotised, as the Alderman's Adam's apple rose and fell. Miles ran his tongue round the inside of his mouth, then said, "Yes, I have. But only as a footnote, as a . . . a reference to an obscurity too obscure even for magicians to care about. A myth, if you will, one of the few for which I have never seen any evidence in my time in the city. But by the way you phrase the question, I imagine I'm about to have to reassess my position quite radically?"

"You might wanna."

"Is . . . this Old Man Bone a factor?"

"When you say 'factor' . . . ?" began Sharon " . . . do you mean like, 'is he going to come screaming out of the earth beneath our feet, bringing plague and doom?' . . . ?"

"*Potentially* bringing plague and doom," corrected Rhys.

"Potentially bringing plague and doom, upon the city and all within it? I mean, I wouldn't want to stake my career on it, because I don't really have the training in this area, and I get that I've got responsibility, but sometimes the responsible thing is to hand it over to an expert, *but* . . . " – she dabbed a rice roll into a pool of brown soy sauce – " . . . if you under-budget and then fail, then that's so much worse than over-budgeting and having a surplus. Except in some areas of local government, where I've heard it's okay, but I never really got how that worked. So I'd say yes . . . plague and doom and all that. Get your footnotes prepped."

Miles ate another wasabi bean. It was, Rhys had to admit, a fascinating performance, a master class given the minimum exertion for each bean followed by the maximum effect as they dropped, one at a time, down Miles's throat. It also, he realised, bought the Alderman time to think up a dazzling reply, instead of falling back on the default allergic reaction that was Rhys's instinctive response to new and upsetting information.

At length Miles said, "I'm trusting, Ms Li, that you and your . . . your friend . . . " – Rhys nearly spat soy sauce across the table, which Miles pointedly chose not to notice – " . . . have a plan to deal with the situation?"

"Well, I . . . I guess . . . we get back Old Man Bone's rusty dagger. And before you give me that look," she added, stabbing a dumpling towards Miles's politely neutral face, "it's not like I'm a fan of ancient mystic items and all the stuff they do, it's just that I can't think of anything better to do right now that'll help, so even if this isn't the greatest idea ever, at least it's progress."

"And how do you propose to find this . . . item?"

Sharon fidgeted uneasily on her high, padded seat. "Well, we . . . we follow the leads, don't we? Did you find B-Man?"

"Ah, yes, now . . ." Miles pulled from his pocket a slim, well-tended smartphone, unlocking it with a faint click of shifting data. "A patient was admitted to UCH three Thursdays back, suffering from high fever and swollen lymph nodes. He had no identification and his face was heavily scarred. The doctors failed to make an initial diagnosis, but a specialist in tropical diseases confirmed bubonic plague. By the time they confirmed the diagnosis, he was in critical care. The patient was then put on antibiotics, and showed signs of recovery, until he died."

"He . . . got better and then died?"

"I'm afraid so."

"He *was* cursed, Ms Li," Rhys pointed out.

"Actually, the cause of death did not appear to be bubonic plague," mused the Alderman, thumbing through the notes on his phone. "But, rather, respiratory arrest. Not associated with the disease itself."

Sharon was fumbling in her bag, digging through several days' accumulation of old sandwich and half-consumed doughnuts, before producing the much-fingered remains of Swift's red-marked map. She tried to unfold it, and, discovering that the table wasn't big enough, gestured at Rhys. With a patient sigh, the druid turned his back so Sharon could lean the map on him, the top drooping down across the crown of his head like a widow's shawl.

"Three Thursdays ago, yeah?"

"That's correct – although he only died a few nights ago."

"And Swift's first little red dot is . . . two weeks last Monday." She ran her finger from mark to mark, squinting at the tiny, messy hand-writing. "So let's just get this straight. Someone pinches Old Man Bone's blade . . . hell, in fact, let's make that incisive leap and say that B-Man pinches the blade . . . gets struck down with plague, which I think is one hell of a reaction, and is admitted to hospital. While he's in hospital, lotsa shoes start appearing all over the city, which I'm guessing we can say is a sign that someone else other than

B-Man is doing the sacrificial thing. Except he's not sacrificing to Old Man Bone, which is kinda a problem, but we'll get to that. Crompton goes to the Midnight Mayor, demanding to get his umbrella back, and Swift goes to the hospital, finds B-Man already dead, even though he's been in hospital now for a few weeks and was recovering. Swift is pissed off, gets spotted by Gold Mnkey and Hobo Grlz, who're there to visit their mate, he storms off to the office, gets the email from . . . from . . ."

"Hacq," offered Rhys from under his wall of map. "That was the email which got him to go to Deptford, then also the address which sent the hex."

" . . . he goes off to Deptford, wham, bam, great big mystic cock-up happens, the woman with the phone ends up dead and in the river, Swift ends up with the Tribe – only Swift doesn't end up with the Tribe, the angels end up with the Tribe, and Swift is . . . God knows where Swift is, but let's say he's not dead yet because the Midnight Mayor's power hasn't yet moved on and no one really wants it to, do they? Meanwhile, Old Man Bone is getting pissed off because he's not getting his sacrifices, and someone is cleaning up the place where the woman died and throwing bodies into the water and that because they've got malign intentions, and B-Man is dead even though he was recovering, which usually I'd say is just bad luck, but hell, let's face it, it's gonna be murder, and so here we are and there it goes, any questions?"

Nobody spoke.

"Great!" she declared. "I'll take it, then, you guys are totally on board with all this. Way I see it, there's only two things left to be answered: who has the blade now, and where the hell is Swift?"

If either man had the immediate answer to these questions, he didn't have a chance to give it, for Miles's phone, already in his hand, rang.

Chapter 42

I Am Where I Need To Be

Where the hell is Swift?

A phone rings.

A maisonette – no one calls it a "flat" – in Hoxton.

Close, but not quite close enough. The one you want, caller, is two doors down, and even if you could reach it, they don't have a land line. Can we redirect your call?

The neighbour, Mrs Phang, answers. She is seventy-eight, and likes to deep-fry her own prawn crackers.

"Hello? Hello? Hello? Hello?" By the fourth hello, most people would have given up, but Mrs Phang is old, and Mrs Phang is lonely, and Mrs Phang doesn't want to be trouble for anyone at all.

"Hello, is anyone there?"

Silence on the end of the line.

"Hello? Can anyone hear me?"

And here it is, a welling up, a bursting out, a screaming up from the darkness; it breaks like surf over the shingle, a sudden roar of foam from a peaceful sea, and it roars:

"GET ME THE HELL OUT OF HERE!"

Chapter 43

When in Doubt, Call an Expert

His name is Mr Roding, and he is a necromancer.

He is also, just in case you're concerned that "necromancer" is the only term by which he defines himself, a keen backgammon player, active in his local Neighbourhood Watch association, member of the Labour Party even though it's all gone to pot these last fifteen years, and regular contributor of letters to the local magazine on the theme of erratic recycling services from the local council and why undertakers weren't doing it right.

There were, it could not be denied, certain downsides to being a necromancer, one of the greatest of which was body odour.

"I can't smell anything!" he exclaimed. They stood in Bunhill Fields — druid, shaman, Alderman and necromancer, while Mr Roding flicked irritably at the yellowing end of a flaking fingernail and sniffed the air and added, "Is this some sort of joke?"

Sharon smiled feebly from behind the protection of her sleeve. When Miles's phone had rang in the sushi bar, she'd hoped for many things. Insight, explanation, enlightenment, or, at the very least, confirmation that the dead woman's river-drenched phone was actually up for use. What she had not hoped for, or even conceived of, was a phone call requiring her presence in Bunhill Fields, a small cemetery lodged between the high offices of Moorgate and the traffic-clogged squalor of City Road: an island of leafy trees, peaceful benches and ancient stones amid the turbulence of EC1. Framed by its tall iron railings, its central path laid with flagstones commemorating the dead, it was a place, she felt, where men and women should sit of a balmy afternoon and drink tea in quiet contemplation, a reminder of life and death encircled by the prowling roar of mundane existence.

That was what it should have been.

What it was, was stinking.

"R-rotting flesh, Mr Roding, sir," stammered Rhys through the jumper he'd put over his mouth to protect against the smell. "Definitely rotting flesh."

Mr Roding seethed, his thin grey arms wrapping round his skeletal frame, his jaundiced cheeks puffing out in indignation. Necromancy was not the healthiest of disciplines, Sharon concluded. Certainly, its practitioners could survive far longer than most wizards of the city, if they were careful about what they did; but when every major spell required the sacrifice of a bit of bone mass or the loss of a kidney in order to fuel it, the art tended to induce a conservatism that reduced the practical activities of its users, as well as narrowing their minds.

However, if he was oblivious to the smell emanating from the torn earth, he could hardly ignore the ground itself. Away from the railed-in path, overlooked by balconied flats and the upstairs room of a quietly churning pub, the green grass had been split apart. Mud had been thrown up with enough force to splatter third-floor windows; age-old tree roots lay tangled in the mess like broken fingers, and, as Sharon peered through her watering eyes, there was no denying it – cracked brown splinters of human bone stuck up from the mess.

The whole convulsion had left a gaping wound in the graveyard, wide enough to park a truck in, and the stench was inescapable. Mr Roding strode forward, slipping down its muddy slope until he stood in the centre of the torn hollow, testing the ground beneath him. Beneath his foot, bones crunched into dust. Rhys and Sharon hung back, and even Miles, usually a bastion of composure, shuddered as Mr Roding rummaged through the foul ground, digging with his fingertips to pull finally, from the remains, half a human femur.

He tutted.

"Lazy lazy job," he sighed, then dropped the bone casually back into the mess. He ran his fingers over the slimy soil, sniffed at it, then sampled it delicately with the end of his pale tongue, rolling the granules around across his teeth. He spat. "No containment, that's the problem," he explained. When no looks of enlightenment dawned at his words, he rolled his eyes, kicking a skull to one side in order to prod a tatty rag of cloth, dyed by the centuries to the same complexion as the soil.

"We're thinking," Sharon's voice was muffled behind her sleeve, "that this has something to do with Old Man Bone."

Mr Roding jerked upright. "Old Man Bone?" he repeated. "What the hell has he got to do with it?"

"You've heard of him, then?"

"I've been a necromancer since before your *mother* was a gleam in her parents' eyes," he barked. "Of course I've bloody heard of him. He's the watchman for the dead, the barefoot undertaker, raggedy man with his cart of skulls – he's also supposed to be sleeping until that time when the city streets are full of the barefoot corpses of the damned, so when I say 'what the hell' I mean it in a more literal sense than you probably understood."

"You're a great comfort to me, Mr Roding."

"You wanted my expert opinion, I'm giving it."

"What's your expert opinion on this?" she asked, gesturing unhopefully at the shattered earth.

Mr Roding sucked in air through the chunky gaps between his yellow teeth. "I never like to use the words 'the dead walk' because I think that 'dead' is a very difficult and overused piece of technical terminology to begin with ..." – the brilliance of Sharon's patient smile was lost on the necromancer as he went on – "... but I'd say you have an explosive release of pent-up mystic energy from within the walls of this pit, which is, of course, a mass grave of some three ... no, *four* ... hundred years old, give or take ... " Here he paused, took another cautious lick of soil off the end of his grimy finger, then spat it out again with the same fervour as before. "Plague pit," he added with a grumble. "I never use plague pits, the energies are too unpredictable, the tangents too interlaced, bloody mess, and you always need to hire a truck to put it back afterwards."

Miles cleared his throat. "I know this isn't the time, sir, but you *have* read the current guidelines on the summoning and commanding of deceased flesh? Only there are consent forms ... "

"Who is this?" demanded Mr Roding, turning indignantly to Sharon.

"This is Miles," she explained. "He's my minion."

Miles greeted Mr Roding with his regulation upward tilt of his chin, one respectful macho man to another. Mr Roding's lips curled outwards, unimpressed.

"I thought Rhys was your minion."

"No, Miles is."

"Then what's Rhys?"

"Rhys is my ... my ... " she looked at the druid, who tried to beam reassuringly from behind his swollen nose and running eyes, " ... my IT manager," she concluded. "But Miles is definitely my minion."

"And why have you got a minion?" he asked.

Sharon shrugged. "Fate of the city, the dead walk, you know, seemed like good resource management for the project."

"Oh." Mr Roding nodded, digesting this information. "Well, that makes sense. About Old Man Bone ... "

"Excuse me?" A new voice, breaking the conversation with the delicacy of a feather duster over crystal glass. They turned.

The owner of the enquiry was short, a little stooped, dressed in a brown waxed coat with a tartan lining, and wearing a grey-blue woolly hat which had the battered look of a thing which had become prosthetic to him over the years. A pair of thick blue trousers ended in an even thicker pair of sensible brown boots. He was leaning for support on a large shovel, and smiled at them as they looked on.

"I'm sorry," he said, "but you seem to be standing in my grave."

Mr Roding's eyes narrowed. "*Your* grave?" he began. "I'll have you know that I have stood in the graves of ..." He faltered suddenly, and seemed almost taken aback, recoiling before the smiling man as if physically struck. "Do I know you?"

"Me, sir?" asked the old man politely. "I wouldn't think so. Do you rob graves round here at all?"

"I do not rob, I ..." Mr Roding paused again, unconsciously scratching a flurry of white skin flakes off his palm. "... Never mind. Probably someone else. Druid! Help me out!"

Rhys reached out, wondering whether it would be rude to cover his hand with his sleeve before grasping the soggy paw offered to him. Mr Roding's skin was damp, and felt loose on his flesh. Rhys's shoulders began to shake with the effort of holding back a sneeze.

Sharon turned to the stranger. "You work here?" she ventured. "You tend the graves?"

"Indeed I do," he replied, holding out a hand. "Name's Arthur."

Sharon's fingers touched his and there was ...

Nothing.

Absolutely nothing. A dead place where perception should have been, a void where all her senses should have told her of the things which had been, and the things which were yet to come, rushing through Arthur's skin. Instead she felt ...

... nothing at all.

The handshake lasted a second too long. Arthur smiled, and eased his cold palm out of hers. Then, turning back to the open pit, he said in a conversational tone, "They threw those who died of plague down here, back in the day. Too many bodies in the street to bother with headstones, and not enough living to pay for the cost, even if they'd had the time or inclination. Nasty time, really."

"Arthur," said Sharon, trying out the name in the hope it would offer an insight which, inexplicably, his touch had not. Revelation bloomed. "You know a man called Crompton?"

"The undertaker? Yes, I know him. Why?"

Mr Roding was brushing himself down, shedding as much loose skin as dirt as he patted off his trousers, but his eyes were still fixed on Arthur's jovial face.

"He mentioned you," Sharon replied. "Said you were an expert."

"That's very nice of him."

"Said you knew about Old Man Bone."

Arthur's smile didn't falter. "Oh, yes," he breathed. "I guess I do at that. You must be with the Midnight Mayor."

"Must we?"

He gestured with the top of his shovel towards Miles. "Man dressed all in black, necromancer wandering round a plague pit and not at midnight, a druid with . . . " – Rhys sneezed, it happened all at once, he couldn't contain himself, and Arthur just smiled on through – " . . . complications, and you. What are you, if you don't mind me asking, young lady?"

Something in Arthur's eyes: a tightness that belied his expression of jolly optimism. "Shaman," she answered distantly. "I'm a shaman."

"Really? I would never have guessed."

"It's the feathers," she explained. "Actually, it's the lack of feathers. The feathers-that-ought-to-be, if you get my meaning. People have expectations. You mentioned the Midnight Mayor – did he come here?"

Arthur's eyes glinted. "Is it too early for a pint?"

Chapter 44

And Heed the Expert's Advice

They had a pint.

Miles bought.

Mr Roding sniffed at his drink and declared that usually, he didn't approve of yeasty products as it did terrible things to his stomach lining; but so long as he took his tablets later, a half might be okay.

Rhys sat between the gently decomposing necromancer and the firmly imposing Alderman, twisting torn-up tissue under the table top.

Evening was settling over London, a cold, damp gloom which drove all but the hardiest post-work drinkers into the pub's noisy interior. It was a traditional London pub in all the most time-honoured ways: the table top was sticky with ancient spilt beverages, the red patterned carpet crunched occasionally with decaying crisps; the average age of the barmen was nineteen and the music was 1980s near-misses, played just loud enough to make it tricky listening to your neighbours. The lighting was yellow and low, kind to acne but cruel to the broken capillaries of the regulars' noses; and across the surface of a fruit machine lights wound in and out of a brilliant maze, promising riches and glory in 20p denominations.

Arthur the gravekeeper sat with his back to it all and heaved a sigh of satisfaction at the dark pint of beer placed before him.

"This," he explained, daubing one finger in the thick froth, "is the drink of kings."

Sharon made herself smile. She would have liked a drink, but staying awake was proving a challenge and somehow, she felt, as deputy Midnight Mayor she was still on duty. So she cradled an orange juice, whose contents were two parts ice to five parts acid to one part remnant of the colour orange, and trod on her own toes under the table in an effort to remain awake. "So Swift came to see you?"

"Is that his name? Matthew, wasn't it?" Arthur took a slurp of beer, leaving a white moustache across his top lip. He grinned, running his tongue round to catch the drops.

"Matthew Swift," offered Miles. "One hundred and twenty-seventh Midnight Mayor, protector of the city, guardian of the night – him?"

"Jesus, he was all that? Looked like just some bloke."

"You clearly know about him, about . . . what he does?" pressed the Alderman.

"Well, yes, used to dabble a bit myself," said Arthur. "Long time ago. Picked up a few tricks, though never did go down the necromancy route," he added, tipping his drink at Mr Roding, whose eyebrows dipped in reply. "I volunteer at Bunhill Fields now because I think it's a bit of calm in a busy part of town. I also do tours of Highgate West cemetery, and I thought about going for blue badge tour guide, but they said I was too old to do the course. 'Not worth my time.' There's an assumption in this society that once you reach fifty-five your brain is somehow inadequate!"

"Do you get patronised?" interrupted Mr Roding. "My news-agent has started asking me if I'll get home all right! Me! And my neighbour tells me to 'ease off a little'. I was looking forward to being old enough to tell people to piss off, but turns out all that happens if you speak your mind is people tell you your mind must be broken."

"God, I know, and I'll tell you something else . . . "

"What did Swift want?" Sharon cut in, before the two gentlemen could swell up indignantly in unison.

Arthur shrugged. "Same as you, I imagine. Wanted to know about Old Man Bone."

"And what did you tell him?"

"The truth, or at least that part that I understand of it. Ancient spirit of the dead, the unwashed one, raggedy man, he-who-walks-barefoot-upon-the-earth, all that. Most people would've been just interested, but this Matthew fella, he sat there looking worried." There was an alert gleam in Arthur's eye, brighter than the lights humming dimly around the walls of the raggedy room. "Something . . . hasn't happened to him, has it? Only I can't help seeing that you fine people are looking worried, too, and if Matthew was perfectly fine, maybe he'd have told you all this himself . . . ?" Arthur let the thought trail away, waiting for answer.

"He's . . . having a rough day," Sharon said. "But I'm sure he'll be okay."

"Really?" Arthur's face turned covertly to one side, listening to all the things Sharon was not saying out loud. "Look," he added, "I don't know what Crompton said. But if there's a problem with Old Man Bone, then I'll tell you what I told Swift – it'll take more than just a Midnight Mayor to do the fixing."

"How about his deputy?"

Arthur spluttered, mid-gulp, and self-consciously wiped the detritus away from his mouth. "A deputy Midnight Mayor?" he cackled. "Well, it's a nice idea, good bit of administration I suppose; but it doesn't mean anything, does it? No power, no magic, probably not even a pension plan, knowing the Aldermen . . ." – Miles avoided both Sharon and Arthur's enquiring glances – " . . . just a great big mess and no way to clean it up! If there's a deputy Midnight Mayor out there, then good luck to him!"

Sharon just about managed to mumble, "Did Swift say anything to you about a rusty blade? Or an umbrella?"

"Sorry, love," said Arthur. "He asked about the blade, of course – Old Man Bone's blade, the rusted needle – but I just told him what I tell anyone. It's a legend. Myth. Crompton seems to think it's important, part of the ritual; but I don't know if I believe it. Seems more . . . symbolic to me, than actually magical. And there wasn't any discussion of an umbrella either."

"Did he say anything at all?" persisted Sharon. "Anything stick in your memory?"

Arthur's eyes turned upwards, as if searching the ceiling for inspiration. "Sorry. He mostly just looked worried. This was before the ground was opening up, but maybe worried was just how he looked?"

"He was quite concerned," admitted Rhys. "But I suppose I never met him when he wasn't being professional. I mean, professionally Midnight Mayor, which I suppose means it was his job to be worried, so actually, maybe he's not naturally worried, maybe it was just . . ." He became aware of eyes on him. "It looks like a high-stress job," he suggested. "And being his deputy is definitely a high-stress job, I think."

Arthur's eyes widened. "Good God!" he blurted, staring incredulously at Rhys. "It's not you, is it?"

Rhys cringed, but was saved from further discomfort by Sharon. "This whole earth-tearing-apart business. If it *was* Old Man Bone clawing his way up from the pits of the dead, which I'm really hoping it's not, but I guess we oughtta budget for it maybe – if it was that, then I don't suppose you could put a timescale on how long we have until the city is stinking and all plaguey?" She wasn't sure about the word "plaguey" but, then again, on the list of things she wasn't happy about in her life grammar was probably a low priority.

"You don't actually believe that Old Man Bone is coming back, do you?" demanded Arthur.

"Um . . . I'm hoping no and assuming yes?"

"But why?"

"He's a kinda grumpy dead dude, so I'm not really down on his reasoning, to be honest with you. Unless, Mr Roding . . . ?"

Mr Roding scowled. "I see," he grunted. "You're assuming that because you're dead, you're grumpy? And that because *I* happen to be a practitioner in a difficult and controversial field, I naturally understand the mentality of all your . . . 'grumpy dead dudes'."

"Maybe the young lady thought you were knowledgeable on the grumpy side, rather than the deceased side?" offered Arthur. His smile was benign, but, at his words, Mr Roding's face twitched. It was hard for a man who was only two parts living tissue to three parts magical graft to flush, but Mr Roding gave it his best shot, a slow splotch of orange spreading like ink through cotton across his cheek.

"I'm sure we've met," he declared, arms folded tight. "You used to dabble?"

"I was a wizard," conceded Arthur, his good nature a bright light in the face of Mr Roding's growing intemperance. "But I gave it up a long time ago. You know how it is – you get older, you get wiser, you start to ask yourself, 'is it any use being able to summon creatures of the nether deeps when I could be watching BBC4?'"

"Where did you do your wizarding?"

"I was with the Westminster Coven for a while. Had a few skills in my day, mind. I made a couple of bob on the side providing blessings and curses for well-paying clients – the company motto was 'Make Your Good Luck Happen', and we ..."

There was a crack. It was the sound of Mr Roding's fingers tightening so hard around his half-pint that the glass splintered, forming tiny lines through which thin wounds of beer began to well. "Make Your Good Luck Happen," breathed Mr Roding, staring not at Arthur but through him, his eyes fixed on some distant place beyond the back of his head. "You're Arthur Huntley."

Arthur's smile didn't falter. "Yes. You've heard of me? How terribly flattering."

Mr Roding said nothing. Then all at once he stood, and began to push his way elbows first, out of the pub, Sharon smiled at Arthur and murmured, "I was thinking of the grumpy, yes – excuse me."

Arthur gestured magnanimously, but Sharon was already heading for the door.

Mr Roding stood outside in the settling gloom of the street, breathing in the evening air. Sharon made her way up to him, and said, "'Make Your Good Luck Happen'?"

The necromancer glanced sideways at her, and it seemed that his scowl was at least habitual rather than a direct insult. She waited. "It was a company," he said. "Run by a bunch of wizards down in Westminster. Dabblers. Not just in magic – in ordinary things. Daily life. People came to them with problems. Wanted a beautiful lover, needed more cash, wanted success in business, respect, wanted their boss to realise how good they were, or maybe to take an early retirement – that sort of thing. None of it was illegal, it was all . . . exertion of influence. The kind of influence you get when you've got a Barbie doll, a lock of a stranger's hair and a very sharp needle."

"Okay . . . doesn't sound strictly fluffy."

Mr Roding let out a rotten-toothed sigh. "Arthur Huntley . . . he was the greatest. The greatest wizard of the Coven. He crafted the circle which contained the sewer crawlers when they came up through the grating at Tottenham Court Road. He put the zephyrs of the BT Tower back to sleep, summoned the Regents Canal wyvern, crafted the Deep Downer's lime-scale armour and forged the Titan's prison at Bank station. It's what wizards do, why they're more useful than bloody sorcerers and that crowd. Sorcerers are all fire and light and spontaneous destruction; but a good wizard, he's about craft, patience and skill. A proper academic, properly working on his subject to create the most beautiful spells you've seen. Stunning. True works of genius, the spells of Arthur Huntley. Then . . . he stopped."

"Why?"

Mr Roding shrugged; it was an awkward gesture, lopsided. "There were . . . rumours. Some said something had gone wrong, a mistake, a spell that backfired. Others said he'd made so much money he couldn't be bothered to work any more. One or two said he was dead, and, to be honest, he'd vanished so completely that was as believable a thing as any other. Truth is . . . no one really knew. Not for sure. And now there he is, in the pub, having a pint. Damn me."

Sharon bit on her fist to suppress a yawn. It wasn't that Mr Roding was boring, or even that she wasn't engaged; it was simply that the desire for sleep was beginning to overwhelm all other instincts. Mr Roding looked at her again, and for a moment there was a flicker of something which might have been concern. "When'd you last sleep?"

"Um . . . few days ago?"

He tutted. "Not sensible, not sensible at all. Sleepy people make stupid mistakes."

"I was thinking I might have a little lie down later . . ."

"Can't be having you making stupid mistakes when dealing with Old Man Bone!"

". . . maybe a hot chocolate and an early night . . ."

"Can't be seen making stupid mistakes in front of Arthur Huntley!"

Sharon's jaw dropped. "You . . . respect him?"

"Course I bloody do!"

She spoke quieter, a thought sneaking through. "You . . . *fear* him?"

Mr Roding shuffled on the spot. She'd never seen him avoid anyone's gaze, even when confronted by the truly profane. "I respect him," he repeated. "Don't say that about many people." Sharon yawned again, despite herself. "You should get some sleep," he repeated. "Can't be unprofessional."

"Yeah," she mumbled. "I guess you can't at that."

Chapter 45

Clear Communication Is Vital to Success

The sun was down over the city, but the mobile phone masts, clinging to the tops of council estates and high, shabby municipal
buildings, never slept.

New SMS

20.59 They're still looking.

21.01 So? What can they find?

21.02 They're being more persistent than I expected.

21.04 But the Midnight Mayor is gone. They can't do anything.

21.07 They're getting closer.

21.08 Spike them.

21.12 They know about the blade.

21.13 You want us to handle it?

21.15 Maybe. If they come too close.

How long will it take you to summon him?

21.21 A few hours. Do you want us to call the meeting?

22.26 Yes. Call it. Let's stop them now.

Chapter 46

Sleep on the Problem

This time, when Sharon walked through the door of her flat, she was very careful about what happened next. She went upstairs and took off her shoes, untying the laces and tucking them neatly away. She went into the kitchen and took out some bread and crunchy peanut butter. She warmed her hands on the toaster as the bread grew crispy, then licked up the crumbs from the plate once the main event had been consumed. She went to the bathroom, brushed her teeth for exactly two minutes fifteen seconds, combed her hair, sat down on the edge of her bed and promptly fell into it. She was asleep within minutes, the light still burning brightly overhead.

A sleep, deep and true, but not entirely complete.

Sharon Li stood in the grey, twisted place of the dream walk, and listened.

Early still, too early for most people in the city to be asleep. Showers were steaming, TVs were flickering in the dark. The youngest children had been put to bed, but many were still huddled under their duvets, reading by torchlight or cowering from thoughts of monsters unseen in the wardrobe. She drifted out of the walls of her room, sinking, soft as lavatory paper, down to the singing flag-

stones in the backyard of the maisonette, and felt the brush of a
jumbo jet passing miles overhead, the passengers settling down to
sleep for their long trip across the ocean. Behind her flat, but visible from her bedroom window, was a great block of single-floor
apartments, nine storeys high, the windows lit up in giddy new con-
figurations every night, figures moving in silence behind the glass.
She turned, and two doors down, Mrs Phang was already asleep and
dreaming of . . .

. . . *the night we danced together, damp grass beneath giant flip-flops* . . .

The shaman turned, drifting back towards her own body, restless
and a little annoyed.

A sound in the night.

A sound, as strange and alien to the grey world of the dream walk
as the silver whispers of dreams were to the bright light of day.

It went . . .

Ring ring!

Ring ring!

An old-fashioned telephone sang out.

She looked, turning this way and that, trying to pinpoint the
source of the sound, before finally walking back through the wall of
her own house and into the living room. The TV was on, a pair of
bright crimson nails, sharpened to a point, reaching out from the
screen to beckon at the fixed stare of Trish, her eyes open wide, her
mouth hanging a little too low, her mind so stupefied she may as
well have been asleep. The TV itself was nothing but a muffled
background buzz in this place, but Trish's mind was as much a display of what was on the screen as any dreamer's might have been.
Ghosts of men and women in scanty, tight clothing, burst and
popped around her thoughts, their features distorted by greed, grief,
joy and hate.

Somewhere in the dark, the phone kept ringing.

Sharon drifted through the house, and out the other side, into
the enclosed crescent of the small estate. She wandered past the
community hall, where ten men and one token female practised a
martial art with great heavy sticks held in either hand, and the
shadows of what they wanted it to be – glorious, powerful, and

physically just a little improbable – danced at their feet as they moved through the rhythms. Still the phone kept ringing.

She wandered past silent patches of wannabe garden turned to must-always-be weed, beneath the arch that sealed off the small parking area for those rich enough to afford such a luxury, and rounded a corner where the graffiti blazed on the wall, to see a small phone box. The glass panels on one side were smashed, and the debris glimmered like frozen diamonds on the ground. A dozen cards offering illicit services cooed and sang at Sharon from the walls, the images coming to life as she approached, women pouting, writhing, calling and crying quietly from the card. A single dull white bulb flickered, brighter than the shadow of the dream walk, calling her closer.

The phone handle was black, shockingly solid in the translucent world.

She reached out and was surprised to find it hard, cold beneath her fingers. She picked it up.

The ringing stopped, and even the twisting figures in the flyers pinned to the back wall seemed to hold their breath.

"Hello?"

Her voice was shockingly loud, almost real.

Silence.

"Hello?" she repeated.

"Sharon?"

A man's voice, distant, twisted through static, uncertain but, undeniably, irrefutably, familiar. She swallowed, then wondered how such a mundane reflex was possible in this unreal place. "Swift?"

The voice of the Midnight Mayor, far away, blurted, "I – I – I can't – I – I – don't know where to they – they us there's – too much noise can't think! Can't think here can't . . ." The words stopped abruptly, a burst of static rushing over the line.

"Swift?" she repeated, turning her back on the now-keenly-staring women in the flyers. "Where are you?"

"I – I – I – I'm here I'm – I'm there here here there I'm – every-where I'm – trapped!" The words crackled, an electric gasp. "Help me!"

"Tell me where you are, what happened?"

"Trapped," he exclaimed. "They – they – they took a part of – of me! Us me us me us us me me SHUT UP! It went like this. 078. 0781 it was 07812 07812 07 it's HELP ME!"

"I'm trying! I don't know where you are!"

"Find me," he hissed. "Find me. Put me back!" The line burst with noise, so loud she snatched the phone away from her ear.

Then nothing, but the busy

beeeeeeeeeeeeeeeeeeee

of the open dialling tone.

Swift was gone.

Chapter 47

A Little Rest Goes a Long Way

Sharon woke with a start.

A phone was ringing.

For a moment, two worlds hung over each other, the living and the sleeping, competing for the best billing.

Reality won.

The ringing of the phone became a tinny cascade of sound effects.

The cascade was the calling tone of her mobile phone.

The light was still burning in her room.

Her mobile phone was still in her trouser pocket.

She eased it out, and looked blearily at the time. 23.10. She'd been asleep for barely an hour.

She looked at the caller, groaned, and answered the phone.

"Hi, Miles."

"Hello, Ms Li – you weren't sleeping, were you?"

"What? Me? No, not sleeping, just thinking about . . . work and that. What's up?"

"Good news from the tech boys, Ms Li – thought you'd want to know. They've managed to recover some of the data on the dead woman's phone."

Sharon's head bounced back against her pillow. For a moment she stared up at the light in the ceiling, and wondered what it would be like if she *could* blow it up with nothing but her mind and a bad temper.

"Ms Li? Ms Li, are you there?"

"Yeah," she groaned. "I'm still here. That is good news." She managed, just in time, to bite off a curse. "Yay for good news."

It took her forty minutes to get to the offices of Harlun and Phelps.

To her surprise, Rhys was already there, waiting in the lofty foyer.

"Oh, Mr Miles was kind enough to text me with an update, and I thought you'd probably be coming here, and so I thought I should come, too," he stammered, "because I know how you like your coffee and I thought you might need some coffee and I picked up a menu for a Chinese take-away on the way because that's something people sometimes do, if they're working into the night, I mean, they have Chinese take-away with chopsticks out of a cardboard box, but you may not like Chinese, so I also picked up Indian which isn't as traditional but I don't think you want tradition, do you, Ms Li, I mean, maybe you do, maybe you hate Indian, and you are sort of Chinese I mean . . ."

She put her hand over his mouth. His body locked tight enough to send shudders down to his fingertips. "Rhys," she breathed, "if I wasn't, like, unbelievably tired, and didn't have this whole fate of the city thing to do with, I'd snog you right now." A tiny whimper escaped him. "As it is," she went on, considering each word, "I never believed as how you should have these work–life entanglements, because it can become sticky and that, and because your professional relationship isn't the same as your social relationships, but seriously, if you ever wanna give it a go, you, me and a big, soppy snog."

Numbly, his ears turning the colour of tomatoes, Rhys nodded, and Sharon pried her hand away from his mouth. "Cool," she said, brushing it down on her trousers in what she hoped was a discreet and non-offensive way. "Let's add it to the to-do list."

There was a polite cough from across the foyer. Miles stood by the open door of a lift. He held a fresh cup of coffee, which he offered to Sharon as she approached. She hesitated, then took it. "Cheers, Miles."

"I'm sorry about the late hour, Ms Li," he said, his eyes barely turning to Rhys as the druid joined them in the lift, "but, as I'm sure you can understand, time is of the essence."

They rode up in silence.

The offices of Harlun and Phelps were busier than usual. Black-clad Aldermen sat at screens or around tables, maps were spread out, and, Sharon was alarmed to notice, guns and blades were laid out for cleaning and inspection.

"We going to war?" she asked.

"If there's someone to war with," Miles replied.

The "tech boys", as Miles had put it, were in an office all of their own. It was all of their own, Sharon decided, because no one else could possibly want to inhabit it. Windowless, brown-walled and concrete-floored, it had the feeling of a converted cleaning cup-board, which a crazed engineer had tried to use as an experiment in how much copper one floor could support before it gave way.

The tech boys themselves were two men in their early thirties; one wore a leather jacket, the other a bright blue hoodie which read Release The Mongoose for reasons Sharon dared not guess. Their work surfaces were saggy with the weight of old coffee mugs, obscure DVDs and green slabs of solid-state circuitry ripped from the bowels of a misbehaving machine, and had barely enough room for the gutted remains of the dead woman's smartphone. One wall was adorned with a thousand pieces of paper offering discount VGA adaptors for the chosen client, pictures of fondly remembered nieces, snapshots of truly embarrassing computers they'd worked on, guides to the easiest way to wire an obscure cable and unread memos lost beneath it all in a moment of well-intentioned efficiency gone horribly wrong.

As the Aldermen entered, one of the two tech boys rose with an expansive smile and held out his hand. The other glanced up, grunted disinterestedly, and went back to his work.

"Ian and Paul," explained Miles. Sharon smiled as nicely as she could and shook the one hand on offer, from Ian, earning a brief flash of

... tomato stew for lunch ...

... click of the camera lens across an empty bridge ...

... fist banging against the wall ...

"Lovely to see you – sorry about the mess, have a chair – have *my* chair."

Paul grunted again. "You here for the phone? It's all there." He gestured at one of a great stack of screens lined up against the wall. Sharon, looking blankly from screen to screen, turned to Rhys for support.

"Um ... that one," he whispered, pointing at one screen among the many.

"Can we get you coffee?" went on Ian cheerfully. "Oh no, you've got some, never mind. I think we have some biscuits here ..."

"Bloody mess," offered Paul, as Sharon shuffled into the chair in front of the screen. "Couldn't get half of it, but what do you expect really when you give us something like that to work on?"

"Paul and Ian are specialists in digital magic," whispered Miles.

Rhys's eyes widened. "Oh!" he exclaimed, turning to the two men. "You're ... you're *Paul and Ian*! It's such an honour, I'm sorry, I mean, I didn't realise but now I know it's an honour, an honour to meet you – meet you both, I mean, I'm Rhys, see, I'm a druid, but I've been working on this app for months ..."

Paul looked sceptical, but Ian's face was at least locked in an expression of polite enthusiasm.

Sharon stared at the screen indicated to her.

It was, she supposed, a not-half-bad recovery from the drowned woman's mobile phone. A series of carefully organised files and folders had been laid out for her scrutiny; and while a lot of the folders were a mesh of empty, skewed-letter jumbles, one or two of them, when examined, still offered up a memory of what had gone before. Part of an address book, the data suddenly turning into gobbledygook around the letter 'G'; the recollection of a London Underground map; the ghost of memo written to self and entitled 'Remember milk and eggs!' A jumble of familiar games to play on long journeys – Sudoku, Scrabble, and one app which attempted to miniaturise golf for a screen four inches by two.

Sharon kept on scrolling. A list of outgoing calls followed – Miles carefully logging the numbers. Then a list of incoming calls, which dissolved halfway down. Sharon looked and suddenly stopped, pointing at one number in particular. "There!"

Miles peered. "What am I looking at?"

"07812 972 2811." Sharon was already reaching for her phone and dialling it.

"I'm sorry, is that number of particular significance? Someone you know . . . ?"

"Maybe."

The phone rang in her hand. It was answered, slowly and blearily, by a voice going, "Yeah? Who is it?"

"Hi, my name's Sharon. You don't know someone by the name of Swift, do you?"

The voice, male, sleepy, grumpy to be no longer asleep, paused. Then, "No – look, do I know you?"

"Don't think so. I'm Sharon, I'm the deputy Midnight Mayor, I'm looking for my boss?"

Irritation flared now in the voice on the other end of the line. "Look, I don't know who you are or what you want, but it's really late so if it's important, yeah, it's just going to have to wait. Bye."

"No, wait I . . ." The voice at the other end, had already hung up. "Well, that's kinda rude," muttered Sharon.

"Not what you were expecting?" murmured Miles.

"Not what I was hoping," she admitted. "What do you know about numbers beginning 07812?"

To her surprise, Paul answered. "Uh, it's a common mobile phone prefix. Millions of people have it."

From behind her smile, Sharon realised that she was going to like Ian far more than this koala-eyed technician, glowering at her from above his coffee mug. "Okay," she said, trying not to let her irritation show. "Well, that's a shame. Still!" She sat up a little straighter. "Maybe send someone over to check this number out? Just in case it's *not* a coincidence?"

"Ms Li," Miles moved round next to her to see her face more clearly. "May I ask what the significance of this number is?"

"Not sure yet," she replied. Then, with a burst of defiance, "Which doesn't make it any less significant! Just . . . a bit unhelpful, is all."

Faced with Miles's restrained consternation, she turned back to the computer screen, glaring at it as if somehow it could be held responsible for her current frustrations. "Did you get any emails off this thing?" she asked.

"We're brilliant, but not that brilliant," replied Paul. "Got her last few internet addresses, though."

He gestured at a file on the screen. Sharon opened it, and scrolled through the web links. Several were map references. One of them, when opened, brought up directions to the Deptford industrial estate where the woman had met her end, another for Scylla Workshops, World's End. Miles reached out abruptly, his hand pressing down on Sharon's, before she could move on.

"Scylla Workshops," he breathed. "Damn."

"Why 'damn'? What are they? How can things get worse?"

"The scylla sisters," he replied. "Manufacturers and enchantresses of all things mystic and magic."

"Great," muttered Sharon. "That's how things can get worse."

She scrolled through a few more links, but the water had eaten more than even a decent digital magician could recover. Finally she stood up, just as Rhys turned to her with eyes aglow and said, "All this time I thought D++ would be the right script to enchant in!"

Sharon looked from Rhys's bright eyes to the patient smile of Ian the digital magician standing at his back, and fell back on her default nod-smile technique. "Yeah, Rhys. That sounds great."

If her words were hollow, they only served to echo off the infinite boundaries of Rhys's joy and goodwill. As they were leaving, a thought struck Sharon. She turned to Paul and Ian, already sinking back into the slow growth of paper and coffee that filled their tiny office. "Hey – the woman whose phone this was. Did you get a name?"

"Brid," replied Ian. "There were messages for Brid, but the phone is registered to Bridget Parr."

Chapter 48

Brid

I only did what needed to be done.

My mother is a witch, my grandmother was a witch, and her mother before then.

We were one of the first families who understood urban magic, one of the first to get rid of the old herbs and cantrips of the trade and learn how to work with this new power, this raw power of the cities. My great, great grandmother blessed the first shovel that dug the dirt of the Metropolitan line, my great grandmother laid a whole chimney of soot devils to rest using nothing more than a bucket of salt water and the shuttle from a weaver's loom! In 1917, my grandmother did the first ever warding of an automobile against rust and in 1940 my mother was born as Silvertown burnt around her; and she had some of that fire in her blood, my mother, some of that stench of brick and smoke and nitroglycerine, and she gave that to me. The old order changes, giving way to the new. I am a witch, and proud, and I did what needed to be done.

He is coming.

Chapter 49

Bring Goodwill Wherever You Go

There was a stranger waiting in the foyer downstairs.

He was waiting in the foyer, because security hadn't known what to do with him.

Back straight, shoulders back, head held up high, he was every bit the proud ambassador, and it was perhaps this pride and force-fulness which the security guards could sense and which, along with his lacerated skin, and flesh punched with metal, held them back from approaching him too closely.

8ft stood in the foyer and glared at it all. He glared at the lifts, at the potted plants, at the bright light and the polished floor, because it was,

"ugly," he explained, as Sharon stepped out of the lift, Miles in tow. The Alderman's expression, usually a paragon of diplomatic inertia, drifted through surprise and then out into open astonish-ment as Sharon held out her hand and the Tribesman carefully grasped it. "its ugly," he added with a grunt. "prty thins 2 disguse slav labor, beatiful wals 2 hid da sin."

Sharon's smile, fuelled by coffee and tension, was unwavering, cheerful and bright. "8ft," she said, "I'm guessing you don't want to come upstairs for a coffee?" He scowled, eyes flickering round the hall like a rat wondering if he should go down the darkened tunnel towards the sweet-smelling chocolate. "Didn't think so," she sighed. "8ft, this is Miles. Miles, this is 8ft."

The Alderman got together something resembling a smile and, overcoming his brief repulsion, even went so far as to offer a hand. The Tribesman glared at it suspiciously. "wat is Miles?" he asked, glancing at Sharon.

"Miles is my minion."

"u av minion?"

"Yes – I was kinda worried that the word had derogatory terms; but actually Miles recommended it himself, and I think if you use it with a sorta tongue-in-cheek attitude then it's almost fond."

"i fought ur druid woz ur minion."

Rhys smiled feebly. "Me, too," he replied.

"is Miles tru?"

"Depends what you mean by true," Sharon replied, eyeing up the Alderman with a fixed smile. "If you mean is he honest, dedicated, determined and hard-working, then, yeah, I guess he's all that and probably making a fortune off overtime. If you mean, has he seen the innate falseness of this world, perceived the lies that we spin over the surface of reality to shield ourselves from the pain . . . then you're gonna have to ask him that yourself."

To everyone's relief, 8ft didn't. Instead, he gestured towards the door. "did wat u wnted," he grunted. "tok tim, tok wrk, but he's ere."

"Who's here?" asked Miles quickly.

8ft spared him only the most cursory of glares. "da mdnght mayor."

The Tribe had put him in the back of a truck.

The numberplate dangled off the front, and the back had no numberplate at all. The blue walls of the vehicle were covered in thick, grey dirt, on which an immortal wit bursting with original-ity had written, in order to fulfil expectations, WASH ME.

Other, more interesting, fingers had written other things. Wards spiralled and spun across the dirt; drawn with fingertips and palm

prints, they swirled in and out of each other in a giddy mess of lines
and sweeps, graffiti-style, sharp contours and jagged shapes which
might have been a word, or an image, or even a very angry idea,
until the necessities of magical binding had disrupted all meaning.
Three nervous-looking Tribesmen were huddled round the back
doors of the van. One carried a piece of corrugated iron, torn and
battered into a crude shield. Burn marks were splashed across its
front like wet black paint. Another carried a wand, crafted from a
broken handle pulled from the end of a circuit breaker, its tip still
smarting with suppressed electrical energy waiting to be
unleashed. A third had fresh burns through her shoulder and across
her neck, the skin red, raw, swollen and bloody, her face beaming
with pride at the injury.

Miles gathered more Aldermen. The neat, black-clad magicians
stared suspiciously at the Tribesmen, who glowered back. Sharon
and Rhys stood between them, smiling until their faces ached. No
one wanted to be the first to open the lock on the back of the truck.

"We just need to get him into the building," said Miles, "and the
office's wards should activate to suppress any dangerous magics."

"'Should'?" squeaked Rhys.

"He's the Midnight Mayor." The Alderman looked pained. "The
wards were designed to protect him, not control him."

"They," corrected Sharon, "are the blue electric angels. I'm not
sure the Midnight Mayor is getting a look-in."

A couple of Aldermen stepped forward. They held syringes and
wore white-latex-gloved hands. 8ft said, "wats dat?"

"Sedatives," replied one, her eyes not quite able to fix on the
Tribesman's face. "In case he's – they're – violent."

The Tribesman goggled. "U fink ... sedtives gonna b gud nuf?"
The incredulity was obvious in 8ft's voice, even if his features were
hard to read. "u is fick!"

"Guys," sighed Sharon, "if we're gonna – and I'm kinda sorry to
be saying this – but if we're gonna be containing a screaming, blue-
fire-throwing, off-his-head, utterly whacked, totally psycho – stop
me when you're feeling freaked, by the way – totally psycho electric angel, then I'm thinking it'd all be way easier if we worked

together. Now, I would suggest a bit of team bonding first, like paintballing or that, but I'm really not sure we've got the time. So let's all try and be united by a mutual fear of spontaneous combustion and oncoming plague, yeah?"

Miles managed to force the thinnest of smiles and even briefly met the eyes of 8ft. 8ft briefly managed to twitch his face into something that wasn't exactly a glower, but couldn't be described as much better. Sharon beamed. "There! Isn't that nice? Now, as no one is rushing in, I'll just do the honours . . . "

She marched up to the door, and wondered if anyone else could see how fast her heart was running, or had noticed the flush of terror spreading over her skin. She put her hand on the handle, and it was warm without being hot, and there was magic in it, the great thick swirling magics of the wards inscribed in the grey dirt on the truck. She felt it strain and warp as she clicked the handle back and, with a long step and a shallow breath, pulled the door of the van open.

Swift – or, rather, the body that should have been Swift – lay inside, head resting against the wall, eyes closed, breathing slowly. His skin was solid, his hands were still, and, apart from the slow rising and falling of his chest, there was no indication in him at all of any living thing.

Rhys peered round Sharon, dabbing at his nose in anticipation.

Swift's eyes opened, and they were blue, brilliant, burning blue, and as they fell on Sharon so his skin split apart. Fracture lines of fire raced along the course of his veins, welling up like lava from inside his flesh. His lips pulled back in an animal snarl and, as Rhys pulled Sharon back, the sorcerer's hair began to stand on end and his fingertips crackled with ultraviolet-bright electric light.

"Give me back to us!"

The words ripped their way out of the truck, hard enough to slam the doors back on the hinges. The wards on the metal began to smoke, dirt shifting and rearranging as the spell attempted to compensate, moving through memories of a thousand words inscribed by fingers over the years, *wash me . . . woz 'ere . . . my other truck . . . spurs 4evr . . . s loves b . . . is also a wolkswagen . . .*

A wave of heat crinkled the ends of Sharon's eyelashes, and something violent knocked her to the ground. She landed heavily, and looked up to see Rhys on top of her. Overhead, where she'd been a moment before, blue arcs of fire lashed at the air, rocking the van from side to side.

"Give me back!" the figure screamed, and at the sound the tyres of the truck burst with gunshot bangs, the tar melted beneath them, the windows in nearby buildings hummed in response to the noise. What had 8ft said about the electric angels? Somewhere between angel, devil and god.

Rhys gasped at where he was and what he'd done, and hurriedly rolled off her. "I'm so sorry, Ms Li, I didn't . . . " Before he could say any more, Sharon scrambled to her feet, even as the Tribesmen and Aldermen scattered for cover. She looked up, and there he was – no, there *they* were, the blue electric angels, stepping out of the back of the truck, skin blazing, blood burning in their veins, eyes wild, hands outstretched. With every step they took, fire danced in sympathy along the wires and cables of the street, burning above, below, sparking from every mains socket and telephone wire. Sharon briefly wondered whether the Aldermen had insurance for this kind of situation, and if it was going to reflect badly on her own role, before the blue electric angels raised their arms again and screamed.

This time, she dived for cover on her own initiative, ducking down behind a bin whose contents began to smoulder and crackle with flame. Windows up and down the street shimmered with reflected rolling blue, casting giddy shapes and shadows, while beneath the angels' feet the road itself began to crack, shooting geysers of water upwards; where spreading pools now rushed for the gutter, maggot-sparks writhed over the surface.

There was a buzzing in Sharon's pocket. It was, she reflected, a bad time for her mother to call. The buzzing kept going even as the Aldermen cowered behind whatever surface they could find. One or two rash members tried raising shields of their own; a woman, her skin shifting to metal as the power of her office imposed itself, dared to raise her head from behind a parked Mini, only for a fist of

white lightning to slam into her chest and hurl her back against the
nearest glass wall, hard enough to crack it like eggshell.

Sharon saw Rhys, hands over his head, knees tucked up to his
chin, huddled into almost the same space as 8ft, druid and
Tribesman briefly reconciled by the bursts of flame spinning out of
control from the blazing man in the middle of the street. Her phone
was still ringing. She prised it from her pocket and looked down.
The number was unknown. Her fingers moved without her willing
them. She answered.

A voice stammered, "D-d-d-d-domine! D-d-d-domine ..."

"Swift?" she breathed.

"Help me!"

"Hear that screaming?" she hissed, waving the phone towards the
street. "That's totally your voice doing that, which makes this phone
call kinda tricky to classify."

"D-d-d-domine ..."

"Any time now."

"Domine dir-dirige nos!"

It came as a gasp, then seemed the only sound the voice could
manage; the phone fell silent in her hand. In the middle of the
street, Swift's body was nine parts fire to only one part skin, his features half lost behind the waves of electric blue light and the
distortion of heat rolling off him. When he raised his arms, the geysers of water building at his feet burst upwards, cracks rushed up
through the glass buildings either side of him, and even the clouds
overhead seemed to spiral a bit faster across the sky. Sharon glanced
over at 8ft, and saw his eyes wide, his mouth hanging open, and
knew he was right. Angel, devil, god, pick whichever one happens
to be in the best mood at the time. Unconsciously, she slipped the
phone back into her pocket, and, as she did so, her fingers brushed
something small and metal, lying unregarded in the mess of fabric
and old receipts. She pulled it out. Tiny, white, a pair of red crosses,
one in the top corner of the other. The badge of an Alderman,
stolen from Crompton the undertaker, who hadn't seemed to want
it any more.

Her fingers tightened around it. As they did, she felt a silver-metal sheen begin to spread. The sensation was cold at first, stiff, awkward, but as it rushed upwards, curling round her arm, her elbow, her back, she found she could still move, even as her spine began to press back against her skin, vertebrae growing out to sharpened points, even as her lips solidified and her teeth began to stretch, as her vision filled with red and her breath began to stink of the smoke she was exhaling. She shuddered, not so much with fear, but as a cat shakes under tension, as the metal skin sealed itself round her body, and looked down to see claws of black at her fingers' ends, and knew that it was natural, and it was fine, and it was right.

She stood up, and her knees bent awkwardly, but with a strength and a springiness in them that her body did not normally possess. For a moment, just a moment, she thought she saw something move in the corner of her eye, in the shadow place of a shaman's seeing, and it was black, and ancient, and it had wings.

Then she was on her feet, even as Rhys called out for her, words lost behind the roaring of blood in her ears, and Swift was turning and, as he did, the fire snapped out towards her and, without thinking, she shifted into the spirit walk, the ghost of the fire bursting around her into hot greyness that ticked across her metal skin; and she saw them. The blue electric angels, their bodies aflame, their wings of electric fire stretching towards the sky. Around them buzzed the essence of their being, a million, million, billion essences of their beings, the life that had made their magic coalesce from a hundred years of . . .

hello, is . . .

   . . . hello?

are you there?

  then I said to him

beeeeeeeeeeeeeeeeeeeeeeepppppppp

   who's calling?

can I

   beeeeeeeeeeeeeepppp

 connect you?

 putting you through

and he said
        oh my God you won't believe
        beeeeeeeeeeee
    operator? Operator?
freeeeeeee

She saw the gods of the telephone line and, in the spirit walk, where all things were true and no one ever dared to look, they stared back at her, and their fires faded.

She stepped towards them, and it seemed to her that something black and heavy moved with her, flexing its muscles in the darkness.

They stared back, but made no move to attack, the flames of their being dancing over their skin. She held out her right hand – talon, perhaps, was the fairer term here – and noted how something moved with it, great and black draping down from her arm – and the twin crosses of the Midnight Mayor were there, blazing scarlet now in the palm of her hand, and she said,

"Domine dirige nos."

The blue electric angels hissed, sparks flying from their mouth, but they did not move.

"Domine dirige nos," she repeated. Then, "I'm thinking you've got issues."

Blue fire flashed across the angels' skin, but still they did not strike. Their eyes moved from Sharon's hand, to Sharon's face, and then upwards, to something at her back. She didn't turn, didn't dare to look, kept her eyes on the painful brightness of the figure in front of her. "So, Swift rang," she went on conversationally and, at his name, their eyes darted back to her, fixed on her face. "I think he's trapped in the telephone wires, which is kinda ironic if you think about it, but then makes sense. Can something make sense and be ironic? I'll have to think about that one, but point is . . . " Another step, she was so close now that the heat was palpable, even in the cool of the spirit walk. " . . . he's trying to find you, you're trying to find him, it's all very upsetting for everyone involved and I sympathise. I mean, I totally sympathise but what I need you guys to understand . . . " She reached out with her scarlet-burning claw, her fingers reaching into the fires dancing round the angel's flesh. The heat was a sauna through her metal arm, the voices that rattled and spun from out of the angels' being, almost deafening.

beeeeeee

    hello? Hello?!

connecting you

       BEEEEEEEEEEEEEEEE

"... what I want you to know is that I think we can get through this together."

She was up to her elbow in the fires now, her hand had almost passed straight through what should have been the angel's arm. There was nothing there, only fire, nothing human left at all, except ...

Her fingers brushed something soft, solid, warm.

A hand lashed up out of nowhere, curling round her hand, grasping it tight. She stared into the brilliant blueness of the angels' eyes and saw their lips move.

"We ... we ... we ..."

The heat from their grip was turning from a smarting to a smouldering beneath her metal skin.

"We ... we cannot ... flesh is ... we cannot ..."

"It's okay," she replied. "You'll be okay."

"Help us?"

"I am. I shall. You'll be fine. Can you sleep? Do you know what sleep is?"

"Humans ... sleep."

"You're in a human body."

"We ... we cannot ... we ... do not ... fear sleep! Fear sleep death sleep death sleep death stopping? Stopping no difference!"

A thought struck Sharon. She tightened her grip on the angel's hand, felt her skin begin to stick, the pain running down to her elbow, to the nerves in her shoulder and back. "Come with me." She turned, and began to walk, pulling them slowly after her. She walked, and they followed, the ground smouldering beneath their feet. She walked through the spirit walk, through the place where things were true and everything could be seen, and then walked a little further, pulling them along, into the deepest darkness of the spirit walk where the past reached its fingers up from the city street, bone fingers clutching at their ankles, bone voices whispering of things which had been, and where the cars were parked beside wheelbarrows and two-horse carriages, and the cobbles were swollen with damp river mud welling up from between the gaps, and then she pulled them deeper, shaking with effort and pain, the air pushing back at her, breath condensing even as the fires of the blue electric angels spat and twisted beside her. She half closed her eyes as her lungs began to swell and contract from the lack of air, pushed one foot forward at a time, each step a leaden shuffle against a wall, until, with a final stagger, she pushed through, into the silver-grey chill of the dream walk.

The blue electric angels followed. She looked back at them, even as they turned upwards to stare at a sky of impossible orange stars. Very carefully, she let go of their hand. The fires began to dim across their skin, shrivelling back into flesh, which closed silently over the wounds. A face, barely recognisable but still, perhaps, human, emerged from the blazing light, and smiled.

"Is this . . . sleep?" they asked, and before Sharon could answer, their eyes closed, and they sunk down to the ground, fast asleep.

Sharon stood and stared, first at the silently breathing body of Matthew Swift, all trace of blue gone, then up at the busy twisting world of the dream walk. She'd never walked into this place before when fully conscious, but the way back seemed no more and no less than the way by which she'd come. Here, the crimson fire on her hand was almost invisible, and the metal skin on her skin shed and grew in great falling flakes, like confetti off a wedding dress. She watched it fall and melt for a second, then straightened up, took a deep breath, and moved again, quickening her pace to the brisk speed of a spirit walk and shouldering her way back through the heaviness between sleep and waking.

She staggered out into the spirit walk and here the pain in her hand suddenly reasserted itself, hot and sharp, a popping, crinkling, in her palm whenever she flexed her fingers, and the metal that covered her hand was black and scarred, all the way up to her elbow, and, as she turned, she felt something move with her.

A pause.

A second to consider.

She took a deep breath, clenched her less-burnt fist at her side, and turned to look.

It stood above her, behind her, around her, wings of black, great red eyes, claws of steel, back of bone, and it was giant, and it was ancient, and it was, for want of a better word, a dragon. She'd seen it before, with its mad flickering tongue and its spined, raised wings. It was the dragon which held the shield of London between its claws on the site of the old city gates, whose shape adorned old walls and bared its teeth from above the porticoes of the churches. It looked at her, and she looked right back at it, and for a moment neither moved.

Then Sharon raised her hand, the Alderman's tiny white badge still gleaming in it, and carefully pried it from her smarting palm. As she did, the metal began to retreat across her skin, rolling down like rainwater, her bones slipping silently back into their proper place, the redness drawing back from behind her eyes; and the dragon overhead began to fade. It looked at her quizzically as it started drifting to shadow. She waggled an unburnt finger at it in polite reproach.

"It's not that I'm not impressed," she explained. "It's just that a girl's gotta prioritise on occasions like this."

The dragon faded into the night, and Sharon Li slipped back out of the spirit walk, and into reality.

Chapter 50

Doubt Never Helped Anyone

She said, "Ow."

"I'm sorry, Ms Li, but you have to let me . . . "

"Ow!"

" . . . apply it thoroughly otherwise the . . . "

"That bloody hurts!"

" . . . the unguent won't have a chance to work!"

Sulky silence.

Sharon and Rhys sat in Miles's pristine office while Rhys carefully applied gel from a bottle that had formerly contained sweet chilli sauce all across Sharon's inflamed right hand. As burns went, it might have been worse. Swelling was definitely to be anticipated, as was blistering: already the skin was shifting loosely over some joints and under several fingers. But there wasn't any blackness, which had worried her, and the cheese-grater effect over some of her skin was, she decided, more an effect of turning into a form of human-dragon hybrid while chatting with an angel. All things considered, it could have gone much . . .

"Ow!"

Rhys flinched. His pain at causing pain almost exceeded Sharon's own sensations in its intensity and fervour. "I'm so sorry, Ms Li, I really am, but this is the best way to ensure it heals." He daubed another dollop of goo under her thumb.

"What's an unguent anyway?" she demanded. "Why 'unguent' and not just Savlon?"

"Oh, druids make all sorts of wonderful remedies and creams. But it's bad professional practice to say 'this is like TCP' or 'this works as well as Sudocrem'. So we give everything interesting names to make it clear they're our own patent."

"Druids . . . patent their cures?"

"Oh yes!"

"Even the mystic ones?"

"Especially the mystic ones. You don't want anyone grinding up the tail of a fox without appropriate training."

Sharon blanched. "Please tell me there's not . . . ?"

"Oh no!" said Rhys, anxious to dispel this fear. "No foxes were harmed to make this, I promise! In fact, you can find most of the ingredients in a well-supplied deep-freeze store. All you do is take one fresh tube of . . . "

Sharon raised her less-burned hand. "You know what, Rhys, just this once I'll let you keep your trade secrets, okay?"

"Oh, my God!" A voice came through the door on a wave of excitement and caffeinated products. The owner followed in a flurry of brown skirt and black jacket, grabbed Sharon's hand by the wrist and held it up to the light. "Is that . . . unguent? Wow, that is so totally druidic I could put it on a pizza!"

Rhys gaped as the diminutive figure of Dr Seah, NHS physician to the gravely cursed and deeply magical, four-foot-nothing of black bobbed hair and epic long stethoscope, sniffed deeply at Sharon's fingers. "Wow," she said. "That is like . . . serious wow. You know, I haven't seen unguent like that since that thing with the seer and the effrit and the kettle lead down in the Brunswick casino."

"Hello, Dr Seah," intoned Sharon.

"Hi, chicken!" called out the merry medic, treating the room to a dazzling display of neat white teeth in a cheery round face. "And, hi, druid!" she added. "How've you been keeping? Not messing around with any wendigos, I hope?"

"Um, no, Dr Seah . . ." A sneeze welled up, all at once.

"Oh, lambkins," sighed the medic. "Are you still on the antihistamines?"

"Yes, Dr Seah."

"Sweetheart, you want to be careful there. If the usual course of treatment isn't working, I'd really suggest seeing a specialist. Have you tried acupuncture? Sticking needles in people: always therapeutic, even if not strictly necessary" – Rhys failed to dodge an affectionate pat on the shoulder – "and you are like, screaming 'therapute me'."

"Dr Seah." Sharon's voice was beginning to show her fatigue. "It's not that we're not really pleased to see you – because we are, aren't we, Rhys?"

Rhys snuffled in reply.

"But it's, like, way past NHS callout hours, and while my hands are a bit blistered, I'm guessing you're not just here for that?"

"Burns are serious," intoned Dr Seah. "But druidic unguent is, like, so the way to go. If you can't get any cling film, I mean, and – how'd you burn them?"

"Uh, the raging electric fire off a furious angel, experienced through the dream walk while wearing the skin of a dragon?"

Even Dr Seah paused. "Okay," she said at length. "Did you run your hands under the cold tap for ten minutes after?"

"Oh yes! Because I remember, that's something you're supposed to do!"

"Fantastic – good call! But I gotta admit, while I'm just tickled to see you all," another brilliant smile, "I was mostly called in by Kelly – you've met Kelly, right. She's so awesome it's, like, I want to be her, you know? – to have a look at the Midnight Mayor." At this, Dr Seah gave a malicious cackle. "Because that's totally new!"

They went downstairs.

Then down a bit more.

There was a basement beneath the basement, a place where the walls were grey, the pipes were thick, and mysterious machinery chugged. Then the walls became less grey. Paint had been sprayed on, some of it still drying: swirling figures and creatures, symbols and runes in the shape of old transport signs, and red triangles declaring STOP. A monkey's head leered out from above a body of spider's claws; a cackling hyena smoked a cigar and, as it puffed, the orange-painted end of the tube flared and shimmered, and black smoke drifted across the wall. Everyone became careful not to let their clothes touch the warm, writhing images and, as they headed down, the stench of magic and chemical fumes became almost overwhelming.

At the deepest part of the darkest corner was a heavy door. Once, meat might have been frozen behind it, or slabs of ice kept for a difficult and expensive social emergency. But now the great door was locked. Outside, 8ft, Miles and the unmistakable cheerfulness that was Kelly Shiring, Swift's PA, stood to something resembling attention.

"Sharon!" exclaimed Kelly, opening her arms almost as wide as her smile. "So lovely to see you! How were the doughnuts?"

Sharon did her best not to gape at the beaming Alderman. "They were . . . lovely, cheers."

"And the umbrella?"

"It was mega-mystic, actually."

"Was it? I thought it might be, though it's so hard to tell. But I knew I could count on you to work it out. 'Kelly,' I thought, 'Matthew has left this umbrella here for a reason, and just because you and the combined forces of the Aldermen's office lack the ability to reason why, doesn't mean that Sharon won't solve it in an instant.' And you did!"

Sharon eyed the locked door behind Kelly, aware of how studiously the others in the passage were *not* eyeing it, as if acknowledging the problem might somehow make things worse. "How about being deputy Midnight Mayor?" said Kelly, radiating satisfaction with the very idea. "Is that working out?"

Sharon looked at Rhys, Rhys studied his feet. She looked up into Miles's expression of consternation, 8ft's scarred face and, finally,

Kelly's brilliant smile. "Actually, I gotta tell you, flattered though I am to be given, like, serious responsibility this early into my career, I don't think this is me being overly humble when I tell you that I'm feeling a bit out of my depth. I mean, I'm not saying never, because one day I'd like to have a decent job with a proper managerial position and a big chair and someone to sort out the taxman for me. But to be honest, at this stage of things, and considering the pressures of the gig, I'm thinking that maybe making me deputy Midnight Mayor was like the most phenomenally stupid thing since... since ..." She hesitated, looking for a comparison. "Since making Swift the Midnight Mayor in the first place!"

There was a polite shuffling of feet. Now no one would meet anyone's eye. Except for Kelly, who, still smiling radiantly, reached out and gently laid her hands on Sharon's shoulders. There was

taste of sushi

sound of laughter, glasses chinking

the flash of a gun firing in the night

walk away, Mr Mayor.

(you can't save yourself)

Then there was nothing but Kelly's smile. "But Ms Li," she exclaimed, eyes wide and bright, "that's why it makes such perfect sense!"

Chapter 51

Matthew

Beeeeeeeeeee . . .
(says the telephone line)
Beeeeeeeeee . . .
(when you listen to the dialling tone)
beeeeeeeeeeeeeeeeeeeeeeeeee
(a waiting signal, asking to be filled, and it says . . .)
beeeeeeeeeeeeeeeeeeeeeeeeee mmmmmeeeeeeeeeeeeeeeee
(Which is not how the song usually goes.)

Chapter 52

Nothing Like a Good Night's Sleep

They opened the door.

They did so very slowly, very carefully; and once Sharon, Dr Seah, Kelly, Miles and Rhys were on the other side, they closed the door quickly behind them.

The room was cold, a refrigeration unit churning somewhere behind, Sharon's breath steaming in the air, skin rising up in bumps. Pipes had been cut short and now hung, crusty with icicles, from the ceiling and walls. The square footprints where great refrigerators had stood still scarred the white-tiled floor. All around, paint shifted beneath the frost on the walls, continually swirling and dancing as the graffiti wards spilt in and out of each other.

"It was painted by the Whites," explained Miles, his breath a thick cloud. "To suppress, contain and control any magics within its walls."

Sharon looked at the one thing within its walls, and found herself wishing for a little more than paint. The body that had once held Matthew Swift lay in the centre of the floor, head tucked into its arms, knees pulled up to its chest, sleeping deep. It looked entirely human, peaceful, almost innocent. Someone had, in deference to the temperature, given it a woolly hat pulled down across the eyes with a pair of fluffy grey rabbit ears sticking out each side, and a pair of thick blue skiing gloves to protect it against the cold. Sharon wondered if this generous soul expected to get these goods back intact, or if they minded them being returned as cinders.

Dr Seah looked at the body and tutted. "Dear me," she said. "If it's not one thing, it's the other. Sick people suck."

So saying, she strode forward, bold as a battleship and, before anyone could stop her, parked herself down on the floor next to the sleeping form and pressed her fingers into its neck. Sharon held her breath, waiting for combustion, explosion, catastrophe, death. None came. Dr Seah reached out and raised an eyelid, peered into the blue depths of Swift's eye, tutted profoundly, pulled out her massive stethoscope, listened to his chest, and then, very carefully, with the end of a drawing pin, pricked the tip of one of his fingers, and observed the blood rise to the surface. A drop swelled up, red and thick, then fell to the ground. As it fell, it changed, bursting into busy, hissing blue fire which hit the floor and scattered, wriggling through the frost like an angry worm, burrowing for the earth. Clucking under her breath, Dr Seah pulled the hat further down over Swift's face, stood up and said, "Right, who's been playing silly buggers with the sorcerer's living consciousness?"

Rhys looked apologetic, Kelly beamed, Miles shrugged. And so, by a process of elimination, it fell to Sharon to say something useful.

"Um?"

"Don't all stand there looking like dead sardines!" exclaimed the medic. "The living human consciousness that should be in this body, who's nabbed it?"

"Uh . . . we were kinda hoping you'd tell us?"

Dr Seah threw her arms up in righteous indignation. "Terrific. You've lost the brain."

Rhys raised a hand in hopeful enquiry. "Dr Seah? When you say we've lost the brain, do you mean as in the actual squishy pink bit with all the neurons, or more as in the essence of intelligence which should inhabit the squishy pink bit?"

Dr Seah glowered. "What do you think?"

"I don't know, Dr Seah," he confessed. "I don't think druids have an unguent for a missing brain."

"I'm guessing you mean the consciousness, right?" Sharon cut in. "I don't suppose you know *how* Swift's consciousness got detached from the pink squishy bit?"

"If I said 'duh, magic' that'd be like, totally unprofessional, right?"

"No, no!" exclaimed Sharon. "It's good to have these basic instincts confirmed, I mean, to get reassurance that this is in fact the case. But the thing is, while 'duh, magic' is an entirely appropriate reply, I was kinda hoping for something ... more ... specific?"

Dr Seah sighed and directed her indignant glare away from Sharon's optimistic expression, back down at the sleeping form of the Midnight Mayor. "Well, if I had to speculate – which I totally hate doing, by the way, because usually I'm like 'just hit with drugs' but that's how you get resistant strains, mutating viruses and the lycanthrope outbreak in Enfield – but if I *had* to speculate I'd say you were looking at a six-, seven-man summoning team minimum? And a mutually resonant casting catalyst to coax the consciousness out, and then maybe, just maybe, you're talking about a storage facility for the brain that'd be, like, *this* big!" – she swayed with the effort of stretching her arms wide – " ... which seriously narrows it down; I mean, your computers don't have the processing power, and your genie bottles totally don't have the processing power; you'd get brain damage and it'd be like, 'pop', hello dopey sorcerer. So I'm guessing we're talking something really big, like the gutted belly of a dead god or maybe the hollowed-out nexus where five train lines met, and even then you'd have to line it with asbestos and ... "

"Telephones." Sharon spoke so quickly, even Dr Seah paused to check that she'd heard. "If I get what you're saying, then to keep Swift's mind alive – I mean, alive but not in his body – you'd need to put it somewhere big, right? Like, able-to-store-consciousness big. How about telephones?"

"Yeah ... " There was a drag on the word which did not bode well. "I guess you could *try* and put his mind into the telephones. But it'd be really tricky; I mean, you'd need a sympathetic catalyst ... "

"He's the blue electric angels," Sharon replied. "That sympathetic enough?"

"I gotta tell you, that'd probably do it, but!" Dr Seah had the grace to look taken aback. "But putting a human mind into the telephones is, like, *way* out there. I mean, there'd be transference issues, and addressing issues, and disintegration issues. Like, I get that the guy's been sharing his body with the gods of the telephone and that, but seriously? One tiny human brain bouncing round the telephone wires? It'd be like – well, put it like this, there'd be psychological things I'd be worried about. Like, *beyond* prescription-drugs kinda things." Few more frightening fates could be presented to Dr Seah, it appeared, than a problem which didn't have a chemical solution.

"Is Mr Swift in danger?" Kelly demanded. "I mean . . . more than having his mind trapped in the telephone wires?"

"Uh . . . *yeah?*" insisted Dr Seah.

"Mortal danger?"

"Depends how you see 'mortal'. Don't give me that look, it's, like, a serious question! Technically the guy ain't dead . . . technically he's just on this wacky extra-sensory field trip. Only, the longer he spends in the telephone wires, the more likely it is that his brain gets splattered, with bits of his mind in, like, Hong Kong, and other bits in Harare, and all chatting to each other over Facebook and that. So, technically, yeah, he'd be dead in the sense that once his consciousness gets split apart like that, there's no putting it back together. But can we call this mortal danger, really? I know it's unprofessional to say this, but damned if I know."

Kelly had gone pale. So, for that matter, had Miles. "Dr Seah . . ." the Alderman's voice was low and grey. "If Swift's mind is broken apart in the telephone wires, but he isn't actually dead . . . what would happen to the power of the Midnight Mayor?"

A pause. Then a shrug.

"You know," Dr Seah mused, "I guess that depends on how ancient primal powers look at death, too. If there's a possibility that the power might stay attached to what's left of Swift's mind in the telephone wires, going round and round the world forever . . . then, yeah, I'd guess there's that chance." Seeing the fallen faces around her, she clapped her hands together and exclaimed, "But don't worry! It's probably, like, a really really small chance. I'm sure everything will be totally okay, and we're all getting worked up about nothing. I mean, look!" She prodded the sleeping body of Swift with her toe. "He's got a woolly hat with rabbit ears on!"

Four mortified faces were as frozen solid as the walls themselves. Sharon cleared her throat. "Um . . . Dr Seah," she said, "I know that you hate speculating, and that this is kinda a bit of an ask, considering your area of professional expertise and that, but do you know how we can stop this? How we get Swift back?"

"Sure. You need to call him."

"We need to . . . "

"Sweetie, he's in the telephone lines. And how do you get into the telephone lines?"

"You . . . pick up a phone?"

"Exactly! Or someone picks up a phone for you, the detail's not that important. What matters is that at some point, somehow, your missing guy must have stood near an open telephone line and got sucked into it, and for the line to be active it must have had a number assigned to it. Dialling code, area code, you know, all that crap. Find the telephone . . . "

" . . . find Swift. Gotcha."

"Only try and do it before his mind disintegrates, yeah?" added the doctor, with a twitch of furrowed brow. "Cos that'll be some serious shit if left untreated."

Sharon stared down at the curled-up body of Swift, sleeping peacefully in its woolly hat. "Yeah. That's all we need."

Chapter 53

Cool and Calm Discussion Is the Sensible Response

They sat round a boardroom table.

Someone brought them biscuits.

Sharon ran her hands over the surface of the table, and felt dismayed. The thing was in the shape of an oval, green-tinted on top, black underneath. It could have easily sat twenty people; as it was, for now, it sat five, who'd managed to spread themselves just far enough apart to make conversation difficult. It was, as boardroom tables went, very managerial, very elegant, and just a bit sinister.

The biscuits, when they arrived, were expensive, sweet and too complicated for the shaman's taste. Rhys frowned at them, too, not sure how to cope with a snack that wasn't from the local supermarket's own brand, or which chose dried apricot pieces instead of ancient, withered raisins to add texture. Nor was he comfortable with someone else making the tea, thus undermining his own role in the managerial structure.

Then Kelly said, "We cannot permit the Midnight Mayor not to die."

As opening statements went, this was startling enough to make the druid utter a faint "uh?" and fumble instinctively in his pocket. Dr Seah had slipped him a fresh packet of tablets on her way out, and though she'd sworn they were the greatest antihistamines man could produce, the lack of any label had left him alarmed. 'Fuck it, you'll work it out!' was not, he'd felt, adequate medical advice.

"We can't permit him ... *not* to die?" squeaked Sharon.

"Please don't get me wrong," added the Alderman. "I want Mr Swift to live, as much as anyone here. His survival and wellbeing are of the highest concern to us all, and as his personal assistant I would feel so ashamed if I let his mind dissolve to the nether reaches of the telephone network. Absolutely our main priority has to be to get his mind back into his body, as quickly as possible.

"However ... " And on that however, how the sound stretched. "If we *can't*, then we do have to consider the possibility that the power of the Midnight Mayor, the force that has guarded this city for nearly two thousand years, may, for the first time in London's history, also cease to be. Or, rather, cease to be transferred onto a successor, which is tantamount to the same thing. And obviously as a PA I'm horrified at the thought that any harm might come to my employer, but we must remember that it's the Midnight Mayor who employs us, as much as any man who wields the spells."

"So what do you want to do?" asked Sharon.

"For now," murmured Kelly, "I think we proceed with trying to find Swift's, uh ... mind. Do you have any – and how exciting it is to use this word! – any leads, Ms Li?"

Sharon squirmed. Her sleep deprivation, which cold, anxiety, burns and coffee had temporarily driven back, was kicking in again as she looked round the large, well-heated room. "Uh, yeah ... " she muttered, trying to think what the hell they might be. "There's, uh ... there's Old Man Bone, who's coming back from the dead, well, the undead, well, the sorta-with-the-dead-but-not-dead ... There's all the shoes, which should be keeping him happy, but ain't. Then there's the Tribe kid who died from the Black Death, for pinching the umbrella, probably. And there's this dead woman, Bridget, who I think was killed by Swift in Deptford, and her phone said she was going to ... *she* was going to this place called Scylla

Workshops, because that was her last maps search, so I guess that's important. And there's this Hacq dude who emailed Swift about the umbrella, which lured him to Deptford but then also sent a viral hex which kinda stinks. And there was this phone call I got on the dream walk which, thinking about it, was really Swift kinda trying to get help which is a really positive thing, because it totally means he knows he's got a problem, and is still hanging on in there. And he gave me a bit of a telephone number although there's probably millions of people whose numbers begin with that, but it's worth checking out.

"And, uh ... yeah, if you ignore the threat of plague and the walking dead things and the shoes hanging off stuff and the missing sacrificial blade and the waking god and the trapped sorcerer and the screaming blue angel in the basement, then I'd say there's lots of really good things we can work with here."

Into the silence that followed, "Great!" exclaimed Kelly. "It's so good to hear that we're making progress!"

There was a polite chorus of "um" and "yeah".

"Someone said something about Scylla Workshops?" added Sharon, turning to where Miles sat. "Something kinda not totally 'whoo-hoo'?"

Miles wasn't a man to squirm. But Rhys, scrutinising him for comforting signs of vulnerability, did detect an instant of unease as the Alderman adjusted his posture. "They're ... very fine enchanters," he said. "There are three of them, sisters, who run the workshop and they are ... very fine."

Sharon's eyes narrowed. "Okay," she murmured. "So, I don't want to go all knower of truth on you here, but I'm kinda feeling that you're skipping something. What's the bad stuff here?"

This time, the squirm was unambiguous. "There are ... those who suggest that having monstrous writhing heads upon hideously bloated bodies from which scaled limbs protrude isn't necessarily a good marketing device ..."

Sharon's mouth dropped. "You mean ... when you say that it's the Scylla Workshops ..."

"Quite."

"As in ... actual scyllas? Like ... half-women, half-tentacled killing machines, with a taste for human flesh and really nasty teeth, kinda scyllas?"

"I wouldn't want to speculate on previous culinary inclinations."

"But that's ... that's kinda cool, isn't it?" She turned to the room for support. "I mean, come on!" She stretched her arms wide. "We're Magicals Anonymous; we're all about people with social issues, and it sounds to me like there's nothing like being a ... monster-headed, bloated-bodied, scaly fiend from Chelsea to cause discrimination! We could totally help!"

"If they want our help, Ms Li," offered Rhys.

"Yes, if they want it of course, but I'm just saying, community outreach, getting to know people, this could be ... " – her eyes glinted – " ... an *opportunity*."

This time, the chorus of assent and approval was even weaker. Sharon slapped her hand on the table. "You guys are so prejudiced! I mean, the worst part is, you don't even know how prejudiced you are, and that makes you, like, even more prejudiced, because you're not even thinking about it. But I know you mean well, and once you guys have noticed the problem, I know you'll all try and deal with it, in your own groovy way."

At length, "Amazing!" said Kelly. "You know, I hadn't even thought about it. Now you point it out, the idea of having tea with a creature capable of rending me limb from limb had been something that bothered me. But now I think about it, that's just a social stereotype, isn't it?"

"Exactly."

"Oh, my God, and I always thought I had such an open mind!"

Sharon and Kelly shared a wide, grateful smile of women surprised to discover comradeship in a difficult time. Elsewhere round the table, Miles, 8ft and Rhys did their best not to notice this moment of feminine unity.

Miles cleared his throat.

"There is also the question of appeasing Old Man Bone ... "

"Yeah," said Sharon, "he's past the sit-down and a cuppa tea stage."

"It can't be easy being the living god of the dead," suggested Rhys, trying to maintain the spirit of open-mindedness.

"Well, quite. Gotta feel it for the guy. Although the whole human sacrifice thing is dodgy."

"Nevertheless," prompted Miles, "without the blade . . . "

Sharon threw her hands up in frustration. "I know: plague, death, bad smells, I see where you're going. But I'm guessing it's not too much to say that whoever pinched the knife – or got B-Man to pinch the knife, whatever – whoever has the knife that was pinched is almost certainly the same guy who ensorcelled the living mind of Swift into the telephone wires, in an effort to get rid of the Midnight Mayor, yeah?"

There was a cautious chorus of, "Yeaahhhh . . . "

"And the dead woman, Brid, was probably killed by the blue electric angels during this same procedure, which makes her kinda a villain of the piece, which isn't to say that it's not sad that she's dead. But she's still tangled up with the whole pinching thing, so I think we can *also*," she was running out of breath, the world hazy with sticky, sleepy thoughts, "we can *also* say that if the last place this Brid looked before she met the angels was Scylla Workshops, then that's probably where we should go looking to find whoever it is who zapped Swift to stop him finding the knife; everyone with me?"

There was a thoughtful silence.

Then, "I am, Ms Li," ventured Rhys.

Sharon beamed. "See! Nothing like working the problem through."

Chapter 54

Wish Hard Enough, and Make Your Dreams Come True

They gathered in their temple.

It was a secret temple, which was good; everyone liked that about it.

But it was also a cold, draughty temple. A temple whose walls weren't finished, and whose furnishings hadn't been put in. A temple which took nearly twenty minutes to get to once you'd left the nearby station, not because it was isolated from transport – quite the opposite – but because the lifts weren't yet running an express service and the stairwell still smelt of fresh paint.

Say what you would, though – the view was amazing.

They gathered.

One said, "But we called on him only yesterday . . ."

One said, "He is strong. He will answer."

One said, "Is it right to disturb him so soon?"

One said, "I have consulted the signs and made the offerings."

One said – who wasn't sure about either the signs or the offerings, and couldn't work out where he'd left his gloves and was feeling less than inspired by the entire course of events, but then, what was a wizard to do? – "I really don't see how this is a problem."

One said, "They are going to the workshops! They will find them."

One said, "B-b-b-but there is n-n-n-nothing to find, is there?"

One said, "The Mayor left a deputy."

One said, "So what? A deputy Midnight Mayor, what does that even mean? That's just the person who does the cleaning up!"

One said, "Not to the Old Man. They spoke."

At this, there was a silence, and even the one who hadn't remembered his gloves, and was beginning to regret it, felt that this might be an unexpected game changer.

Then she said, and really, on this, her word was final, "I'll do it. I'll call him."

That was a bit of a relief to everyone else, as it made what followed somehow inevitable, and not their fault after all.

Chapter 55

Always Face Adversity with a Smile

It was called World's End. This had always confused Sharon, since, clearly, the world didn't end there. Certainly it was a bitch to get to, but anywhere in London that required both a train *and a bus* was, to Sharon's mind, pushing things too far. Perhaps once it had been a place where the houses stopped; but surely, by the time London had reached this corner of Chelsea, the city's builders should have noticed that the development of its streets was far outstripping their ability to find appropriate names.

Whatever the reason behind the name, in the small hours of the morning this part of King's Road did feel like an apt location for a quiet, entropic Armageddon. Towards Sloane Square, the street was a pulsing heartland of designer shops and well-lit galleries, in which every portrait of a red wall on a white background was priced at £15,000 upwards and the only drinks worth having had been pre-served for twenty-five years before the bottle was opened. Down here, though, where the shops ran out, World's End was a hallowed paradise for old gentlemen with many letters after their names; for wealthy bankers who enjoyed rowing on a Saturday, polo on a Sunday; and for families who believed in having groceries delivered, and felt no need for a corner store. The streets of white houses led down to the river's edge in high-ceiling decorum, heavy silk curtains pulled across sash windows; immaculately tended hedges and perfectly raked gravel paths. If World's End could choose to be anywhere, it would be a tiny, lavender-scented village in the Lake District, with all the amenities of Manhattan.

Sharon, Miles and Rhys walked through the quiet streets and tried not to make any noise. In other parts of London, noise wasn't merely a constant; its background hum was almost a reassurance that you were never really alone. Here, where the rose bushes stood upright against a background of Volvos and Mercedes-Benzes and every other streetlight was an adapted historical relic from Victorian times, it was hard to talk in more than a polite murmur.

As they went, Sharon felt the shadow walk drift over her, an easy slipping into invisibility. It was happening almost instinctively now, with her thoughts so tired. She was finding it hard to be herself, to be anything more than a part of the city, just slipping into the city, becoming . . .

"Ms Li!"

Rhys's voice snapped her back to wakefulness, and full visibility.

"What? . . . Was I vanishing?"

"You were vanishing, Ms Li."

"Was I?"

"Yes, Ms Li. Which isn't to say you shouldn't . . . I mean, when I said you vanished what I was trying to say, actually, was . . . "

Miles politely cleared his throat. "I think," he murmured, "if I understand our druidic friend, he was going to enquire as to whether you were *aware* of your impending invisibility, and, if you were, he wished you to be aware that as a state of both physicality and visibility, that was entirely acceptable with him. Am I correct, Rhys?"

Rhys seethed. The seethe became a sneeze, which might have been a "yes".

"Uh, cool," said Sharon. "Thanks for that."

The three walked on in silence.

Then Miles said, "Forgive me mentioning this; about the scyllas,

I mean. But I'm not sure if it is prejudice. Is it prejudiced, for example, to suggest that sharing the sea with a great white shark might be a bad idea?"

"You're comparing scyllas to . . . great white sharks?"

"In a way, yes."

Sharon drew in a slow breath, and Rhys, bracing himself, nonetheless felt a shimmer of satisfaction at what must come next.

"So . . . you're comparing a rational being who can, I grant you, rend people limb from limb, but who makes a perfectly respectable business enchanting mystic goods from a workshop in World's End, you're comparing this probably-council-tax-paying entity who had no choice but to be born with a monstrous head and a taste for raw flesh, with an oceanic creature who gets chemically incensed by the smell of blood and so can't control their own instinctive animal reactions? Is that what you're saying?"

Miles's black shoes tapped sharply on the pavement as they walked.

"I do see your point, Ms Li," he murmured.

"We do cautiously concede," Sharon replied, "that vampires may drink our blood, banshees may pulverise our brains with the shriek of their voice and scyllas may suck the marrow from our broken bones. But what we have to do is respect the fact that they are currently choosing not to use these abilities but are trying to adapt to circumstances imposed on them through no fault of their own."

"Yes, I do see that . . . "

"Prejudice," she added, "is what you get when stupid people go around judging the whole rending-talons thing without bothering to see if the talon is actually holding a fucking ice cream!"

Her voice echoed off the houses.

"Anyway," she muttered. "That's just what I think."

Miles was silenced, and Rhys, to his surprise, found that he was no longer sneezing.

Scylla Workshops was in a mews.

The former stables were now a mixture of tactfully disguised garages and elegant front doors; a place where night-time noise wasn't merely unwelcome, it was practically impossible. The former entrances for servants had been converted into softly lit portals with hanging flower baskets, and notices above the letterbox warning against junk mail. At almost every step, motion sensors caught the passage of strangers down the cobbled street, creating a rolling pathway of light which rippled with them all the way to the far end. There, a single black door in a single white wall declared on a small silver plaque:

Scylla Workshops

Sharon said, "Do you think they'll mind how late we are?"

"With all due respect, Ms Li," murmured Miles, "you are the deputy Midnight Mayor, seeking to save London from a fate worse than . . . well, many alternative fates of dire import. I'm sure they'll forgive you."

"Cool," muttered Sharon, and knocked.

Her knuckles rapped on the door, and the door swung open. It should, Rhys felt, have creaked, but in this part of town nothing creaked that wasn't meant to. They stood there, staring at the narrow dark gap beyond the door.

Sharon said, "Okay, so, anyone else freaked out by this, or am I overreacting?"

"I'm a little freaked, Ms Li." Rhys fumbled automatically for the reassuring presence of his antihistamines.

"Perhaps it's a customer feature?" suggested Miles. "Our door is always open – that sort of thing?"

Sharon turned to stare at the Alderman. "Okay, I get it," she said. "You *are* freaked, and all this 'it'll be okay really' stuff is how you manifest it, right?"

Miles gave an expansive shrug from the elbows out. "You are a knower of the truth, Ms Li."

"That's cool," she replied. "It's a defence mechanism. Defence mechanisms are way better than repressing."

She pushed the door back all the way, and felt a moment of nausea while crossing the threshold, as of the world being twisted to one side. There was an impression of a wood-panelled corridor, a stair leading upstairs, an umbrella stand, and then there wasn't.

Then there was simply a wood-panelled corridor and a stair leading, very definitely, down, and a long way down at that.

Sharon looked back, and the world behind the open door seemed a long way off; Miles and Rhys, framed in the portal, looked tiny, though they were only a few paces away. She gestured at them to follow, and for a moment they were small, and then they were very large again, right by her side, nearly knocking her into the stairwell.

"Interesting," murmured Miles. "Not so much an illusionary disguise as a spatial distortion?"

"I guess down is the only way to go," Sharon muttered, and began to descend.

Bright lights shone at regular intervals above the staircase. As Sharon reached the bottom of the stairs, her foot crunched on the broken plastic and glass that had been ripped from one of the bulbs overhead. The light swayed above her, with the screw of the bulb still tight in its fitting and a black electric scar running up one side of the wire. "Right," she murmured. Then, "Okay. Rhys?"

"Yes, Ms Li?"

"You got your antihistamines?"

"Yes, Ms Li. But they make me drowsy if . . . "

"I'm not saying take them yet. Just . . . have them close."

So saying, she pushed back a cream-coloured velour curtain and stepped into a low, windowless reception area. Like the rest of the building, the walls here were panelled in light-brown wood, and there were two cream-upholstered sofas where guests might sit, and read the magazines laid out on the low glass-topped coffee table. A poster proclaimed, "**All Our Enchantments At Scylla Workshops Come With A Guaranteed Three-Year Warranty!**" Other picture frames held gold and silver certificates, announcing that in the years 2001–2013 Scylla Workshops had been the proud winners of some of the most prestigious awards for material magic manipulation, and were an industry-standards leader.

A small white door led away from reception, to what could only be the workshops. Next to it a formal sign proclaimed, 'Personal Protective Equipment COMPULSORY Beyond This Notice'. To illustrate the point, a figure of a man had been drawn, demonstrating his hearty boots, his strong plastic hat, his high-visibility waistcoat and his neutral-density charm bracelet.

The reception desk itself was unmanned. In the middle of it sat a brass bell. Sharon dinged it. Nothing happened.

Rhys said, "Um?"

Miles said, "Perhaps we are a little late ... "

Sharon dinged the bell again, louder.

Silence.

Silence in the reception, silence in the workshop, silence in the stairwell, silence in the street. Thick, World's End silence, that brooked not an atom stirring out of place, not a footfall on unclean soil.

"Right!" exclaimed Sharon. It was the "right" of righteousness, of problems to be solved and adventures had, of mysteries to be unlocked and – yes – for grave and terrible dangers to be endured in the cause of ... well, of equal opportunities, open minds and broad community support. So saying, the shaman marched forward to the small white door, paused by the sign warning her about all the protective equipment she should be wearing, considered her options, shrugged, and pushed the door open.

It, too, opened easily. At once the smell of strong cleaning products hit Rhys and slithered their throat-drying stench down to the pit of his lungs. Grey energy-efficient light, this time for illumination rather than art, deadened the space beyond the door with its dull glow. The thick carpet of the reception area became harsh concrete; the walls were painted a deep green. Sharon pushed through a hanging barrier of rubber straps like the entrance to a butcher's shop, and stepped out into a cavern.

It was a cavern, she decided, because the ceiling was high overhead – far, far too high for Chelsea – but the floor was so far below, a darker blackness almost out of sight, tiny and pinched in by the weight of wall above it. Gantries and stairs zigzagged between each other, creating dozens of slot-in floors hanging off chains from the walls, and, on each new level, technical and occasionally mystical apparatus had been neatly set out: great blue-glowing refrigerators and the polished ivory of a siren's skull, bleached peroxide white; trays of plastic pipettes and rubber gloves, and the engine torn from the heart of a still-smoking wreck. The stairs, Sharon suspected, were purely for show: great shipwright-thick lengths of chain dangled between every floor, their rusting iron coated with traces of a blue-grey slime that might well have come from tentacles curling round the supporting metal. Rhys peered over her shoulder, gasped, "Well, no one seems to be . . ." and stopped. His eye fell on something hunched and grey, one rolling curve just visible above the edge of a table top.

Sharon moved forward, the metal stair ringing loudly beneath her feet, the first gantry swaying ever so slightly as she stepped onto it. The shadows of this place were full of echoes, almost strong enough to be visible. The flash of a crowbar as it struck the floor, discharging the spell which had run out of all control within the tortured metal. The smash of glass as a beaker exploded, spilling out still-burning oil which rippled into the grinning features of a petrol elemental who leered and spat before worming his way into freedom. The slither of great bloated bodies, supported on huge tentacles that sucked and clung to the chains strung between the room, as three scylla sisters cracked jokes about cracking bones, and cackled together as they worked.

Something else, too.

Half listen and there it is, the tiny, almost imperceptible *chink, chink, chink,* as of glass still falling. Not then, not even in the near future, but *now.*

Sharon rounded the table and there she lay, a scylla, tentacle-legs spilt around her like the shawl of a skirt, great bloated belly and chest flattened by their own weight as they lay across the floor, grey skin of scales encrusted with mineral growths and fungal crustations, dull and matt in the dim light. She'd fallen on her side, eyes open, jaw apart, her hairless head resting on the metal floor, but her face, tiny above the swollen mounds of her body, was human, old, lined with frowns and laughter, and her blood, where it dripped through the grating beneath her, was crimson-black.

Miles, Sharon noticed, was growing talons at his fingers' ends;

she herself felt a sudden chill from the white and red badge in her pocket, and the burns still smarting on her bandaged hand. Rhys was turning his packet of antihistamines over and over, his feet tapping with sudden nervous energy. Sharon stepped between the splayed tentacles of the scylla, and peered closer at her flesh. Somewhere overhead, glass tinkled in the gloom; a chain swayed from side to side.

Something glimmered in the scylla's neck. Sharon reached down and eased it out. A shard of glass shimmered in her palm, the blood still bright and wet; and as her fingers ran along the cold surface there was,

FATHER!!!

The scream came so loud and suddenly in her mind that she dropped the piece of glass. It tumbled through the grate beneath her feet, bouncing and spinning its way down until, several floors below, it hit a metal table and shattered into dust.

Metal still swayed in the gloom. There were shadows overhead, above the bulbs that illuminated the workshops. Deep shadows that ran into jagged lines across the ceiling, among gantries where the lights hadn't been turned on. Or couldn't be turned on. Sharon stared up at them, looking for a shimmer of something, a hint of . . .

"Ms Li!" Rhys's voice, sharp and urgent. He was at the foot of the stairs down from the gantry where she stood, pointing. Two floors below, just visible through the grating, two more bodies lay, one on its back, the blood from its sister above dripping onto its belly; beside was another, face-down.

One of the sisters was still moving.

They clattered downstairs, Miles's skin casting a silver gleam. The two scyllas between them occupied nearly all the gantry, a mess of tentacles and swollen, crusted flesh. They had managed to twine their tiny stunted fingers into each other's hand, and lay there side by side, the barely living and the dead. Blood was everywhere, and on the back of the sister who had died, Sharon saw, through the welling blood and lacerated flesh, the glimmer of more glass. She tried to focus on the faces, saw a far younger sister, the mirror of her deceased siblings, staring up at her. Glass was lodged in the scylla's chest, in her throat; tiny embedded fragments glinted in her cheeks. Her breath came in great shudders which rolled through all her body. Sharon knelt beside her and whispered, "It's okay, we're here, we'll help. Miles!"

Miles was already fumbling for his mobile phone. "I'm calling Dr Seah."

The scylla's eyes were wide, her nostrils flaring. She tried to speak, and blood burst around the wound in her neck. Sharon looked desperately along the scylla's body, searching for somewhere obvious to begin, some wound that was worse than the others which she could treat. To her surprise, she found Rhys kneeling beside her. He reached out, and took the scylla's hand. "Hi," he whispered. "I'm almost a druid of the first circle. May I take away your pain?"

The scylla gave a slight nod, and even that caused her face to contract, her breath to heave, her body to ripple with exertion. Rhys half closed his eyes, and breathed out slowly. As he did, it seemed that the creature herself also began to exhale, to deflate, just a bit more than the requirements of normal breath. Sharon glanced down at the druid's hands and saw the tiny white plastic of the anti-histamines packet between his fingers. Two pills were missing.

"There," murmured Rhys. "Nothing to be worried about."

"Dr Seah is on her way." Miles's voice overhead was hard and worried. Something tinkled onto metal in the roof. The scylla's eyes snapped upwards at the sound.

"A doctor's coming," breathed Sharon. "You'll be okay."

A tiny twist of the neck, a tightening of the fingers held in Rhys's hands. "No . . . Life . . ." Her voice was soft, warm; surprisingly light, coming from such a giant creature.

"Don't be daft, of course you'll live."

"No . . . life! Without my sisters."

"What happened here? Who attacked you?"

"We made . . . "

"Yes?"

"We made him."

"You made who?"

The scylla's face tightened. Her breath was a high-pitched wheeze. "We kept!" she managed. "Kept it! Lied to them, kept it!"

"What did you make?" breathed Sharon.

"We made . . . *him*."

A swaying of chain, a tinkling of glass, closer now, it seemed; a breath of a breeze that should not have been.

"We made . . . god."

Something overhead went, *ting!*

The note was high and clear. It hummed away through the metalwork of the cavern. Sharon looked up, and something was looking back down at her. Something translucent, that shimmered in the night. Something which twisted, and turned, and had two bottle-green eyes, and fingers that clattered over each other as they flexed. Something alive.

For a second, she looked at it, and it looked at her, and neither moved. Then it turned its head, raised its back and burst into brilliant light.

"Run!" yelled Sharon. Leaping up, she dived straight into the grey embraces of the shadow walk. Miles was already turning silver-grey, the metal skin spilling across his body, black talons growing at his fingers' ends, ears drawing back, carbon smoke beginning to twist from his nostrils as, overhead, the creature raised itself on all fours, curved its back like a cat, and dropped.

It dropped down, straight through the grating, its body shattering into a thousand parts to fit through the holes, then coalescing back together as it landed, almost too fast to see. And its body was glass, and its head was glass, and its fingers were three pieces of curved crystal glass that slotted over each other like the armour of a knight's gauntlet, and its heart was blazing light and its eyes were green and shimmering like emeralds, and as it reassembled itself on the gantry before them, it opened its arms wide, like a welcoming mother, and roared.

Sharon dived down beneath the nearest table top as a torrent of shattered crystal glass erupted from the creature's belly and burst from its parted lips. It tore through the air above her, slamming thousands of bright splinters into the wall at her back. She raised her head and saw the light churn and twist in its middle as it opened its mouth again, and it occurred to her that invisibility wasn't the same as invulnerability.

Then something hot and metal leapt onto the creature's back, and tore at its face and neck with black talons and teeth, legs wrapped around its midriff as it bit and slashed and screamed. Somewhere beneath the spell, Sharon thought she saw the shape of Miles as he clung to the creature's back, but for all that he scratched and pounded and tore, the glass bones of the creature remained smooth, polished and bright, its attacker's claws sliding off like a sponge over stainless steel.

The creature turned on the spot a few times, bewildered by this half-dragon assailant on its back, then seemed to grow bored, and shrugged. The shrug sent Miles backwards, with his legs and arms flailing. Slamming shoulders-first into the opposite wall, he tumbled head downwards, onto the floor below. He landed with a crack, and stayed there, motionless.

The creature turned to Sharon. Though she was still in the shadows, it saw her, as clearly as she saw it. She gasped and dived deeper, scrambling away into the depths of the spirit walk, where the ghosts of the dead scyllas writhed and twitched around her, where the shadows of enchantments made and spells gone awry burst and popped in the air like myriad fireworks and here –

– here the glass creature blazed all the brighter, a lighthouse pushing back the dark, too bright to look at; as bright, perhaps, as the blue electric angels, except –

except here, when she looked, the body, which was evidently that of a man, here seemed to be that of a woman. And the light that consumed it wasn't so much light, as fire.

Then the creature opened its mouth, and the light in its belly twisted and rose upwards into a cloud of glass. Sharon gasped, and seeing nothing to hide behind, dropped.

She dropped straight through the gantry beneath her, as if it wasn't there, and landed one floor below, flopping clumsily onto her hands and knees while reality wobbled around her, trying to work out if it was really up for all of this. She looked to one side and saw

Miles sprawled at the bottom of the staircase, the dragon-skin retracted from his bones, eyes shut, a leg splayed out at the wrong angle.

Rhys was there, too, by the Alderman's side, having scrambled down a floor during the melee. He looked straight through Sharon, unable to perceive her, and then up, to where he very much could perceive the monster as its body split again into a thousand parts which rained down through the grating. It reassembled into its perfect, smooth glass body on the floor below, and straightened up to glare at Sharon.

She turned, looking for a way out, a wall to run through, and, as she did, Rhys straightened up, a confused look on his face. "Rhys!" she shouted, and for the first time, he too could see her.

"Ms Li?"

Then the glass creature opened its mouth and the air filled with razored raindrops, and there was no way to hide, and no time to hide, and no place, and there was . . .

"Um, now, this is rather awkward."

Sharon turned. Rhys stood between her and the creature, his hands raised, and he wasn't sneezing, wasn't coughing, wasn't snotty, but had before him a thin grey wall of liquid writhing concrete which had sprung from his fingers like a shield, deflecting the blizzard of glass to either side.

"The thing is, Ms Li," he explained, as the creature snarled and drew itself back for another blast, "antihistamines are wonderful things, but they do make me drowsy . . ."

This time, the force of glass against his concrete shield was hard enough to send him staggering back, his feet scrambling for purchase on the floor. Sharon slipped into visibility behind him, hissed, "Move towards Miles!"

"I'll certainly try, Ms Li." The glass creature hissed in frustration, and raised its hands in a gesture that, Sharon felt, could only result in bad news. The temperature in the room began to drop, and ripples ran through the monster's skin as the solid glass of its flesh began to liquefy, now bound together only by its own viscous weight. Shards of glass began to detach from it and rise, spiralling upwards to form a cocoon whose motion grew faster, and faster. Sharon grabbed the unconscious Miles by the arm, and Rhys by the sleeve.

The spinning mass of glass had grown so dense, she couldn't even see the figure behind it, could barely hear above its furious gnat-jangle of noise.

"Deep breath!" she exclaimed, and with a desperate gulp of air she pulled the two others through the nearest wall.

Chapter 56

Be Grateful for the Luck You're Given

Thickness.

Weight.

Depth.

A moment – a brief, eternal moment, as the air began to run out and the weight of reality closed in – when Sharon wondered if this was it, this was the wall too far, a wall that was in fact nothing more and nothing less than a sidestep into the earth's crust itself, where they would be crushed and buried, lost and out of sight for the rest of time.

Release.

It came, cold and sudden. She fell forward onto the damp ground, gasping for air as Rhys and Miles flopped down beside her. They were in darkness, black and unbroken. But the sound of her breath was hollow and the air was damp and frozen. She felt stones beneath her feet, thick and dirty, smelt ancient black dust, and, as she reached out tentatively to either side, her fingers brushed something metal. Smooth on top, rusted beneath. She ran her palm over the shape of it, and jerked her hand back with a gasp.

"Bloody hell!"

Her voice whispered back at her, *bloody hell, bloody hell, bloody hell,* as it raced away down the tunnel.

A flicker of tungsten-yellow light burst from Rhys's palm, faint and unsure of itself. He laid it to the surface of the metal thing, which burst with dull yellow light along its length, describing a straight bright line, off in either direction into the dark. Then he yawned, and gasped, "I'm so sorry, Ms Li!"

Sharon climbed to her feet, and stared down the tunnel. Contrary to her fears, there was no live rail on which she might have put her fingers, but, rather, a single track running between ancient, crusty brickwork. "It's okay, Rhys," she murmured. "You can't help it, if you've had your antihistamines."

He yawned again, managing both to expand his jaw and collapse his face in shame.

"How's Miles?" she asked.

Rhys crawled over to the unconscious Alderman. "Um . . . I think his leg is broken, Ms Li."

"Breathing?"

"Yes."

"That'll have to do. Now . . . where the bloody hell are we?"

Rhys looked up and down the tunnel. "Maybe it's disused?"

"Yeah, because that's all this evening needs to get better. You, me, an unconscious Alderman and a disused tunnel God knows where under the city. Your phone working?"

Rhys checked it. "No signal, Ms Li."

"Great."

"What do you want to do? I don't think we should move Miles. But if that thing . . . "

Sharon glanced back at the thick wall through which they'd passed. "I gotta say, if it can come through that, then it deserves to get us."

"Does it?" whimpered Rhys. "Ethically, I mean?"

To his surprise, Sharon grinned. She pressed her back to the wall, and slid down to the ground, tucking up her knees. "It's okay," she said. "I've got a plan."

"Do you, Ms Li? I mean, I don't doubt that you do, it wasn't a 'do you' as in I can't believe it, it was more of an enquiry ..." Rhys's words dissolved into another yawn.

Sharon's smile widened. "It's a great plan," she replied. "It involves sleeping."

Chapter 57

Scylla

We are
    the scylla sisters.
    We love
    each other
    so much
    though sometimes it hurts
    and sometimes it is joy
    and always
    together.
    We love each other.
    Because no one else will.

Chapter 58

It Will Come to You in Your Sleep

Sammy the Elbow was careful about what he dreamt. Dreams, after all, were dangerous bloody things, liable to get you into trouble if you didn't keep an eye on them. People could learn all sorts of shit from your dreams, but, most importantly, people could think they'd learnt all sorts of shit from your dreams. And then get it wrong. And then tell you you had a problem when, really, dreaming about fire-breathing hamsters had a perfectly rational explanation, if only they weren't so hung up on everything being complicated and . . .

Point was, if you were a shaman, and into the truth of things, you just had to set a few standards. And dreams, the undigested stuff of the subconscious mind, were about as true as true could be, even if no one quite knew what to make of that truth.

He was, therefore, rather surprised when, dreaming a particularly sagely dream about waiting for the 17 bus at Archway station with a chinchilla in a top hat and a woman who kept on saying "'blueberry!" at the top of her lungs, he felt someone tap him on the shoulder.

Sammy turned, and looked up into the smiling, grimy face of Sharon Li. Why his apprentice's face was grimy when she dream walked he had never really gone into, save that sometimes the unconscious mind manifested certain truths which even the sage-liest of sages found it polite to ignore.

"Oi oi," he blurted. "What you want?"

Sharon beamed. It occurred to him that, even for someone in the full throes of a dream walk, she had a particularly otherworldly quality.

"Sammy," she said, "how'd you like to be a hero?"

Chapter 59

Rest and Rejuvenate

There was a light at the end of the tunnel.

The light bounced up and down a while, and finally exclaimed, "Oi oi, soggy-brains!"

Sharon blearily opened her eyes. Somehow she'd fallen asleep against the wall of the tunnel, her head resting on Rhys's shoulder. Miles still lay unconscious on the track beside them, and as she struggled towards consciousness, an awareness suggested, through the cold in her fingers and numbness in her toes, that time had passed, and she had slept, and both these things had been fine. No – more than fine. Something more, something . . . safe. She sat up. Rhys smiled wanly, his shoulder bearing a Sharon-shaped indent.

"Oi!" The shrill voice of Sammy the Elbow, second greatest shaman to walk the earth, echoed down the tracks. "I do not make it a habit to rescue any apprentice what is too bloody thick to rescue themselves!"

For a moment, Sharon wondered if it would be all right to go straight back to sleep, right there.

"Soggy-brains!"

She crawled to her feet, bones grinding and limbs aching as

blood returned to her extremities. "Sammy!" Her voice bounced away down the tunnel. "Miles is hurt!"

More lights burst up behind the torch which Sammy was carrying. By their relative height about the goblin's light, the bearers were most likely human. Mostly. Then something great and grey and shambling briefly eclipsed the torches, and it was huge, and it was familiar, and it was . . .

"Gretel?"

Gretel, seven-foot-nothing of gourmet troll, her skin a lightly spined leather across flesh of pure muscle, each component of which had taken on the expectations of the universe and challenged them to get massive.

"Hello, Ms Li!" Gretel's voice rumbled down the tunnel, like the sound of trains once gone before. "Mr Elbow invited me to assist him in saving the day. I hope that's all right?"

Moving behind the goblin and the troll were more figures, Aldermen dressed in black, a couple carrying a stretcher, one marvelling at the fact that he had finally found a corner of the city where he couldn't get a signal on his mobile phone. "Mr Elbow," went on Gretel cheerfully, "said that you might be in need of a . . . a . . ."

"Great big lumbering wall of physical capability!" Sammy sang out. "That's what I said, innit?"

"Yes, Mr Elbow," murmured Gretel, not sure if that was how the goblin *had* phrased it. "Something like that."

Sharon sighed. Her mentor, despite having experienced, she felt, some really rather damaging prejudice, showed not just undeniable social defects in his daily life, but an attitude of casual contempt towards any other creature so pungent that she was sometimes worried it might rub off onto her.

Aldermen now filled the tunnel. Towards the unconscious Miles, they manifested an extraordinary professionalism and cool, which suggested that among the things they dealt with, injury was hardly novel. Sharon lurked in the dark as one of the Aldermen, a pleasant-faced woman wearing latex gloves, examined her for injury.

She said, "How's Miles?"

"Broken leg; possibly some fractured ribs. They're taking him to hospital to have a scan of his skull – just a precaution." The Alderman added, "I'm sure it'll be fine. He's a very strong young man."

They drifted out of the tunnel. It was a long way, Sharon discovered, particularly in the torch-crossed dark. A rusted metal door, narrow and forgotten, led to a tight, twisted stair which wound up and up through damp, mould-covered walls to another metal door, where the chain had been broken and the padlock torn away to let it open in a brick wall set almost where they had begun: Sloane Square. The lights of the nearby theatre still shone, inviting audiences to enjoy the latest hit; the department stores and designer outlets were illuminated beneath the tall trees; the traffic lights blinked around the crowded one-way system. The sudden brightness, though mostly just from streetlights and their orange glow reflecting off the clouds above, hit almost as hard as the smell, or, rather, the non-smell, the cessation of the tunnels' damp, sticky stench. The Aldermen had claimed a section of road for their own by the tunnel entrance; on the double red no-parking lines there stood a couple of cars and a small utility truck, complete with kettle and a tiny TV. Four orange cones, and some yellow tape around this scene of illegality, warned any traffic warden to steer clear.

Kelly Shiring stood in front of the truck, ready with a cup of tea. With her was Sammy the Elbow, his head barely reaching her hips, the grubby sleeves of his hoodie trailing at his side. As the others emerged from the darkness, Kelly exclaimed, "Ms Li!" and thrust the tea into Sharon's hands.

"You must be exhausted, just exhausted, what a terrible night. Now, I've arranged rooms in the nearest hotel I could find. It's only four-star, but they've opened the kitchens for you and I've asked that they heat the bath."

Sharon's mouth was dangling open. So, she noticed, was Sammy's, with rather more profound effect, as it revealed the dental nightmare of the goblin's gullet for all the world to see.

"A room . . . in a hotel? Why does she get a room in a hotel?" he squealed. "I went and bloody found 'em both, didn't I? I did the whole 'they're in this tunnel thing needin' rescuing' crap, I'm the teacher, I'm the hero of the frickin' hour! Why do *they* get a frickin' hotel room?"

Kelly's face opened in horror and consternation. "Mr Elbow, sir, you're so right! I do apologise, I hadn't even considered – how senseless of me. Would you find a single acceptable, or shall I try for the suite?"

Sammy's eyes narrowed, searching the Alderman's earnest face for some symptom of mockery, of sarcasm, of a practical joke being played. Finding none, he mumbled, deflating a little, "No, it's okay, I wouldn't want anyone to go to trouble for me, not the hero of the hour, not the second greatest shaman ever, you don't worry . . ."

"Oh, but Mr Elbow! I absolutely must, I insist, I feel so guilty about having not even considered it, the best – absolutely, the best. Do just give me a moment . . ."

So saying, she pulled out her mobile phone and, treating them to one last dazzling smile, turned to find a quiet corner and make the arrangements.

Sharon, Rhys and Sammy stood on the pavement by Sloane Square, as Sharon's tea grew cold. Sharon said, "Well." This not quite hacking it, she added, "You know, maybe being deputy Midnight Mayor isn't so rubbish after all."

"Hah!" exclaimed Sammy, gesturing with his arms to express the indignation his vocabulary couldn't muster. "It may be all hotels and tea and stuff now, but just you wait 'till it's blood and screamin' and gettin' stuck down in dirty tunnels beneath the city; then you'll come runnin' again, just like you always do."

"Do I? Have I come running before?"

"Yeah! You came runnin' with the Tribe, ain't you?"

"Yes, but then you didn't come with us."

"I showed you the way."

"But we faced the Tribe, and Swift, and Old Man Bone without you."

"I did the important bit! Facilitating, that's what I did! Look . . ." Sammy hopped from foot to foot, nostrils puffing. " . . . I could've just left you down in that tunnel with the squelchy Alderman and the snot-nosed druid . . . "

"Oh, I don't know if that's really . . . " began Rhys.

" . . . but I didn't, did I? Cos even though I'm basically undervalued by all you ignorant nits, I still got class even when no one else got none of their own!"

Sharon considered her options. There was a part, a not insignificant part, which was tempted to argue back, to turn round and say, yes, of course, saving us from being stuck in a tunnel was really good of you but, actually, class would be doing it and not shouting about it afterwards, that's what class is, a kind of casual brilliance rather than a lot of hard work, which isn't to say we're not grateful, of course we're grateful, it's just that gratitude is a finite commodity and you're really . . .

What she actually said was, "I've never been to a four-star hotel before."

Which, for now, would have to do.

Chapter 60

Wake and Feel Restored

She wakes and she screams.

She screams and screams and screams until her father holds her and she says, "I'm sorry I'm sorry they fled they fled I didn't know where they went I couldn't see they just ran and they were gone and I was scared and so tired so tired and they ran away and I couldn't I couldn't make them . . ."

He strokes her hair and whispers, "It's all right. You did very well. I'm very proud of you."

"Daddy?"

"Yes, my love?"

"Are they going to come after us now? Now that I've failed?"

"No, my love. They won't."

"But they ran. They ran through the wall and I couldn't, I couldn't, it wasn't . . ."

"They won't find us. And if they do . . . I'm ready for them now."

Chapter 61

Everyone Needs Me Time

It was a four-star hotel.

She could tell it was a four-star hotel, because the bath was bigger than the bed she usually slept in, and from the windows – many windows, no less – in her room she could see the London Eye and Big Ben.

Someone had warmed the bath in advance.

She sunk into it as the sun began to rise over London, and wondered if it was bad form, considering the death, and the torment, and the lingering threat of catastrophe hanging over the city, to go to sleep for a bit. What would *Management for Beginners* suggest? She felt fairly certain that working your team to death wasn't an efficient use of human resources. Then again, she also felt certain that deadlines had to be met, and achievements achieved, even if this sometimes forced senior management to make hard decisions. Certainly, not getting into the great double bed, warm and soft and turned down in one corner ready for her presence, was going to be a tough decision, possibly the toughest so far. Then again, that was the whole point. That was why she was in charge.

Someone – almost certainly Kelly – had laid out warm, fresh

clothes on the end of the bed. She climbed into them, one limb at a time as the sun slipped upwards over the city, and the sound of buses fighting with taxis for space in the streets below drifted up through the trees. She had to sit on the edge of the bed to put her shoes on, and the mattress was soft and deep, a great big soft falling waiting to happen beneath her, an infinite warmth of . . .

There was a knock on the door. "Good morning, Ms Li!" sang out Kelly's indefatigable voice. "Meeting in the breakfast room?"

They had a meeting in the breakfast room.

Kelly had arranged for a part of the room itself, a great hall of crystal glass and ivory ceramics, to be separated off from the general dining area with a panelled screen, permitting Sammy the Elbow to shimmer into full and unwashed visibility as he perched on his seat at the end of the table, and for Gretel, usually masked behind the perception-blurring walls of a chameleon spell, to unmask and proclaim, "Is that . . . pâté?"

Gretel the gourmet troll, for whom the diet of old cheeseburgers and undercooked rat was no longer quite good enough, sat on a chair which could barely accommodate her bulk, held cutlery between her fingers like a toothpick in a titan's hand, and tried her very best not to splatter fresh yoghurt up the walls as she ate. Sharon was, to her mild embarrassment, the last to arrive at the breakfast table, which, besides the troll and the goblin, consisted of Rhys, Kelly and two other Aldermen she didn't recognise, but who seemed determined to minute everything that was said and quite possibly every cup of coffee that was drunk, on little laptops balanced on their knees.

"Hi, there!"

Kelly Shiring gleamed with hearty good-morning vibes as Sharon took her place at table. "Good morning, good morning," she added, impaling a piece of watermelon on her fork, and waving it in greeting. "Please, tuck in!"

Sharon cautiously did so. Rhys was already on his second dish of scrambled eggs, and showed no sign of slowing for the corners. Sammy had managed to steal three tubes of toothpaste since arriving in the hotel, and was now carefully sampling each one on the end of his tongue. Gretel was seeing if green grapes and bacon worked together as a combination, and, by the expression on her face, was making as thorough a mental note of the outcome as the two Aldermen with their laptops.

"You'll be thrilled to know," Kelly explained as Sharon hungrily speared a sausage, "that we've sent a team to seal off Scylla Workshops and, on inspection, there have been no sightings of . . . how did you describe it, Rhys?"

"A great big glowing glass monster?" suggested the druid.

"Exactly! Of a great big glowing glass monster."

"It's gone?" queried Sharon, wondering if it was okay for senior management to talk and eat at the same time.

"It's gone!" concurred Kelly. "Although when I say 'gone' I have no doubt that it will reappear in suitably frustrated and furious form at some point yet to come. But for now, I think we can all feel very satisfied."

"But . . . it *killed* the scylla sisters."

"Yes, that is very sad. We do have a team arranging a suitable burial and flowers, don't we?" she added, turning to the two Aldermen with their laptops. A brisk nod was all the reply she received.

"How's Miles?"

Kelly's smile didn't alter, so much as lock into place. "He's fine," she said. "He's going to be in a cast for a while, and I don't think he's going to be helping with the investigation for a little, but he's fine. He'll be . . . fine."

She added, "I'm sure everyone will be delighted to hear that Mr Swift – or what's left of him – hasn't destroyed anything organic in the last few hours, although we have had a few complaints about noise pollution. So all that's left is the decontamination of the workshop facility and a consideration of our next plan of action."

There was a silence. It was the busy silence of people chewing their food in the hope that this would be contribution enough. Then Rhys raised a hand. "Um, excuse me?"

"Of course!"

"I know I'm only an IT manager," he said, "but there's something about people all in black saying decontamination, see, which really makes my nose itch."

"Actually," mumbled Sharon, through a mouthful of toast, "I'm kinda with Rhys on this one. It's like when people say 'terminated' and they mean 'dead', or 'on leave' and they mean 'fired', and that."

"Oh no!" exclaimed Kelly. "Absolutely not! I mean, there's a whole volume, isn't there, on the value or otherwise of these politically correct phrases – I, for example, would far rather discuss vampires *passing on* instead of being staked through the heart with a sharpened stick, as it just gives such a negative spin on proceedings. But when I say decontaminate in this context, what I mean is that the workshops are such a den of mystic afterglow, we'll be lucky if there aren't twelve-foot-long sewer worms evolving beneath it as we speak!"

Sharon whimpered, "Twelve-foot-long sewer worms?"

Sammy kicked her under the table. "Don't be thick! Obviously, twelve-foot-long sewer worms! Don't show me up by being a pink squishy ignorant nit!"

Sharon's expression of disgust dissolved into one of displeasure. "If I don't know important stuff," she said, "it's because you haven't taught it to me yet! Don't go round blaming *me* for being ignorant!"

"I hadn't heard of sewer worms either," offered Rhys. "But I'm sure they're quite rare, aren't they?"

"Oh yes!" exclaimed Kelly. "Well, quite! Well, in some places!"

In the silence that followed, the goblin glared at Sharon, Sharon glared at Sammy, Rhys kept his head down and Gretel politely paused in eating. Kelly cleared her throat, and added, "Let's think of the decontamination as merely an aside, shall we? Perhaps if we focus on . . ."

"Actually," said Sammy, smearing toothpaste onto the palm of his hand, ready to be licked clean by his great grey tongue, "I think decontaminating the workshops is really thick. Just saying."

"Do you, Mr Elbow?" Kelly's look was as earnest as ever. "Of course, your insight is always welcome at this table!"

"Just saying, shamans – even marshmallow-brains over there," another kick at Sharon's shins, "aren't so hot at seeing shit once you've gone and decontaminated a thingy. You wanna leave it all messy and raw, then we can go in there, see stuff you're all too pig-stupid to pick up on, solve everythin' and bugger off home again, proper professional like."

Kelly's eyes drifted from Sammy, to the rather more reassuring face of Sharon. Sharon shrugged. "Look," she said, "it's not like I was given many options when it came to picking my mentor, okay? And, I'm not gonna lie here, it would've been nice to have someone tall, handsome, maybe just a little bit rugged, who could've come and swept me off my feet while saying, 'Hey there, Sharon, you're, like, totally a shaman, let's get it on' or something. Which isn't to say . . . point is . . . Sammy may be small, and smelly, and have the manners of a verruca, but he is usually right about this magic shit."

Kelly's smile could have guided a lost ship home on a stormy night. "Fantastic! Then I guess we hold off on the decontamination, and go for shaman power instead! More melon, anybody?"

Chapter 62

Time Stands Still for No Man

The sun crawls up over London, and in a basement deep beneath an office in the Golden Mile, a no-longer-man lies on the floor and dreams of . . .

we we we we we we we beeeeeee

beeeee

beeee weeeee

weeeee beeeeeee

free?

No. Not quite right. Not any more. It had been true once, but now, in this place, suffocating under the weight of painted magics, drowning on the floor, it is something else, it is, it *is* . . .

weeeee beeeeeeeeeeee

trapped?

burning?

breaking apart?

Dying.

It is not a fit concept for a god, and so they do not name it. But that is what it is, what will come, if only they had the humanity left inside them to comprehend it.

*

And on the edge of the old plague pits of Bunhill Fields, Arthur Huntley, sometime wizard, turned gravekeeper, stands with his scarf tied over his nose and mouth and looks down at the freshly turned earth in which the white bones are beginning to pop out from the tattered, stinking soil, and half imagines he can see the thousand writhing microbes of the bubonic plague as it wriggles out from the rotted flesh of its victims, buried so long ago, and wonders, if he was a shaman, and into that thing, whether he would hear the racing heart of Old Man Bone as he stirs beneath the soil and whispers, and roars . . .

GIVE ME WHAT I'M OWED!!

And in a telephone exchange in Zambia, a line clicks and a string of words flickers across a screen, on their way to somewhere else.
help me help me help me help me help me
    Simultaneously, a lawyer in New York City is surprised to receive a text message which cries out from an unknown number in a far-off land
help me!
    while a computer server in New Delhi tries, and fails, to block a firewall intrusion that briefly turns all the screens in the office black, then blue, then bursts the glass from the inside out, on its way to somewhere else.
    This disruption, this global decay, has been going on for several days now. If anyone had bothered to monitor it, they would have considered it a curious example of the pervasive, global nature of telecommunications and the errors, the rogue signals, which can sometimes be produced. However, owing to the very same global nature of the network, no one does, and so no one did.
    If someone had, they might have also been interested to notice that the signal was getting weaker.

And in World's End, in fact nothing more nor less than an unremarked corner of zone two of the London transport network, Sharon Li stood once more outside Scylla Workshops in the hard light of day, and reminded herself that just because her last encounter with the place had ended in broken glass and blood, that didn't mean today would go the same way.

The reassuring bulk of Gretel loomed behind her, and Sharon wondered at what point in her career the presence of a troll had become a comfort. She took a deep breath, and strode forward, down into the gloom of the workshop.

Aldermen were everywhere, many of them prominently armed. Sharon wasn't sure what good their weapons would do, should the glass man choose to return. But then, as Kelly had pointed out . . .

"If this glass monster is able to destroy *all of us* as well as your good self, Ms Li, then frankly there's nothing to be done and we may as well not worry about it! Isn't that a comforting notion?"

At the shaman's side, Sammy now grumbled and sniffed. "Enchanters. Never tidy their auras up afterwards, amateur wankers."

Sharon sighed. The bodies of the three scylla sisters had been removed, tidied away to who knew what fate. She hoped it was a good one, nothing medical, maybe a nice plot, or, rather, three plots, all together, with flowers. "All right, Sammy," she said. "Whatcha see?"

"Enchantment enchantment enchantment wank," he tutted, knocking against tables and scorning apparatus as they made their way through the bowels of the workshop. "This is interesting, though." They'd come to a wall, where a blast from the glass man's lungs had left shards embedded in the very stones. Sammy picked at one, muttering, "Magic magic magic spell spell glass glass glass ow!"

He snatched his finger back. A tiny bead of blood welled up at the end. "Bloody monsters and their bloody weapons of destruction! Tossers!"

"When I looked at the glass man in the spirit walk," explained Sharon, patiently handing the goblin a tissue, "he looked like a girl."

"Yeah," sighed Sammy. "Elemental construct like that'd probably take the shape of the thing what feeds it."

"Elemental construct . . . and feeding it? I mean, there's a 'what the fuck' at the start of that, but I figured you'd know that."

Sammy gave a sigh of exasperation. "Don't talk so loud," he hissed. "I don't want everyone else knowing how pig-ignorant my student is; *mine!* People'll think I'm no good!"

Sharon glanced over her shoulder at where Gretel was doing her best not to look like an overly interested bodyguard. She lowered her voice and her posture to a more convenient level for the goblin and hissed, "Okay. So tell me."

"Thing what attacked you," grumbled Sammy. "Made of glass, kinda unstoppable, force of deadly death and that?"

"Yessss . . ."

"Glass elemental. Summoned thingy, like tossers sometimes summon neon elementals or copper elementals or that shit. Glass is tricky to summon, I mean, to summon it right that is. Needs a lot to fuel it, to keep it moving, keep it ticking over."

"To feed it?"

"Yeah."

"I'm guessing we're not talking lamb bhuna and a coupla poppadoms?"

Sammy glowered. "You ask thick questions because you know the answer, right, but are just hoping you're wrong, yeah? I mean, you're not *actually* thick, are you, it's just this stupid human thing, yeah?"

Sharon's smile was old and worn out. "You're the knower of the truth, Sammy."

He grunted, then said, "The feeding it. Yeah, you gotta feed an elemental to keep it alive. Neon elemental you gotta feed with light; copper you feed with electricity; but glass elemental . . . glass elemental is kinda tricky. Gotta feed it with something better, something bigger."

"Like . . . ?"

"Bit of this, bit of that. Touch of blood, years of life, dollop of mortal bodily strength, you know. Depends on the binding, innit. What you're seein' – this girl you thought you seen in the spirit walk . . ."

"I did see her, she was there."

"Yeah, whatever. You probably saw the bird what's feedin' this thing. Givin' it her life, so as it can live. Nasty wizarding stuff, very shoddy, but I never got the human thing anyway."

"So the creature's being controlled?"

"Duh. You're tired, right, not thick?"

"I am," she agreed. "Very, very tired."

"You gotta look out for that. Easy to cock up when knackered."

"Thank you, Sammy."

"I'm here to mentor and shit."

"Ms Li?" The voice came from Rhys, and it came from above. "Ms Li, I think you should look at this!"

Rhys was waiting at the very top of the stairs. A door, which in all the excitement of the night before Sharon hadn't even noticed, stood ajar in what she supposed had to be called the ceiling of the cavern. "Ms Li," the druid exclaimed. "You have to see this!"

Sharon followed him through the door. Beyond was an office like any other, but at its far end a pair of enterprising Aldermen had pulled open a heavy door, metal, thicker than her bedroom wall. The wards that had guarded it were still fizzing angrily around the hinges and lock. Beyond the door was what could only be termed a vault.

Shelves lined every wall, ten rows high. On some were ledgers, records, notes of monies received and spent, ranging from commissions for crafting items of great power, through to last week's receipt from the grocery order delivered to their door; for the scylla sisters were hardly great attendees at the local supermarket. Beyond that, the shelves sagged under the weight of what could only be magical artefacts. There, a jar containing the stolen light snatched from the dying embers of the last gas lamp to go out; here, a pot of living, writhing coal dust seized from the chimney stacks where the flames had fanned the dirt into a living curse. There, a penknife whose blade had been anointed with the blood of the albino pigeon, whose very sight induced terror in its enemies. The gutted remains of an ancient piano, whose strings, bound up carefully in a padded box, still sung the tunes from the old music halls. The collapsed fender of a car which struck the acrylic-painted flank of a unicorn as it crossed the road, and whose driver died from the dehydration induced by his own tears. The black wing of a raven from the Tower, still beating against the glass that held it, though no body was attached. The torn-off claw from a wendigo: Sharon briefly wondered, which wendigo, how fresh the claw? A few fibres from a pinstripe suit once worn by the Death of Cities, before he dissolved into the single parking penalty notice, kept beneath three layers of lead and two of magic at the very back of the very highest shelf. The ground-up grains of devil's blood, hissing against the white ceramic that held it; the ring that had been pulled from the finger of a dead sorcerer who'd been flung from the top of a tower off Tottenham Court Road; a tiny shimmer of yellow fairy dust, which stirred against the glass and whispered, *alive*...

Anything and everything which hissed, glowed, tinkled or seethed with magical potential, the sisters had collected over the years, snatching traces of one thing to create another, piling their shelves high with the tools of their trade and creating in the process a veritable Manhattan Project of mystic goods. And there, at the centre of it all, wrapped up carefully in oilskin and with a paper label hanging off it, a very thin, rusted blade. A neat hand had written of it:

Handle With Care

Sharon's eyes fell on it instantly – even in this place, it hummed with power, almost audible to her. The thing was barely a blade at all, but had over the years been honed down and down to a sharp point, which could have fitted perfectly into the end of an umbrella.

No one seemed to want to touch it.

"Okay," said Sharon. "Sammy?"

The goblin spluttered. "What with me being so sensitive to the basic forces of the universe, you'll understand if I don't go around handling mystically charged objects!"

She turned to Rhys. "Rhys?"

"Oh, um, well, if you want me to touch the sacred blade of the god of the plague pits which has been used for sacrificing living people for thousands of years, then I suppose I will because someone should, but, um, if that's what you want ..."

Sharon threw her hands up in despair. "You guys are so . . ."

Gretel picked up the blade. For a second, the world held its breath, waiting for the troll to vanish, combust, explode or anything else which would have seemed mystically appropriate. Gretel considered the thing in her hands then said, "Is this what all the confusion has been about?"

Rhys sneezed.

"Uh . . . yeah, basically," muttered Sharon. "You're not . . . feeling the urge to take your shoes off, are you, Gretel?"

Gretel stared at Sharon, struggling to comprehend this new and unexpected enquiry. Then, just to confirm her own opinion, she looked down at her feet, then back up at Sharon. "But I'm not wearing any shoes, Ms Li."

"Good point."

"Would you like . . . ?" She held out the blade, and the room recoiled in horror.

"No, no!" cried Sharon. "I think . . . I think you should definitely hold on to it! I mean, where better, in fact? Just . . . um. Just don't cut yourself. Or anyone else with it, will you?"

"All right, Ms Li," replied the troll amiably. "I wasn't intending to anyway."

"Shouldn't we give it back to Crompton?" hissed Rhys in Sharon's ear, as Gretel turned to examine the rest of the shelves. "I mean, if it *is* the blade of Old Man Bone . . ."

"What, so he can go around sacrificing people again?" Sharon demanded. "That kinda sounds wank."

"But the plague pits . . . the foul odours . . . the death . . . ?"

"I'm not saying I've got a better idea," she replied. "I'm just saying we shouldn't go rushing in with a cry of 'whoopee human sacrifice'. Besides, we still don't know what the fuck the blade is doing here, with the scylla sisters."

"Maybe they stole it?"

"Yeah, because there's nothing like three dead scyllas in Chelsea to make you think 'case closed'."

Rhys looked dismayed. "Oh dear. Does this mean we can't go home yet?"

Sharon patted him on the shoulder. "I think you've been, like, really good, so far."

He beamed with delight. "Thank you, Ms Li. I mean, I'm only trying to fulfil my job obligations, and of course, I'm immensely satisfied to be contributing to the wider community . . ."

"Oi oi, dribble-nose."

Sammy stood in the door, holding up a small plaster slab.

"Soggy-brains!" shrilled the goblin, and this time it was a command, as much as an accusation. Sharon peered closer. The plaster slab, larger almost than the goblin's hands, contained an indent which was, unmistakably, the same size and shape as the rusted blade now in Gretel's hand.

Chapter 63

Keep an Open Mind

"Absolutely not!"

Arthur Huntley, ex-wizard and part-time scholar, stood in the doorway of the small warden's hut in Bunhill Fields, and lectured. He lectured three people who he could see – Rhys, Sharon and Kelly, and perhaps he sensed, or at the very least smelt, the fourth and fifth, Sammy and Gretel, lurking just below perception in the shadowlands where the shaman walks.

"The idea is ridiculous!" he exploded. "Talk to Crompton; he'll tell you!"

"Yeah, the guy who sacrifices people for an undead god?" muttered Sharon. Her nose wrinkled as she contemplated the gathering clouds overhead. They threatened rain, proper downpour rain which turned the streets into bubbling waterways and sent sheets of water pouring over the sides of bus shelters. Perhaps, she thought, it would at least help wash away the smell, which in Bunhill Fields was growing so intense it threatened to wipe away even the prevailing stench of unwashed goblin. Rotting flesh, it turned out, trumped poor bodily hygiene.

"The notion," exclaimed Arthur, "of anyone making a *copy* of Old Man Bone's blade is absurd."

"Why?"

This question seemed to appal Arthur, mostly because he didn't have an answer. He floundered for a moment, before exclaiming, "Because what would it achieve? If you copy over the enchantments from Old Man Bone's blade to another vessel, then all you'll do when you use it is feed more souls to Old Man Bone. So what's the point?"

"Maybe there's something wrong with the original blade?" offered Rhys.

"Then why was Crompton all worked up about it?" mused Sharon. "What if they altered it somehow, I mean like . . . what if they used the enchantment on the original blade, and copied it to a new blade, but adapted it."

"Absurd," insisted Arthur. "Ridiculous. Dangerous."

"But what would it achieve? If it could be done?"

He hesitated, as the first drizzle began to slide in feathery silence from the skies. It was still early in Bunhill Fields, the traffic rushing by outside, men and women heading to work. Finally, "I don't like to speculate."

Sharon sighed. Magicians, she was beginning to suspect, were as petty and prideful as university scholars when it came to their academic reputations. "Fine," she grumbled. "We'll ask Crompton, and maybe get Mr Roding to have a look at it."

"It?" There was a sharpness in Arthur's voice, an alertness that cut through the rising tap dance of the rain. "So you have the original blade?"

"Pretty much."

"Excellent! Please, give it to Crompton at once – the stink here is becoming overwhelming."

Sharon smiled thinly. "Yeah," she muttered. "Kinda noticed that."

As the rain became heavier, they huddled in a downwind doorway from Bunhill Fields. Sammy and Gretel slipped back into brief visibility, before Kelly cried, "Oh, but think of the neighbours!" at which point they vanished again, to nothing more than voices on the breeze.

"Should've kept the umbrella," Sharon grumbled, as the rain began to drum on the paving stones and burst from the mouths of downpipes.

"Do you really think the sisters copied the blade?" asked Rhys. "I mean, it doesn't seem very wise . . . "

"Rhys, I swear I'm working on a worst-case scenario kinda vibe here, since it seems that's all we're good for."

"Ms Li." Kelly's voice was forthright without being overkeen; determined without being stressed. "What do you propose now?"

Sharon thought about it. "Okay, so I think it's probably best if Gretel hangs on to the blade for now, just cos she's got no shoes to throw over things, and she's a seven-foot troll, and I kinda think this makes her seriously qualified. Sammy? Can you stay with Gretel, please? Just to keep an eye on the unseen stuff?"

"I am not," grunted Sammy, "an errand goblin!"

"Yeah." Sharon fixed her best smile on the empty space where she felt Sammy's face most likely to be. "You're a wise, brilliant, clever, generally groovy goblin, and I'd only trust someone as amazing as you are to keep an eye on this mega-mystic artefact with Gretel, so if you don't mind . . . ?"

Sammy's silence was expressive in both its sulkiness, and consent.

"Are we going to talk to C-C-Crompton?" asked Rhys.

"Not yet. Can you get in touch with Mr Roding? Ask him to have a look at the blade, and maybe also the workshops, see if he can pick up on something we've missed? And maybe drop Kevin and Sally a line."

"The . . . vampire?" enquired Kelly. "I mean, I don't want to judge, of course, but perhaps . . . ?"

"I'm just thinking ahead, which is like . . . managerial and that," Sharon replied. "I'm thinking we nearly got ourselves kicked to shit last night in the workshops, and someone's summoned a glass elemental, and maybe copied a mega-mystic blade from a mega-mystic umbrella, and this is exactly the kinda time when you wanna have a vampire, a banshee and a necromancer all on standby with a packet of digestive biscuits, a cuppa tea and a bazooka."

"Oh!" Kelly brightened with satisfaction. "I can provide both tea and bazookas, in liberal quantities!"

Sharon's smile didn't falter. She had the exhausted look, Rhys mused, of a woman who was standing up only by an accident of gravitational neglect. "Well," she said, "I'm thinking we might need lotsa both. Also, if the Aldermen can, like, go through the scylla sisters' records and see if they can find anything which says 'massive commission to replicate mystic artefact here' or something, that'd be, like, totally helpful."

"Of course. We shall go through the receipts with a fine-tooth comb. What about yourself, Ms Li?"

Sharon smiled wanly. "Well, judging by the smell round here, I'm guessing it's time to go Midnight Mayory on this shit. Rhys?"

"Yes, Ms Li?"

"You're with me."

Chapter 64

Lay Out Your Agenda Clearly

Sharon stood by the churned-up graves of Bunhill Fields, and tried not to retch. On the edge of the tree-shaded graveyard – on the upwind edge – Rhys was on his mobile phone, calling up every member of Magicals Anonymous who might be useful against a rampaging glass monster, or know something about plague, or who just felt like an interesting evening out of the house/flat/lair/den, and he was trying not to look concerned. He tried not to look concerned even when, out of the corner of his eye, he saw Sharon crouch beside the gash of mud and broken bones torn up nearby and cautiously run her fingers through the soil, nor when she started to go invisible.

Meanwhile, Sharon whispered, "Righto, chummy, we gotta chat," and slipped the whole way into invisibility.

The city turned to grey around her, and all things which the eye did not want to perceive were now visible. She looked down at the earth, and the dead stared right back at her. Thousands of them, piled up beneath her feet, grinning their lipless grins, flesh tunnelled by worms, bones woven together to form a pyre beneath her feet; the dead of the city, thousands of years of dead, turned in their graves, and were watching.

The air was heavy with their stench, even here, where usually everything was cold and clear and, as she moved, thin grey-green vapours stirred around her, the stinking smog of Old Man Bone, rising from the ground, imperceptible to the naked eye, but undeniable to a shaman's gaze.

"Right," she murmured, as flesh shifted beneath her feet. "Okay." Then she raised her voice. "Oi! Old Man Bone! We kinda gotta have a talk!"

Her voice fell away.

She cleared her throat, got a pungent whiff of the dead, and regretted it. "Seriously, Old Man Bone, I get that you're annoyed, but there's other shit going down here. And I know it's not fair for you to have to take some of the crap for that, but in these difficult times we all gotta pull together, so if you could, like, hold off on the unleashing of the plague pits and that, it'd be totally amazing of you."

Beneath her feet, bone creaked, and those few faces of the dead that had eyes left in their sockets stared at her in eyelidless surprise. Sharon sighed. "Oh yeah," she went on, "I think, like, someone's copied your sacred blade and is feeding on the power which should sustain you."

Something moved beneath her feet, the ground shifting. Skulls twisted aside, ancient brown ribcages split like twigs, soil broke and spluttered black clouds upwards, great plumes of stinking fog rose like geysers from the earth and all at once he was there, bursting from the ground like oil from the well, vapours spinning around him, off him out of his ragged clothes, his tendon-tight skin rippling into place over his hunched old bones, his bare toes digging into the grime of rotting flesh and dirt beneath his feet. He burst out right in front of Sharon, splattering her with mud and she dared not think what else, and in the spirit walk he was blazing with fury, rolling clouds of stench and dirt spiralling round him like a whirlwind that lashed and twisted his ragged clothes with every word as he snarled, he roared,

"THEY WOULD NOT DARE!"

Sharon waited for the noise to pass. Then, unable to stop herself, she coughed, the cough of someone whose nose had been assaulted too recently by too much, and who, having no "off" switch for smell, was falling back on mere exhalation. "Sorry," she spluttered, flapping ineffectually at the vapours wreathing round her head, even as Old Man Bone creaked and twisted before her, the grey boundaries of reality rippling before the might of his indignation. "Totally unprofessional moment here . . . "

She fumbled for a tissue, and spat into it; then muttered, "Uch. That was, like, totally useless." Old Man Bone, incredulous, billowed before her, flesh knitting and unknitting in uncertainty as his rage tore at the air. Sharon folded the tissue, put it in her pocket, smiled up wanly at the raging creature and said, "Hi again. So, um, I don't know if you've noticed, what with being . . . you know . . . busy and that, but everything's kinda gone to crap and I really, really would be sooooo grateful if you didn't unleash plague on the streets for a little bit longer, you know?"

It wasn't often that a living essence of the buried dead could be surprised, but Old Man Bone now seemed to show symptoms. The clouds of stench which tore the air around him seemed to diminish, and his jaundiced yellow eyes, rolling in his withered skull, twisted from side to side before settling back on Sharon, as if he just needed to check that his own senses weren't playing some hideous trick.

Sharon's smile grew a little wider, and a lot thinner. "Is that all sorta . . . okay by you?"

"What . . . are you?" His words were a bare hiss on the air, a rattle of thin tongue across bony jaw.

"Me? I'm a community support officer."

"You dare to . . . "

Sharon raised a finger, and waggled it. "I'm also deputy Midnight Mayor," she added. "Which I only mention because sometimes you gotta throw these things out there, even though, personally, I think you should respect me for me, rather than for what I do. And I'm not saying it in a kinda 'I'm deputy Midnight Mayor so don't fuck with me' kinda way, because you're like a raging undead monster thingy, and I'm, like . . . you know . . . not . . . which isn't to say I judge, but I just mention it so you get that when I say please don't fuck around with this plague thing for just a little while longer, I'm asking you on behalf of lotsa seriously concerned dudes who've got access to the bigger picture and that, rather than just as some random shaman who thought she'd stop by for a chat, because that'd be kinda weird, really, even though I know I said you should respect the individual, but, seriously, there's conventions, you know?" She sighed again, shoulders sagging a little under the burden of society and all its foibles. "So, yeah. Basically, if you could gimme a bit more time to get the real Midnight Mayor back, and sort out all this crap, that'd be, like, amazing, and I'd really appreciate it, I mean, me *and* the city and that, if you see what I'm saying?"

Was it possible to surprise a god into submission?

Old Man Bone stood on the torn earth of the graveyard, his rags swirling around him, fingers curled up in rage, ready to strike, and then, at once, seemed to sink. His head sunk down, his shoulders sagged, his knees bent, and the earth opened up beneath him, beginning to suck him down again into its bone-latticed depths. His voice drifted up, though his eyes did not, as he descended.

"You have two days. Then I'll have your shoes."

The ground closed over him, and swallowed him down.

Chapter 65

Make Sure You're on the Same Page

Three hours, one shower and two doughnuts later, and Sharon sat with her feet up on Miles's perfect desk, drinking coffee and proclaiming, "You know, this would all be so much easier if we could just convince the primal forces of nature to get over their cryptic ego stuff and talk to people using reasonable language that everyone could understand."

"Yes, Ms Li."

"I mean, I get that if you're, like, thousands of years old, you've probably earned the right to say what you want, how you want to, but this automatic resorting to threat and unleashing the pits of hell upon the earth is just such an overreaction. Whatever happened to the middle ground? Start with a stiff letter of complaint, then build up to the dead walking, that's all I'm saying."

"Yes, Ms Li."

Sharon glanced over the rim of her coffee mug, to where Rhys was sitting on the floor, methodically going through reams of paperwork shipped over from the Scylla Workshops, with all the furrowed-brow determination of a mole in a wet field.

"Rhys," she said. "How long have you been looking at the scyllas' receipts?"

"Um ... I don't know, Ms Li."

"But it's been a while, right?"

"I think so, Ms Li."

"You know there's ... Aldermen who are professionally trained in this stuff? I mean, who are all, like, 'we're qualified and tough and brave' and that."

"Y-yes, Ms Li. But ... you're management, and I'm only IT support. Besides," he insisted, "the fate of the city is at stake, and I really feel that sort of thing is important."

Sharon deflated, back into her chair. "Yeah," she muttered. "But you can't be saving the city all the time, can you?"

"You can try," he replied with the firm tone of the righteous.

Sharon scowled. As a senior management figure, she was entirely in favour of striving for the good of all. However, she couldn't but feel that when it came to project "save the city", there was a serious need for diversification of roles.

On the floor, Rhys kept on patiently going through the scyllas' receipts. Being a scylla, he concluded, wasn't just socially challenging, it was also practically demanding. Tailoring, for example, was a significant cost, as was the electricity bill for refrigerating an intimidating amount of raw meat. Professionally, the workshop also seemed to involve a lot of wining and dining for customers; champagne and canapés for visiting important guests, and a rolling series of receptionists who didn't mind an eclectic clientele and unusual hours. Enchantment materials were carefully registered and the receipts for their purchase logged for VAT purposes; letters from the local bank informing the sisters that an ISA was due to mature had been marked with "check the allowance" while another from the council reporting that a new parking regime was about to come into force had been annotated neatly with "what about client vehicles?" The sisters were, in short, running a business like any other; it was merely that their business involved the manufacturing and, possibly, replication of mystic artefacts.

And then, without any warning, Rhys said, "Oh look. That's ... odd."

Sharon opened one eye, then the other, and realised she hadn't noticed when they'd closed. "Uh?"

He held up a card. It was small, yellow, and proclaimed in bright orange lettering –

Get Your Perfect Tan Today - Bring A Friend And Get 20% Off Your Treatment!

"Okay," said Sharon carefully. "So the sisters were big on tanning?"

"I don't know," said the druid. "I didn't think they looked very tanned, did you?"

Sharon took the card from Rhys's hand, and for a moment there was

can we make this quick?

an impression of heat and light and fear,

which passed as her fingers tightened over the cardboard. "I dunno," she murmured. "As triumphant leads go, I'm not sure if this is really it."

"But ... we followed the lead of an umbrella with no end on, didn't we?" Rhys ventured. "And that revealed an ancient undead waking god? And we followed a lead of shoes-over-things, and of a map on a mobile phone, and of blood going into a sewer, and that all went very well, I thought. I mean, not well, exactly, but it made progress, didn't it? And maybe this is something else, I mean, something else we can use, like another ... c-c-c-c-clue?" Even as he stuttered over this last word, he recalled just how little he'd enjoyed pursuing all the other clues they'd encountered so far.

Sharon hesitated. Then she shrugged, and reached for Miles's phone in a corner perfectly squared off on his immaculate desk, and dialled the number on the back of the card.

A voice sang out, "Sunrise Spa and Tanning, how can we help you today?"

It had a professional cheerfulness, a vibrant, eager-to-serve quality that Sharon automatically associated with expense. "Yeah, hi," she said. "My name's Sharon. I'm with ... the community support service. I was wondering if I could ask you a couple of questions?"

"Is this a professional or a personal call?"

"Uh ... professional?"

"Please hold while I transfer you to the manager. Thank you!" The high, upbeat voice was replaced by the sound of water tinkling over doubtless serene rocks beneath a glorious sky.

Sharon glanced over at Rhys. "They're playing soothing sound effects at me," she hissed; "it's kinda getting me down."

Before Rhys could respond, someone else picked up the line. This voice was male, business-like; concerned to please but in no great hurry to indulge. "Hello, this is Barry, can I help you?"

"Hi there," she sang out, trying to raise her spirits to something matching the voice on the other end of the line. "My name's Sharon Li, I'm with the community support service, do you mind if I ask you a couple of questions?"

"Of course, we're always happy to help local government."

"Great. So you, uh ... you run a tanning booth, is that right?"

"Sunrise Spa and Tanning," corrected Barry, in the tone of an artist slightly annoyed at not being recognised as such, "is a relaxation and therapy spa catering to all the needs of its exclusive clientele."

"Great! And are you, uh ... do you cater to a cross-section of the community? Like, diversity and that?"

There was a pause as the manager considered the notion of "diversity and that". Finally, "We have a wide range of clients with varied needs. If you're asking whether there is any sort of ethnic or religious discrimination, then of course I'd have to tell you absolutely not – have there been complaints?"

"Complaints? No, no. Just checking up on that sorta thing. So you don't mind where a client comes from?"

"Not at all."

"Do you have ... any disabled clients?"

"One or two."

"How about ... difficult clients?"

"I suppose it depends what you mean by difficult."

Sharon gave up. "Look, this is gonna sound a bit out there, just stick with me, okay. You haven't given tans to three scyllas recently?"

Silence.

Then, "Pardon?"

"Scyllas? You know, great big scyllas, creatures of the blackened deep, rend you limb from limb, raw blood and meat – that sorta thing?"

"I cannot say we have, no . . ."

"Ah well. Worth a shot. Thanks for your time . . ." Sharon moved to hang up, but Barry's voice cut through.

" . . . are you sure you don't mean striga?"

Slowly, with a rising sense of doom, Sharon put the phone back to her ear.

"Come again?" she said.

Chapter 66

A Little Sunshine Will Brighten Your Day

The tanning salon was just off the Edgware Road, in that transitional world where offices with tatty ceilings were scarcely a party wall away from multi-millionaire apartments in the same grand stuccoed terraces; where squares shaded by great plane trees lay next to busy streets with every other shop selling Turkish Delight and shisha pipes, and where the bus was always late, and full when it arrived. It was a part of town where everyone was everything, and always only passing through.

For that tiny proportion of people who did put down roots in this changeable area, there was Sunrise Spa and Tanning. It, like the local NHS dentist and the neighbouring solicitor's office, had set up shop in a converted apartment block. An unassuming brass plate by the front door was the only indication of commerce at work behind the spiked black railings that lined each neat side street.

Sharon rang the bell, and the door buzzed almost immediately, swinging back a centimetre from its magnetic lock. She looked at Rhys, Rhys shrugged, they went in. A corridor, white tiles on the floor, magnolia paint on the wall, led like any ordinary corridor in any ordinary house, past some closed doors to a flight of narrow

stairs. The stairs led up past a closed sash window looking down
into a flagstoned courtyard where the rubbish was put out. Round
the corner of the stairs, and up again, and another magnolia corridor led to an open white door where there was music of infuriating
blandness and the air smelt of eucalyptus, a breath from a celestial
temple. Beyond this door stood a woman, guarding it and the sacred
odours. She had short, dyed black hair, and wore a white tunic,
white trousers and white shoes. She gave a thin-lipped smile as
Sharon and Rhys entered, and a half-bob of the head that might, in
an older time, have been a bow.

"Welcome," she intoned, and her voice was as soothing as if
gentle chimes drifted onto the scented air from a concealed speaker.
"Are you here for a treatment?"

Sharon fixed her most professional smile in place. "Yeah, hi, we're
looking for Barry."

"Of course." The woman was somehow able to appear serene and
zephyr-like, moving without seeming to lift her feet. She drifted to
a desk on which sat a single purple orchid, designed perhaps to reas-
sure the visitor that their feng had been truly shuied; and pressed an
invisible button. "Mr Barry will be with you soon. May I get you a
herbal tea while you wait?"

Sharon's nose crinkled at the prospect of herbal. "Uh . . . thanks,
no. We'll be fine."

The woman's smile quivered the barest millimetre. She stayed
motionless, like a heron waiting to grab a recalcitrant fish, her gaze
locked on Sharon's own: implacable, irresistible, a force of nature in
white-clad form. Then, from the door on the opposite side of the
room, a cheerful voice called out, "Lesley! Is that the community
woman?!"

For a second, the white-clad woman's zen faltered. Then her
composure recovered, and she drifted over to the door, eased it back
and breathed, "Yes, Barry. You were expecting?"

They were sent in. "In" was an office, and it was a mess. In a room
barely large enough to accommodate its owner had been crammed
bits of old computer, creaky filing cabinets, sagging posters, forgotten wall charts, broken lamps, legless chairs, and even a couple

of calendars dating from 1999 to 2001, all stashed away with a cry of "it might come in useful ... one day". At the centre of it all, in a marvellous curvaceous chair, was Barry. His top half wore a vanilla-coloured wool jacket and open-necked blue shirt, while his bottom half was wrapped up in what Sharon supposed had to be a sarong. Pictures of swaying palm trees and still ocean waters blazed out in blues and greens from the folded fabric, while on the desk ...

Sharon wanted to say that he'd "put his feet up" but to do so implied that Barry had feet to put up. Instead, where his top half was human, his bottom half was what could only be called a tail. A big, coiling tail, covered in translucent blue-black scales, which protruded out from the bottom of his sarong and wrapped itself, first round the chair, then up onto the desk itself. The end twitched gently from side to side, as a cat's might do; but, thicker than a human thigh and longer than the length of Sharon's own body, it was still, unmistakably, the tail of a snake.

"Hi! You must be the community support people!"

Sharon realised her mouth was hanging open and, instinctively, trod on Rhys's foot. It seemed to that small part of her brain which was still functioning socially, that, if she was looking surprised, Rhys must be looking astonished. She managed a rictus smile.

"Hi!" she exclaimed. "Yeah, that's right, I'm Sharon, this is Rhys ... and it's really good of you to, uh ... see us, yeah?"

Barry shrugged, the effect rippling down his body in great scaly pulses. "No problem!" he exclaimed. "We're always happy to help the local authorities. Now, which of our services can we tell you about?"

Sharon chose a chair which looked like it would survive being used, and eased herself into it; Rhys lurked in the doorway.

"I guess we'd like to hear about the services you offer for mystic dudes."

"Mystic dudes – haven't heard it put like that for a while."

"I figured, no point dancing round the subject, right?"

"Absolutely! Well, as we're talking 'mystic dudes', let me think ... at the most basic range we do all the standard services; massage, aromatherapy, tanning and so forth. However, we pride ourselves on our customer service and do try to individually tailor each package to meet our clients' needs. We have an effrit, for example, who only tans at three hundred and forty-four degrees Celsius: and every lunar month the acupuncturist does a session for werewolves. We do aromatherapy for vampires who are on the 'low blood, low carbs' course, hydrotherapy for naiads, hypnotherapy for medusas' hair and, of course, ashtanga yoga on Tuesdays for genies – hatha on Thursdays. Our products are popular with the more ... comfortable ... members of society; but we have also received medical referrals. I remember one very pleasant young wizard with terrible allergies, who was sent to our masseuse to solve his sneezing problem, and a rather less agreeable gnome with just the most appalling ..."

"Excuse me?" Rhys's voice held a note of keening need. "Allergies? Wizard? Masseuse?"

"Yes, of course. Is this ... a problem?"

The druid's mouth was hanging over. "Allergies?" he squeaked. "Wizard? *Masseuse?*" Salt water welled in his eyes, and his nose began to glow.

"Do you have a website with details of all this on?" asked Sharon, before Rhys could burst.

"Of course, though we do prefer direct client contact, to assess their needs."

"But you've never treated scyllas ...?"

"No, I'm afraid not. Do you know some who might be interested?"

"No," she murmured. "Not any more. What about this ...?" She pushed the card across the table, advertising discounted tanning for the sun-deprived connoisseur.

"Yes, this is our card," said Barry. He passed it back across the table towards Sharon. "Is there ... has something happened? Is there a problem?" His tail quivered with the nervousness his face would not show.

"No, no, not at all," she replied. "Well, actually, yeah. See, I'm kinda working for the Midnight Mayor ..." Barry's tail curled sharply in on itself, an almost audible drawing in of breath. "Well,

I guess he is my boss, but I'm also, like, deputy Midnight Mayor, you know, which isn't to say there's, like, a problem, because I totally approve of what you guys have got going here, but just to say ... there's kinda a few dead people, and, like, some missing people, and this thing involving glass and shoes and all of that, and some of the dead people ... well, they had your card and we figured we should be thorough, you know, so I'm like ... this ringing any bells for you?"

He spoke very slowly, eyes wide, fingers tight; and it occurred to Sharon that he might actually be scared of her. "No," he murmured. "Not at all. Obviously we'll be happy to help the authorities however we can. Client privacy is hugely important but then ... did you say you're his deputy?"

"Yeah."

"Of course," he blurted. "Of course. Anything you need, we'll happily oblige."

Sharon could almost feel Rhys's astonishment at her back, matching her own incredulity. "Uh ... seriously?"

"Anything! Anything at all!"

"That's, uh ... that's great. Well, I guess the first thing to ask is, have you seen a great big glowing glass elemental that spits shards of broken glass?" Barry's silence was eloquent. "Okay, how about a raging undead god from the plague pits?"

"I'm really sorry, I can't help you there."

"What about a rusted blade? Anyone come in here lately waving one of those about? Or a pair of shoes tied together at the laces?"

It was only Barry's deep confusion, she felt, which was saving her the trouble of his disbelief. "No ... "

"Nothing ... glowy, zappy, zippy or zoomy of any suspicious nature at all?"

He thought it through. "No, I'm so terribly sorry."

Sharon deflated. "Ah well. Guess we had to try."

"I'm so sorry I couldn't be of assistance."

"No, no worries. I mean, it was kinda a long shot. Thanks anyway." She stood up, making to go. "Love this place, by the way; totally recommending it to all my friends."

"Thank you!" As she passed through the door, Barry sat up a little straighter, tail swishing to one side, nearly knocking a cup of herbal tea into the bin. "Excuse me? Ms Li?"

"Yessss . . . ?"

"Thinking about it, one of our clients did start screaming uncontrollably last week during her facial."

Sharon paused, one hand on the door handle. "Okay," she said. "Is that . . . common?"

"Well, Mrs Greyfoot does tend to see things from the nether regions, but sometimes she takes her medicine, sometimes she doesn't . . ."

"So . . . she screams a bit anyway, I mean?"

"Yes, but this time she screamed *at* a client, which isn't very common and was highly embarrassing for the establishment."

Sharon hesitated, eyes narrowing as she turned back in the doorway. "And what did she say?"

"She said, 'I will have your shoes'. Which I did think rather odd at the time, as Zhanyi wasn't wearing any shoes."

Sharon's smile was a quivering arrow notched to the bow. "I think Mrs Greyfoot may be a smarter lady than you know."

Chapter 67

The Truth Hurts

Her name was Zhanyi.

She'd been a client, according to Barry's logs, for over four years; but recently she'd stepped up her attendance at the spa and was, the owner concluded, looking much better and happier for the same.

Then a few weeks ago, Mrs Greyfoot, who saw things that others didn't want to see, had spotted Zhanyi on her way to the tanning booth, and screamed, and screamed, and screamed. And in between the screaming, one of the things she'd screamed was, 'I will have your shoes', which everyone agreed was a sure sign that Mrs Greyfoot needed more of her medication. And Zhanyi was . . .

" . . . a really sweet young lady, really lovely, it's such a shame about her condition."

"Which is?"

"The poor thing, such a pity. By day, I swear, never anyone nicer."

"And by night . . . ?"

Barry looked pained. "It's not so much a question of the solar cycle," he explained, "as the intensity of illumination. Obviously in winter it's much harder for her, poor dear. Much harder indeed."

"So," Sharon pushed out the words one at a time. "What happens to her when it gets dark?"

Barry told them.

Sharon's smile didn't falter. "Yeah," she said. "I can see how that might be a bit of a bitch."

He gave them her address anyway, just in case.

It was late afternoon by the time Sharon and Rhys got off the Underground in Hammersmith, to the sound of "Ms Li?"

"Yeah?"

"You know how we're keeping travel receipts, see, for the Aldermen?"

"Yesssss . . ."

"What if you're on pay-as-you-go auto top-up?"

There was silence in reply to this. Amid the panoply of things going wrong with life, magic and her new job, Sharon hadn't considered the question of reimbursement for expenses incurred.

"Maybe . . . we can send a memo?"

"It's not a problem, though," insisted the druid; "I don't want to cause a fuss!"

Sharon smiled feebly, and strode out into the grey afternoon light.

Hammersmith was not her favourite part of town. It was a great ugly junction where great ugly roads collided: a one-way nightmare of horns, traffic lights, pressed-in pedestrians on narrow pavements, and giant shopping mall depths where schoolchildren in pink and grey tried to look tougher than their peers even while buying latte frappuccino and a cinnamon bun. The place was at once rebuilt and run-down, with so many conflicting personalities that it possessed no character at all. Sharon sniffed, and thought she detected just the tiniest scent of rotting flesh. A shiver ran through her.

Two days. Then I'll have your shoes.

They headed south, into the no-man's-land of samey terraced

streets where buses tended not to run, and the corner shop was a rare beacon of enlightenment.

They walked on. Occasionally Rhys sneezed. As they slowed down in front of a perfectly ordinary door on a perfectly ordinary street, Rhys declared, "W-well, this is for the good of the city . . ." and made no move to knock on the door.

Sharon sighed, marched up the crazy-paving path that ran all of three foot past the dustbins and hammered on the front door, with its black iron knocker. The sound seemed dull, hollow, loud, in the quiet street. She glanced at the neighbouring scene: a ground-floor bay window populated with cut-out pictures drawn by infant children whose parents just knew that their offspring was the next Picasso; family cars wedged in nose-to-tail; and rubbish bins carefully marked out for trash, paper, card, glass and aluminium by owners who loved the environment and feared the council. As she looked around, it occurred to her that the door where they were standing was probably the only one in Fulham which had bolts on the outside.

A chain moved somewhere inside. The door opened an inch and an eye peeked out. A timid voice whispered, "Hello?"

It was as soft as rabbit fur, hushed as a vicar at a funeral. Somehow its incredible meekness propelled Sharon to enthusiastic confidence. "Hi there!" she sang out, then realised the eye had recoiled from the door in dismay. "I'm Sharon, this here is Rhys . . ."

"Hello."

" . . . we're here to save the city, rescue the Midnight Mayor, appease the ancient gods, prevent plague spreading through the streets and get a decent night's sleep at some point preferably without having clocked up too much overtime. Can we come in?"

At length, "I don't think you should."

Sharon found her confidence dented. "But . . . fate of the city?" she suggested. "The walking dead? Or actually, *not* the walking dead, since we want to avoid that, don't we, Rhys?"

"Oh yes, Ms Li."

" . . . and *not* the plague on the streets, which is all kinda related, because we're anti-plague too ... So really, with that kinda brief, I don't see what the problem is."

The eye cringed. It wasn't easy for a single sensory organ to express horror, dismay, distress and terror all at once, and through a gap in the door, but this eye managed it. Sharon tried beaming. This seemed to make it worse. She switched to a more diffident smile, one she'd always thought was a winner, expressing in every quiver the hope that things will be all right really and, if they aren't, that nobody's going to be blamed.

"Um ... excuse me?" Rhys shuffled forward. "You're not ... part of an evil conspiracy, are you?" he asked tentatively; and this time the blinking of the eye was accompanied by an intake of breath. "Only, I was thinking that after all the victims and distressed friends we've met, maybe we were going to encounter someone actually malign? Only that would explain, I think, why you're being very reluctant to open the door. Only it's okay!" he added. "Because even if you are part of an evil conspiracy, we're mostly harmless, aren't we?"

"Oh, yes," replied Sharon. "Mostly."

"Though we do have frightening friends."

"Do we? Yes, I guess we do. And I'm the deputy Midnight Mayor, which from what I can tell doesn't mean shit in terms of actual mega-firepower; but did I tell you, Rhys, I met a dragon?"

"No!"

"Yeah, totally! I was kinda busy at the time ... "

"When did this happen?"

"Oh, when I was luring the blue electric angels to sleep. I had to go into the dream walk, yeah, and take them with me which was, can I add, bloody hard work, not that I'm asking for sympathy here, it's just that Sammy doesn't give me any credit when I do these sorta things ... "

"Oh no, Ms Li, I completely understand ... "

" ... so there I was, in the dream walk, and the blue electric angels were sleeping and I looked at my hand and I do think the Midnight Mayor left some kinda mark on me, even if it's nothing actually useful in day-to-day evil-battling, because when I looked up there was a dragon. And it was the city. And it's insane. But in kinda a groovy way. So, yeah." She paused, head on one side, struggling to recollect through the fogs of exhaustion, sleep deprivation, caffeine-saturation and adrenalin. "That was my big moment."

So saying, she turned back towards the door.

The door was closed, and the eye had fled.

"Oh bollocks," she sighed. "I thought we were being so friendly."

Chapter 68

Bathe in the Light of Revelation

There was a moment.

The world blinked.

When it opened its eyes again, Sharon and Rhys were standing inside the locked door, where, in fact, they'd been all along because, really, it was that or the universe had a lot of explaining to do.

The corridor they stood in was painted white.

White, glossy walls, white glossy floor. Lights lined the ceiling, downlit the walls, glowed upwards from the floor like emergency strips in an aeroplane. White stairs led upwards to the open door of a large white bathroom; a white living room with white padded walls had a white metal grille pulled shut across the windows, the gaps wide enough to let in streams of light. There were no curtains, but more lights burnt, uncomfortably bright, in the ceiling, the wall, the floor, anywhere electricity could be coaxed to reach. Rhys wandered into a white kitchen, where padlocks had been fastened across the drawers and more white grilles were stretched across the windows. He tried the back door to the garden; it was bolted, inside and out.

"Um . . . ?" he said.

Sharon shrugged, and pointed towards the staircase. They climbed upwards, past the white bathroom with its white bath, toilet and tiles; past the view into a white bedroom with a lock on the door and grille across the window, and a white desk on which were laid out a soft white hairbrush, a box of plain white tissues and a book. Sharon glanced down at the book, and froze.

The title of the book, in large, reassuringly pastel letters, was *You Have a Secret*.

Rhys followed her gaze.

"It's . . . the secret!" Sharon's voice was hushed and reverent. "The secret to being happy with yourself! I am beautiful, I am wonderful, I have a secret, the secret is . . ." She sighed, remembering the glories of that time when this simple truth had meant the world to her, there being not much else in her life that meant anything better. " . . . the secret is me. It's a self-help book for . . . anyone. To encourage confidence and teach you that you're actually wonderful even if you feel shit."

"I see," murmured Rhys. He was trying not to look too neurotic as he swivelled his gaze, watching every door, window and inch of wall for the death that must surely lurk behind all this high-gloss paint. "And . . . is this a clue?"

"I spent months reading this book," breathed Sharon, reaching towards it. "It was like my Bible, like the thing I went to because I was . . ."

Her fingers touched the cover and her face changed. Her mouth twisted, shoulders hunched, knees bent; animal-like for a second, her face darkened into a mockery of human form. Her head swerved towards Rhys as she hissed, "Turn out the light!"

Then her hand was swept by its own weight off the surface of the page. At once, the look was gone, her back straightening, her head lifting upright again. She staggered back, dizzy and confused. Rhys caught her by the arm, and yelped with surprise as she grabbed back at him, clinging on for support. Gradually her eyes focused. "Bloody hell," she whispered. Then, "We gotta find her."

Rhys could feel the warmth from her skin on his; for a moment her face was so close, he could see every eyelash. He felt her breath against his cheek.

It occurred to him that this was a moment.

He wondered what he should do with it.

Then the moment passed, and so did Sharon, marching for the door, taking the stairs to the top floor two at a time. Rhys followed, between more white walls and under more bright lights pumped up to full wattage, round the corner, to where there was one door – just one – blocking their way. It was large, white, metal, reinforced with heavy rivets forced through great hinges thicker than Rhys's fist, and very much locked. It put him in mind of a bank vault although perhaps a better description was . . .

. . . prison cell?

There were bolts on the outside, pulled wide open, but the door, was locked from the inside. She hesitated, then rapped politely with her knuckles.

"Hi!" she called out. "Really sorry to be breaking into your house like this, but, seriously, this whole plague in the streets thing, it's gotta take priority here. And I know that's a bit like saying, in times of trouble all the laws go, and we all know where that leads, and I think we should talk about this, like, afterwards, I mean, like, have a proper sit-down and maybe a consultation and that, but for now, really, I'd just like to talk, okay?"

Silence.

"Look, I know you don't wanna hear this, but I can just walk straight through this door. I mean, it's not a big deal, it's just this thing I do, but I don't want to violate your privacy or anything like that."

At length, quietly, muffled through the great wall of metal, "I don't want to hurt you!"

"That's great!" exclaimed Sharon. "I don't want to hurt you either! You don't wanna hurt me, I don't wanna hurt you, I really think we could have a dialogue here!"

Silence. Then, "I can't tell you anything!"

"That's okay, that's okay! I think we can work through this together, you know?"

Another silence, even longer than the last. The voice said, "Can you really just walk straight through?"

"Uh, kinda yeah. Unless the door is warded, but I'm not feeling like this door is warded, are you, Rhys?"

"No, Ms Li. Just a perfectly ... ordinary ... reinforced prison vault door in Fulham."

"So, yeah, I could totally walk through it. But I don't want to do it and, like, violate your civil rights or anything."

"Unless you're an agent of evil," suggested Rhys.

"Unless you're an agent of evil, or merely a kinda adjunct of evil, or like evil's PA or that, in which case I actually think there's an argument to be had."

Again, silence.

"Okay then," concluded Sharon. "Well, I guess we gotta come through the door now, haven't we, Rhys?"

"If you say so, Ms Li," he conceded.

"So stand back, sorry about this ..."

She grabbed Rhys by the arm. The druid screwed his face up tight against the discomfort of being pulled bodily through a solid surface, and Sharon marched them both through the locked door.

A moment of coldness, and they stepped into the room beyond.

White padded walls, white padded floor, white padded ceiling; even the inside of the door was padded, but this hadn't stopped something, something angry and heavy and mad, something with ten razored claws, five on either limb, and ten pinpoint-sharp toe-nails with deadly curved points, from lacerating a large part of the padding, which now dangled in yellow foamy strips off the con-crete-reinforced fabric of the building. The lights in this room, as in all others, were blinding, brilliant white, bright enough to make Rhys's eyes sting. Crouched against the far wall, head bowed against the glare, was a woman.

She was only a few scant years from being a girl, and certainly the way she hid her head behind her hair, tucked her chin into her chest, curled her shoulders down and inwards, suggested in every way a teenager barely escaped from the hormonal torture of that age. She wore a bright purple T-shirt, denim shorts over black

leggings, and a pair of puppy-eared fluffy slippers. Her hair was
long, straight and black, her skin almond-brown, and as she cringed
back against the wall she covered her body with her crossed arms
and wailed, "Go away! Go away, please! Go away!"

Rhys glanced over at Sharon, and saw the shaman recoil in surprise and dismay. It occurred to him that the two women didn't
merely share the same reading material and ethnic origin, but they
were not so far apart in age. Sharon said, "Um . . . hi," and even for
Rhys, who'd seen the shaman in all sorts of socially distressing circumstances, her greeting sounded inadequate.

"Go away, please, you have to leave . . ." whimpered the girl.

"I'd love to, I mean, seriously, but the thing is . . ." Sharon edged
closer, and squatted down in front of the girl. "The thing is, you
kinda look like you're unhappy and, like, in distress and that, and I
was wondering . . . would you like an intervention?"

Slowly, the girl looked up. "An . . . ?"

"Intervention?" offered Sharon. "It's this thing, like, where if you
get into a really bad way, then people who care about you sorta
intervene? I mean, like if you're locking yourself into bright white
barricaded rooms, then things are kinda not perfect, but . . . have
you heard of Magicals Anonymous?"

"W-w-what?"

"Magicals Anonymous? It's a community support group for
people with mystic issues? I'm the boss," she added with a flare of
pride. "Although really I'm just there to facilitate."

"You're . . . here to promote a self-help group?" Even in her cowering state, the woman's voice couldn't hide a shrill of incredulity.

"Yeah. Well, no, we're here to talk about the fate of the city, but,
yeah, we're also here to talk about how you don't have to be alone,
and how there's, like, people out there with issues like yours and
that. So . . . um . . . can we help you at all?"

The girl stared into the shaman's eyes, with the open wonder of
a mouse debating if this cat was really sincere about its new vegan
regime. Then she bowed her head again, clutched her knees to her
chest and whispered, "You should really leave."

"And we'd love to, but we kinda can't."

"You should leave," she repeated. "Before it comes."

"It?" Rhys was never slow to pick up on a sense of doom. "Not ... a big glass, glowing, angry sort of 'it'?"

The girl's eyes flew to him, and there was recognition there, no question. But she half shook her head. "No. *It*. The *it* in *me*."

"You're a striga." Sharon said it so matter-of-factly that both the druid and the girl were taken aback. "Your name is Zhanyi, you're twenty years old, you go to a tanning booth in Marble Arch as often as you can afford to get your weekly burst of high-intensity light, and when you're tired, and your spirits are low, and you haven't been in the sun for a while, and the lights go out, you turn into a striga. Which, by the way, must really hurt, because I don't know how it feels having every bone in your body rearrange itself to form a hunched carnivorous killing machine, but I'm, like, that's gotta hurt. But!" Sharon brightened. "I totally respect that you've got this place ... " She gestured expansively at the padded room. "To, like, keep others safe. I think that's a real community spirit you've got there and actually, I was wondering, did you get a council grant for this? I mean, like, how if you're disabled you can apply for extra financial support with things like bathroom handles and that, I think it could be so useful to have a panic room for metamorphic trans-formation – Rhys!" Her head snapped round to face the druid.

"Yes, Ms Li?"

"You gotta remember this for me, cos my brain is, like, dribbling out my nose I'm so tired, but local authority assistance for meta-morphic transformation safe rooms – add it to next week's to-do list!"

"Yes, Ms Li."

The girl – Zhanyi's – mouth was hanging open. "You're ... not here to arrest me?" she squeaked.

"Arrest you? God, no!"

"Or ... imprison me?"

"We'd never! I mean, you're handling your condition so well, don't you think so, Rhys?"

"Yes, Ms Li."

"The padded rooms, the lotsa lights, the books about being at one with yourself – God no, I'd never imprison you! You know, only a few months ago, I was like, 'who the fuck am I and what the fuck can I do?' and now I realise that it's okay to walk through walls and be the knower of truth, so why the hell should I judge you?"

To Rhys's surprise, Zhanyi was beginning to uncurl a little, raising her head to look into Sharon's face. "I thought . . . you said the Midnight Mayor . . . "

"Oh, God, that!" Sharon exclaimed. "Seriously, I wouldn't get the wrong idea from it. I know that the job description has this kinda 'boom' reputation . . . "

"Very 'boom'," muttered Rhys.

" . . . but we're so much more people-orientated, at Magicals Anonymous. The Individual," Sharon proclaimed, "Is At The Heart Of What We Do."

"You're . . . not here to hurt me?" whimpered Zhanyi.

"Hell, no!"

"Even . . . with the blade?"

Sharon hesitated. "Weeellll . . . " she conceded, "I can't say that we're not having issues right now with a whole stolen mega-mystic rusty blade thing. But I'm sure that whatever you've gotta tell us, we'll be happy to listen patiently and hear it from your point of view."

"You . . . will?"

"Absolutely."

And for the first time in what might have been far, far too long, Zhanyi smiled.

Chapter 69

Zhanyi

My name is Zhanyi.

And I'm a striga.

I thought it was a night/day thing – by day I'm me, and by night I'm . . . it. The creature, this thing inside my bones. But it's not. It's a light/dark thing. When the lights go out, when the city is silent, when the shadows get too deep . . . that's when it happens. I can feel it, inside me, when I run home in the winter and the sun is going down. I glare at strangers and don't know why, start to scowl at people who smile at me in the street, shove onto the bus, curse under my breath, muttering, muttering all the time, and then people look at me and I get so mad when they look at me, so mad that I want to scream and it's not me, it's not me who's screaming: it's . . . it.

That's how I know it's coming, I can feel it, feel myself doing it, know it's stupid, know it's wrong, but I can't make it stop. And then it comes, and it is so angry. That's all it is – anger. It screams and howls and tears things up and I thought it might be a kind of freedom but all it is is anger, pointless, frustrated, endless anger, with nothing that can ever make it stop, make it better. Frustration, I guess. Frustration without cause, without end.

I do try to control it. I'm trying to save enough money to move to an equatorial climate, where the days are long and hot. It's really hard, living in a northern latitude, especially when the days are short. But getting a job, keeping a job, saving – that's hard, too. People say you should just do it, just move, take the plunge. But what if something happened on the aeroplane, at the airport, what if it . . . ? And if I move I need to go somewhere safe, somewhere I can control it, if it emerges, keep it safe, and so I . . .

. . . it's hard.

And I go to the tanning booth, because I learnt that sometimes I can sorta . . . get a reserve of energy, you know? Like I can store up on light and that might make it harder for *it* to come out, keep it buried deeper inside me? And I practise breathing exercises, and try to cook nice things and learn to knit, but nothing really . . .

I don't know what to do.

Don't know who to trust.

Don't know how to make it stop.

Don't want to . . . hurt anyone else. Don't want to. Can't make it stop.

Then one day I'm at the spa, and this woman – Brid – she comes up to me and says she's been watching me a while, thinks I look really sad, and she's really nice, and most people when they find out the truth, they just freak out, like they don't dare be in the same room as me – and I don't blame them – but Brid, she wasn't like that. You're special, she told me. Someone does love you. You don't have to be alone. And I thought that was really nice, and she invited me to meet some of her friends, and they were really kind, everyone was really kind and they were having these . . . services, but they were always at night, so I couldn't attend, but Brid said, that's okay, don't worry about it, we'll come to you during the day, bring you cake, and they did, they were really good about it! Then one day Brid calls and says she needs me to do her a favour, and it's in day-light hours so that's okay, and she gives me this address in Chelsea and I go down there and there's . . . there's these sisters. Three sisters. And they're . . .

. . . and I'm terrified of them, but I think that's stupid because if the lights were low I could be just like that, I could be just like them, but they give me this thing, this thing in a box and it's a really long, thin box, and I know I shouldn't look and I do and it's . . .

Beautiful.

Glass – clear glass – but, like, bright, like it has its own internal light, like there's a light all the way through it, woven into the glass itself. And the sisters say, "you should be careful with that, don't cut yourself" and I ask why and they just look at me and say, "do you know what it is, this thing you worship?" and I say, "I don't worship anything" and they say "you shouldn't tamper" and I'm scared again, but I think they're trying to be kind, and I go back to the spa and Brid is there and I give her the blade and, as I'm leaving, Mrs Greyfoot sees me and she screams. She looks right at me and she screams, "I will have your shoes, I will have your shoes, I will have your shoes!"

Brid says it's fine.

That I mustn't be afraid.

That I mustn't answer the door to strangers.

Keep faith.

Believe in her.

Because she's my friend.

And to believe in *him*, too. To believe in . . . in the one who is coming, and never breathe to anyone the secrets of the glass blade. And I promise I won't, of course I won't, because Brid is my friend, and he will make everything better. But deep down I know, somehow I just know . . .

. . . we're doing something wrong. We're doing something evil. We're making a . . .

Chapter 70

There Is No Need to Fear the Dark

The striga stopped, mid-sentence, eyes flashing up towards the still-locked door of the vault. "Did you hear . . . ?" she began.

Sharon strained, and murmured, "Uh . . . no?"

All three pairs of ears strained.

Silence in the glowing house. "You said you were making something?" murmured Sharon.

Doubt and guilt twisted their ugly path across Zhanyi's round features.

"A god," she whispered. "A new god."

A pause.

Rhys hiccupped.

Sharon said, "Okay, I gotta tell you, it's not every day that people say that sorta thing. I mean, maybe it's everyday for you, but for me, it's kinda a new experience. What . . . kind of god?"

"A new god," repeated Zhanyi, in the far-off tones of one remembering a mantra. "A beautiful god, a god of the city, a god from the streets, a perfect, immaculate god. A glass god."

Sharon paused. She said, "Tallish guy, skin of glass, body of glass, spits glass everywhere?"

Zhanyi's eyes widened. "You've seen him?"

"Seen him, had a row with him, run away from him."

"He is ... he is coming! He is growing stronger, from our worship, from our love, from our magics. He's becoming ..." She stopped, listening for something beyond the door. Then, softer, "... he's going to be the new lord of the city. The Midnight Mayor, Old Man Bone – they're old magic. They say they're new, urban gods born from the street. But they're the old streets, the old ways. Our lord is new, he is perfection, he'll sweep away the old ones."

"Okay," murmured Sharon. "As deputy Midnight Mayor, I really don't know what that says for my job prospects. You mentioned a blade ..."

Zhanyi flinched. "He ... must be fed."

"Fed?"

"There must be ... sacrifice."

Sharon's face darkened. "*Sacrifice?*" she echoed. "*Fed?* Like ... you feed Old Man Bone?"

"Hacq said ..."

"Who's Hacq?"

"The high priest."

"You have a high priest already? That's kinda keen."

"He's the head of the coven."

"And Brid?"

"She's a priestess."

Sharon took this in. "I don't want to be the bearer of bad news here, but she's kinda dead." Zhanyi's hands flew to her mouth. "It wasn't me!" Sharon insisted. "Or Rhys, for that matter!" Rhys nodded, and tried to smile his most harmless, sweet-natured smile.

"But, point is, it's all going a bit wrong, and if I understand you right ... if you're *feeding* this glass god of yours, then that is kinda putting you in the shit, and, actually, does seriously undermine this whole dialogue we've got going here. The glass blade you collected from the scylla sisters ..."

"You know about the scyllas?"

"Yeah. They're dead, too, by the by. Your glass guy – he killed them."

Zhanyi let out a gasp. "No! He's kind, he loves us . . . "

"Kinda didn't love the scylla sisters. Or Rhys, or me. Anyway, this glass blade . . . I'm guessing you don't have it now?"

"No." Her word was a bare whisper.

"You gave it to Brid, right?"

"Yes."

"About . . . what, three weeks ago?"

"Yes." Zhanyi's eyes were downcast, her body huddled in tight to itself, curled up for protection against the world and its accusations.

"And did Brid tell you what she wanted it for?"

"She said there had to be sacrifices."

"She tell you what kind?"

"She said . . . shoes."

Sharon forced her smile to remain intact. "Shoes," she repeated. "And you took this to mean . . . ?"

"I thought . . . we burnt shoes?"

"You *burnt* them?"

"As an offering to the glass god! To show our devotion! I burnt three pairs," she added, with an air of regret. "Hacq said that the loyal would walk barefoot over glass. He showed us the scars on his feet."

Nothing could keep the smile on Sharon's face fixed any longer. "So I'm guessing he didn't mention something about the people who were *wearing* the shoes?"

"N-n-n-n-no!" Zhanyi's voice was almost a scream.

"Great." Sharon straightened up, and said, "Look, I'm really sorry about this, I can see that you probably didn't mean any harm even though, I gotta tell you, things are really kinda crap and you're gonna have to do a lot of rethinking about your lifestyle approach in the future. But the thing is, there are dead people all over this business, and that's, like, something I was hoping to avoid this early in my career, so actually, if you don't mind, I'd like you to . . . " Her voice stopped abruptly. "Rhys?" she murmured.

"Yes, Ms Li?"

"Did you open the vault door?"

"Um . . . no, Ms Li." He turned, following her gaze to where the heavy metal door, through which they'd walked a few minutes since, stood ajar. "Uh . . ." he began.

The lights went out.

"Uummmm . . ." The sound was long, slow, careful. It came from the very pit of Rhys's lungs, as if every part of his body was willing, in that single sound, for things not really to be as bad as they seemed. In the absolute darkness, he looked to where he felt Sharon ought to be, and fumbled in his pocket for something which might glow, or pop, or even shimmer, or do anything at all that didn't involve standing still in a pitch-black room with a . . .

. . . yes, with a creature that made a sound like . . .

"iiiiiiiiiiiIIIIIIIIIIIIIIIIIIIIIII'M COMING!"

His fingers closed round an old plastic bottle into which he'd poured a potion. At a command it glowed with the golden light of not-quite-rinsed-out baby shampoo, and as he raised it to see, his gaze brushed across Sharon, turning towards the open door, then fixed on the shape rising up from the floor behind her, the source of the sound, of the voice which had only a few seconds ago been so quiet, so human, and which now shrieked,

"IIIIIII'MMMM FREEEEEE!"

By the thin glow of his shampoo bottle, Rhys saw Zhanyi rise up on her haunches, shoulders hunched forward, chin twisted down like an old crone's, back arching, knees twisting out to the side; and as she looked up through her loose black hair, the tresses on her head began to tangle and knit together, lashing themselves into coils of metal rope which spun and slashed at the air around her, with gleaming, sparking tips. Her fingers stretched, and stretched again, fine strands of wire sprouting in place of the hairs on the back of her hands, needle-thin, needle-sharp; and her eyes – her eyes were widening, expanding so they seemed to fill her face, other features displaced, and Rhys could see the capillaries in her irises straightening and pulsing with blood, forming ridged criss-cross patterns like a circuit board, banishing the whites of her eyes, and in each great pupil he thought he could see shapes moving, bursts of light flaring up and withering away into the inky darkness of her

stare. Then Zhanyi rose up even as her knees snapped backwards
with a snicker-snacker of realigning bone, and stretched out her fingers – if fingers were what they could be called any more – and,
with a shriek, leapt straight at Rhys's face.

Something fast knocked Rhys out of the way and held on to him,
its momentum carrying him to the floor and then down *through* the
floor itself, landing with an explosion of papers and card in a mess
of boxes below. Rhys groaned as the shock rippled all the way down
to his toes, and looked up blearily into Sharon's dimly illuminated
face.

"Uh?"

She rolled off him, slid through a pile of boxes to the nearest
piece of clear floor, grabbed him by the arm and said, "Antihistamines!"

"Oh, um . . ." Rhys started fumbling in his pockets even as something fast, bounding fast, galloping on all fours, thundered across
the floor overhead, claws tearing at wallpaper and wall as it passed,
and screamed the hunting cry of the striga.

"Antihistamines, antihistamines . . ." stammered the druid, patting
down pocket after pocket. "I'm sure I had . . ."

Sharon let out a groan, grabbed him by the sleeve and dragged
him out through the nearest wall, even as the door burst back and
Zhanyi – or the creature which had been Zhanyi – tore into the
room. Her head was held high on a great, thickened body of wire-
encrusted skin; her hair lashed around her, tearing scars in the frame
of the door; and her metal claws were still growing to their full
length on her elongated fingertips. For a second the striga stared,
bewildered, at the empty room as Sharon and Rhys passed through
the nearby wall; then her nostrils flared and with a cry she turned
and leapt down the stairs, her body uncoiling cat-like as it sprang.
Her claws gouged mortar dust from the wall where they struck, and
seized it, so that she now hung suspended, head turning this way
and that as she searched out her prey.

One floor below, Sharon and Rhys passed into the shadow walk,
the druid mumbling, "Maybe the other pocket . . . ?"

But even from the shadow walk, the golden glow of Rhys's potion was faintly visible. Zhanyi shrieked again and, propelling herself backwards off the face of the wall, she threw herself claws first at the glow passing the bottom of the stairs. Her leap struck something which fell, tumbling first to the landing below, then out of visibility entirely and into the full obscurity of the darkened house. The striga raised her head triumphantly, crouching on the fallen body of her prey, and looked down into a face which was . . .

. . . altered.

A silver metal skin had laid itself over once soft features, a red, glowing madness was intruding itself across formerly almond eyes, and from the parted lips of the striga's intended victim, a black puff of smoke curled around a stretching lizard tongue. Confused, the striga looked down to where, by rights, her claws should have punched straight through rib and lung, and saw instead that her intended victim's spreading metal skin was now complete, thickening before her eyes; and even as she looked, she saw something darken in the face of the creature beneath her.

Then Sharon, the Alderman's badge tucked firmly in her right fist, clenched her dragon-skinned fingers tighter around the hot little source of magic, and hit Zhanyi as hard as she could across the side of the face.

The striga flew backwards, head knocking against the wall, as Sharon rolled onto her feet, head aching, vision pulsing a scarlet red, the whisper of . . .

domine dirige nos domine dirige nos domine dirige
    i'm freeeeeeeee!
I bought you doughnuts . . .
        come be freeeeeeeeee
    and this umbrella!
domine dirige nos domine dirige nos
    and congratulations!

. . . rushing in her ear. She looked at Zhanyi. In the gloom of the whitewashed hall, softened by Rhys's potion, she saw a striga, a monster of the dark, a creature out of nightmares, fed on the forbidden things that happen when there is no one there to perceive them. And she knew that her own fingers were the fingers of the dragon, her blood was the blood of the streets, her breath was fire, her judgement was fury, her authority was absolute, go on, go on, go on, kill the monster . . .

Then Zhanyi picked herself back up and snarled an animal snarl and for a moment, Sharon saw as only a shaman can see and there was a girl standing in front of her and even as she screamed the hunting cry of the untamed beast, a voice drifted beneath it, barely audible in the shadows, and it whispered

I am beautiful, I am wonderful, I have a secret . . .

And for a second, Sharon hesitated.

Then something moved in the corner of her eye, a shadow heading for the front door, and in that instant, that moment of divided attention, Zhanyi leapt. Sharon threw up her hands in front of her and was surprised, and then again, not that surprised, to see that her fingers had the claws of the dragon, and her arm was growing tendrils of metal which spread around her and lapped at the air like pennants in a breeze, and as Zhanyi threw herself at the shaman, Sharon stepped to one side and threw the full force of her combined fists into the side of the striga. The blow knocked Zhanyi across the hall, and into the door of the whitewashed living room, nearly colliding with Rhys, who was picking himself up from where he'd fallen at the bottom of the stairs. The druid gave a whimper and scurried into the living room itself, carrying his potion with him, but Sharon was surprised – and then again, not so surprised – to discover that the scarlet haze across her sight required little in the way of light for her to see by, and even as it richened, deepened, it seemed that the striga grew brighter in her eyes, every pulse of blood through her body visible, every puff of breath a great expulsion that distorted the air. Sharon thought she heard the front door slam, but there was no time to think about it as Zhanyi got to her feet and, cautiously now, began to back through the living-room door, eyes locked on Sharon, teeth bared and claws out. Sharon advanced carefully after her, opening the fingers of her left hand to reveal the black claws that had also grown from her skin, fuelled by the badge of the Aldermen.

"Zhanyi," she murmured, her voice rasping metal scraped across fresh blood, and the striga's head twisted in hatred at the sound of her own name.

"Zhanyi, we can help. Rhys?"

"Y-y-yes, Ms Li?" As the three of them moved round each other, the druid was trying to keep himself as far from the striga as possible without, that was, necessarily putting Sharon between it and him.

"Can you get us more light?"

"I can try, Ms Li."

Zhanyi hissed at the idea, a plated black tongue flicking from between her deformed lips. "Iiiiiiiii," she breathed, the sound beginning only as an exhalation struggling to be shaped. "Iiiiiiiii aaaaaammm freeee!"

"Well, now, that's an interesting and complicated thing you said there," murmured Sharon. As if these words were an insult, the striga leapt again, a great clawed fist lashing at the side of Sharon's head.

The shaman vanished, then reappeared a heartbeat later to one side of Zhanyi even as the striga staggered behind the force of her own blow. "But I'm guessing you're not really up for that discussion right now," she added.

Zhanyi shrieked in frustration, and spun again, even as Rhys clutched his glowing potion and, wiping away snot and tears with his sleeve, started whispering words at it, urging more light to come out of the soap-smeared bottle. Again the striga lashed out at Sharon, and again the shaman vanished. Zhanyi flailed at the empty air; but now her fist connected with something hard, knocking Sharon out of the shadow walk and back into full visibility. The shaman's ears rang from the blow, and her vision flared with static as she staggered and tried to catch her balance. Zhanyi gave a shriek of satisfaction and launched herself onto the shaman's back, wrapping her legs round Sharon's middle and her arms across her throat, the sheer weight of the striga pushing Sharon onto her knees. Sharon tried to vanish, and the striga vanished with her, plunging into the shadows of the spirit walk; and here, where all things were true, Sharon saw human fingers wrapping round her throat, felt human flesh pressing at her back. Zhanyi's arm tightened around her neck, her feet dug in tighter against her ribs and the whisper in Sharon's ears became a roaring, a screaming, and it screamed,

domine dirige nos domine dirige nos
I looked up and there was this dragon
            I am beautiful I am wonderful I have a secret!!!
and it was insane
                        the secret is me
and it was the city

She scrabbled at Zhanyi's flesh, and here, in the spirit walk, even though Zhanyi's mind and eyes and voice were the striga's, her skin was soft, and warm, and human, and it tore easily beneath Sharon's fingers, blood running down her arms in hot bursts, spilling onto the floor. But the striga roared in rage even as the human Zhanyi sobbed in pain, and Sharon was bent double beneath the weight of the human-striga. Through the blur of suffocation and pain she looked up and there it was

congratulations!

There it was.

Just on the edge of perception.

The black dragon that guarded the city streets with its mad red eyes and its wings of night.

It looked at her, and she looked at it, and it really didn't give a damn.

From elsewhere a burst of light cut through the shadows, bright enough to banish some of the twilight of the shadow walk: a brilliant, baby-shampoo golden glow. Even as Zhanyi looked up, Sharon gave a groan of effort, braced her back against the striga's body and heaved. The two rolled, falling over each other, with the spirit walk breaking around them and shattering into reality. Zhanyi was bleeding from great claw marks on her arms, and Sharon was wounded, too, her neck on fire, and hot blood seeping from a cut above her ear. As they tumbled across each other Rhys raised his potion higher and the light grew with it, a burst of illumination filling the room to almost unbearable gloss-finish whiteness. Sharon tumbled over Zhanyi and saw the striga's eyes begin to narrow and felt something hot beneath her fingers before she rolled away.

For a second, shaman and striga lay where they fell. Sharon looked down at her hands, still clad in dragon-silver, black claws grown from her fingers, and saw a smear of crimson. She turned her hands this way and that, and the smear was a great rupture of redness on the palms of her hands. She scrambled back instinctively, the metal sheen vanishing from her skin as she examined her body, patting herself down for cuts, tears, wounds. Every part of her ached, and as the metal skin retreated to reveal her own, a flush of sensory data and burst of hormones added to this sensation. But for all the bruises, grazes, cuts and bumps which now covered her body like rags on a wandering beggar, there was nothing to explain the blood clinging to her hands.

Then someone whimpered, "I ... didn't mean to?"

She looked round. Zhanyi, pinned like a butterfly beneath the light of Rhys's potion, lay on the floor beside her. The striga was already vanishing into Zhanyi's skin, driven back by the illumination. Her hair became soft again, her eyes receded to their normal size and shape, her skin regained some of its lustre – but only some. The tears across her arms were still bleeding, slow and steady, the blood spreading across the floor. What drew Sharon's attention was the redness welling from between her ribs and seeping through her clothes like water through a dried-out sponge.

For a second she stared, unable to speak. Zhanyi let out a sudden, shuddering breath. Sharon saw blood fleck her lips with the passage of the air, then, with the inhale, a surge of blood from her torso. Then Rhys was by her side, whispering, "Shall I call an ambulance, Ms Li? Ms Li?"

Sharon didn't answer.

Rhys fumbled in his pocket and pulled out his mobile phone, fingers shaking as he dialled. Zhanyi's eyes flickered from Rhys, to Sharon, and then finally to the potion still clutched in Rhys's free hand. She smiled. "Oh," she said. "Baby ... shampoo?"

"I need an ambulance right away!" As Rhys babbled down the

line, Zhanyi's head turned slowly from the potion, to Sharon, and her smile faltered.

"Did . . . did I . . . hurt you?" she whispered.

Sharon shook her head.

"Didn't mean to," added Zhanyi. "Didn't mean it."

"We need to put pressure on the wound!" exclaimed Rhys, the phone still pressed to his ear.

Sharon reached out uncertainly, and pressed her bloodied hands over where she thought the wound might be in Zhanyi's side. Zhanyi flinched, face, eyes, contracting tight, breath rushing faster, thinner. "Didn't mean," she whimpered. "Tried not. Didn't mean."

"Please hurry!" cried Rhys into the telephone.

Sharon felt something chilly brush against her fingers where they pressed down over Zhanyi's chest. She glanced down and saw the fingertips of Zhanyi's hand close around hers. "There's a temple," the striga breathed. "The highest. The brightest. The newest. Palace fit for a god."

Her voice faded.

Her eyes began to close.

"Rhys?" whimpered Sharon.

The druid fumbled for the striga's pulse. Zhanyi's eyes closed.

"Rhys?!" It was nearly a scream, a cry caught somewhere between a whisper and an explosion.

The blood, rushing up between Zhanyi's ribs, began to slow.

Somewhere in the distance, a siren sang.

"Rhys?" A question this time, which barely made it past Sharon's lips, and didn't want an answer.

He put the phone to one side, and carefully pulled Sharon's hands back from the striga's wound. He felt for a pulse on Zhanyi's neck. First one side, then the other. Then he checked a wrist. He bent down low and listened for breath, for the rise and fall of her chest.

The siren dirge crept closer.

"We have to go," he whispered.

Sharon didn't answer.

"We have to go!" he repeated, grabbing her by the arm.

Still no answer.

He pulled her bodily to her feet and through the living-room door. The front door was standing ajar. Rhys wrenched it back all the way and dragged Sharon out into the night, turning first one way, then the other, hearing the siren come closer, as she staggered behind him, into the dark.

Chapter 71

Regret Never Helped Anyone

They were guarding the rusted blade.

They weren't quite sure why they were guarding it, but Mr Roding, when he looked at it, was afraid, and that told the others quite enough.

They waited where it had begun; in the small downstairs office by Coram's Fields. Sally, Mr Roding, Gretel and Kevin had holed up for the night, four guards to one rusted blade. Mr Roding had laid out pillows on a couch, and somehow managed to find blankets in a cupboard in the back of another office. Sally hung suspended from the ceiling, wings folded in over her face, one eye open and staring at nothing, like a nesting duck waiting for an aggressive cat. Gretel sat hunched by the disused fireplace, while Kevin sat at Rhys's computer, a pair of headphones pressed to his ears, watching BBC downloads by the grey-blue light of the flickering screen. Sometimes Kevin exclaimed, "Oh my God, she is totally not wearing *that*?"

Mr Roding grunted and rolled over on the couch. He'd given up trying to get Kevin not to exclaim out loud; the vampire, he was forced to conclude, didn't even notice his own actions. The only light in the room glowed from the computer screen, but sodium streetlights each cast a glow from outside, and created conflicting versions of the window's shape across the ceiling and floor.

Sally the banshee swayed gently from her ceiling roost. She wasn't particularly comfortable inside confined spaces, not least as small walls tended to amplify her ear-shattering voice to the point where even she found it unbearable; but this was the office of Magicals Anonymous, one of the very few places in London where it was okay to let her wings down and stretch out those talons. It wasn't that banshees were social creatures – far from it – but in the busy urban environment Sally had been forced to reach the same conclusion as every mage, magus and magi from Acton to West Ham: that in the city, everything changed. Especially people.

A key turned in the latch.

Sally stirred beneath her roost. Kevin, eyes still glued to the computer screen, sniffed the air unconsciously. Mr Roding rolled onto his side, head turning towards the door.

The front door opened.

Footsteps fell in the corridor outside.

In the room, no one stirred.

They were hunters, all of them, in their different ways. And sure, in recent years they may have chosen antibacterial hand wash over hot blood, and Impressionist art over raw pigeon, but there was a reason they had been asked to guard Old Man Bone's rusted blade.

A hand fell on the door to the room, started to push it back. Gretel stirred on the floor, Kevin's eyes darted up from the computer screen. Outside the opening door, someone hesitated. Then someone sneezed.

"Um . . . guys?"

Mr Roding groaned and rolled back across the couch, pressing his head into the cushions. "It's the druid."

The door eased back further, revealing Rhys and, just behind him, the grey-faced shape of Sharon. Gretel rose slowly to her feet, an oddly courteous gesture from the troll, and murmured, "Good evening . . . morning, Rhys. Good morning, Ms Li, I hope you are both well?"

Rhys smiled wanly. Sharon drifted towards her desk, and slumped into the chair without a sound. Sally eyed her from the ceiling, and didn't move.

"No ... trouble?" asked Rhys. "No evil vapours, outbreaks of plague, glass gods?"

"It was fine until you two bloody showed up," grumbled Mr Roding from the couch.

"I'll put the kettle on ... " said the druid, even as Kevin glanced up again from his screen and sniffed the air. The vampire's face blanched.

"Oh my God!" he exclaimed, ripping the headphones from his head and spinning to stare at Sharon. "You're, like ... covered in blood!"

Sharon stared at Kevin for a long hard moment, not moving from her chair. Her hands were clean, washed in the bathroom of Zhanyi's house, but traces of blood still clung to her clothes, her nails, her thoughts; and as the vampire leapt to his feet with a rising shriek of "Oh my God, and it's striga blood, it could be, like, contaminated!" she hit him with a look so hard he almost staggered.

"Are you all right, Ms Li?" rumbled Gretel.

Sharon didn't answer.

Kevin, never one to let a point go, hopped nervously from foot to foot. "Striga blood!" he wailed. "It doesn't even have a measurable rhesus value! Oh, my God." Another thought struck, more terrifying yet. "What if there's airborne particulates? What then?" So saying, he grabbed his large shoulder bag, and started rummaging through it. Mr Roding, usually professionally disinterested in all things which weren't several weeks into decomposition, sat up to observe as Kevin pulled out bottles of alcohol wipe, sterile pads and surgical gloves. Snapping on a blue medical mask, he offered the packet round for anyone else afraid of inhaling something untoward. Then, pulling on a pair of latex gloves, he very carefully pushed the sterile wipes towards Sharon's desk, trying at once to keep as far from her and as close to the medicines as he could. "Babes," he added, as she stared unseeing at the packet before her, "I know it's gonna seem like an overreaction, but I'd totally get yourself checked out first thing tomorrow morning. These things are easier to deal with if you get them in the incubation period!"

"Tea!" Rhys's voice was too loud and too jolly as he poured steaming water into a chipped cup. "Who's for a cuppa?"

Amid silence, Gretel raised a giant hand.

"Marvellous!" exclaimed Rhys. "Biscuits?"

"Where's the blade?" Sharon's voice was as empty as the look on her face, sucking all feeling and sound into it so that, for a moment, the others wondered if she'd spoken at all.

"Your goblin mate's got it," murmured Mr Roding.

"Where is he?"

"He's right . . . oh." Kevin looked round the room, his gaze drifting from face to face. "Well it *smells* like he's still here."

Sharon sighed with exasperation and, without seeming to move, vanished.

It was almost too easy, now. Before, when shifting into the shadow walk, she'd had to move physically, matching her pace with that speed at which travellers through the city all seemed to walk, that precise I-know-where-I-am walk of the commuter on a weary journey, the walk that made you invisible to the world, no more and no less than a part of the city as a whole.

But now, in the dead of night, her eyes heavy, her head sinking down, her fingers dry from too much soap to wash off too much blood, it was simple. Just a falling – that was all that was required. A falling without moving into the shadow walk, then a falling without moving into the spirit walk, and then a falling without moving and she was on the edge of the dream walk, still sitting in the chair by her desk and in this place, where all things which were true were finally evident. She looked, without much interest, and saw skin flaking off Mr Roding like snow, revealing the rotting flesh beneath, bound together by muscle fibres and runes; she saw the air ripple around the great umbrella of Sally's wings where she hung from the rafters; and she heard the rattling on cobbled streets outside of the costermongers who had gone before, and the belching of the cars that would be tomorrow, and the whispering of the walls which had seen so many people come within their grasp to try, and fail, and pass on by, and all of it was . . .

. . . largely irrelevant at this stage in the proceedings.

She looked, without rising from her chair, and saw Sammy the Elbow, a tiny figure on the very edge of the dream walk, and in this place, with his back turned to her, she could see the shadows of his life, hovering at his back, swimming beneath his feet, a whole history spread out wide in the shadowlands of Sammy's past: a great black horde, a whole tribe that flickered and swirled behind him, forming a cone of ghosts that rippled and swayed like a whole, living thing, avoiding his sight. Sammy had always said that a shaman needed a tribe, but had never told her what had happened to his.

Then he turned, and there was something in his hand, and the ghosts of his past shimmered away behind him, blown apart by the smallest movement. Whatever it was the goblin grasped between his tiny fingers, it was whispering, speaking, words without a language, a voice with no mouth, calling, begging, imploring, and as it whispered it dripped black drops of blood onto the ground, and every drop as it fell spread outwards and became a face, twisting its features briefly up from the paving stones, before it was swallowed whole into the earth.

Sharon rose, and walked towards the goblin's back, until she stood almost beside him. Looking down, she saw that he held the rusted blade of Old Man Bone, its point turned towards the earth, black blood dripping off the cracked orange iron. His eyes were fixed on it – no, not quite – fixed through it, staring down at his own bare feet.

"Sammy?" murmured Sharon. The goblin didn't stir. "Sammy?"

Nothing. His arms were shaking, which effect seemed to shake his entire body, the thin hairs quivering on the top of his head. "Sammy," she murmured, "I think you oughtta give me the knife now."

He turned to stare at her, and there was a look on his face that she had never seen before. If he had been human, she might have called it . . . sorrow? Then he grabbed her by the sleeve, raised the knife, and, point first, drew it down through the air before him. The greyness of the spirit walk seemed to crack, creating a black tear in the world, through which, before she could protest, he pulled her.

They stepped out into a street – any street in any place in the city – white terraced houses either side, shops below. The greyness of the spirit walk was still on everything they saw, but the street-lights burnt through, sodium-yellow, filling the world with their sickly colour, and lights from within the houses gave off the same dull glow. Sharon turned, taking it in slowly, then followed Sammy's gaze upwards. Wires criss-crossed the street, where every Christmas the residents had hung fairy lights and coloured banners against the bleakness of short days and long nights. But where their purpose had been festive, now they were hung with something else entirely. Shoes, some laced, some Velcro, the straps pressed together to form a bond, dangled across the street as far as she could see, hundreds – thousands – of them. There, slung overhead, the stiff black leather shoes of an undertaker, their laces joined in a neat bow. Here, the brown loafers of a busy estate agent who never got a chance to sit down, nor ever would sit down again. There, the sensible navy shoes of the old lady who went out to get her shopping and never returned; the white sneakers from a trendy jogger caught out late at night; the fashionable branded trainers of the young man who spat in the street, and vanished. Here, the suede shoes of an off-duty constable on his way to buy milk; there the ankle-high lace-up boots of the partygoer who missed the last bus.

And more: they stretched back further, and as they zigzagged across the street, they grew older, relics of another time, hanging off ancient pieces of rope and bent branches pulled across the street. There, the shoes of the Inns of Court solicitor, disappeared in 1896, may he rest in peace; the tall boots of a highwayman, the buckles strapped one to the other; the rough, laced sandals of the night-watchman who rattled his staff to declare the hour – the shoes stretched off into the night beyond the reach of sight, a thousand years and more of empty, silent remnants left by people gone.

Sharon looked up at them, hanging like washing from a line, then down at the silent street. She expected ghosts, echoes, the shadows of those who had once inhabited them, but there was . . .

. . . nothing.

Silence.

The absolute, perpetual silence of the vanished.

Nothing but shoes remained.

Neither shaman spoke.

Then Sammy said, "I didn't . . . it weren't meant to be this many."

Silence.

"Weren't . . . meant?" Sharon's voice was loud, painfully so, in the dead silence of the dead street. "Weren't . . . *meant?*"

"The city is alive," muttered the goblin, eyes fixed upwards at the shoes strung across the street. "It has to feed."

He turned the blade slowly in his hands, and, yes, it was still there, the tiniest whisper, a voice that came through to the mind without bothering with the ears, which whispered,

give me
   give me
      give me
         give me
            what I'm owed!

Sharon looked away. "I don't think I want this any more," she murmured. "I don't think . . . I want to know."

Sammy grunted. "Tough. Coward's way that is, not knowing. You know, and it's proper that you know, because knowing is . . . is what's left. Someone's gotta know, someone's gotta care, no damn reason why that ain't you. Gotta be done. Gotta be a truth, and it's gotta be known. You're a shaman. Deal with it."

"How? How'd you deal with it and be . . . ?" She hesitated. Then, "I killed a striga."

"She gonna hurt you?"

"Yes . . ."

"Then you did what you had to do."

"She was . . . nice. She was . . . like me."

"You mean to kill her?"

"No – no. I swear, I didn't, I didn't mean . . ."

"Deal with it."

"I don't think I know what that means."

"Cos it means nothing. Ain't an easy way to deal with it, ain't no map or nice book or any of that shit that tells you what you gotta do. You just gotta do it. Whatever it is."

Silence.

Then, "There are a thousand ghosts at your back, Sammy."

"Better at me back than in my face."

"Is that how you deal with it?"

The goblin's head snapped round. His eyes locked onto Sharon's. For a moment they stared at each other, in that dead street beneath the shoes of the vanished. Then he looked away. "Everyone's gotta find their own way. Knower of the path, that's our job. Seer of the truth and knower of the path. No one said it were ever easy."

They stood there, beneath the shoes, and stared at nothing, and said nothing.

Then Sammy turned and, with a muttered, "Come on", started to walk away.

Sharon hesitated, even as the goblin began to vanish back into the spirit walk, her gaze playing involuntarily over the shoes hung across the telephone lines. Then she, too, began to walk away.

Something flashed in the corner of her eye, bright and blue. She paused, looking back. A flicker of blue rippled along a wire overhead, dancing between the tied laces of the shoes suspended there. It vanished into the wall of the house on the opposite side of the street, flickered again, then bounced back and forth before earthing itself down a pair of laces and into a pair of brown walking boots suspended by a double bow. More flashes of blue rippled across the lines overhead, dancing round each other, thickening and spinning like courting insects, writhing over and under each other, dripping in great sparks, an electrical rain falling down from above, coalescing on the ground and forming a convulsing pool of electricity that spun, thickened, grew, stretched, thickened again and that, slowly, cautiously, the corners still sparking and rippling over each other as the whole settled, became a man. His body was misshapen, many parts not placed quite right, and his eyes blazed with an inhuman light; but if you looked through these things, through a skin trying to disintegrate into electric nothing about his face, beneath a head of dark hair writhing in a perpetual blue flame, the man was human, and the features were familiar.

"Help me!" Sparks dribbled from his lips like undigested food as he spoke, and he was looking straight at her, and he was the sometime Midnight Mayor, the human mind whose body the blue electric angels precariously inhabited, and he was Matthew Swift.

"Help me," he whispered again, and at his feet blue electricity rippled and sparked, grounding off him as he tried to stagger forward. Even that small movement nearly collapsed him, back into electric nothing as he moved, contained with a gasp that seemed to draw his being back together again in crude, changing shapes.

"0781273 . . . !" The sound was nearly a shriek, pushed out between lips that could barely hold their human form.

"07812 . . . " he tried again, and his legs dissolved with the effort, collapsing beneath him into swirling blue sparks.

Sharon moved towards him even as his flesh parted and co-alesced again, skin breaking into flame, flame thickening into skin, each motion now happening almost too fast to see.

"Matthew?" she murmured.

He tried to pull himself out of the pool of blue electricity which was all that remained of his legs, leaning on his arms, which them-selves threatened to crumble into sparks under their own weight. "Help me?"

"Matthew Swift?"

He looked up, and for a moment, even through the unnatural blue of his eyes, there was something real, human and desperate, staring up at her. "Sharon?"

Cautiously, she knelt down by him. The sparks of blue fire leapt up to run over her skin, play around her hands, her wrists, and flow in little eddies around her knees, but they weren't hot, and they didn't bite, but carried with them instead the thousand cries of . . .

hello, hello?
I'm trying to reach . . .
      the voicemail of
lols xx
      r u comin 2nite?
and she said but I said and then he said
      hello!!

A hand, or what was left of a hand, the fingers crumbled into whispering flame, brushed her own. Its touch, warm and human, surprised her. She unfolded her own hand and saw, floating on her palm, the ghostly twin crosses of the Midnight Mayor, a reminder of the job promotion she'd never wanted. Then the hand that touched hers opened in surprise, and there were the real marks of the Midnight Mayor, two vivid red scars, defiantly crimson in a dissolving palm.

She took the hand, and held it tight, even as the skin gave way beneath her grasp. "Domine dirige nos," she breathed. "Domine dirige nos."

The grip within hers increased. She looked into Matthew Swift's face and saw a smile, so brief as to be barely brighter than the sparks into which it was dissolving. Then it faded. "07812732 . . . 732 . . ."

The hand crumpled in her own, dissolving into sparks which wormed and writhed away. The face dripped away, taking the words with it, dissolving into blue flame that splashed harmlessly across the floor. "I'll find you," she breathed. "It's okay. I'll bring you back."

The last features dissolved into nothing, and sunk down, into the earth.

Chapter 72

Sharon

My name is Sharon Li.

I am a shaman.

I am one who sees the truth of things, and the truth is that there are no absolutes any more. There is no absolute right and absolute wrong, there is nothing for which a reason cannot be found, a cause observed. For every murder there is a story, for every birth there is a consequence, and nothing – nothing at all – is simple, especially the truth.

I am a knower of the path. I chose the way I look at the world, but, in choosing, I know all the other paths I could have taken, all the other choices I could have made. That is what it means, that is what shamans have to do.

I am deputy Midnight Mayor. Protector of the city, guardian of the night. I didn't know what this means, but now I do. I'm the one who makes the choices, because someone has to.

And that's fine.

Don't think, just because I am all of these things, that I can't be me.

Chapter 73

Seize the Day

Sharon sat on a beanbag in a corner of Magicals Anonymous furthest from the window, nursing a cup of coffee. She said:

"I think it's like this. Someone – probably some guy called Hacq – thought it'd be, like, a mega-cool idea to make his own god. He got together a bunch of guys to help him, including Brid, the witch we picked up from the river, and ... and Zhanyi. He probably said something like 'this'll be really cool, come on, guys, let's make a god' and instead of saying 'that sounds like a bloody stupid idea' they seemed to go with it and they're dead now so I guess it's too late to ask them what the fuck they were thinking but I guess it was ... I guess they were scared. And they wanted something more. Needed something more. So they went with it.

"But," she paused to slurp coffee as Sally, Gretel, Rhys, Kevin, Sammy and Mr Roding waited, watching her in the slow pale creep of dawn. "But you can't just go around *making* a god. I mean, you need time, you need power, right? And where do you get that power from? I'm guessing it's not enough to sacrifice a chicken or anything like that; you need something bigger. And they look around and they see Old Man Bone and they're, like, 'hey, this dude, he's kinda like a god, and he gets fed on human lives and stuff, and wow! He's got a magic blade, because that never goes wrong for anyone; let's pinch it and use it for our stuff, there's gonna be no consequences in pissing off an ancient god of the dead, yeah!'

"But they've got a few brain cells to rub together, because someone clearly says 'whoa there, I'm not sure about stealing the blade of Old Man Bone, I'm thinking there might be some curses attached', so they get this kid – B-Man – to pinch it for them. B-Man is one of the Tribe. He pinches the blade, and, sure enough, gets the Black Death for his trouble. But by the time the Tribe are sitting up noticing that one of their kids is growing black lumps under his arms, these glass-god guys have already got the rusted blade. But they've still got a problem, haven't they? The rusted blade of Old Man Bone is still only good for feeding Old Man Bone, they can't use it just like that to make their own god. They need a new one, something modelled on the basic principle of Old Man Bone's blade, but crafted to their own purposes.

"So they go to the scylla sisters, who use the rusted blade as a template to make something new. A new, glass blade, something which mimics the effect of Old Man Bone's magic but, obviously, without actually chilling out the dead guy. And they might have got away with it except, by now, other people are interested. Crompton's noticed that he's lost the blade, and he goes running to Swift. The Tribe have also noticed that B-Man's got the Black Death and so when Swift turns up in the hospital trying to chat to the kid, the Tribe sit up and take note, because, let's face it, where Swift goes, explosions usually follow and so it's only sensible to pay attention to that sorta shit. And Miles said that B-Man died, but it wasn't the plague that killed him, which kinda suggests that Brid and that crowd . . . did it. Killed him, to stop him talking to Swift.

"But that's still not stopping Swift, and by now he's noticed that there are shoes being thrown over high things but Old Man Bone is getting pissed. And he's kinda dumb, but he's still Midnight Mayor, and actually he's got this special kinda dumb that really makes him a bit scary. So I figure that the glass-god crowd are all a bit 'oh fuck' and they decide they need to get rid of him.

"But here again, they've got a problem. Cos it's all very well killing the Midnight Mayor, but even if you manage to get rid of the guy, the magic is still gonna linger on, it's gonna get inherited by someone. And, bloody hell, I think we all don't want that to happen because I'm not happy about this deputy Midnight Mayor stuff, and even if it doesn't mean anything for my pay grade I'm seriously thinking you should have more qualifications for the job of Midnight Mayor other than 'the other guy said so'. I mean, whatever happened to proper management techniques, it's the twenty-first century, for Christ's sake . . . but anyway. Yeah. Killing Swift isn't really gonna hack it. But then they figure . . . he's not just the Midnight Mayor, is he? He's the blue electric angels, he's got this mega affinity for the telephones; maybe they can use that to somehow . . . bind him? Like, to trap his mind while leaving his body harmless? Because that's not death, not really, and it'd take out the Midnight Mayor without some other bugger taking over the job.

"So they send him an email. 'Hey, we've found Crompton's umbrella!' they say, 'come collect!' I mean, they probably dress it up a bit, but based on what we found on Swift's computer, that's my best guess. And Swift, he's dumb, but he's not totally dumb, so even as he's thinking 'sure, I'd better check this out', he's chatting with Kelly and he's all 'if something happens to me, make Sharon my deputy'. Which, like I said, is majorly flattering but professionally seriously flawed. And then he trots off to Deptford and these guys try to bind and compel him or whatever and it goes wrong. Majorly, majorly wrong. I mean, it works in the sense that they do incapacitate the Midnight Mayor, if you count a rampaging blue electric angel with no restraining human consciousness as a victory. And I think we can say that the angels kill Brid, during the whole cock-up that was that bit of business, before they go totally off the rails and end up running to the next-nearest off-the-rails guys they can find – the Tribe. Which is obviously where we come in."

Sharon paused to let out another sigh and take in another slurp of coffee. "So, like, most of what Rhys and me do is catch up with what Swift's already done. Which is, I think, even more proof, like you needed it, that memos are good. But eventually we catch on to the whole scylla sisters thing and off we trot to World's End and I'm guessing by now someone's noticed that we're getting close and . . ." Her voice trailed off abruptly.

"Actually, I'm not totally sure about how someone worked out that we were getting close. I mean, I've got a few ideas, but it's not really something I gave much thought to at the time, what with all the death and fuss and that. Anyway, point being, whoever's behind the glass-god business clearly decide they need to tidy up their loose ends, so they kill the sisters and nearly kill Rhys, Miles and me, and that's another thing, actually. Because when I last checked, people served their gods, not the other way round, but this glass dude who we met in Chelsea seemed to be totally on board with the other guys' agenda, and I'm thinking it takes more than just a bit of prayer to do that."

"'A god'," sniffed Sammy, his nasal hairs quivering with indignation at the notion. "In the old days all you needed, to be a god, was to be unexplained. The sun comes up and we dunno how? It's a god! The moon waxes and wanes and it's a goddess! Gods are always made up by people, to serve people; it's what they do. Ain't no such thing as a god . . . just an idea with a purpose, that's all, and usually some bloody stupid bloody naïve purpose made up by people what ain't got the brains to figure shit out for themselves."

"If we are hypothesising," offered Mr Roding, idly peeling a thin layer of translucent skin off the palm of his hand as he talked, "that the mechanism by which Old Man Bone's blade works has been mimicked, and adapted onto a new weapon by the scylla sisters, then it is no great logical leap to assume that the object being fuelled by the blade has been modified accordingly. Thus, where Old Man Bone is an independent entity with his own will, whatever has been created by this new blade need not, in fact, have an independent consciousness of its own. 'God' could merely be a term representative of some imposed physical and spiritual properties, rather than an indication of actual theological purpose."

Sammy turned to stare at the necromancer. "That's what I bloody said!" he shrilled. "People are always like that. I say clever shit and then humans repeat it bloody slowly and stupidly, and people are, like, 'that's a great idea' and I'm sitting right here! It's racist, that's what it is!"

Mr Roding stared long and hard at Sammy, as if trying to work out whether he wasn't the victim of an inexplicable goblin joke. Then his gaze turned back to Sharon. "Your training as a shaman," he said. "Is it a certificated course?"

Sharon smiled wanly, even as Sammy shot her a glare more expressive than any shriek. "Let's say for now," she murmured, "that 'god' isn't the right way to talk about the big scary glass dude. Let's say ... glass guy or glass ... construct or something like that. Anyway, that wasn't the only odd thing about him, because, sure, he looked like an unstoppable glass dude all the time he was trying to tear us to itty-bitty pieces. But, actually, if you saw him from the spirit walk he was ... well, he was sorta more a girl."

All eyes shifted to Sammy. "Oh, now you want my opinion, do you?" sniffed the goblin. "Now that you ain't got a clue what it means, you come running back to Sammy for answers. Well, they always do, don't they?"

"Do you have any?" asked Mr Roding.

"Not ... right now," admitted Sammy. "But that's only cos I ain't got enough information to work off, ain't it? 'He looked like a girl' is bloody useless."

Rhys shuffled closer to Sharon, hoping his mere physical presence would offer a wordless reassurance to complement her locked, tired smile.

"Whatever this glass guy is," she said, "I think we can say he's connected to the glass blade that the sisters made, and that this thing is modelled on Crompton's umbrella. And if it is, then it means it's making people ... disappear, with their shoes thrown over the nearest telephone line, and that whoever made it is also responsible for killing B-Man and for trying to do shit to Swift. And while we're talking about Swift, I think we also gotta pay attention to the fact that his human mind is still stuck in the telephone wires, and, while he's doing okay, I can't imagine that's gonna be a helpful thing

for anyone. So the sooner we get him out, the better. He's given me
the beginning of a telephone number ..."

"You've talked with the Midnight Mayor?" blurted Mr Roding.

"Yeah, but it was a kinda wires-crossed moment. Anyway, there's
the beginning of a telephone number, which I think makes a kinda
sense, since if you were going to get him into the telephones you'd
probably need a phone or something with an open line to do it
with. So I think it boils down to this: find the guy with the glass
blade; find the guys who summoned the glass god; find the mobile
phone that Swift's so hung up on – sorry, didn't mean for it to come
out like that – and then ... yeah ...That's kinda that."

Into the silence that followed, there sounded the slow, careful
scribbling of wipeable marker pen on whiteboard.

Excuse me? I have a question?

Sally the banshee held up her small whiteboard for inspection.
Satisfied that no one was about to object to her enquiry, she turned
it over to reveal:

How do we find these individuals, or individual, or culpable
party?

Silence.

Then, "I've got an even better question," grunted Mr Roding. "If
this glass god – or not-god, or whatever he – it – is meant to be, is
so tough, and has been fuelled by the sacrificial blood of people
snatched away in the night, how exactly do you suggest we deal
with it, when we meet it?"

Another silence. Sharon said, in a voice suddenly high and
bright, "Well, I think this is a lot for us to think about so if anyone
wants another cup of coffee ..."

Wordlessly, Rhys took the mug from her hands.

"Could Mr Swift handle it?" asked Gretel. "I don't mean to
impose any difficulties upon him, I'm sure he's already very imposed
upon. But as I understand it, the blue electric angels are themselves
very ... temperamental ... individuals, and perhaps if they could be
convinced to interact with this glass entity ...?"

"I'm not sure the blue electric angels are in a convincing mood,"
murmured Sharon. "Which isn't to say it's not a great idea," she

added, as Gretel's great face began the slow collapse of an ice sheet
from a glacier. "It's just getting them on board without blowing up
the train, if you see what I'm saying."

Gretel nodded the slow nod of the mildly dejected.

"The A-A-A-Aldermen seem very big on heavy artillery?" ventured Rhys.

"Yeah, I was kinda hoping to get through my first month at work
without breaking out the grenade launchers," sighed Sharon. "But I
guess it's all part of senior management, learning to adapt to difficult circumstances and that."

"Challenging," corrected Rhys automatically.

"Sorry – yeah. 'Challenging' circumstances and that. Like, so it's
challenging to know the graves are gonna crack open, plague's
gonna flood the streets, the dead'll walk among the living and Old
Man Bone will have my shoes."

Rhys hadn't thought it was possible for the dejection in the room
to deepen, but somehow it managed it. Then Sammy said, "We
could just give Old Man Bone his blade back?"

"Yeah," grunted Sharon. "I guess we should at that."

If this was meant to lighten anyone's spirits, it didn't.

I hate to offer such a stand-offish approach, wrote Sally, *but
perhaps this isn't the time to consider the matter?*

All eyes turned to the banshee, who scrubbed out her note and
wrote in a hurried scrawl,

*Of course the dead walking is a grave concern, but if everyone
in this room is tired and rather fraught, perhaps any decisions
made regarding the fate of the city would be more construc-
tively made after a little recuperation?*

At the stunned silence in the room, Sally beamed a deadly-
toothed beam and added, with a scrub of her sleeve across the board
and a scribble of pen,

It's important to recognise one's own limitations, yes?

Sharon looked at Rhys, and Rhys smiled what he hoped was a
smile of utter faith, confidence and dedication, mixed with an overwhelming, soul-deep desire to sleep. Outside, the grey light of dawn
was drowning out the sodium glow of the streetlamps, which started

to flicker and die. The silence of the streets was yielding to the distant grumble-hiss of rising traffic. It occurred to Sharon that she couldn't remember the last time she'd slept, or even what sleep felt like; only that it was good and it was blissful, and that it seemed entirely inappropriate.

"Maybe a couple of hours," she conceded. "Then we . . . totally get on this thing. Fate of the city and that."

Rhys sagged with relief. Sally's wings twitched in approval.

"Besides," added Sharon, "I'm sure the Aldermen will have things to do."

Chapter 74

Management Is the Art of Delegation

Kelly said, "I see." She listened a little longer. "I *see*." And listened still. "Of course. Well, naturally."

The black-clad Alderman stood with a phone pressed to her ear, and nodded, and smiled, even though the speaker on the other end of the line couldn't see the expression of goodwill and optimism that was, Kelly felt, a good default position for any personal assistant.

"So . . . if I understand you . . . we need to find a secret temple to a not-entirely-glass god, within which will be a group of probably anti-social magicians armed with a blade copied from Old Man Bone's own? And in order to destroy said glass god, we must find a telephone whose number begins with 07812 and free the Midnight Mayor from his captivity in the lines? Is that about correct?" Her smile was fixed, her voice light and pleasant.

"Uh . . . yeah." Sharon's voice was as far the opposite of Kelly's as it was possible for a voice to be. "That's kinda it."

"And meanwhile you're . . . ?"

"I figured I might have a shower. And maybe . . . a nap. Not," added the shaman, "in a kinda lazy-off-the-job way, because that's not what this is, and I really don't want you to think that I'm fobbing you off with this because, like I said, as soon as I can speak without dribbling then I'm so totally on this deputy Midnight Mayor thing, but also, my brain is, like, coming out of my ears and Rhys looks really tired, too, and the guys are on it with looking after Old Man Bone's blade and Kevin's got a fresh pint of O- blood to see him through the day and I really think . . . I *really* think that this would be . . . like . . . a really good idea?"

Silence, as Sharon waited for condemnation and reproof.

"Ms Li!" Kelly's voice soared high as a bat above an epic forest. "I think this is a marvellous idea! It's all very well and good taking responsibility for the fate of the city, and may I say you've done it just brilliantly, inspirationally, even – but really, if we *are* having to fight a glass god . . . "

"Dude."

"What?"

"We – that's Magicals Anonymous and that – figured 'god' had a negative connotation? Particularly when it's got the words 'have to fight' before it."

"Of course, a thousand apologies. If we're going to have to fight a glass dude and all his confederates, then of course, but of *course*, a good night's sleep and some clean clothes are entirely prudent!"

On the other end of the line, Sharon nearly collapsed with relief. Her eyes stung with a sudden heat which could not, absolutely *could not*, be tears, since she wasn't upset, wasn't angry, wasn't even near chopped onions or posters about lost kittens, and yet there it was, a hysterical, burning wetness building up around her eyes and she blurted, "Thanks. I didn't want you to think I wasn't . . . "

"Of course not, Ms Li! We'll get on with finding this glass temple and you just put your head back and relax."

"It'll only be a nap . . . "

"Nonsense and tosh, Ms Li. Your overtime must be extensive by now, and I'm sure that if shamans were unionised there would be rules about having eleven-hour breaks between every shift of truth-seeking. So I really must insist that you take your health seriously and have a sleep. After all, what is there you can practically do right now?"

Sharon hesitated. Somehow she felt she no longer had to say the words, 'well, I *could* dial every single mobile phone whose numbers begin with 07812 732???? and see if, nine thousand nine hundred and ninety-nine calls later I get lucky and the Midnight Mayor picks up ... or I could walk round and round the city trying to find a temple to an angry glass god ... or return Old Man Bone's blade to Crompton or check my email because, actually, these things add up, or organise the witches' bingo night or write a letter to my MP about discrimination against djinn in the workplace or ...'

"Sleep?" she squeaked. "I could ... I could sleep."

"Absolutely, Ms Li. Sleep and a sound meal. You just leave all of this in our hands."

"That's great," she sighed. "You're amazing."

Later, Sharon wasn't sure if she'd bothered to hang up before her head hit the pillow.

Chapter 75

Teamwork Is the Key to Success

Kelly set to work.

Or, rather, the Aldermen worked and Kelly supervised.

Supervising, it turned out, was also very hard work. Sure, Kelly Shiring had always suspected that management was tougher than it looked from the outside, not least as, in her capacity as personal assistant to the Midnight Mayor, she'd seen just how much paperwork landed on Swift's desk every day and, more importantly, just how badly wrong things could go when he failed to deal with it. And obviously, it wasn't her place – not at all – to make decisions for her boss. She was merely the vessel, she informed herself, through which these things passed. But then again, if a decision had to be made, and someone had to make it, and if Swift *wasn't* going to deal with it but it really had to be done then, really, as a PA, as someone close, if that was at all possible, to understanding his state of mind, perhaps she was the only person who actually . . . could. . . make decisions after all?

And so, quietly, and without anyone really noticing, Kelly had slipped up through the ranks of the Aldermen, from merely a PA given a job which no one else would touch with a fully charged iron wand, to quietly running things, for the good of everyone else. Not that her pay grade had improved; but then again, it seemed too cheeky to ask. Not least as she'd probably have to ask herself.

So when Kelly turned to the assembled Aldermen of Harlun and Phelps and uttered the immortal words, "hello team – I'm looking for a glass god, any ideas?" somehow no one questioned her right to command.

She sat and supervised, and, in its own way, it was rather fun.

Chapter 76

A Good Night's Sleep Clears All Woes

Sharon woke at 3.34 p.m., sat upright in bed and exclaimed, "Of course they shouldn't charge VAT!"

The words rang round her room in the tiny flat in Hoxton, ripping through the afternoon sunlight drifting in through the dirty window, and caused the person sleeping on the floor by the foot of the bed to sit bolt upright, too, a potion bottle clutched in one hand, a pillow in the other, and cry out, "Did they, where?"

There was a moment. It was the moment in which two waking minds shook themselves down, brushed themselves off, took a steadying breath and, like released prisoners curious to see if the world is as they remembered, opened their eyes to their surroundings.

Sharon was sitting in her small bed in last night's clothes. The blanket was a shuffled mess at her feet, the pillow a pounded lump. She'd been planning to hold Magicals Anonymous' first ever singles night (no enchantments, glamorous or polymorphic transformations please) at the local community hall, and at 3.33 she'd been hit by the thought that they couldn't possibly be charging her VAT for the night. The sudden rush to consciousness was merely an inevitable by-product of this nagging little doubt, which had been scratching at the back of her mind for weeks.

The resulting flash of triumphalism faded, as a recollection of everything else flooded back in oppressive detail. Her gaze drifted to the floor, as her ears contributed their penny's worth and declared that it wasn't usual for her bedroom to respond to her thoughts by shouting answers of its own.

Rhys sat on the floor by her bed, his eyes swerving round the room as he struggled with his own revelations. Revelation the first – contrary to all expectation, he was still not dead, in itself a remarkable achievement. Revelation the second – his back hurt, his neck had a crick in it, his nose itched and somewhere just proud of his vocal chords a deep-throated sneeze was forming. If none of this brought him contentment, then revelation the third – that he had spent the last six hours sleeping, amid a mess of thrown-down duvet and pillows, on the floor of Sharon Li's bedroom – brought a stab of adrenalin that nearly knocked his head from his shoulders. And there she was, Sharon Li, staring down at him from her bed, mouth hanging open as her brain tried to work out how he'd got there and why.

"Hello, Ms Li," he managed to say.

"Hi."

He looked round her room, then realised that looking round a girl's room might be considered ungentlemanly, so stopped looking, and stared at the floor. This, he concluded, might be construed as disapproving, since it was a lovely room really, and not that messy all things considered, and he didn't want Sharon to get the wrong idea. So he looked up again, this time at the ceiling, and as he looked some deep, dark voice inside, which had been with him for as long as he could remember and only ever said one thing, whispered . . . *you idiot* . . .

He sneezed.

Then sneezed again.

As the third sneeze approached, he scrunched up his face, stuck his chin down to his chest, and . . .

... a box of tissues appeared beside him. The shock of relief at being proffered such blessed objects briefly suppressed the allergic instinct. "Thank you," he gasped, and grabbed a handful. Then he worried that he'd seized too many, and unstoppably, inescapably, inevitably ...

... he sneezed.

Sharon said, "You know, I can't actually remember how I got here?"

"Um ... you fell asleep in Magicals Anonymous," said Rhys, dabbing at his nose. "And Gretel said she'd carry you home and Mr Roding said that was a stupid idea and Kevin ordered a taxi and I put you in it and you were kinda awake, Ms Li, but you were mumbling something about bingo and plague and community support schemes, so we took you home and you said you had to call Ms Shiring and you did that and we put you in bed and I didn't want to leave you alone in case anything bad happened so I um ... I stayed here."

A pause. Then, "Okay, Rhys, I feel like there's a few things I oughtta say right now."

Rhys braced himself for retribution. Sharon took in a long breath, then blurted, "So, yeah, it's, like, really bad management to get involved in relationships in the office and that, and I do not believe – I mean, it's just a bloody stupid idea, isn't it? – but I do not believe that just because you've been through hell together and people have tried to shoot, stab, cut, fry, strangle, suffocate or blow you up or whatever, that going through all that trauma together is a proper basis for a relationship. But ... " – she stopped to heave down another breath – " ... all this besides I figure sometimes you just gotta take a plunge so, when this is all over and that, I mean, if we live that long, do you wanna ... get a drink sometime?"

For a moment, Rhys's mouth worked silently, even as his nose and his ears flushed the colour of ripe tomatoes. Then, in a voice which was meant to be cool and savvy, but which came out as a squeak, he blurted, "Um ... yes, Ms Li? That would be ... very nice?"

"Great. Then maybe you can also start calling me Sharon."

"Yes, Ms Li – I mean, Sharon – sorry, Ms Li."

"That's sorted then."

Only later did Rhys realise that he'd got through the entire exchange without a single antihistamine.

Chapter 77

Embrace the Inter-Connectedness of All Things

The city moved on.

It moved from the saggy part of the day, that mid-afternoon lull when children slumbered in the classroom and teachers regretted having that extra portion of potatoes; the post-lunch-hour sag when shop assistants drifted between the shelves, waiting for the evening rush, and the Underground breathed a sigh of relief as the platforms stood reasonably quiet, reasonably empty, in expectation of the great punch of people bursting to go home – towards dinner time. The sun twisted the shadows across the streets, sinking down until the reflection of its rays cast new shadows as they shone back from the high windows of the office blocks and flashed off the roofs of elongated lorries, and the coffee shops pushed their staler products to the front of the shelf, ready for the sugar-craving at the end of the day. Schools were released with a great clattering of bells, and on the top deck of every double-decker bus girls and boys with ties askew clamoured to be loudest and widest as they sprawled across the back seats, furthest from the stair.

In the high offices of Harlun and Phelps, dinner was announced by the delivery of sandwiches to the desks of all employees as they worked on towards the night. Every sandwich had been handcrafted by skilled artisans, Kelly assured them, and provided gratis by the firm in grateful acknowledgement of their labours.

This, Sharon realised as she sat in the great oval-tabled office where so regularly the Midnight Mayor had failed to attend board meetings, was management on a different level. Kelly Shiring had even arranged salad for the gluten-intolerant members of her team, and knew precisely how many cups of tea the office required.

Sharon Li, in fresh clothes and looking a few hours less like a sleep-deprived panda, sat at one end of the boardroom table, eating a bacon and lettuce sandwich which was eight parts lettuce to only two parts bacon ('healthy living, Ms Li!') and said, "*How* do you know how many gluten-intolerant Aldermen there are, Kelly?"

Kelly Shiring looked up from her tablet computer. "Well," she said, "I suppose it's just something I picked up."

Sharon wondered what she herself had failed to pick up as head of Magicals Anonymous. Beside her, Rhys's sandwich lay untouched. The druid, Sharon noticed, had been wearing an inane grin all the way from her flat down into EC1, and was still beaming brightly, at not much in particular. She suspected his mind wasn't entirely on the job at hand; certainly his merry disposition seemed incompatible with the direness of the situation. Even more alarmingly, she hadn't seen him sneeze for a good hour and a half. He just sat there, calm and cheerful as reports came in for Kelly's attention, remarking whenever pressed that wherever this glass-god-dude chap was, he was sure it'd all be all right.

Sharon took another watery bite of sandwich. Positivity was, according to *Management for Beginners*, an absolutely vital component of any office environment. There was no such thing as too much positive thinking, since a positive attitude could almost invariably find a way to overcome all managerial problems up to and including bankruptcy. At least, that seemed to be what the book suggested. She tried to imagine unleashing Rhys's overwhelming good nature on Old Man Bone. Somehow she couldn't picture it going well. The slow, deadening revelation that, actually, modern management

techniques could not, as the cover claimed, be applied to all aspects
of her life, was a realisation only slightly dented by the thought that
during their initial research the authors probably hadn't considered
the problem of ancient plagues and walking dead. Then again, if
management was a philosophy – or at least a quirky lifestyle
choice – then it was rather disappointing how little its techniques
were helping her now.

And then, without any ceremony or triumphant fanfare, Kelly
said, "Oh my. Look at that."

The Alderman sat upright in her chair, an email open on the
screen in front of her. "Are you concerned that Big Brother might be
watching you?" she asked, bright-faced as ever.

Sharon shifted uneasily in her seat. In all truth, she *was* a little
concerned that Big Brother was watching – not necessarily an all-
seeing organ of state security, but some higher power with a twisted
sense of humour, or possibly just a bored wizard with a scrying glass
and a limited understanding of the rules of privacy. However, what
Kelly meant was . . .

"Do you know that every time you touch in and touch out with
your Oyster card on the Underground the system records your journey? And that every credit card transaction is traceable to a specific
location, and every time you use your library card there's a note on
a system which says so and whenever you log into a computer or
access a wireless network or use the internet or book a cinema ticket
or enter the congestion charge zone in a vehicle with carbon emis-
sions of more than . . . ? I can see that you do."

Sharon wasn't convinced that Kelly could see that she did, but
the Alderman, with a remarkable sense of self-preservation, had
clearly decided not to press the point. "Now let us suppose," she
went on, merry as a mead-soused monk, "that you take all the last
known movements of the witch, Brid, and all the last known
movements of the striga, Zhanyi, and you map them together.
Everywhere they travelled, everywhere they drew money from a
machine, everything they bought which was similar, every journey
which brought them into contact . . . what do you suppose you get?"

Sharon looked at Rhys. Rhys beamed. Sharon looked at Kelly.

Kelly beamed. Sharon suddenly felt rather small and alone in the world. "Um . . . the hidden path and the misty truth?"

"You get *congruence*," explained Kelly, and she clearly enjoyed the word "congruence" so much that she said it a few more times, just to see whether it was as good on the repetition as it had been on the first delivery. "A few places where their journeys collide. Of course we knew about the spa in Edgware Road; naturally their journeys collide there, it's where Zhanyi passed the glass blade to Brid . . . and over a few months they've each passed through the centre of town because, frankly, who doesn't . . . ? But then there's this."

She pushed her tablet towards Sharon, who stared muddy-eyed at the map which had appeared on it. It was covered with blue and red bubbles which, she guessed, marked every time Brid and Zhanyi had appeared on the vast electronic systems on which the city ran. Here was a purchase for £4.99 at a coffee shop in Piccadilly; there a deduction of £2.90 for an Underground journey made between zones; here a location request from Brid's mobile phone as she tried to work out which of the exits from Elephant and Castle led to somewhere better. A great electronic mess of dates and times had been built up by the Aldermen, as Sharon slept, and overlaid on a map of London. But only in one place, for all the near-misses and could-be coincidences, did the various bubbles of Zhanyi's and Brid's activities collide, same time, same place.

Sharon looked up at Kelly, and saw that the Alderman was still, unaccountably, beaming. "Okay," she said. "But maybe they're just changing trains?"

"Oh, but Ms Li, look at the timings. Two and a half hours between touching out and touching back in? Even by Transport for London terms, that's a very long time to get a connection."

Sharon thought about it. Kelly, she had to admit, had a point.

Chapter 78

Build Your Towers High . . .

It is a temple.

Not many people would realise that was what it was, looking at it, which was odd, as anyone passing within a fifteen-mile radius of the place really couldn't help *but* look at it, even on a cloudy day; especially on a cloudy day, in fact, when the very spire of the temple vanished into the vapours drifting overhead.

But, passing through its great shadow, which turned like a sundial across the city with the passage of each day, if any of the millions of people living beneath its might had paused, and stopped, and considered it, they, too, might have realised what the select few already knew: that it *was* a temple, glorious, majestic, mighty and new. A worthy tribute to a great god, a new god of glass and light; a palace fit for a deity, a hall of worship, a monument to power and might, a dedication to an idea greater, richer, taller than any mere mortals might aspire to by themselves. It is the temple of the glass god, and it is nearly finished.

Chapter 79

Gather Ye Forces While Ye May

Rhys said, "Oh, I see!"

Kelly said, "Do you think they would?"

Sammy, a voice from the shadow walk wherein he dwelt said, "Wankers."

There was a chorus of assent at this, causing Sharon to glance back, into the shadowed mists of invisibility where lurked . . .

. . . a goblin, a troll and a banshee. The banshee, her whiteboard hung by a piece of string around her neck, waved uneasily at Sharon from the depths of the shadows which hid her from human sight. Getting Sally onto a bus for the short journey from Harlun and Phelps to London Bridge station had been, to Sharon's surprise, incredibly easy. The banshee had been so enthused by the prospect of taking a human form of transportation that the shaman had barely been able to keep up with her, running the risk of a fully fledged and fanged banshee springing into full existence on the top deck of the 17 bus from Archway, and causing, if not commotion, then certainly comment. As it was, the bus driver had been very confused by the multiple tickets dutifully touched in as the invisible troupe boarded the bus, and peered at the empty air even as a voice shrilled from the void, "One pound thirty-five?! I remember when it was forty fucking pence!"

Sammy the Elbow, while no stranger to public transport, certainly wasn't going to invite it over for tea any time.

Sharon was hardly comforted by those of her companions who felt socially respectable enough to wander around in full visibility. Kevin the vampire had been convinced to put aside his surgical face mask for the duration of the trip, so long as every window on the bus was opened, and he was allowed to sit on a sterile plastic bag. Mr Roding the necromancer had grumbled that he was old enough by at least forty-three years to have earned a freedom pass, and it was only council bureaucracy and narrow-minded attitudes towards the necromantic regeneration of the flesh which meant he had to pay a full fare. Kelly had tutted and sighed and explained that before the financial crisis she would have just hired three bullet-proof vans and a catering unit for the trip, but that even the Aldermen had to move with the times.

To prove this point, five surly-looking men in long black coats had joined the expedition, bent under the weight of fresh sandwiches, flasks of coffee, surgical bandages and sub-machine guns, all zipped up with a cry from Kelly of, "you never know what you'll meet!"

On paper, Sharon realised, she had a commando-sized force of serious firepower, both chemical and mystical. On paper, two shamans, six Aldermen, one druid (still smiling inexplicably), a vampire, a necromancer, a banshee and a troll of the Dartford Crossing Clan, created an undeniable impression of diehard strength. It was only in reality where the sound of "Oh, my God, blocked drain, blocked drain; oh, it's, like, fungal breeding ground one-oh-one *disgusting*" undermined the otherwise positive impression.

She looked around them, at the approaches to their destination. Like a lot of central London just south of the river, the predominant sound was of traffic and trains. Borough Market was a painted-iron roof on thin columns where, by day, smoked salmon, organic vegetables and cake so sticky you could use it to glue submarines together were sold for only five pounds fifty above the national average cost, to the tradesman's cry of "apples, apples here, organic hand-picked apples, three a pound, three a pound!"

Beyond the other side of Borough High Street, London Bridge station was a churning mass of travellers heading south to Gatwick, Croydon and Kent, juggling briefcases, travel cards, and white cinnamon mocha soya skinny lattes with added sprinkles and foam. As stations went, London Bridge wasn't much – a flat iron roof above metal tracks which splayed out like the fingers of a pianist's hand from a concourse where benches were a luxury and the update board assured you of a delay, but never admitted how great this delay would be.

All that, however, was slowly changing, and the walls were adorned with gleaming pictures of the newer, better, brighter, whiter London Bridge station that was yet to be, a glowing glass footnote to the main event which now dominated the area, and whose soaring walls now held the attention of Magicals Anonymous, assembled beneath it.

"Well," said Mr Roding at last, staring up – and then up a little further. "Not sure what Gaudí would say."

In the shadow walk, Sally scribbled furiously on her board, holding it up for the inspection of Sammy and Gretel:

I think he'd regard it as a rather inorganic, if triumphantly conceived, architectural venture.

Alas, Sally's artistic insight, apt as it may have been, was wasted on the only two people who could see it.

"Are you sure this is it?" asked Sharon. Already her neck was starting to ache from the strain of staring upwards. "I mean, I'm just saying, if I was a secret cult I'd want my temple somewhere . . . more secret."

"But it's perfect, Ms Li!" exclaimed Kelly. "It's got glass, it's got majestic worship-here vitality, it's got symbolism, it's got an absolutely incredible view, and frankly, who'd ever suspect it as a site for mystic worship?"

Sharon thought about this. To her irritation, the Alderman had a point. "Besides," Kelly insisted, "this is the only place where the journeys of both Brid and Zhanyi regularly intersected, and what did Zhanyi say?"

"Highest. Brightest. Newest," murmured Sharon, barely aware that she spoke. "Palace fit for a god."

Kelly threw her arms up for emphasis, a gesture somewhat dwarfed by the scale of the thing it was trying to encompass. "You see?" she declared. "It's perfect!"

Sharon bit her lip, but still couldn't find fault with the argument. "Okay," she said. "I guess we'll give it a go. Um . . . guys?"

There was a mutual chorus of grunts, grumbles and grimaces from the assembled Magicals Anonymous members.

"So uh . . . anyone here got a problem with heights?"

Chapter 80

... And Your Dreams Higher Still

It is called the Shard.

As names go, at first impression this is perhaps deceptive, as "shard" commonly implies a piece of a thing, perhaps small, perhaps broken, perhaps sharp round the edges, but generally associated with it getting underfoot, or becoming lost down the back of the sofa.

This is not like that.

Shard might imply other notions: perhaps a piece of glass, uneven but inclining towards a sharpened point. A certain reflection of light through crystal, a certain smoothness of surface, a certain brightness of reflection – these could be implied in the word, but still it would not do credit to what the Shard actually is.

A billboard at the base of the building itself gave more details, but they were numbers, ideas without any real connection. Seventy-two floors from the surprisingly narrow square base to the tip of the pointed spire; ninety-five if you counted the array of infrastructure, machines, cogs and pipes that sustained life within the building. Three hundred and ten metres, give or take a little from the anten-nae and warning lights that sat upon the top against any low-flying aircraft; the tallest building in the European Union – certainly, the figures gave the actual size of the building, but, even so, they failed to do credit to the thing itself.

What it was, was a tower – no, more than that – a spire. A spire made of glass, not a concrete surface in sight as you looked up, and then up, and then a little further to where it pricked the sky. Another tower like this, more than twice as high as any neighbour, might have loomed over the city, a redefinition of what greatness meant. But as much as it was tall, it was also slender, a finger pointing towards heaven. And here it was again, the thought that Sharon couldn't quite shake off as Magicals Anonymous slipped invisibly past the security guards in the unpainted foyer, only a few weeks from completion – spires and heaven, majesty and glass, people called the Shard a monument, a temple to architectural ambition and financial expense, and they said these things in jest, or as a turn of phrase, the words used and discarded as quickly as they came. But it was, she realised, of all things, the place most fit and proper to pay homage to a new god of glass.

They rode the lift up in silence.

The lift was functional, but not yet up to speed, and one wall still consisted largely of metal frames and cardboard fillers, as the builders waited for panels to arrive. The car itself was large enough to hold all of Magicals Anonymous, with room to spare, built for early morning commuters rushing up to the seventy-second floor, a whole journey into the sky in and of itself. At the fifty-third floor, Sammy's impatience finally broke through.

"I hate heights!"

All eyes turned to the diminutive goblin. "I *asked* . . ." began Sharon.

"Didn't think I hated heights cos I've never been very high," countered Sammy. "But now I think about it, I think I hate heights."

"You're in an enclosed vehicle! You can't even see how high you are."

"I," he replied, arms wrapped around himself, the sleeves dangling from his wrists, "have got so much frickin' insight and wisdom that I don't need to see shit to know it's there. That's how frickin' shamanly I am."

"Well, I'm sorry," exclaimed Sharon. "But it's too late to stop now!"

"I'm not sayin' I won't be fine when we get there! I just wanted to let you know how grateful you oughtta be to me for stickin' with this."

"I think it's very interesting," offered Gretel. "I am looking forward to seeing the view."

"We're not here for a sightseeing trip!" wailed Sharon. "Fate of the city, glass gods, missing Midnight Mayor, scary odd worshipping people, can we stay focused, please?" Gretel hung her massive grey head, and Sharon relented. "Which isn't to say," she added, "that we can't take something positive from this experience."

"I think it's disgusting," offered Kevin. "Working inside a sealed tower like this? Breathing other people's recycled air day in, day out? I mean, even with a proper air-conditioning system it's just foul. Air-conditioning units are breeding grounds for all sorts of vile pathogens."

"Are they?" exclaimed Kelly. "What kind?"

"Babes! Legionella, TB, aspergillus . . . A vamp's gotta think about all the stuff floating about in a bleeder's veins, you know? I won't touch the red stuff of anyone who works in an office tower unless the windows open, even if they eat organic."

The door wheezed. One day it would probably ping beatifically; but for now, without access to its full operating systems, it wheezed, and a voice with a cold that bordered on the terminal proclaimed, "Sthandth cler. Drths opnin."

The doors opened.

Sharon looked out on a small, unpainted corridor. A single mop in a bucket stood on the floor. A small pile of newspaper had been laid out beneath a stepladder, where someone had left an unplugged working light and a screwdriver. A few panels were still missing from the ceiling, revealing cables and pipes tangled above. At the end of the corridor was a glass wall, through which they could see the city. Not just the City, not the locale of offices and streetlights that made up the commercial district of London; but *the city*, from the Thames below to the darkest borders of north London where the lights clung to the edge of Highgate Hill and Hampstead Heath, where the streets became wide and the trees tall, the pavements clean and the houses spacious – *the city* – spread before them like an upside-down galaxy across the world. Sharon heard Gretel draw in a breath, felt a pre-emptive quiver on the air as Rhys swallowed a sneeze.

She edged forward, scanning the corridor: a place of doors not yet attached, of nooks where some day potted plants might flourish. The very top of the Shard was narrow to the point of bare functionality, a floor squeezed in where society ended and pure architecture began. Sharon led the way past toilets whose seats were still covered in plastic; beneath light fittings waiting for a bulb; and round a corner to another place where floor met wall, and the wall was pure glass, beautiful and cold, the vein-clenching chill of it a testimony to how cold the wind was that raged inaudibly on the other side. She looked out and saw all the places she'd known from below, their dimensions tiny, even great monuments small enough to be pinched out between her finger and thumb.

The lights in the Shard itself were out, or not yet fully installed, but the glow of the city below was bright enough to see by. And as Sharon looked, she realised that not *every* light was off. A passage ran along the window's base, and, at its far end, a door stood ajar; a piece of paper attached to it proclaimed, "Caution – Wet Paint". Through the gap in the door, a light glowed, scarcely daring to spill into the corridor, as if embarrassed to be caught blazing at this time, in this place. Sharon walked towards it, fighting the urge to slip into invisibility. Behind her, Kelly gestured to the Aldermen: two to guard the lift, another to keep watch at the end of the passage. Two more were on what Sharon guessed a commando would have called "on your six" and which everyone else probably called "at the back". As she neared the door she felt a chill in the air beside her as Sammy slipped silently into the shadow walk. She couldn't hear any voices, but the air was warmer here, and as she pushed the door back she saw people.

There were maybe two dozen of them, kneeling. Their faces were lit by two large yellow floodlights, but their eyes were turned towards the city. Breathless and motionless, they were bent forward like supplicants in prayer, their gaze all locked on the one same thing.

And there he was. Body of glass, a crystal glow rippling beneath his perfect, smooth skin, but faint now, far less than when he had killed three scylla sisters and breathed out jagged glass. The glass god, or dude, or whatever description was least politically incorrect, now stood before his congregation, arms at his side, head bowed, body loose – or as loose as a construct of glass could be – light playing round and over and through him, and his people worshipped.

For a moment, no one moved, no one spoke. No one seemed to have noticed that Sharon was there.

At the front of the group of people – men and women, all ages, no uniformity in their clothes – a man finally looked up. He saw Sharon and his eyes narrowed. He stood, thereby causing a ripple of activity through the worshippers; a few of the bolder risked a furtive glance, then an outright look, then a hostile stare towards Sharon and her crew as the room realised its meditations were being interrupted. The glass man didn't move. There seemed to be no animation in his body, no life in his limbs, just the slow, steady pulsing of light, like a computer switched to standby.

As more worshippers noticed Sharon, at length the whole congregation looked up and round. A barely audible gasp went through them as Gretel peered over Sharon's head to get a better view; then surprise converted to suspicion as Kevin, fangs politely tucked away, and Mr Roding, who at least wasn't decaying at that moment, shuffled into the room. Suspicion, however, became animosity as Kelly stepped round the necromancer and, looking at the room, exclaimed, "My God! A secret religious order! A real secret religious order! I'm so excited!"

"Who the hell are you?" demanded one man, the first who'd looked round. By his proximity to the feet of the glass god, Sharon guessed he had to be a figure of authority. If so, he was something of a disappointment, lacking any flowing robes, or exciting face paint, or even ceremonial knives. Instead he wore a white cotton shirt, with the sleeves rolled up to reveal an expensive chrome watch, and black cotton trousers ending in bare pale feet. Sharon's eyes roamed over the congregation, and, yes, there wasn't a single shoe to be seen on any one of the worshippers.

"Well, I'm Sharon . . ." she began, and then paused, waiting for the 'hello, Sharon' which traditionally greeted such a statement. " . . . Well, yes, I'm Sharon, I'm the head of Magicals Anonymous, a discreet and courteous service for the mystically inclined. This is Rhys . . ."

Rhys waved.

" . . . my IT manager, and Gretel, who's very excited about the view, and Mr Roding, who isn't, and this is Kevin . . ."

"Hi guys!" Kevin tried to infuse his voice with a cheery sense of friends-yet-to-come, and failed.

" . . . and somewhere in the nether realms is Sammy, my teacher, and this is Kelly who—"

"What?" the man with the expensive watch interrupted. "What the *fuck* . . . ?" he tried again, struggling with every aspect of the conversation. "What the mother-fuck," he concluded, "are you fucking doing here?"

He was met with silence. This was not the attitude or language which Magicals Anonymous traditionally condoned.

"Well," Sharon ventured, "I was gonna try and interest you in joining our bingo night, but I guess we're already a bit past that? But I wanna keep this civil, so how about you tell me your name?"

The man stared at her, speechless from a great range of emotions, none of which seemed pleased to see her.

"Okay," she went on. "How about I make a stab in the dark – sorry, not in a scary knives way – but just, you know, language and that. Your name is Hacq, and I think you've walked barefoot over glass in honour of your god."

There was a stir in the room which was all the confirmation Sharon needed. "That's great!" she exclaimed. "I mean, a bit wacko, all things considered, but, still, great. Um, I don't suppose we can talk privately?"

Hacq glanced across the congregation, sampling the mood. The mood, which hadn't been good to begin with, was beginning to be tempered with something else – a dangerous hint of fear. "What the fuck do you want?" he hissed.

"Excuse me?" Gretel rumbled, easing forward into the room. "I don't think you're being very polite to Ms Li."

Hacq, to his credit, or perhaps as a man with not much evolutionary potential, squared up to the troll and did his best to stare her down. "Don't think I'm scared of you," he hissed. "Of any of you!" he added, shooting a glare towards Kelly. "Our lord will protect us, our lord is come, our lord is . . ."

"Inert, by the looks of it," offered Mr Roding. "Now that I actually *see* your glass god, I think . . ."

"Elemental construct!" sang out Sammy's voice from the empty air.

" . . . indeed, fed by the looks of it with a . . ."

"Direct point-to-point blood bond inscribed in . . ."

"The silicate level of the core, yes, I was saying all that . . ."

"You were saying it frickin' slow, necromancer!" offered the goblin.

"Blasphemy!" interrupted Hacq. "You stand in the presence of a god, of the new god, of the . . ."

"Shall I hit him?" asked Gretel, staring down at the man. "I know it's not polite, but I'm afraid I'm not aware of the socially acceptable alternative options."

"Lay a finger on me," breathed Hacq, "and our lord shall rip you apart."

Rhys leant over to Sharon, and whispered, "It *could* rip us apart, Ms Li. You saw what it did to Miles."

Sharon looked from the motionless glass figure to the man before her, who trembled with adrenalin and rage. Behind him, a woman, slightly built, painfully pale, cowered as Sharon's gaze passed over her. There was something familiar in her face, something . . .

"Are you *sure* we can't talk in private?" she asked. "I kinda feel like, talking in front of all these people . . . hi guys!" she added with a wave towards the congregation, " . . . is hyping you up and might not lead to totally rational decisions or free discussion."

"Every person in this room has seen our lord's majesty and is loyal to his cause."

"Uh, babes, that's, like, such an unfashionable attitude you've got there," offered Kevin.

Hacq was visibly shaking now with emotion threatening to burst through his skin like blood through a broken eardrum. "You . . . you defile his temple!" He managed to keep his voice a bare squeak below a shriek. "You bring creatures of darkness into his sacred space, you abuse his name, you . . . you . . . you . . . "

"Mr Hacq, if you please."

The voice came from the middle of the room, from one figure, unremarkable among the many. It was dry, old, soft, but loud enough to cut through even the vibration of Hacq's rage, and Sharon recognised it at once. It was the voice of Arthur Huntley.

Wizard, scholar, expert in the magics of Old Man Bone, and sometime groundskeeper at Bunhill Fields, the small, stooped man, in his brown wax coat and grey woollen hat, stepped out of the crowd and laid a comforting hand on Hacq's arm. The younger man deflated at the touch, the breath and the rage rushing out of him, leaving him almost as inert as the glass god himself. Mr Roding took a step back as Arthur approached; and all the while the ex-wizard smiled, patiently, into Sharon's eyes.

"Ms Li," he breathed. "A pleasure to see you again."

Sharon waited before she answered, running through a mental checklist – mouth not hanging open, arms not flopping uselessly at her side, face not locked in a stupid expression of blind ignorance and startled revelation. To her surprise, she looked Arthur Huntley in the eye and said, "I can't see this conversation ending well, can you?"

Arthur smiled, a slow, tolerant smile. "That, I think, is dependent on how we handle this situation. But perhaps your initial idea was correct; this may not be a conversation to have in public. May we?" He gestured towards a doorway at the far end of the room where they stood, a space which might one day be an office, the highest in Western Europe. Sharon hesitated, then followed. Glancing back she said, "If anything goes whoops, go boom."

A mutual nod from the assembled Magicals Anonymous suggested that this tactical command was duly appreciated, as Sharon Li followed Arthur into the gloom.

Chapter 81

Hacq

God is shit.

I prayed all my life to god, and what did he do?

He took everything from me.

My job.

My family.

My home.

I worked and I was good and I did everything that god fucking said I should, and I looked at the world and I saw rich fuckers get richer and poor fuckers get poorer and I thought, this isn't god. This is just people, fucking people doing their fucking thing and no one looks out for yourself unless you do, and if you do it properly, then you're a fucker so we're all damned and going to hell in this life or the next no matter what we fucking do.

Then he came to me and he said, "let's build a god", and I thought he was out of his fucking mind but he said, "the old god is one of floods and fires, the old city is of stones and shadows, but that's not how the world works any more. Let's build a new god for a new world, and he will be like the new world, heart of glass, skin of glass, perfect, polished, smooth, immaculate, flawless, the flawlessness of machines, and he'll show them. He'll show all those fuckers just what it means to be fucked up by fucking creation. Because we made him, and he is ours."

Chapter 82

Take a Slow Breath and Try Again

They passed through the congregation, and the congregation parted to let them by.

As they went, a girl, tiny, with a pale face, skin far too young, eyes far too old – reached out to grab at Arthur's arm, pleading, perhaps? Or asking for advice? She was brushed off, her hand falling to her side, her eyes cast down.

Another bare room. Arthur moved to its centre, not bothering to see if Sharon followed, and waited for the door to swing shut behind him. One day this place might be a dining room or a restaurant, if the Shard catered to giant dignitaries from Brobdingnag and their hungry offspring. A glass god, if he bothered to stand up here, would be able to see the lives of eight million people moving beneath him, each spark of life smaller than the distance between the nail of his thumb and the skin of his finger, whole boroughs blotted from view with the palm of his hand.

Arthur stood with his back to the city and said, "I think it's customary to offer tea under these circumstances. However, the machine hasn't been put in, but I hoped you'd appreciate the thought."

Sharon scowled. "Even if there weren't this mega-deathy vibe going down here, I gotta tell you, we're probably past the cuppa tea stage of polite chitchat. I mean, here you are ..." – she turned back the way she'd come, pacing across the room, the shadow walk close and inviting, promising invisibility at the tiniest step to one side – "... the guy who we went to for information about shit, actually being involved in shit and actually, I'm like, what happened to you being a trusty pint-in-the-pub kinda guy?"

"I didn't deceive you, Ms Li. My information regarding Old Man Bone was entirely accurate."

"Apart from failing to mention being part of the guys who stole his blade – hey, you all got a name?"

A flicker of eyebrow, the tiniest quiver of a lash. "A ... name?"

"Yeah. Like, we're Magicals Anonymous, and Kelly out there is with the Aldermen. And you're clearly part of a secret cult and that, so you got a name?"

"Officially," murmured Arthur, "we are the Modern Temple of Illuminated Heavenly Mysteries."

"Does that have an acronym?"

Muscles twitched around Arthur's mouth, which in other circumstances might eventually have crossed an evolutionary barrier and become a smile. "Most members refer to us as ... the Illuminated."

"That's cool," Sharon murmured, still pacing, still listening to the shadows, toes nudging the very edge of invisibility. "It's like the Illuminati only less European. It kinda gives off this 'we know shit bet you wish you did too' vibe without being totally in your face about it. I like it."

This time, the smile was almost palpable. "And yourself, Ms Li? After your visit to my graveyard, I asked a few questions regarding Magicals Anonymous. I must admit, your ambition is ... remarkable."

"No it's not," she replied. "Thanks for the thought, but, seriously, pissing off an ancient undead god, nicking his sacred blade, imprisoning the Midnight Mayor in the telephone wires, sacrificing people to make a new god, killing scyllas, turning the lights out on a striga – I mean, next to all that, I'm just organising a piss-up in a brewery and even then it's mostly froth, if you get what I'm saying."

Arthur said nothing. The smile, however, remained, hovering over his lips like a gunship over open ground.

"You *did* do all that shit, right?" Sharon persisted. "You got B-Man to pinch Old Man Bone's blade; trapped the Midnight Mayor in the telephones, sent your glass guy to kill the scyllas ... how's that holding up doctrinally, by the way? I mean, I get that when we talk about a glass 'god' this kinda implies omnipotence, omniscience and theological things, but then Sammy says that your glass guy is nothing more than a glass structure, an elemental composite animated through other means, but, still, 'god' has gotta come with some sorta implications, right?"

Arthur sighed the patient sigh of a busy teacher. "Tell me, do you *like* Old Man Bone? Do you enjoy what he is? Once upon a time I'm sure he served a function within the city, when the graveyards burst and the sewage flowed in the street. Once upon a time I'm sure we needed a ghoul come from the pit to carry off the corpses of the dead, to wash away the water swimming in cholera and pry the boots from the swollen, rotten feet of the bodies turned black by the roadside. He was important once. But now? You're a modern woman, Ms Li, you've seen how things are. We have antibiotics now! We have sanitation, industry, local government, recycling centres – and still Old Man Bone will have his sacrifices? He'll have his blood? Do you think he *deserves* it? Do you really think he's somehow *better*?"

Sharon kept on walking, as she considered his words. "I dunno," she said. "I'm not a big fan of Old Man Bone, I give you that. But, thing is, where I'm stood, this chat weren't never about him and all his shit. It's about you. You and the things you've done, and trying to make it out like you're somehow ... something bigger, to make it sound like you're doing this cos of Old Man Bone or for the city or any of that shit ... that's a plain, crappy lie, and I ain't going for it. Don't matter what you think about Old Man Bone, or what I think about him. What matters is the things you've done."

"You seem to know a great deal about it already, Ms Li. What exactly have I done?"

"What have you done?" She paused, and looked at Arthur in disbelief. "You take that patronising tone, asking me what you've done? Because, like, the only reason we're having this chat is so we can find some way to deal with this without the Aldermen going all submachine gun out there. I don't tell you stuff; you tell me stuff. And you do it, if you don't mind me saying, in a really 'shit I'm so sorry we've killed at least four people and nearly killed you and turned the lights out' – turned the fucking lights out on one of your fucking own, and Zhanyi was nice, you know? I really fucking liked her, she was . . . she was trying and she cared and you turned the fucking lights out on her and I had to . . . so you don't get to fucking smile!"

She was shouting, and hadn't noticed; the blood throbbed in her face. If anything, Arthur's smile widened. "You really are out of your depth, aren't you, deputy Midnight Mayor?" he breathed, and there was something about him, Sharon noticed, an edge of something that clung to him as he moved, a shadow beneath the shadow, which turned beneath his feet, barely visible except to a shaman's eyes.

"I mean, I heard that the real Midnight Mayor was something, a real firecracker, and when we stripped his mind from his body I thought, that's it, we've done it, we've sorted the problem. But you know what? His body kept on going, even though he wasn't in it any more; it tore Brid apart like that." He snapped his fingers so loud Sharon jumped.

"The *real* Midnight Mayor was something – but even though he kept fighting, even though he ripped Brid to pieces, I knew that this was the best the city had to offer, and we'd already beaten it. And then you turn up, sent by Crompton – *Crompton* – the blithering idiot servant of an ancient, outdated god, and you're the deputy Midnight Mayor, and, well!" He chuckled, the smile spreading, pushing against his ears, crinkling up beneath his eyes. "Look at you. A little girl with a grown man's job. All . . . empty words and bingo nights. I am impressed by Magicals Anonymous, whether you realise it or not. All those damaged lives, all those heartfelt, aching problems, and you know what it is? You know what you made? It's a really good place for all the little people to go and be small together. Take your people and go, sweetheart. You're out of your league."

Silence. Sharon stood still, eyes fixed on some point far behind Arthur's shoulder.

"Did you just call me . . . *sweetheart?*"

Arthur rolled his eyes.

"No, but seriously, I just wanna get this clear," she said. "I'm not saying that I object to the term necessarily; I can see how it might be endearing in, like, the same way I might call a bloke 'mate' or 'pal' or an endearing personal nickname or something. But I'm just saying, it's about the context, yeah, and in the context where you're, like, 'you're so weak and pathetic so fuck right off', ending the sentence with 'sweetheart' is *exactly* the kinda attitude that gets you into trouble. I mean," she added, before Arthur could interrupt, "would you call a raging male sorcerer 'cupcake'? Would you walk up to an angry djinn and say 'how's it going, duckling?' Course you wouldn't, and I gotta say I think that the way we use language is actually half the problem here so why the hell . . . ?"

She vanished. Arthur blinked, his mind struggling to reconcile what *had* been with what suddenly was very much *not*. A second later something slammed into the side of his head, hard enough to knock him to the floor – something fast, heavy and possibly bagshaped. He crumpled, his arm automatically covering his head. Above him, Sharon reappeared. "It's not about political correctness!" she exploded, swinging the bag by its strap round her wrist. "It's about – respecting – the other guy's – point of view!"

Arthur looked up, as blood seeped through his fingers and made dark rat's tails of his hair. The shaman stared at the gravekeeper, and for a moment neither moved.

His eyes narrowed. A second before it happened, Sharon saw the impending change, and dived back into the invisibility and cold embrace of the shadow walk. Then Arthur threw his hand up, still red with his own blood, and the air was thrown with it, thickening and twisting, condensing round his fingers and bursting outwards with the force of a tidal wave breaching a dam. Even in the shadow walk the blast knocked Sharon off her feet, slamming her face first into the floor, and back into full visibility.

She hauled down a breath and, scrambling on all fours, she tried to regain the safety of the shadow walk, even as Arthur, grunting with the effort, pulled himself to his feet. She saw the air shaking around him, twisting and spiralling.

"Don't!" he roared, and the air roared with him, slapping Sharon back down to the floor like a scarecrow in a storm.

"Talk to me!" he added and the glass windows of the Shard hummed and creaked, warping under the pressure of his voice as it filled the room.

"Like!" One step, and the floor groaned beneath him, the cityscape misshaping at his back as every glass surface flexed and bent.

"I'm!"

Sharon briefly struggled up onto her hands and knees, crawled a few paces into the comforting embrace of invisibility, felt the shadows twist and thicken around her, the pressure of Arthur's voice recede; but he threw his hands up and the room seemed to lurch like a freefalling lift, picking her up and throwing her back down.

"A fucking!"

He was almost on top of her, and his eyes blazed, his skin shimmered with the haze of magic tumbling off it.

"*Child!*"

She looked up and Arthur Huntley, ex-wizard, sometime grave-keeper, former member of the Westminster Coven, stripped of his powers, so Mr Roding had said, for deeds unknown, was brilliant with power, enough to sizzle the air, to twist the wires, to make the glass in the windows sing. He reached down and caught Sharon by her shirt, hauling her up, twisting her clothes hard enough to cut into her spine, slice across her neck, and his eyes were bright and furious. "The young never listen," he hissed, drawing his other hand back, the fingers filling with fire, the knuckles clenching into the shape of a spell.

"Too bloody right," said a voice at his back.

The voice was nasal, small, shrill without being feminine, smug without being pleased, and carried with it, not just sound, but an unmistakable aroma of ... rotting rubbish? Arthur half turned and there he was, Sammy the Elbow, four-foot-nothing of goblin in a dirty green hoodie, and at his back there were ...

Shadows was too loose a term. Shadows implied merely the absence of light. These weren't that. These were echoes, dragging out of the shadow walk and given solid shape, living memories, shadows in that they had been cast by something else, but the things which had cast them had been life itself, and now they twisted and writhed and they were ...

the purple-green spirit who nested in the lights that burnt off the old NatWest Tower in the city below

zephyr of stolen wind who was trapped one day during the building of the Shard. It came in to have a look, and when it tried to go out again, it found the windows had been sealed

angry rush of the engine wind from the planes that whooshed overhead

echo of a spanner which was dropped and fell seventy-two floors before it hit the ground hard enough to shatter paving stones

slither of the eel-like ghosts that nestled in the turning tide of the river below

multifaceted gaze of the staring spirits who perched with the pigeons to study the patterns of the night-time cities, reading their fortunes in the runes cast by the changing traffic lights

shadow of a dragon, wings black, eyes red, raging mad, watching, always watching from the city streets

They stood behind him now, all the shades that dwelt in the shadow walk, all the hidden truths that only the shamans were meant to see, they writhed and twisted and scattered the light around them, and they were visible even to Arthur's eye, and they were real, as they always had been, and they were angry.

"Yo," said Sammy as Arthur's eyes widened in revelation. "Squishy-brains."

He didn't point, didn't say anything, make any sign, but with a silent shriek of delight, the spirits at his back leapt forward, blacker than the reflective black on the rain-washed tarmac, brighter than the heart of the sodium lamp burning alone against the darkness, hotter than the pipe at the back of the overheating bus, colder than the depths of the damp water pipes below the city streets. They threw themselves at Arthur, wrapping themselves around him and some had claws, and some had fingers, and they gashed and tore and screamed.

Arthur dropped Sharon, who sagged to the floor, slipping into the shadow walk; and now she saw them all, perfectly, all the spirits that Sammy had summoned, clinging to Arthur, who staggered beneath the weight of them. Staggered – but did not fall. His skin blazed with a burst of something bright, white flecked with gold, and, as she looked, something thin and translucent began to spread across his face. At first she thought it was water; then oil; but as it thickened and grew stiff she recognised the perfect smoothness of crafted glass, sliding over every part of him. She looked round, and saw Sammy, right above her. The goblin grabbed her by the hand. "Scarper!" he called out with a merry, gap-toothed grin, and before she could protest, he pulled her to her feet, and straight through the nearest wall.

Chapter 83

Chaos Is Nature's Solution

There was chaos among the congregation.

The sounds of battle in the room next door had produced, at first, an awkward shuffling, as each person looked at their neighbour to double-check that their impression of things going wrong was, in fact, correct. No one wanted to be the first to start throwing spells, or bullets, or talons, or heavy fragments of local architecture, but at the same time, if that was the direction things were going in, no one really wanted to be left behind. As much as anything, it would have been bad teamwork.

In the end, it fell to Kelly to take charge, which she did with a rousing cry of "All right, team, now, I know that this doesn't seem good . . ."

Someone in the congregation threw a spell at her.

It wasn't a particularly good spell, it wasn't particularly well crafted. It was a stinky ball of blue-green flame, which, scientifically assessed, would probably have been rated at gas mark five on the oven scale. Even so, it was almost certainly hot enough to melt flesh, which made it all the more remarkable that Kelly, seeing its approach, reached out with one hand and, like a baseball player catching an easy feed, grabbed the fireball between her fingers, her arm recoiling as she did so. She held it there for a moment, staring at the fire dancing in the palm of her hand, before snuffing it out. Then she looked up at the congregation. She said, "The city of London shall have all the old Liberties and Customs which it hath been used to have. Moreover we will and grant, that all other cities, boroughs, towns . . . "

Someone in the congregation laughed. Someone else – someone who knew far better, shouted – "Bewitchment!"

This was roughly the moment that chaos broke out.

Sharon fell through the wall, Sammy in front of her, as the room where she'd left Magicals Anonymous exploded into madness. She stumbled onto the floor and looked up to see Gretel calmly hit a member of the congregation hard enough to send the bare-footed man flying backwards into two of his peers, and knocking all three to the floor. Mr Roding's hands were moving through the air, trailing crimson sparks even as his hair began to thin on his head and his skin shrivelled around his mouth from the effort of his enchantments. Someone was summoning great wheels of metal wire up from the floor, cracking through the concrete and the freshly laid carpet, while another person was directing huge gouts of steam towards the Aldermen, dragged out of the air in hot prickly bursts. Kevin was holding a surgical mask over his mouth with one hand, while with the other hand, in a white latex glove, he grabbed a still-incanting witch by the throat.

The air burst with hot and cold as spells fired and misfired; the floor was heaving, the ceiling sagging, the glass walls singing and warping under the rapidly changing air pressure in the room. Sharon's ears popped as she staggered to her feet and looked round. There stood the glass god, still inactive, with his back to the city. The girl with the pale skin, who'd reached for Arthur's arm as he'd passed, was squatting by the glass being's feet, her arms wrapped round her thin body, rocking back and forth from heels to toes. And as Sharon looked, a fist, skin thickened by concrete, speed enhanced to piston-pump, slammed by her face, nearly taking her ear off. She ducked, dropping back into the protection of the shadow walk even as Rhys leapt past her, hands blazing, crying out an incoherent sound which might, once upon a time, have been considered a battle roar. She felt the floor shake, a great rhythmic thump, and, glancing back, saw the wall through which she'd just passed buckle, fresh white mortar dust spreading from a dozen hairline cracks. Then Hacq was there, right in front of her, his face wild, his hands raised, electricity writhing between them as he drew back his fingers for another spell. His eyes were fixed on Kelly, who stood aloof at one side of the room, calmly chanting,

" . . . No freeman shall be taken or imprisoned, or be deprived of his freehold, or liberties, or free customs . . . "

The words cut through the great gaseous roar of an enchantment that burst black smog from the shrieking mouth of a witch. There was a weight to them, a density; shadows twisted around Kelly, the echoes of things gathering and listening as the words tumbled from her lips, building a spell in the air around her, thick and ancient and mighty. Hacq drew his hands back to strike and Sharon threw her bag at him, catching him across the head and neck, knocking him to one side, the spell fizzing out between his fingertips. He staggered and she hit him again, slipping in and out of visibility as she struck and, around her, magics burst and opened and flared and died; and there it was again, the red burning in the palm of her hand, the shadow of the Midnight Mayor's mark, and something watching, something black and ancient, drawn in by the sound of Kelly's spell, by the twin crosses on Sharon's palm, by the stench of magic and, Sharon thought, simply by the view.

Too little time to look; Hacq fell to the floor and Sharon was on top of him, swinging her bag wildly into his face. He shielded himself with his arms, but she just batted them aside even as Kelly's voice rose to proclaim,

" . . . nor condemn him, but by lawful judgement of his peers, or the law of the land . . . ", and as Kelly spoke, the fires of spells in the room flickered and dimmed, crushed by the greater, weightier spell starting to press down upon them, and Hacq's arms were battered aside beneath Sharon and his nose cracked as she slammed her bag against him one more time, and there it was: the great black dragon with its wild red eyes, looking down at her from the deepest places of the spirit walk, and Sharon looked down at herself, too, and saw that her skin was silver and her nails were black and the world she perceived was crimson-red and Kelly's voice didn't have words to it any more, it was pure roaring, a dragon's roar, the spell swelling to a pitch as she proclaimed, " . . . we will not deny to any man either justice or right . . . !"

And it occurred to Sharon that, though she wore the dragon-skin of an Alderman, she'd somehow left the Alderman's badge, stolen from Crompton, in her *other* pair of trousers.

Then the wall behind her burst.

Dust and moving air and torn-up breeze blocks and steel blasted through the air with the force of a jet plane coming into land. It knocked all before it to the ground, tore up skin and shattered bone. Those nearest the wall were smashed down before it; those furthest away dived to the ground, covering their heads as the dust slammed through the room. The windows, pushed already to the point of tolerance, cracked. Snapped. Twisted. Balanced for a second, the panes of glass were held together by their own internal friction more than any chemical force, then finally shattered, exploding outwards in a silver storm, falling away, and cascading down and down into the night.

Sharon peeked out from the shelter of her arms, spitting out dust, her head spinning, the silver skin that covered her own creaking from stress. Her stomach felt sideways, as if her whole body had been pushed but only some parts had managed to catch up. The ground was strewn with bodies; some moving, several not. Kevin lay a few feet away, blood on his face, on his chest, his mask knocked to one side. Rhys coughed and tried to pick himself up, but someone else had fallen across him, pinning him down, hard to tell if it was a man, a woman, dead or alive – merely a soft shape covered in dust. The wind rushed in from the outside, thin and shrieking, lifting up giddy vortexes of mortar dust and pulling clouds of beige-white out into the void below.

In the place where a wall had been stood a man; or, rather, not a man. A had-been-man, until his skin was glazed over with glass, burning itself into the flesh; until his hair dissolved into solid, pulsing silicon, until his arms crackled as they moved, until his breath was sealed within glassy lips, the condensation of his gasps puffing in and out over the plug across his mouth. He should, by rights, have been dead, but instead Arthur Huntley blazed before them, the air burning, his body blazing, his hunched back pushed erect by the new skin which had grown over it, and, in a moment of realisation, Sharon knew what the glass blade had really been for, and who had used it, and why.

Then Arthur spoke, his voice both muffled and amplified by the glass around his lips, and he exclaimed, "YOU *MORONS!*"

Sharon saw Kelly, over by the door, struggling to pick herself up, and looked for Sammy, but couldn't see him amongst the spinning dust and raging winds of the otherwise still, shattered room.

"YOU *IDIOTS!*" roared Arthur, and with every word the room shook again, the sound of his voice fracturing amidst the wreckage. "WHY DOES NO ONE EVER LISTEN TO ME?!"

Someone – an Alderman, if his dust-covered clothes were indeed black – tried getting up. With a single swat of his arm Arthur knocked the man off his feet and threw him against the nearest wall like a scrunched-up bill into a wastepaper bin. Something soft stirred next to Sharon. Hacq, sometime high priest of the Illuminated, groaned; blood was rolling in streaks down his face, muddied by mortar dust. Sharon looked at him, then looked again. As he'd fallen, he'd landed on one side, disturbing something lodged in his pocket. A screen had lit up electronic white, and through the thin stuff of his pocket a little message declared,

    1 New Message

Carefully, looking around her and hardly daring to move, Sharon slipped her hand into Hacq's pocket and pulled out his mobile phone, then clambered to her feet. As her finger brushed the screen of the phone, the image changed.

    1 New Message
    From: Unknown
    Message: Found Me

She looked up, and her eyes met Arthur's, and he recognised the look in her eye, and she recognised the recognition in his. He roared, threw back a hand that blazed with electric fire, even as Sharon threw the phone across the room towards Kelly and yelled, "Get it to . . ."

Something hot and blazing struck her full in the chest and knocked her backwards. Pain burst behind her eyes, hot and popping, and she rolled back across the floor, wheezing for breath. Arthur's gaze turned to follow the phone, now in Kelly's hands, even as the Alderman staggered to her feet and lunged for the door. Arthur reached out again and a great burst of electricity snarled across the room, only for a pasty white hand to reach out and grab it, pulling it like so much string into its grasp.

Mr Roding had staggered to his feet. His skin was rumpled, flaking away around his chin, neck, fingers, revealing raw red muscle beneath. His eyes were shot with bloody capillaries, and he swayed where he stood, but he held steady nonetheless and looked Arthur in the eye. "Wizard," he hissed, "make your good luck happen."

Arthur snarled and hurled a fistful of crackling flame popping with static and hissing with radio-trapped fury. The necromancer threw his hands up and deflected the spell in a burst of hair-prickling electromagnetism that wriggled and writhed through the floor. Kelly, with the phone in her hand, burst out through the door, and Arthur shrieked with fury, sending another spell after her which, again, Mr Roding intercepted.

"YOU CAN'T STOP ME!" Arthur roared. "I AM A LIVING GOD, I AM . . ."

Something bright orange and liquid burst against his side, spilling to the floor. He stared at it in surprise, and then recoiled as a thin coat of rust began to spread across him, expanding like lichen over stone. Rhys stumbled upright next to Mr Roding, an empty packet of antihistamines falling to the floor and another potion bottle ready in his hand. "Go, Ms Li!" he shouted. "Get the phone out of here!"

Sharon staggered into the spirit walk. The rust on Arthur's skin continued to thicken and grow, smothering him, covering his face, his hands, locking his arms in place, a stiff, solid coating – but one which couldn't hold. Even as it grew, it cracked, and the light from Arthur's glass skin was breaking through. As Sharon stumbled towards the door, out of the corner of her eye she saw something else move; and there was the pale-faced girl, right in front of her, staring *at* her, chin up, face defiant. Behind the girl was the glass god, raising his heavy, heavy head; and he, too, was looking at Sharon now, his serene, crafted features mimicking the girl's own. As Sharon swerved to avoid him the girl turned to follow her, and shrieked,

"Don't you hurt my daddy!"

And it seemed to Sharon that the glass god opened his mouth to scream these words, too, his body twisting as the girl's did; and here, in the place where all things were real, even if they were not perceived, she looked again at the glass god as he came to life, and he was a she, and always had been, and he was opening his mouth to scream and he was screaming broken glass.

"Get the phone!" roared Arthur, and the girl – and the god – seemed to agree with each other.

Sharon tumbled through the wall even as it thudded with the impact of glass behind her; then she raised her head and ran.

Chapter 84

Take Your Life into Your Hands

Kelly was at the bottom of the hall, clutching Hacq's mobile phone. She was waiting for the lift.

Seeing this, Sharon shrieked, "You're kidding me!"

"You want to take the stairs all the way down?" suggested Kelly.

A thud behind them, then a roar, suggested that even the stairs might be one of their least harmful downward options. Sharon looked back the way she'd come. "Got any spells for making lifts appear?"

"No, but we really should develop some," sang out the Alderman with a cheerfulness that was starting to sound strained.

A glowing yellow light cut through the gloom of the unlit corridor, coming nearer. There were footsteps, heavy, sluggish, but growing lighter, as of a creature coming to life.

"Um . . ." began Kelly, even as Sharon grabbed her by the sleeve and pushed open the door to the emergency stairs.

"Glass god woke up!"

"Why'd he do that?" exclaimed Kelly as they bounded down the stairs two at a time.

"I think he's being powered and controlled by Arthur's daughter. I mean, 'don't hurt my daddy' isn't something I was geared up for hearing, you know?" They spun round another corner even as the door they'd just come through burst open, and the glow of the glass god's body filled the stairwell.

There was a gentle tinkling of glass. Sharon grabbed Kelly by the sleeve and pulled her through the wall as the glass god's body disintegrated, tumbled down the stairwell and reassembled on the landing below them. The air spun with glass.

In a moment of displacement, Sharon had pulled Kelly out halfway between floors. They fell the last two and a half feet, Kelly landing with a thump of knee and bone, Sharon staggering onto all fours. Behind them, the wall buckled and shook with the impact of the glass god's fists.

"Where now?" gasped Kelly.

Sharon looked, and found no easy answers.

"Obviously I'd be honoured to die fighting nobly for you and your cause," said the Alderman. "But if you have any useful advice on the most productive manner in which I could heroically lay down my life for the sake of others, it'd be greatly appreciated . . ."

Sharon stared into Kelly's smiling, breathless face. "You know, I get as how this isn't a great time to ask, but are you *ever* actually kidding?"

Kelly opened her mouth to answer, and the door at the end of the office burst open, spinning off its hinges. A roaring cloud of glass filled the room as the god burst upon them.

Sharon squeaked, grabbed hold of Kelly and pulled her back through the wall they'd just breached. As they staggered out onto the staircase, she looked up, into the face of the small, skinny girl in a small, skinny floral-patterned dress. "Her!" Sharon yelled. "She's controlling the glass guy!"

Kelly lunged towards her, but the girl gave a shriek and threw up her hands, and a burst of crackling hot air slammed the Alderman and Sharon away from her. Finding herself and Kelly trapped between the girl and the god, Sharon groaned, and pulled Kelly back through the wall, onto the floor they'd just departed.

"Oh, Ms Li," the Alderman exclaimed, "thrilling as this is, I don't feel our situation is improving!"

Sharon looked around. Empty space, empty floors, empty walls, no weapons – not even a handy sign of the cross – to hand. Then she saw something grey pass quickly across the windows outside. "Gimme the phone."

"Are you sure? I'd hate to . . ."

"The phone!"

Kelly handed over the mobile to Sharon, who said, "Okay, so you go for the girl."

"This . . ."

The glass god burst back into the hollow room, still reassembling his component spinning parts. Sharon turned to him, waving the phone over her head.

"Hello!" she sang out. "Found me!"

The creature fixed its eyes on Sharon and strode towards her, the last few pieces melting back into its form as it advanced. Sharon grabbed Kelly and pushed her back through the wall, into the stair-well, her fingers parting from Kelly's frame as the Alderman reappeared on the other side of the wall. Then she darted back, waving the phone at the glass creature. "Come on!" she sang out. "Come to Mama!"

The god opened its hands, a great spinning vortex of splinters spreading between its fingers. Clutching the mobile phone, Sharon grinned, turned and, slipping easily now into the shadow walk, she ran.

She ran across the office floor, away from the walls, away from the doors, and, head first, out through the nearest window.

Chapter 85

Choose Your Battles Wisely

Some four floors above the place where Sharon Li had chosen to plunge to an almost certain death, things were not going well for Rhys and Mr Roding. It wasn't just that Mr Roding's skin was falling away in grey sagging sheets, or that Rhys was beginning to feel drowsy; it was that their opponent appeared unperturbed by everything the druid and necromancer could throw at him. Spells which would have eaten the flesh of lesser creatures, enchantments to addle the minds of all but a genius devil, he absorbed, considered and shook off like a dog drying itself after a paddle. It wasn't simply frustrating; it should have been, *must* have been, impossible.

And yet there was Mr Roding, his limbs giving out, every gram of strength sapping from him as he deflected another spell, sagging to his knees. Only a few strands of hair still clung to his head; his eyeballs were white spheres sagging from their sockets. He had suddenly become a man of more than a hundred years; and the stench of decay was gone from his flesh, because all the flesh that was left was his own, and it was ruined. Rhys was too late to deflect another reverberation of power as it slammed into him, ripping through his defences like a tiger through silk, sending wave after wave of pain through his nervous system. He toppled to the floor, his body locked in agony.

Above him he felt Arthur moving, and looked up to see the face of the gravekeeper. Rhys tried to speak, but no sound made it through his closed-off throat. He tried to move, and only the toes on his right foot seemed willing to obey. He tried to think, but the thoughts came too many to be understood.

"You," breathed Arthur, his voice resonating through the glass shell. "Never appreciated."

What it was he hadn't appreciated, Rhys wasn't sure. But it seemed to matter enough to Arthur for the wizard to raise his right hand, and to reach with it *through* the glass shell, which rippled around him like liquid to let his fingers pass. He reached inside his jacket and pulled out something wrapped in velvet. It was long, thin. It gleamed as Arthur unwrapped it. A glass blade, the same size, the same shape, the same bite of magic on the air – a copy of the rusted dagger of Old Man Bone, shimmering in Arthur's hands.

"Don't worry," murmured Arthur, as Rhys struggled to fight, to scream. "You won't feel it."

"Oi. Squishy."

The voice was faint, worn out. It belonged to Sammy. The goblin was swaying with exhaustion. His face was bloody, his skin covered in dust, the green hoodie torn in a dozen places to reveal knobbly bone and leathery flesh. He blinked bleary-eyed at Arthur, and coughed dust, a tiny hacking sound from a tiny pair of lungs.

"Little thing," breathed the wizard. "Aren't you *cute*."

Sammy's eyes narrowed. "Me," he wheezed. "Second . . . greatest . . . shaman . . . ever!"

So saying, he dragged his arms upwards, and then down, fast. Sammy vanished.

So did Rhys, Mr Roding, Gretel, Kevin and the Aldermen.

And so did the floor.

Chapter 86

Take the Chances Life Gives You

If Kelly was surprised to be pushed bodily through a wall by Sharon, before the shaman herself vanished to face off against a presumably indestructible glass god, her astonishment was nothing compared to that of the pale-faced girl in the floral dress who now found herself opposite the Alderman.

The two women stared at each other, mouths hanging open. Then the girl shrieked and raised her hands again, to shape the beginning of a spell. With the sense of priorities that she considered essential to a good PA when organising a disorganised life, Kelly swung forward with her fist, and caught the girl squarely on the chin. The girl flopped backwards with a shriek of indignation. Before she could get back up, Kelly threw herself upon her, drove her knee into the girl's chest, wrapped her fingers round her throat, pushed her head back against the stairs and hissed, "One move and I'll pull your windpipe out through your nose!"

The girl froze. So did Kelly, surprised that this anatomically implausible notion had crossed her mind, let alone her lips, and a little disappointed by its biological inaccuracies.

Riding the moment while it was still high, she added, "Who are you?"

The girl didn't answer.

Behind her, Kelly felt something move. She didn't have to look to know what. The glow of the glass god, golden-white, filled the stairwell. The magic rolling off it was palpable, heavy, a force waiting to be unleashed. Kelly kept her eyes fixed on the girl's. "If it touches me," she breathed, "I'll kill you. And I don't think that would be good for anyone. You'll be dead, and I think that means it'll be dead, too, and I'll be dead. And when the crime scene investigators come to piece all this back together they'll be very confused, and I don't feel that's fair to them, as they're just trying to do their job. Besides," she tightened her fingers against the girl's throat, " . . . we want an amicable solution, don't we? So, hi, I'm Kelly, I'm the Midnight Mayor's personal assistant. Who are you?"

"V-V-Victoria," the girl wheezed.

"Hi there, Victoria, lovely to meet you. Sorry about the windpipe through your nose business, it's really not the image I like to give but, then again, one must adapt, mustn't one? Now, this glass gentleman behind me," she murmured, still keeping her eyes fixed on Victoria's face, anywhere, in fact, but on the creature at her back. "You're controlling him, aren't you?"

Silence. But, then, the girl didn't really need to answer. She was young, Kelly decided – far too young to be playing with elemental constructs – possibly only fifteen years old, and even as she crumpled her face into an expression of bravery, the tears were welling up. "Would you mind making him back off a little?" said Kelly. "Only my feng is getting a little un-shuied and . . . "

A crash caused her to look up. So did Victoria, her eyes rolling back in her skull to try and see the source of the disruption. It came from a seven-foot troll bursting through the doors upstairs, Sammy tucked under an arm, Mr Roding slung across a shoulder. Neither party looked fit to provide their own forward momentum, so Gretel supplied the effort for both. Shuddering down the stairs in tow staggered a bloody, groggy-eyed Rhys, one arm thrown across Kevin's shoulders.

Kelly sighed. "Please hold that thought," she murmured at Victoria, and felt the girl's throat contract and expand beneath her fist. Gretel swung round the corner, saw Kelly, saw Victoria, then saw the glass creature towering behind them. The troll stopped so suddenly that Rhys and Kevin slammed straight into her back. Bleary-eyed, Sammy raised his head from beneath Gretel's arm, took in the situation and gave a dry cackle.

"*Stuffed*," he wheezed. "Buggery."

"Friends!" exclaimed Kelly. "As you can see, you've arrived in the middle of a . . . "

Above them, the wall burst apart, raining mortar and concrete down the stairwell. Arthur Huntley, his glass skin blazing, fire dancing round his fingers, had lost patience with doors, people and the world.

His voice roared down the stairwell. "YOU CANNOT RUN!"

"Uh, can we, like, totally ignore that?" squeaked Kevin.

Kelly turned back to Victoria. "Hi there," she breathed. "This is shockingly unethical, but would you mind calling for your dad?" She pressed harder into Victoria's throat, causing the girl's eyes to bulge. "Now, please?"

"Daddy!" whimpered the girl, her voice wavering up the stair. "*Daddy!*"

From above, abrupt silence.

"Hello there, Mr Huntley!" called out Kelly, gesturing at the rest of Magicals Anonymous to press around her. "I'm so embarrassed to do this, but I fear that unless you back off, I shall have to kill your daughter."

Silence.

"It's not something I usually do," she went on, "and I suspect my employers would frown on it, were they aware of the situation. But as it is, they aren't, and so, you see, I really will."

Silence.

At her back, the glass god swayed, fingers twitching at his side.

Then, "Vicky?" Arthur's voice drifted down, softer now, more human.

"Daddy?"

"You're a good girl."

Pinned to the stairs, Victoria smiled even as the tears ran down her face. "Yes, Daddy!"

"You've done very well, sweetheart."

"Yes, Daddy."

A moment, a pause. Kelly listened to it, and perhaps heard something in the silence, an intake of breath; for her eyes widened.

Then Arthur's voice rolled down the staircase. "Make me proud."

Victoria smiled, and closed her eyes. At Kelly's back the glass god raised its head and opened its mouth, even as Rhys called out a warning. Fragments of glass were splitting off from its skin, from its innards, its glass fingers, filling the void between its glass lips, jagged great bursts of silicon flooding the air like a sandstorm. It reached out for Kelly, the glass exploding, tearing through the air and there was . . .

A very soft crunch.

A slight crack.

A gentle tinkling.

Shards of glass tumbling to the floor, spinning, falling. Fragments tinkled down the gap between the stairs, cascading end over end, a crystal rainfall. The light behind the glass god's skin went out, fading like the last red filament in a blown bulb. His head leant forward. Its weight tore at the neck. The neck began to split, to crack. Dragged by its own mass, it tipped forward, tumbled forward, tumbled down. The head fell from the body, and bounced away; cracks in the neck, where it had separated, spread with a slow ripping throughout the god's frame, splitting each arm in two, its chest into five, severing its legs at the groin, shattering its knees, sundering its glassy feet apart. With a heave of breaking bonds and a sheer of sliding parts, the glass god disintegrated.

Kelly stood slowly. Beneath her, Victoria's head was turned to one side, eyes open, staring at nothing. There was blood on her throat, and blood on Kelly's hands. The black talons of the Alderman-dragon were glistening at the end of Kelly's silver-coated fingers.

Silence, apart from the gentle falling of broken glass.

A sound.

It started soft, a bare gasp on the air.

A tiny exhalation, which became trapped in the vocal chords of a stranger for just a moment, before passing on by.

Another.

Breath which could not stop itself from being breathed.

Another again.

Kelly wasn't smiling. "Run," she murmured.

The others stood, frozen.

"Run," she repeated again, so soft, so quiet, and this time they didn't need telling. Kevin ran, and the others followed, Gretel carrying the goblin and the necromancer, Rhys staggering behind, Kelly at their rear.

A cry in the hollow stairwell.

It bounced from wall to wall, rose up to the summit and echoed down seventy floors to the earth below. It started as a choke which became a sob which became a scream, a scream of grief, a scream of vengeance, a scream of retribution and regret. And tearing before it like clouds before a storm, they ran, feet crackling over broken glass.

Chapter 87

Victoria

Daddy has always been good to me.

Always looked after me.

They said he did something wrong – or something that the others said was wrong, even though it wasn't – and Daddy stopped being a wizard, and they took his powers, and tattooed runes into his skin and burnt scars into his bones so he couldn't be strong any more, so he couldn't look after me and he said,

Now you must be strong, too, Vicky.

The others took Daddy's power, but not his knowledge. So I learnt.

When I was seven I summoned my first efrit from the red-hot remnants of a tungsten lens. When I was ten I ensorcelled the minds of Daddy's enemies, of all the people who'd done him wrong. They said that I was too young, that it was . . .

. . . dangerous . . .

. . . did damage, that I'd see and hear . . .

. . . but Daddy said I was special, that I'd make him proud, and he spent every day with me, and he'd never spent time with me before, because he was so busy, but now he did and I wanted to do better

even when the voices were loud
and my head hurt
and things talked to me in my sleep
but he said be strong
be strong
be brave
try harder
And he said, make a glass elemental for me and it was hard, it was
so hard but in the end we found a way and I gave it
my blood
fed it on me
but Daddy said he is a god and people will worship him
but shush it must always be our secret
because there are people who hate us
people who will never understand
so try
a little bit
harder
and give it your soul.
So I did.
I just want to make him proud.

Chapter 88

Every Journey Must Have an End

It was Kevin who collapsed, which caught the others by surprise. He fell, and rolled, and hit the floor, and they dragged him through the door into another empty space, an office waiting to be filled, and he lay there and wheezed and pulled his hand back from his belly and there was blood, cold red blood, seeping through his clothes.

"Be honest with me," he whimpered. "Does it look like there's . . . *dirt* in the wound?"

Rhys collapsed onto the floor beside him. He didn't know how many stairs they'd descended, how far they'd run, the roar of Arthur Huntley at their back, his grief and his magic blazing in the air, but now they could run no further. "Well," said Kelly encouragingly, as she sank onto the floor by the vampire, "the good news is that you haven't been staked through the heart."

"And the bad news?" gasped the vampire. "Be honest, babes."

"The bad news is that sometimes death *is* the easy way out."

Kevin stared at her, goggle-eyed. "What kind of fucking bad news is that?" he shrieked.

"Just trying to find something positive here."

"I'm feeling a little drowsy . . ." offered Rhys through a profound, antihistamine-fed yawn.

Gretel carefully deposited her charges on the floor. Sammy lay on his back, staring up at nothing much; Mr Roding just lay, his withered flesh scarcely moving; the only sign of life was the press and shrink of his ribs against bare, shrunken skin. The troll considered her companions, then gave a great shrug and marched back towards the door.

"Where are you going?" exclaimed Kelly.

"I intend to hold the wizard gentleman off for as long as I can," replied Gretel. "So that you may yet escape."

A roar filled the staircase, and a crash of glass. No one had dared look back as they fled, but neither could anyone deny that Arthur Huntley was getting closer. "That's really sweet of you," said Kelly, "and I think we all appreciate it, don't we, team?"

This was confirmed by a groan of approval from Rhys.

"However," went on Kelly, as a flare of light from the stairwell briefly stabbed through the door, "while I am all in favour of noble gestures in suitable causes, the fact that we shall *all* soon be eliminated by an enraged and grief-stricken wizard is going to make it hard for anyone to report back on the nobility of gestures made. Thus, arguably, undermining any such gesture."

Gretel thought about this. "But . . . it doesn't have to be *known*, to be noble, does it?"

"No, of course not; I'm just saying, if we're all about to be obliterated into little pieces, no one will notice."

"But that's a terrible thing to say!" declared the troll. "Why would anyone do anything noble if it was all about the . . . ?"

Behind her, the door burst open. So did a large part of the wall. Arthur Huntley, his feet barely touching the ground, his glass skin smeared with blood, blazed, too bright and too hot to look at. He didn't speak, didn't scream, didn't make any noise or draw any signs, merely threw his arms out towards the gathered refugees and unleashed a wall of rolling golden glass that tore through the air like razored locusts. Gretel threw her hands up to cover her head, a futile gesture before the moving wall of debris. Kelly raised a hand in an attempt at a shield, which buckled even before it was raised. Mr Roding simply closed his eyes. It was, Rhys reflected, if nothing else a reasonably quick way to die.

The glass sliced through the air, spreading out thick and wide to encompass the room, sheering straight towards the Magicals . . .

. . . and burst apart before their eyes into a thousand motes of dust. An invisible wall curved up before the frozen crowd, pulverising the blades and needles of glass before they could strike, and smashing them into a harmless drizzle which trickled to the floor. Stunned, Mr Roding opened his eyes, his thin tongue tasting the air like a lizard. Kelly's mouth dropped open. Sammy sniggered, though even he couldn't say why, and Arthur Huntley, enraged, turned towards the source of this new frustration, who said,

"You guys know the lifts are working?"

Rhys coaxed his head round to see the source of this intrusion.

Emerging from the entrance to the lift were two shapes. One, shorter than the other, had straight black hair, dyed with streaks of blue. She stood, glowering at Arthur Huntley with almost matronly disapproval.

The other figure, who seemed barely able to stand, had dark brown hair, pale skin that threatened to freckle at the least exposure to sun and eyes bluer than blue. He swayed a little, and, as he raised his right hand in greeting, a pair of crosses, carved in the skin, shimmered with a flicker of blue, burning blood.

"So we thought about the stairs," he added, reaching out with his left arm to grab support off the figure by his side. "But did I mention . . . lifts?"

Rhys looked from one face to the other, and found himself smiling.

"So, yeah," said Matthew Swift, sorcerer, electric angel, 127th Midnight Mayor, protector of the city, guardian of the night. "Basically . . . hi."

Chapter 89

Spread Your Wings and Soar

There had been a moment, many, many moments ago, when Sharon Li held a mobile phone close to her heart, turned and ran.

She had run from a glass god, run from an angry wizard and his daughter, run from danger, destruction and despair. In the process, and with a not insignificant pang of guilt, she'd run from her friends.

But mostly, what she'd done was run straight through the nearest window, and out onto the empty air.

And say what you would for the Shard, there was a *lot* of air around it to be empty.

For a moment, this seemed a very silly idea. Her feet kicked at nothing, her head tilted down, her legs swung up, her belly leapt into her throat, her throat crawled into her nose, her spine retreated towards her knees, and all things which had been in proportion, spun and twisted and for a moment she thought, this was it, this was how she was going to die, what a bloody stupid cock-up and what would her mother think? Her parents would never know, never understand, she'd just be a footnote, a squashed footnote, an empty coffin in a muddy grave and the graves would crack and the plague would burst up from the earth and Old Man Bone would walk the

streets in the pestilent fumes of the dead and no one would stop the
glass god and the Midnight Mayor would wither and perish, his
mind destroyed and scattered among the telephone wires and it
would all be her fault and the bingo night would never get organised and Rhys would be ...

And something grabbed her under the armpits and tried to pull
her arms out by their sockets.

Where there had been one body, two bodies now tumbled
through the air. Great wings were beating against the roaring wind,
trying to get leverage against total nothingness. Acid burst from
Sharon's stomach into her mouth, her eyes rolled in her skull and
claws bit into the soft skin under her arm as, with a great heave of
muscle and effort, spinning round and round in a vortex of her own
beating wings, Sally the banshee caught Sharon as she fell.

Even the most aerodynamically graceful creatures could not have
sustained the balance of shaman and banshee in full flight for long,
and Sally's wings stretched and strained as she beat furiously against
the air, trying to hold Sharon up. Forward or up or side to side was
impossible; but like a parachute Sally spread her wings to hold
Sharon in her descent, and instead they twisted round and round
like a hula hoop, rushing towards the ground, great blasts of air
pressing against Sharon's face as Sally fought all the laws of nature.
The pavement spun up beneath them like water up from a plughole,
spinning, filling the world; a swing to one side and Sharon's legs
slammed hard against the side of the Shard; a swing in the opposite
direction and it seemed they would land in the river, straight down
into the rushing waters of high tide. Sally's mouth opened in a silent
scream, but there must have been a sound since Sharon felt her ears
pop, her nose run, her eyes water at the ultrasound shrill of effort
that burst uncontrollably from Sally's lungs as, with a final heave of
leather and claw, the banshee flopped the last few metres to the
ground.

They dropped, a tangled mass of shaman and banshee, limb
struggling against limb. Sharon felt her knees graze, her arms graze,
every part that could scrape, slam or jolt fulfilling its mission with
an indignant cry of bone and skin against hard, fast earth, and she

rolled, pressing herself into the ground for fear that the ground might try to go away again, while Sally tumbled across the paving stones beside her and, with a gasp, they were still, and they were down.

They lay there, each trying to breathe, trying to control racing hearts, shaking wings, the urge to vomit. Sharon half turned her head and saw Sally, her wings shuddering against the ground, her arms curled into her chest, like a cripple cradling broken limbs. "You okay?" she wheezed.

Sally nodded, and did no more.

"Thanks."

Another nod, a flash of fish-fang smile.

Still not moving, Sharon carefully unwound her fingers. In her right hand, gripped so hard it hurt to unclench, she held Hacq's mobile phone. The screen said:

1 New Message

From: Unknown

Message: HELP ME!!!

Groaning, she rolled onto her hands and knees. Her left leg gave out, and for a moment she lay, face-down, wondering if this was it. Next to her, Sally stirred, with a rustle of concern. Sharon tried again, made it to her hands and knees and then, groggy, nauseous, onto both feet. "Can you fly?" she asked Sally.

The banshee thought about it, then shook her head. She scrabbled for her whiteboard, usually on its string round her neck, but somewhere in the chaos of their descent she'd lost it. A shaking claw, instead, scratched at a paving stone.

Muscle pulled. Take-off unlikely. Very very sorry.

Sharon managed a ragged smile. "Don't worry about it," she wheezed. "I'm totally on this."

1 New Message

From: Unknown

Message: GET ME TO US NOW!

She cradled the phone tight again to her body. "Right," she wheezed. "I'll get a cab."

Chapter 90

Do Not Act in Haste . . .

There was a cab.

It was London Bridge station – there were always cabs, even at this late hour.

The driver took one look at her and told her to take the bus.

To her surprise, she said, "I am Sharon Li, deputy Midnight Mayor, protector of the city, guardian of the night! I have seen things you cannot imagine, witnessed horrors, unleashed magics beyond your comprehension, and I demand . . . "

Then an American pushed in by her and asked if the cabby could take him to King's Cross, and the driver said sure, get in. So when the next cab came by her in the taxi rank, she said, "I – I – I'm really sorry my – my – my friend is in trouble and I need to see him before it's too – too late . . . "

He told her to hop right in, and she felt only a little dirty as the door slammed shut behind her.

London Bridge. Traffic at Monument, curling round the mess of one-way systems.

St Paul's Cathedral lit up white; white walls, green-grey dome, the cross on the top massive and gold.

Narrow byways heading north, remnants of an older street plan, guilds with ancient names and quaint mottos, fluorescent lights burning behind glass windows in offices where no one lived, perfect, silver, smooth; the ride was £8.90 and the doorman at the office paid for her as she ran by. The phone vibrated in her hands, one new message, hurry, please, hurry, so close now, so close. She ran through the foyer of Harlun and Phelps, took the stairs down two at a time. There was blood running down her left arm from a thick gash she hadn't even noticed; there was blood on her knees, seeping through her trousers, blood in her hair though she had no idea where it had come from, dust in her lungs, cracking on her lips, dirt in her eyes; but she rounded the corner and here it was, the corridor of a thousand graffiti, wards against magic, wards against angels, wards against invasion, wards against disaster. A heavy metal door; a room too cold to be borne, ice on the ceiling, ice on the floor, a figure, huddled in a corner, blue fire in his hair, blue fire in his eyes, awake – he was awake; the blue electric angels opened their eyes as Sharon approached, and opened their fingers ready to fight and they were mad, quite, quite mad as they always had been, always would be and in that moment, all they knew was that they were hurt, and trapped, and in pain, and they reached out and . . .

A phone rang.

The blue electric angels hesitated. The skin of the body they wore opened and contracted, opened and contracted, bursts of blue electric light slicing in and out of the flesh as it tried to decompose, tried to heal itself around the creatures that resided in it. The face that had once belonged to Matthew Swift stared, first at Sharon Li, then at the phone in her hand.

Her hand was shaking.

She held the phone out to them.

It kept on ringing.

Caller: Unknown.

"I think it's for you," she said.

They hesitated, not moving, their hair writhing about their head, skin rippling with blue fire, ready to burst. Then, very slowly, they reached out, the fires receding from their hand as, gingerly, holding it by the fingertips, they took the phone from Sharon, and, like a child with a new, delicate toy, the blue electric angels answered the telephone.

Chapter 91

... Unless Speed Is of the Essence

"So, yeah," said the Midnight Mayor, as Arthur Huntley blazed with fury before him. "Basically ... hi."

Arthur hesitated, weighing up this unexpected development. Then feelings overwhelmed rationality, and with a flick of his hands he hurled spinning glass wrapped in jagged electric sparks towards Swift and Sharon, where they stood by the entry to the lifts.

The glass dissolved before it reached them, the electricity fizzing out into nowhere. Swift took a cautious step forward, swayed a little, and Sharon caught him under the arm. Arthur's face darkened. "Don't think," blurted the Midnight Mayor, before the wizard could move, "that I'm in any way intimidated by this whole ... magic thing you're doing! This," he gestured at his own shaky body, even as Sharon tightened her grip on his arm, "is merely the result of not being used to having legs for a while. I mean, we've had legs, of course we've had legs, but I haven't had legs, and not having legs has been very disconcerting ..."

Another blast of fire from Arthur was swatted aside like an irritable wasp, barely interrupting Swift's speech. " ... but we're feeling better now. It's been an experience . . . enlightening, educational, a little disturbing but . . . "

A roar, a tearing jagged blast of bundled static and microwaves, which fizzled through the wall as Swift batted it aside. " . . . but basically I feel that we've . . . what did you call it, Sharon?"

"Grown as a person," offered Sharon.

"Grown as a person!" agreed Swift with manic cheerfulness. "I like that. It's like growing as a mushroom, or growing as a bit of mould in a damp bathroom or something, only better."

"Much better," Sharon assured him, as his left foot tried to be where his right was at the same time as his right tried to get with his left. "If you carry on like this, you'll end up happy in yourself before you know it."

"Will we? I suppose we will!"

He giggled, a hyperactive sound; and as he giggled, he flicked out a hand, absent-mindedly. Arthur was picked up off his feet and slammed back against the wall. A shiver rocked through his body, and where his back had impacted with the concrete a single, tiny fracture wiggled like an ancient riverbed across a bare landscape, through his shell of glass. "Oh look!" exclaimed Swift. "He's all, um . . . what's the word I'm going for here? Uh . . . "

"Hyped up?" suggested Sharon.

"That's it! That's exactly it! Sharon, you are brilliant! Have I promoted you lately?"

"No, but actually, about that . . . "

With a roar, Arthur staggered upright, the crack spreading as his hands came up to form a spell. But before he could do so, Swift raised his own hand again. A cage of electricity twisted up out of every plug, every wire embedded in the floor or cable running through the ceiling, spinning around Arthur and spinning Arthur around, a giddy vortex of UV-bright light that ended when the wizard slammed down hard into the floor.

"I should promote you," said Swift. Then, with a moment of realisation, "Am I . . . high?"

"We gave your body a lot of sedatives . . . "

"You did what?!"

"You were screaming and threatening to tear the sky down."

"Were we?"

"Um . . . yes."

"Why on earth were we doing that?"

"Stress-management issues?" said Sharon.

In the moment of surprise it took for Swift to process this idea, Arthur crawled back onto his feet. The cracks were spreading, moving visibly now, through his glassy skin. He staggered as he rose, stared down at his hands in surprise, mouth moving in a silent O, and even that was enough to cause the lines to spread, rippling out across his body. He raised his head, looked at Swift, at Sharon, his face twisted, like that of an angry animal.

"I'll . . . I'll . . . show . . ." he wheezed, cradling his arms across his chest.

"I really don't understand anything that's been going on," said Swift, and, with a roar, Arthur flung back his arms.

The glass skin across his body splintered, cracked, shattered, burst apart in a moving wall of glass and light and heat. It tore through the wall behind him, a flying shrapnel, splitting the concrete through in great gaping holes. It blasted the panels out of the ceiling, ripped up the fresh carpet from the clean floor, shattered every windowpane, blowing them out like exploding plastic bags. It burst apart, too bright and too white to look at, a heat that sizzled Sharon's hair and made her skin contract; instinctively she dived for cover, cradling her head against the straining floor. Meanwhile, Swift, grinning like an idiot, squinted against the glare.

On the other side of London Bridge, a sleepy street cleaner looked up to see a burst of whiteness erupt from the forty-fifth floor of the Shard, and wondered why, and went back to cleaning. On the railway lines of Waterloo East, the supervisor of the night railway crew heard a bang, and looked round sharply to see who had dropped their tools on the in-progress track. In a flat in Blackfriars, a musician's dream changed from Brahms to Tchaikovsky, and she rolled over in her little bed to dream of cannon and overtures; and in the concrete concourses beneath the Shard itself it rained shards.

The silence was a long time in coming.

When it finally asserted itself, it wasn't even a silence of all things coming to an end. Rather, it was the rush of wind dancing through broken windowpanes, tinkling the shattered glass dust across the floor, pushing it in eddies and forming Zen-garden patterns in the torn-up mess of mortar and sand that had twisted across the room. Sharon listened to the wind, and when it became evident that the wind wasn't about to go anywhere and neither was she, she opened her eyes.

Swift stood in the centre of the room, his shields still palpable around him as a bubble where the writhing dust didn't go; and even those were contracting back into him as, swaying a little, he surveyed the damage. Kelly was there, peeking out between her fingertips; and Gretel, her large body braced between the sorcerer and the still-prone shapes of Sammy and Mr Roding. Kevin, too, already fumbling with one bloody hand for his emergency packet of sterile wipes; and Rhys the druid, struggling against drowsiness, antihistamines and adrenalin in equal measure, his features at once swollen and contracted, bursting and withdrawn. Sharon climbed to her feet, staggering with the effort, every part battered, dirty or bloody.

Swift grinned. "So," he sang out, "I'm guessing I've got some catching up to do?"

Sharon looked round the room, searching for the one last person who should, who needed to be there.

Arthur Huntley was gone.

Chapter 92

Adversity Is Merely Opportunity in Disguise

The sun rose over the city.

The day crew, come to inspect the Shard, were first alarmed, then bewildered, and finally infuriated to find a snowstorm of shattered glass scattered all around the base of their building. Infuriation turned to outright rage as the building supervisor, inspecting the floors for structural damage, stumbled upon whole rooms gutted, stairs scorched, carpets torn, ceilings buckled – a veritable redecoration with grenades.

If the structural engineers felt outrage, the managing directors, on discovering several dust-covered, bewildered men and women on the very top floor, groggily trying to worship a shattered window and a lot of cracked dirt, were so utterly perplexed that all they could do was reach for the nearest handy lawyer.

The sun pressed up over the buildings of the Square Mile, pushing the shadow of St Paul's down towards Fleet Street and throwing a great open-armed hug from the figure of Justice on top of the Old Bailey, out across the city below.

The sun stretched through into the offices of Harlun and Phelps, and into one office in particular where a voice said,

"Ow." Then, "Ow!" And finally, "Ow, do you mind?"

"Now, Mr Mayor, this is very important, we really need to make sure that you are physically healthy after your ordeal."

"I'm fine, I'm . . . ow! – I'm giddy."

"That's very reassuring, Mr Mayor, but if you don't mind I'd like a professional medical opinion on this subject."

"And you think . . . OW! – that Dr Seah is the right person to give that?"

"Hey, sweetheart, if you wanna meet the unprofessional me," sighed Dr Seah, "I can totally arrange that."

A moment, as Matthew Swift considered this. Then, "Okay, fair enough."

Kelly Shiring beamed. She was, all things considered, satisfied with her job performance. A temple had been destroyed, and while structural damage had been suffered during the process, at least it was very highly insured structural damage, which was always a source of comfort to her when doing the paperwork, and her boss was back in the office after an unscheduled absence, which meant . . .

"Now, I know you'll want to ease back into things, Mr Mayor, but you do have a lot of email to catch up on . . . "

"You are kidding me."

"The cogs of the city don't stop just because you're having an out-of-body experience, Mr Mayor."

"I thought you'd be . . . " Swift's voice trailed off. " . . . you know . . . "

"Mr Mayor?" Kelly waited politely.

"I thought you'd . . . handle all that stuff," he said, shamefacedly staring at the floor of his grubby, paper-strewn office.

Kelly waited, a beatific smile on her still-grimy face. Swift cleared his throat, then said, "So, uh, Kelly . . . "

"Yes, Mr Mayor?"

"I've been thinking about management . . . stuff . . . and I was actually wondering. How do you . . . uh . . . see your place in the organisation?"

"My place? Why, as your personal assistant, Mr Mayor!"

"Yeah, but I mean, like . . . what do you want to be in five years time?"

"I really don't understand," she exclaimed. "I am *personal assistant* to the *guardian of the night*. If my careers officer could see me now! She always said I should go into government . . ."

"Kelly!" Swift threw up his hands in despair. "What I'm trying to say is . . . how'd you feel about promotion?"

"A . . . promotion?"

"Yeah. To something more . . . you know . . . more managery. Something with a big title, with a bigger office. And a pay rise. And dental."

"This is still Britain, despite the government," chided Kelly. "You only offer dental in countries where there is no NHS."

"The kinda job," replied Swift, eyes narrowing, "where you get to offer *other* people jobs, with dental or without depending on your personal discretion."

Kelly thought about it. "Still reporting to you?"

"Christ, *yes!*"

She thought a little longer. "Just one thing . . ."

"Go on?"

"Would I still have to wear black to work?"

Chapter 93

From Our Trials, We Grow Stronger

She said, "Hey, Miles."

The Alderman looked up. One leg was suspended before him, held up by pulleys and cables. The other was tucked away beneath a clean white sheet. A portable tray on wheels had been pulled across his bed, and bore a plastic jug of water, a small tablet PC and a copy of *The Economist*. The Alderman raised his head from this latter, saw Sharon, and his face split into a smile.

"Ms Li!" he exclaimed. "How delightful to see that you aren't dead yet!"

Sharon shuffled between the curtain that separated Miles's hospital bed from its neighbour, and sat down in the padded chair that threatened to overflow from its tiny space. "I was gonna say something like that to you."

The new day had brought, if not healing, then clarity as to the extent of cuts and grazes across Sharon's body, and while she wasn't actually suspended within a plaster cast from the ceiling of an NHS hospital, barely three consecutive inches were free of a plaster or ointment. When the Aldermen's first-aid kit had run out of big pink fabric plasters, they'd gone to blue catering plasters. When the blue catering plasters had been used up, Kelly had been forced to break out her secret stash and now, dotted over the cuts and abrasions, several large Winnie the Pooh plasters greeted the day with a happy smile and jolly teddy-bear faces.

"So, yeah," said Sharon, "I brought you grapes." A brown paper bag of grapes was deposited on Miles's tray. "Then I thought you mayn't like grapes, even though they're traditional and that, so I got you blueberries, too."

A pot of blueberries was duly revealed.

"But then the blueberries were on special offer, and it seemed kinda stupid not to do it, because it was, like, two for three quid, you know? So I got raspberries . . ."

Which were deposited before Miles.

" . . . but then I thought maybe you don't like red fruit, because people sometimes don't, like, it makes them sick and that, so I got you a KitKat." This last was laid with ceremonial care before the stricken Alderman. Sharon waited as Miles inspected his haul. "So, um . . . hi," she concluded.

"Ms Li . . ." breathed Miles. "You didn't have to!"

"Yeah, I know, but it was this or flowers, and I don't think girls are meant to get guys flowers, even when they're stuck in hospital, which is actually stupid, if you think about it, but I guess one social battle at a time, you know?"

Miles looked patient and smiled. "How are you, Ms Li? I heard there was an incident."

"Yeah," she admitted. "Like, with the Shard blowing up and that? I thought Kelly was gonna be so mad about it, but apparently it's okay when stuff is insured."

"I was thinking of yourself. You look a little . . . tired."

"Tired?" she echoed. "I guess I am a little knackered, you know. Well, there's this bingo night to organise, and this social, and the guys want a singles' night for polymorphically unstable individuals seeking a meaningful relationship and . . ."

"Have you considered a holiday?" interrupted the Alderman.

"What?"

"A holiday?"

"But ... I've only been in the job for a few weeks! I can't take time off now! What would that look like?"

"How about an assistant?" he suggested, before Sharon's indignation could begin to swell. "Or ... a partner?"

" ... You mean, like a boyfriend?"

"That's exactly what I mean."

Sharon sat back in her chair, staring up at the ceiling. "I dunno," she said at last. "I guess it isn't just up to me, is it?"

"Ms Li ... " Miles sighed. " ... I'm hardly in a position to offer you good advice, but if I may suggest ... you perhaps have more options than you are aware of."

Sharon looked at Miles, Miles looked at Sharon.

She started to smile.

Chapter 94

Share Your Burdens to Make Them Less

Magicals Anonymous assembled.

"I've had to pull out everything I had saved up: potions, lotions, organs – how's my skin doing? Is it setting nicely?" asked Mr Roding.

Thank you for your enquiry, my left wing has healed very well, and Dr Seah assures me that I will have full flight with my right soon. In the meantime I have been using Boris bikes for my transportation needs. Tell me, do you know of an easy way to locate the nearest bike parking station? I seem to spend a lot of time pedalling in circles trying to find a place to lock my bike.

"And I was, like, 'do not worship your false gods, babes!' and they were, like, 'fuck you, vampire' and I was, like, 'oh my God, that is so judgemental' and they were, like, 'unleash the glass god' but I stayed cool, you know, I held the guys together . . ."

"Personally," said Gretel, "I think the entire thing was overblown. If we could have just discussed it over a good meal, I'm sure we could have found an amicable solution."

"Apparently there are antihistamines which *don't* cause drowsiness!" Rhys breathed, his eyes glowing at the thought. "Imagine it!"

"Hey, guys!" Sharon's voice cut across the hubbub. Slowly, mugs of tea clasped in hand or talon, Magicals Anonymous settled down. Sharon stood, waiting for their attention, ragged notebook in hand. "Just a few housekeeping things before we start," she said, when the silence had settled. "If you're wearing a chameleon spell on arrival, can you please be careful about recharging the sigils before you leave. I get the need to be discreet, but we've had a couple of you putting your sigils into the microwave to recharge and I gotta remind you it's six hundred watts for your average chameleon recharge, and our microwave is seven hundred watts so if you could just keep an eye on that, that'd be great. Um ... if anyone else wants to sign up to go with Kevin and the gang to the blood donor centre on Wednesday, then please book your place sooner rather than later as there is a high demand for appointments during the middle of the day, and remember to drink plenty of fluids before and after your donation. As you can see, we've started a biscuit kitty – a few pennies here or there really go a long way – and Rhys will be taking you through the 'comments and suggestions' leaflet at the end of the session. I see a couple of new faces here tonight, so let's begin like we usually do. I'm Sharon ... "

"Hello, Sharon!" sang out the room.

" ... and I'm a shaman ... "

Chapter 95

Companionship Is Society's Greatest Gift

The meeting came to an end.

They drifted out, some by themselves, some in little groups, heading for the buses, trains, bikes and, in a few cases, skies, of London, slipping back into the shadows from which they'd so briefly emerged for tea, biscuits and shared lives.

In the end, only Sharon and Rhys were left, closing up the office, turning the lights out.

Sharon's key clicked in the door as she closed it behind them.

Rhys said, "Um . . . "

Sharon turned to stare at him. "You okay?"

The druid nodded. "Uh?" he managed.

She waited.

"I uh. I um." He gestured furiously to fill the space his words couldn't achieve, and finally sneezed.

"I saw Miles this morning," Sharon put in, and Rhys froze, even his sneeze seeming to suspend itself. "He's doing okay, you know. I mean, beat up, but who the hell isn't? But doing . . . all right. He said I should get myself an assistant, but I don't think I need one. Then he said I should take a holiday, but I don't think that'd give the right message. Then he said I should get a boyfriend, which I think is actually a bit of a leap, you know what I'm saying?"

Rhys nodded furiously.

Sharon nodded, too, slower, which seemed to calm Rhys's furious head-waggling.

"So, yeah," she concluded. "All things considered . . . yeah."

" . . . Yeah?" asked Rhys.

"Yeah."

"Yeah?" he echoed again, checking the sound, making sure it was everything he'd thought he'd heard.

"Uh . . . yeah."

"Really yeah?" His voice rose to a squeak.

"Yeah!"

Rhys shuffled forward, a quickstep his body made before his brain could reject the idea, and stood now, a nose distance away from Sharon. "In that case," he said, "Ms Li – Sharon – in a strictly not-professional way, can I . . . buy you dinner?"

"*Yeah!*" The sound bounced off the streets around as Sharon threw her hands to heaven.

"Can I buy you dinner . . . *now?*" asked the druid.

She thought about it, but only for a second, and then, quieter, took his hands in hers. "So basically," she said, "yes."

Chapter 96

Leave No Loose Ends

There was one thing left to do.

Sammy said, "Ain't no body, innit! And I'm not saying as how it's impossible for a guy to just explode into glass and stuff. I mean, maybe he did, maybe there's no squishy bits left behind, but, as a goblin in the know, I'm telling you – there *should've* been squishy bits left."

And Swift said, "I've got legs! I mean, sorry, that wasn't what I meant to say, what I meant to say was fate of the city blah blah blah epic struggle blah blah blah battles against evil blah blah blah but look! Legs!"

And Miles said, "It sounds like he's gone to lick his wounds."

And Rhys said, "I'm sure it'll work out all right."

And Kelly said, "I've got a pay rise! An actual pay rise! Can I buy you dinner? Can I buy you a really *expensive* dinner?"

And it occurred to Sharon, as she listened to all this, that somehow, without noticing how or why, the task had fallen to her.

He walks, angry and alone.

He has become a nightmare on the lonely streets, the man people cross over to avoid.

He shuffles, checking the payphones for any spare change, the stink of sweat and disappointment ingrained on his skin, and as he walks he whispers to himself,

"I'll show them, I'll show them, I'll show them ..."

Once upon a time, this man shuffling along had power, he had strength, he had respect, people looked up to him, asked his opinion, valued his advice ...

But that was then and this was now. Now he is old and alone, and people ignore him, as though time had stripped away all he ever was, could ever be.

"I'll show them, I'll show them ..."

Now they call him "old man".

"Bag of bones."

They took his magic from him.

They took his strength.

They took his respect.

They took his daughter.

But they never took his mind.

"I'll show them, I'll show them, I'll ..."

Passing by the red postbox, on the corner of the road where shadows stretch between the bubbles of the streetlamps, he feels something press against his thigh, and turns in indignation.

No one there and, as he brushes his leg, he can't feel any blood, and is already wondering if he imagined it. Perhaps he did. He's had a long day, a long week, and in the darkness of the lonely streets it's easy to imagine things stirring in the night.

He walks on, past the shuttered convenience store and the locked-up laundrette, beneath the painting on the wall of the glowering, long-nosed rat, a top hat on its head, a fistful of dollars held in its claws, and beneath the glowing arches of the railway line, where domes of coloured lights ripple from blue, to green, to red and back again. He turns the corner towards the graveyard, his fists clenched at his side, his head throbbing and his back bent, walks three more paces, and pauses.

Stops.

Stares at nothing in particular, then down at the ground.

His hand brushes his thigh again, where he thought he felt something in the night, and this time there is blood there, a tiny streak of crimson, seeping through his trousers.

He raises his head, looks around at the empty dark.

"I know you're there."

His voice is a whisper, a bare gasp. He doesn't move, frozen in place; and she is there, without a sound, without a sigh, where she had been all along, standing beside him.

Arthur Huntley doesn't turn, doesn't move his head, seems to stare straight ahead at nothing, his body frozen in place, his hand still held up, blood turned brown beneath the dull yellow streetlight; but his eyes dance in his face, straining round to see her at the edge of his sight. "Have you . . . ?" he breathes, and she doesn't answer. "Did you . . . ?"

"I didn't see you fall," she replies. "And there wasn't a body. Swift says that you're not a threat now, that as soon as he's worked out how to walk again, he's going to hunt you down and do the sorcerer thing. But I thought about it, and I realised that wasn't his job."

She moves round a little further, so he can see her clearly now, Sharon Li, with her Winnie the Pooh plasters, and her green shoulder bag covered in badges. She stands before him on the empty street, and there is something in her hand. Something thin, ancient, reddish-black. A blade of rust, gripped beneath her fingers, the point hanging down loosely by her thigh. Arthur's body shakes with the effort of not moving, every breath a swell in his chest that is gasped out before it can be drawn fully in.

"I guess I oughtta ask you why," she murmurs, wrapping the rusted blade carefully up in a plastic bag. "Why you did all this, why you let so many people die, why you killed, why you lied, why your daughter . . . "

Arthur jerks at the words, but his feet don't move, rooted to the spot. Sharon pauses, eyebrows raised, waits for the moment to pass, keeps on wrapping. "Why you let your daughter," she continues, "give her life, her body, to the glass god. Because that's what she did, you see. I saw it when I looked at the glass god in the shadow walk, in the spirit walk where all things are real, and true; and there, he was a she, and she was your daughter, giving her very life to sustain this lie of yours. And that got me thinking ... if your daughter was sustaining the glass god, then what the hell was the point of stealing Old Man Bone's blade? Why'd you get a copy made, why'd you need to waste all that time and effort? It's not for kicks, it's not for worship, so what's the point? And then we had all that stuff in the Shard, and you went mental and as you went mental you went mental in a glassy way and I thought, shit. He hasn't been killing people to feed the glass god. He's been killing people to feed himself."

She finishes wrapping the blade, slips it into her bag, and, for the first time, looks Arthur in the eye. "Mr Roding had your number, right from the beginning. An ex-wizard, he said, and I never stopped to think, what must that be like? To have been the guy at the top, and find yourself suddenly the guy at the bottom. And talking to you, when you were busy being whacked out, I mean, it was like all you really cared about was that people knew how big you were, and how important, like nothing else mattered and I thought, yeah. That's the kinda guy who might just do it. That's the kinda guy who might be arsehole enough to steal the blade of Old Man Bone, and make himself a copy, and go around stabbing people with it and feeding on their deaths, like Old Man Bone has fed, but you ... you're just a guy, just a man, an old, broken man and Old Man Bone ..." – she sighs, shoulders sagging forward a little, bag swinging by her side – "... he's not. He's part of the city. Like rats, and sewage, and death. Ain't pretty and ain't nice, but that's what it is. So, yeah. I figured it was time to finish it. Sorry about that."

So saying, she turns and begins to walk away.

"Sharon!" The sound jerks out from Arthur's throat, a bare crackle on the air. She stops, turns to stare back at him. "You ... you can't ..." His voice strains on the very edge of speech.

She hesitates, then shakes her head. "You know," she murmurs, "if this whole ... deputy Midnight Mayor thing sticks, and I, like, get lumbered with this job forever, then people are gonna talk about me and Swift, and how we worked and that. And everyone's going to be, like, 'wow, Matthew Swift, he's such a bad-ass, such a firebrand, look at all the stuff he blows up' and they're gonna go 'jeez, Sharon, she's so like "let's work through our issues" and shit and so kinda "cuppa tea in the afternoon" and that' and they'll be right, of course, because that's what I'm like and that's what I think people should do.

"But the thing is, you gotta remember that all this doesn't make me the good cop."

Walks away.

"Sharon!"

His voice rings out among the railway arches and the high apartment blocks.

"Sharon!"

Drifts down through the open drains and tangles upward in the buddleia sprouting through the old dark stones.

And Sharon is gone.

Arthur stands alone in the dark, his thigh smarting, his fingers sticky with the tiniest smear of his own blood. He doesn't move. His own weight is pushing him forward, trying to force the next step. He stays frozen, chest heaving now with a rush of air, eyes turning this way and that. Spells rise and fall unbidden to his lips, but they are ash, hollow, futile. He whispers wards and summons shields, begs spirits and calls for aid, and nothing comes, and, pressed on by the forward slope of his own back he . . .

steps.

Another pace.

Walks.

His shoes are old, sensible, brown loafers.

Another step.

The laces are newer than the shoes themselves, threaded not two months ago, when one pair snapped.

Another step and he straightens now, eyes gleaming, pushing his back upright and he can't stop himself: another step, walking stiffly down the street, a proud old soldier on parade, another

step

step

step

stop.

And it suddenly appears to Arthur that everything he's known up to this point has been meaningless. All that was has passed him by, and all that remains is everything which is, and yet to come. He has had such profound thoughts before. He thought it when the Westminster Coven stripped him of his powers; when his wife left him alone with his baby daughter, when his little girl cast her first spell and it was nearly good enough. He thought it when he first held Old Man Bone's rusted blade between his fingers, and felt it again when he finally received the new blade, the glass blade, forged by the scylla sisters. He experienced something close to this sense when Brid died, torn apart before his very eyes by the blue electric angels; thought he felt it when he turned the lights out on Zhanyi and heard the striga's scream, or that moment when his daughter fell silent. Silent and crumbled, a stillness in the dark.

All of it, meaningless.

He looks down at his fingers and is confused to find them stained with blood. He wipes them clean on his trousers. His thigh stings a little, though he cannot say why, and doesn't believe that it matters.

And so, for tomorrow can only come if we let go of today, he reaches down to his shoes and carefully slips them off his feet. He flexes his toes on the ground, feeling the sudden damp chill of the paving stones rise up into the soles of his feet. He picks up his shoes, carefully unpicking the knot in the laces; then, once they are free, ties the laces back together, one shoe to the other. He raises his head, looking for something suitable for his purpose, and sees a lamppost with a long neck sticking out over the street. He steps back a few paces, to get a better line of sight, then, whirling his shoes overhead, spins them like an Olympic champion and with a great heave of his arm, lets the shoes fly. They tumble through the air, one over the other, and hook across the neck of the lamppost, tangling a few times round as they come to rest, to form a noose of lace across the metal top.

And, like that, he is gone.

extras

orbit

meet the author

KATE GRIFFIN is the pseudonym of Carnegie Medal–nominated YA author Catherine Webb. Her first novel for adults was *A Madness of Angels*, introducing the sorcerer Matthew Swift. She lives in London. Find out more about the author at www.kategriffin.net.

introducing

If you enjoyed
THE GLASS GOD,
look out for

CHARMING

by Elliott James

John Charming isn't your average Prince...

He comes from a line of Charmings—an illustrious family of dragon slayers, witch finders, and killers dating back to before the fall of Rome. Trained by a modern-day version of the Knights Templar, monster hunters who have updated their methods from chain mail and crossbows to Kevlar and shotguns, he was one of the best. That is—until he became the abomination the Knights were sworn to hunt.

That was a lifetime ago. Now he tends bar under an assumed name in rural Virginia and leads a peaceful, quiet life. One that shouldn't change just because a vampire and a blonde walked into his bar... Right?

Chapter One

A Blonde and a Vampire Walk into a Bar...

Once upon a time, she smelled wrong. Well, no, that's not exactly true. She smelled clean, like fresh snow and air after a lightning storm and something hard to identify, something like sex and butter pecan ice cream. Honestly, I think she was the best thing I'd ever smelled. I was inferring "wrongness" from the fact that she wasn't entirely human.

I later found out that her name was Sig.

Sig stood there in the doorway of the bar with the wind behind her, and there was something both earthy and unearthly about her. Standing at least six feet tall in running shoes, she had shoulders as broad as a professional swimmer's, sinewy arms, and well-rounded hips that were curvy and compact. All in all, she was as buxom, blonde, blue-eyed, and clear-skinned as any woman who had ever posed for a Swedish tourism ad.

And I wanted her out of the bar, fast.

You have to understand, Rigby's is not the kind of place where goddesses were meant to walk among mortals. It is a small, modest establishment eking out a fragile existence at the tail end of Clayburg's main street. The owner, David Suggs, had wanted a quaint pub, but instead of decorating the place with dartboards or Scottish coats of arms or ceramic mugs, he had decided to celebrate southwest Virginia culture and covered the walls with rusty old railroad equipment and farming tools.

When I asked why a bar—excuse me, I mean, *pub*—with a Celtic name didn't have a Celtic atmosphere, Dave said that he had named Rigby's after a Beatles song about lonely people needing a place to belong.

"Names have power," Dave had gone on to inform me, and I had listened gravely as if this were a revelation.

Speaking of names, "John Charming" is not what it reads on my current driver's license. In fact, about the only thing accurate on my current license is the part where it says that I'm black-haired and blue-eyed. I'm six foot one instead of six foot two and about seventy-five pounds lighter than the 250 pounds indicated on my identification. But I do kind of look the way the man pictured on my license might look if Trevor A. Barnes had lost that much weight and cut his hair short and shaved off his beard. Oh, and if he were still alive.

And no, I didn't kill the man whose identity I had assumed, in case you're wondering. Well, not the first time anyway.

Anyhow, I had recently been forced to leave Alaska and start a new life of my own, and in David Suggs I had found an employer who wasn't going to be too thorough with his background checks. My current goal was to work for Dave for at least one fiscal year and not draw any attention to myself.

Which was why I was not happy to see the blonde.

For her part, the blonde didn't seem too happy to see me either. Sig focused on me immediately. People always gave me a quick flickering glance when they walked into the bar—excuse me, the pub—but the first thing they really checked out was the clientele. Their eyes were sometimes predatory, sometimes cautious, sometimes hopeful, often tired, but they only returned to me after being disappointed. Sig's gaze, however, centered on me like the oncoming lights of a train—assuming train lights have slight bags underneath them and make you want to flex surreptitiously. Those same startlingly blue eyes widened, and her body went still for a moment.

Whatever had triggered her alarms, Sig hesitated, visibly debating whether to approach and talk to me. She didn't hesitate for long, though—I got the impression that she rarely hesitated for long—and chose to go find herself a table.

Now, it was a Thursday night in April, and Rigby's was not empty. Clayburg is host to a small private college named Stillwaters University, one of those places where parents pay more money than they should to get an education for children with mediocre high school records. This sort of target student—an underachiever with upper-middle-class parents—not surprisingly does a lot of heavy drinking, which is why Rigby's manages to stay in business. Small bars with farming implements on the walls don't really draw huge college crowds, but the more popular bars tend to stay packed, and Rigby's does attract an odd combination of local rednecks and students with a sense of irony. So when a striking six-foot blonde who wasn't an obvious transvestite sat down in the middle of the bar, there were people around to notice.

Even Sandra, a nineteen-year-old waitress who considers customers an unwelcome distraction from covert texting, noticed the newcomer. She walked up to Sig promptly instead of making Renee , an older waitress and Rigby's de facto manager, chide her into action.

For the next hour I pretended to ignore the new arrival while focusing on her intently. I listened in—my hearing is as well developed as my sense of smell—while several patrons tried to introduce themselves. Sig seemed to have a knack for knowing how to discourage each would-be player as fast as possible.

She told suitors that she wanted to be up-front about her sex change operation because she was tired of having it cause problems when her lovers found out later, or she told them that she liked only black men, or young men, or older men who made more than seventy thousand dollars a year. She told them that what really turned her on was men who were willing to have sex with other men while she watched. She mentioned one man's wife by name, and when the weedy-looking grad student doing a John Lennon impersonation tried the sensitive-poet approach, she challenged him to an arm-wrestling contest. He stared at her, sitting there exuding athleticism, confidence, and health—three things he was noticeably lacking—and chose to be offended rather than take her up on it.

There was at least one woman who seemed interested in Sig

as well, a cute sandy-haired college student who was tall and willowy, but when it comes to picking up strangers, women are generally less likely to go on a kamikaze mission than men. The young woman kept looking over at Sig's table, hoping to establish some kind of meaningful eye contact, but Sig wasn't making any.

Sig wasn't looking at me either, but she held herself at an angle that kept me in her peripheral vision at all times.

For my part, I spent the time between drink orders trying to figure out exactly what Sig was. She definitely wasn't undead. She wasn't a half-blood Fae either, though her scent wasn't entirely dissimilar. Elf smell isn't something you forget, sweet and decadent, with a hint of honey blossom and distant ocean. There aren't any full-blooded Fae left, of course—they packed their bags and went back to Fairyland a long time ago—but don't mention that to any of the mixed human descendants that the elves left behind. Elvish half-breeds tend to be somewhat sensitive on that particular subject. They can be real bastards about being bastards.

I would have been tempted to think that Sig was an angel, except that I've never heard of anyone I'd trust ever actually seeing a real angel. God is as much an article of faith in my world as he, she, we, they, or it is in yours.

Stumped, I tried to approach the problem by figuring out what Sig was doing there. She didn't seem to enjoy the ginger ale she had ordered—didn't seem to notice it at all, just sipped from it perfunctorily. There was something wary and expectant about her body language, and she had positioned herself so that she was in full view of the front door. She could have just been meeting someone, but I had a feeling that she was looking for someone or something specific by using herself as bait… but what and why and to what end, I had no idea. Sex, food, or revenge seemed the most likely choices.

I was still mulling that over when the vampire walked in.